CLOSE MY EYES
SOPHIE MCKENZIE

**SIMON &
SCHUSTER**

London · New York · Sydney · Toronto · New Delhi

A CBS COMPANY

First published in Great Britain in 2013 by Simon & Schuster UK Ltd
A CBS COMPANY

1 3 5 7 9 10 8 6 4 2

Simon & Schuster UK Ltd
1st Floor
222 Gray's Inn Road
London
WC1X 8HB

www.simonandschuster.co.uk

Simon & Schuster Australia, Sydney

Simon & Schuster India, New Delhi

A CIP catalogue copy for this book is available
from the British Library.

ISBN: 978-1-47111-173-0
Trade paperback ISBN: 978-1-47111-172-3
E-book ISBN: 978-1-47111-174-7

Typeset by Hewer Text UK Ltd, Edinburgh
Printed and bound in Great Britain by
CPI Group (UK) Ltd, Croydon, CR0 4YY

CLOSE
MY
EYES

Sophie McKenzie is the author of over fifteen novels for children and teenagers including the multi-award winning *Girl, Missing, Sister, Missing* and *Missing Me*. She has tallied up numerous award wins and has twice been longlisted for the prestigious Carnegie Medal. This is her first adult novel. Sophie lives in London.

Find Sophie online at www.sophiemckenziebooks.com, on twitter at @sophiemckenzie_ and on facebook at www.facebook.com/sophiemckenzieauthor

For my mother

I used to like stories, especially the stories Mummy told me when I was little. The Special Child was best. It's a bit of a babyish story for me now but I loved it the most back then. In The Special Child, *there's a child that grows up all happy with a mummy and a daddy who are the king and the queen and then a wicked witch from the next kingdom comes and takes the Special Child into a prison and the mummy and the daddy are really sad but the Special Child does special fighting and kills the witch and escapes back to the mummy and daddy.*

We used to do stories at school. Sometimes we had to read them. Other times we made them up. I remember I wrote down The Special Child *and did pictures.*

Mummy used to say it was only a story but that sometimes stories come true. She said the wicked witch in The Special Child *was only a lady in a story but that there were Bad People in real life too. She said you can't tell from looking at them and that sometimes they will be smiley and saying all nice things and maybe offering sweets and toys but underneath they are still Bad People.*

For a long time I never met any Bad People in real life – but then Ginger Tall and Broken Tooth happened and after that everything was different. Just like Mummy said.

CHAPTER ONE

I'm late.

I hate being late.

I'm supposed to meet Art at 5 p.m. and it's already quarter to. I race down the corridor to the staff room. I can't remember the new code for the door, so have to wait outside until another teacher lets me through. I shove my spare photocopies in my pigeonhole then deposit my register in the box. As I reach the exit, Sami, the head of Humanities, reminds me that tomorrow morning's class is cancelled due to building repairs. I make a mental note then fly out of the Institute doors and half run, half jog along Great Queen Street to Kingsway. It's grey and gloomy, the clouds swollen with rain. There are no cabs. I should get the tube to Oxford Circus, but since 7/7 I avoid using the underground when possible. Anyway, I've always preferred the bus. Art hates buses. Too slow.

I charge round the corner to the bus stop, negotiating several uneven pavements and a swarm of Italian teenagers as I run. Good, I can see a number 8 trundling towards me along High Holborn. That'll take me to John Lewis. I can race up to Harley Street from there.

Inside the bus I press my Oyster card against the pad and lean with relief against a post. The woman next to me – young, straggly haired – is wrestling with a baby in a buggy.

'Sit down, for fuck's sake,' she hisses under her breath. There's so much anger in her voice I have to turn away and move up the bus.

I arrive at the clinic at quarter past five. Art is waiting by the door. I see him seconds before he sees me – smart and suave in his suit. It's dark grey, Paul Smith – his favourite. Stylish and simple, he wears it, as usual, with a plain open-necked shirt and no tie. Art looks good in those kind of clothes. He always has. He turns and sees me. He's tired. And irritated. I can see it in the way he raises an eyebrow as I walk up.

'Sorry I'm late.' I raise my face and he kisses me. A light, swift brush of the lips.

'It's fine,' Art says.

Of course the truth is that I'm not really sorry and he isn't really fine. The truth is that I don't want to be here and Art knows it.

I follow Art inside. He shrugs off his jacket as we cross the entrance hall. The shirt he's wearing has a tiny nick on the inside of the collar. You can't see it but I know it's there, just as I know Art is pissed off with me from the way his arms hang stiffly at his sides. I should feel guilty. After all, I'm late and Art's time is precious. And I'm aware that this is hard for him as well as for me.

Art stops as we reach the waiting-room door. He turns to me with a smile, clearly making a huge effort to overcome his mood.

'Mr Tamansini was here a minute ago. He's very pleased we're back.'

'You've spoken to him?' I'm surprised; the consultants rarely leave their rooms during appointments.

'He just happened to be in reception when I arrived.' Art takes my hand and leads me into the waiting room. It's classic Harley Street: a row of stiff chintz armchairs and a matching couch. A

3

fireplace with dried flowers on the mantelpiece and a terrible piece of modern art above. Certificates, licences and awards are positioned in glass frames all around the walls. I catch sight of my reflection in the mirror in the corner. My jumper is creased and my hair looks like it hasn't been brushed for a week. It really needs cutting: the fringe is in my eyes and the ends are split and dry and curling shapelessly onto my shoulders. Before Beth, I had highlights and a trim every couple of months. I straighten my jumper and smooth out my hair. My eyes shine bright blue against the pink of my cheeks, flushed from running up the road. I used to go to classes at the gym as well. Now I never seem to have the energy.

'He's on time, but they sent the next couple in ahead of us as you weren't here.' Art's tone is only faintly accusatory.

I nod again. Art runs his hand up my arm.

'Are you okay? How was your class?'

I look at him properly. His face is still so boyish, despite the fact he turned forty last week. I don't know whether it's the soft curve of his jaw or the dimple in his chin or the fact that his eyes are so big and eager. I stroke his cheek. The skin is rough under my fingertips. Art has to shave twice a day but I have always liked the shadow on his face. It gives him a rougher, sexier edge.

'The class was fine.' My throat tightens. I *so* don't want to be here. 'I'm really sorry I was late. It's just . . . being here again.'

'I know.' Art puts his arm around me and pulls me against his chest. I bury my face against his neck, squeezing my eyes tight against the tears I don't want to let out.

'It's going to work this time, I know it is. It's our turn, Gen.'

Art checks his watch. He's had it years and the face is scratched and worn. It's the watch I gave him – my first present to him on his birthday, three months after we met. That evening Art let me buy him dinner for the first time; I'd insisted, seeing as it was his

4

birthday. It was a mild, spring evening – the first warm night after what felt like months of winter and, after dinner, we'd walked along the Embankment and across Waterloo Bridge to the South Bank. Art told me about his plans for Loxley Benson . . . how all his life he'd been searching for something to believe in, something worthwhile to put his energies into, something to drive towards.

'And your business means all that?' I'd asked.

Art had taken my hand and told me 'no', that *I* was what he'd been looking for, that our relationship was what he wanted more than anything.

That evening was the first time he told me he loved me.

I pull away now and wipe under my eyes as discreetly as possible. Quite apart from Art, there are three other couples in the waiting room and I don't want them to see. I sit down and close my eyes, my hands folded in my lap. I focus on my breathing, trying to take my mind away from the turmoil raging through my head.

Art still loves me. I know he does. If he didn't, he wouldn't have stayed with me through the long, terrible year after Beth. Not to mention the six failed IVF attempts since.

But sometimes I wonder if he really listens to me. I've tried to explain how tired I get of these visits to the clinic. The highs and lows of IVF. It's been nearly a year since our last attempt. Back then I insisted on a break and Mr Tam – as he's known on the online infertility forums – supported me. Art agreed – we both hoped I'd get pregnant naturally. There's really no reason why I shouldn't – at least not one that anyone's found. Just as there's no reason to explain why every single attempt at IVF has failed to produce a pregnancy.

Art's been angling for me to undergo more treatment for the past few months. He even made this appointment for us. But

I can't bear the thought of another round, and the physical side effects and psychological battering it will bring. I've been there too many times: starting a cycle, wasting an opportunity to start one because you're away, going to the clinic every day to be tested, taking the drugs at specific times on specific days – all only to find your follicles aren't big enough or plentiful enough, or else that the embryos don't survive. Then resting a cycle or two, obsessed with when you ovulate, when you menstruate, before you start again. And on and on. And none of it, none of any of it, can ever bring her back.

Beth. My baby who was born dead.

I want to tell Art all this, but that means talking about Beth and she's shut up in my head in a safe place along with the pain and the grief and I don't want to go in there and start raking it all up again.

'Mr and Mrs Loxley?'

Art leaps to his feet. The nurse smiles at him. It's hard not to smile at Art. Even before he appeared on *The Trials* on TV people smiled at him. All that boyish charm and energy. I'm sure that's half the secret of his success with Loxley Benson, that way he looks at you, his eyes blazing, making you feel special, as if nothing matters more than what you're about to say or do.

The other half's a different story, of course. Art's smart. Shrewd. And completely driven. Mum saw it when she met him. Before he'd made his fortune, when he'd just set up his business – an online ethical-investment company – with no money and no security. 'That one,' she said. 'That one's going to set the world on fire.' Then she'd given me that wry smile of hers. 'Just make sure you don't get burned while you're trying to keep up.'

Mr Tamansini's desk is as big as a ship – all embossed brown leather with brass studs around the edges. He looks lost behind it – a small, olive-skinned man with a pointy face and delicate hands. He's pressing his fingertips together, which he always does when he speaks. He gazes at me and Art sitting next to each other on the other side of the desk.

'I'm going to suggest you try ICSI this time,' he says slowly. 'That's where we inject sperm *directly* into the egg.'

'See?' Art nudges my arm like we're in the back row of a classroom. 'I told you there'd be something new.'

I stare at Mr Tamansini's fingers. Weird to think they've been inside me. But then the whole idea of being a gynaecologist is weird. On the other hand, I like Mr Tam. I like his stillness. The way he stays calm even when Art is at his most forceful. He was my consultant for four of the six failed IVF attempts. I guess you could say we've been through a lot together.

'ICSI's not new,' I say, looking up at Mr Tam. 'Why that? Why now?'

Mr Tam clears his throat. 'ICSI is often used in cases where the sperm is of poor quality. Of course, that isn't the case here, but ICSI is equally useful when couples present with low rates of fertilization and a low yield of eggs at egg retrieval, both of which do apply to you.'

'Won't that cost more than ordinary IVF?' I ask.

At the mention of money Art stiffens. It's a tiny movement, but I recognize it well. It's like when an animal pricks up its ears, listening out for warning sounds. I stare back at Mr Tam's desk. The brass studs around the edge are gleaming in the light. I wonder, idly, whether somebody actually polishes them.

'It *is* more expensive,' Mr Tamansini acknowledges. 'But it will undoubtedly increase the chance of a viable pregnancy.'

'So what does ICSI involve?' Art says. His tone is neutral, but I can hear the steel in his voice. He's not going to let himself – or me – get taken for a ride.

Mr Tam smiles. 'As far as the two of you are concerned, there's

7

really very little difference from standard IVF.' He starts talking about the procedure. I tune out for a moment. I already know about ICSI; it was one of the options I pored over several years ago.

'. . . which works like a cleaned-up software platform,' Mr Tamansini finishes. 'All ready to program a new computer.'

Art laughs. He loves Mr Tam's metaphors.

'So what do you think?' Mr Tam asks.

'Absolutely.' Art looks at me. 'We should go for it.'

For a second I'm furious that Art is speaking on my behalf. And then I remember that I agreed to come here, that he thinks I'm up for this, that I haven't talked about how I really feel for ages . . .

'I don't know,' I squirm. 'I mean . . . I don't know about IVF any more. Let's face it, in a few months I'll be forty which . . .'

'. . . is *not* too old.' Art turns to Mr Tam. 'Tell her, please. It's not too old.'

Mr Tam takes a deep breath. His face remains calm and professional, but underneath he is surely wondering why I'm here at all if I've got such doubts. 'Of course, Mrs Loxley, you are right. There are no guarantees. But you became pregnant once before, which is a positive sign. And forty is not that old in IVF terms. Indeed, one might say it is not as old as it used to be.'

I stare at him, at his soothing, gentle smile.

'I don't think . . .' My voice trembles. 'I'm not sure I can cope with . . . with going through it all again . . .' My voice breaks and I look down at the carpet. There's a brown stain by the far desk leg in the shape of a kidney bean.

Why is it so hard to say what I want? How I feel?

Art's voice is low in my ear, as intense as I've ever heard it. 'Gen, we have to keep trying. Don't you see? If you like, I'll do a full risk assessment on the ICSI stats, I promise, and I'll work out the odds, and if that pans out then we'll make it work together, just like we always make everything work.'

I look up. Mr Tam has walked across the room, to the intercom by the curtained-off area. He is talking to someone in a low voice. Giving me and Art a moment to pull ourselves together.

I turn to Art. His eyes are dancing with this new hope. I hate myself for not feeling it too.

'I know that it's hard for you, all the drugs and the appointments and everything,' Art continues. 'And I know we've been through it before five times . . .'

'Six,' I correct.

'. . . But it would be worth it,' Art presses on. 'Don't you think it would be worth it?'

I shake my head. I thought that once, maybe, the first few times we tried IVF after Beth. But the pain of trying and failing *wasn't* worth it.

Art frowns. 'I don't understand why you don't want to try again,' he says. He's trying to sound sympathetic but there's a note of impatience in his voice. 'If the percentages pan out, I mean.'

I take a deep breath. 'It's not the percentages and the risk factors and the drugs.' I look into his eyes, hoping I'll see that he understands. I lower my voice to a whisper. It's still so hard to say her name out loud. 'It's Beth.'

His eyes express confusion. 'You mean it's being disloyal to her memory to try again?'

'Not exactly . . .'

'Oh, Gen. This isn't being disloyal. If anything, it's a testament to how much we loved her . . . that we want so much to . . . to replace her.'

Replace her?

Mr Tam is back at the desk now, fingertips pressed together.

9

Art's words are still ringing in my ears. I stare down at the kidney bean stain again, blood drumming at my temples.

'I guess we need a bit more time to think about all this,' Art is saying. His voice sounds dull and distant.

'Of course.' Mr Tam is smiling. I can hear it in his voice, but I'm still staring at the carpet stain. 'At this stage it's just a suggestion. I think we should take it one step at a time.'

I look up. 'That's a good idea.'

Art puts his arm around my shoulders. 'Absolutely.'

A few minutes later we're outside the clinic and heading home in a taxi. Art refuses to travel any other way. He could have a driver if he wanted one, now that Loxley Benson is so successful, but he hates any appearance of elitism. I tell him taxis are just as elitist but he says they're a practical solution – public transport being so slow and Art's time being money.

We don't speak. I'm still reeling. Suddenly I realize he's speaking to me.

'Sorry?'

'I wish you wouldn't do that.' He takes my hand and holds it between both of his.

I look down. The nail on the first finger of my left hand is bitten right down and the skin around the nail is chewed and red raw. I curl it over, out of sight. I hadn't even realized my finger had been in my mouth.

Art's fingers exert a soft pressure. 'Why did you let me make the appointment if you were so sure you don't want any more IVF?'

Through the taxi window, the sun is low above Regent's Park. A perfect burning orange disc against a clear navy sky with no sign of the earlier clouds. I turn back to Art. His eyes glitter in the soft light and my heart lurches with love for him. For all his ruthlessness in business, Art's fundamentally the kindest man I know.

'I'm sorry about the appointment,' I say. 'I know it's not fair . . .' I tail off, wishing my thoughts weren't so confused.

'You know you're nuts, don't you?' Art says affectionately.

We stare at each other for a moment, then Art leans forward. 'Can you at least explain to me what you're worried about, Gen? Because I only want . . . that is, everything I do, it's all for you, you *know* that. I just want to understand, because I can't see how *not* trying again is the right thing.'

I nod, trying to work out what to say. How I can explain what feels so muddled and fragile in my own head.

'I can't think in terms of "replacing" Beth,' I say.

It hurts to use her name. But not to say it denies her existence, which is worse. My stomach twists.

'I didn't mean *replace*.' Art dismisses his previous word with a shrug. He sits upright. '*Obviously* we can't replace her. But we *can* have the experience of being parents, which her dying cheated us of.'

'I don't know.'

Art fingers his collar, feeling for the hidden nick in the cotton. 'Then let *me* know for both of us.'

'What about the money?' I frown. 'We've already spent so much.'

Art waves his hand. 'That's the least of our problems.'

It's true, though I still can't quite get used to how much Art is earning. It's not that we were struggling before: Loxley Benson has been doing well for a long time, but it's really taken off this year. In fact, right now, it's one of the fastest-growing small businesses in the UK.

'I don't mean the amount,' I say. 'It's the whole thing of sending good money after bad and—'

'Jesus, Gen, it's not *that* much money. Just a few grand. And me doing *The Trials* is getting us more work every day. A woman at a client meeting the other day, she's involved in some government initiative and she wants to talk to me at the Brussels meeting tomorrow about bringing me in. We're doing really well, Gen, like I told you we would. We're about to go *massive*.'

'But . . .' I stop, unable to say what I truly feel, which is that Art's business success makes me feel inadequate. It's not fair, when he works so hard for us, but being pregnant made me his equal. Like I was making a proper contribution to our marriage at last. And now, the reminder that he makes money hand over fist highlights how I have failed to keep my end of the unspoken deal between us.

'You *have* to want this, Gen. We can do it. I will find a way.'

The words, the set of his mouth, his whole body . . . it's all utterly convincing. And, I know from experience, virtually impossible to resist.

'You really want to try, don't you?'

Art shrugs. 'What's the alternative? Adoption?'

I shake my head. That's one thing we've both always agreed on at least. If we're going to have a baby, it should be *our* baby.

'Exactly.' Art leans forward. 'I do want this, Gen.' He pauses and his mouth trembles. 'But not unless you want it too.'

For a fraction of a second he looks vulnerable, like a little boy, and I see how afraid he is that I will never move on from Beth dying and that our love will slip away from us because of it . . . because one day I will have to choose between letting go of Beth and letting go of Art.

'I want to do this *with* you, Gen,' he whispers. 'Please try and see that.'

The taxi slows to a halt at the traffic lights separating Camden High Street from Kentish Town Road. Art and I met in Camden, fourteen years ago at a big New Year's Eve party I'd gone to with my best friend, Hen. Art was twenty-six and in his first year of running his own business. He'd blagged his way into the party with a bunch of his colleagues because he thought there'd be useful people there. I was just up for free drinks and a laugh.

We met at the bar, when one of Art's colleagues – Tris – bumped into Hen and it turned out they were old uni friends who'd lost touch. Of course, Hen introduced me to Tris who, in turn, introduced me to Art. Art bought a round of drinks, most of which I knocked over on my way back from the Ladies. He was sweet about that, immediately buying another round, even though – I found out later – he could barely afford to eat at the time. We got chatting. He told me about Loxley Benson, how he'd set up the business with a good friend just months before, how he wanted to ride the new wave of online trading, how passionately he felt about making sure the investments his company supported were ethical and socially and environmentally responsible.

I told him how I worked for a boring homes magazine, writing about kitchens and paint schemes, but how one day I wanted to write a novel. I remember being blown away by how driven he was. How he was prepared to take any risk and suffer any setback to get where he wanted. How it wasn't so much about making money as making a difference.

Even then, I knew that whatever Art wanted, he was going to get.

Including me.

'Gen?'

I bite my lip. It's dark outside now, the street lamps starting to glow as the taxi drags its way past the dreary shops and crowded pavements of Kentish Town High Street. If he wasn't married to me, Art would probably have four kids by now. He should have this. I shouldn't stop him from having this.

'It's the hope,' I say. 'I can handle anything except the hope.'

Art laughs. I know he doesn't really understand what I mean. But he loves me and that's enough.

'Why don't you check out the ICSI stats,' I say. 'See what you think. Then we can decide.'

Art nods enthusiastically and reaches into his pocket. A second later his phone buzzes and I realize he must have had it turned off for most of the last hour. I can't remember the last time he turned it off for more than a few minutes.

He's still talking on the phone as we reach Crouch End and walk into the house. Lilia, our Slovakian cleaner, is just leaving. As I shut the door behind her I notice the post piled up by the hall radiator. I pick it up and wander into the kitchen. We don't use the other downstairs rooms that much. It's a big house for just two people.

I flick idly through the mail. There's a postcard from my mum, who's on holiday with her latest boyfriend in Australia. I set that down on the kitchen table, then take the rest and stand over the recycling pile, chucking the junk mail on top of it. I put aside two bills and an envelope bearing the logo of Art's solicitors. More junk mail follows: magazines, takeaway flyers . . . How can we receive so many pointless bits of post in just one day?

Art is still talking on the phone. His voice – low and insistent – grows louder as he passes the kitchen door, then fades again. As I throw a couple of catalogues onto the recycling pile, it teeters and finally collapses.

'Shit.' As I pick everything up, Art reappears.

'Gen?'

'How on earth is it possible for us to generate this much paper?' I say.

'They've brought forward tomorrow's Brussels meeting, so Siena's booked me onto an earlier flight.'

'When?'

'The meeting's at ten. I'll be leaving here just after six, so I was wondering about an early night . . .' Art hesitates, his eyebrows raised. I know what he's thinking. I smile. At least it should mean the subject of IVF gets dropped for the rest of the evening.

'Sure,' I say.

We have dinner and I watch some nonsense on TV while Art makes a couple of calls and checks various spreadsheets. My programme segues to the *News at Ten*. As the first ad break starts, I feel Art's hand on my shoulder.

'Come to bed?'

We go upstairs. Art drops his clothes on the red-and-orange-striped rug and shakes back the duvet. He gets into bed and grins up at me. I lie down and let him touch me.

To be honest, I like the idea of Art wanting to have sex with me more than the sex itself. Our conversation about the IVF is still running through my head, and it's hard to let go and relax. I move a little, trying to be turned on, but it's just not happening. Art approaches sex pretty much like he approaches everything else – when he wants it he goes and gets it. Not that I'm saying he's ever been unfaithful. And I don't mean he's *bad* in bed, either. Just that he didn't have much idea when I met him, so everything he does now I taught him to do. And he's still doing it, exactly like I showed him fourteen years ago.

'Gen?' Art's propped up on his elbow beside me, frowning. I hadn't even noticed he'd stopped touching me.

I smile and take his hand and put it back between my legs. I will myself to respond. It works, a little. Enough, anyway. Art's convinced I'm finally letting go and eases himself inside me.

I let my mind drift. My focus turns to the pile of recycling downstairs. All that paper. I know that what really bothers me is the reminder of all the written words out there – the endless magazines and books competing for space on shop shelves. And that's before you include the internet. I used to be part of it all: I wrote and published three books in the time between marrying Art and getting pregnant with Beth. Sometimes the amount of published material in the world feels suffocating – squeezing the air out of my own words before they have a chance to come to life.

Art moans and I move again to show willing.

It's not just the paper stuff either. Art's 'Mr Ethical' and insists we are ultra-green, with separate boxes for everything: aluminium, cardboard, glass, food waste, plastic . . .

Sometimes I just want to chuck it all in a black bag like we did when I was growing up. My mind slides to a memory from childhood. I'm struggling to carry a bin bag across the back garden, the grass damp under my feet. I'm hauling it towards Dad, who's on a rare visit home between tours. The grass smells sweet and fresh. Dad has just mown it and now he's making a compost heap with the cuttings. I want to help. That's why I'm carrying the contents of the kitchen bin out to him. He laughs and says most of the contents won't rot so we make a bonfire instead. I can still remember the smell of the fire, my face burning hot while the cold wind whips across my back.

Art's kissing my neck as he thrusts harder into me. I just want him to get on with it . . . get it over . . . As soon as we're done he'll fall asleep and then I'll get up and have a cup of tea.

Art's breathing is heavier now, his movements more urgent. I know he's close, but holding back, waiting for me. I smile up at him, knowing he'll know what I mean. A minute later, he comes with a groan and sinks down onto me. I hold him, feeling him slide out of me and the wetness seeping out onto the bed. I love the way he feels so vulnerable like this, his head on my chest.

I wait . . .

Art nuzzles into me, sighing contentedly, then rolls off, leaving just one arm draped over my chest. His breathing deepens and I slip out from under his arm. It's one of those things that I know, but don't want to face: our sex life has got into a rut. Unsurprising after so many years, I suppose. And it's certainly a lot better than during the years when I was obsessed with getting pregnant. I know Art felt under pressure then, having to do it at the right times, and I hated how trying to conceive took all the fun and spontaneity out of it. I stopped checking when I ovulate ages ago but maybe all that history has taken its toll. Or maybe it's just classic, married sex: predictable, comfortable, safe. I'm not complaining, though. One day I'll talk to Art properly about it. He'll listen, I know he will. He'll want to make it better. Which means he will. I've never known Art fail at anything.

Art's iPhone rings from his trouser pocket on the floor. He wakes with a start, then sighs as he reaches over the side of the bed to retrieve it.

As he starts talking, I get up and go downstairs.

I wake up. The bed beside me is empty. Art is long gone, headed to Heathrow. A damp towel lies across his pillow. Irritated, I push it onto the floor.

Half an hour later I'm dressed and spreading butter and Marmite on my toast. The day stretches ahead of me. My normal Wednesday morning class has been cancelled and I have no appointments. Not even coffee with Hen. But I have this niggling sense that there's something I'm supposed to do today.

You could write, says a voice in my head.

I ignore it.

The doorbell rings and I pad to the front door. I'm not expecting anyone. It's probably just the postman. Still, you can't be too careful. I hook on the chain, open the door and peer through the crack.

A woman stands on the doorstep. She's black and plump and middle-aged.

I instantly assume she's a Jehovah's Witness and brace myself.

'Are you Geniver Loxley?' Her voice is soft, with a hint of a Midlands accent.

I stare at her. 'How do you know my name?'

The woman hesitates. It seems unlikely that a Jehovah's Witness would have this kind of detail, so I'm now assuming some kind of invasive mailing-list scenario. Still, the woman lacks the bravado of the sales-trained. In fact, now I'm looking closely at her I realize she's nervous. She's wearing a cheap suit made of some kind of nylon and sweat stains are creeping out from under the armpits.

'I . . . I . . .' she stammers.

I wait, my heart suddenly beating fast. Has Art been in an accident? Or someone else I know? The door is still on its chain. I open it properly. The woman presses her lips together. Her eyes are wide with fear and embarrassment.

'What is it?' I say.

'It's . . .' The woman takes a deep breath. 'It's your baby.'

I stare at her. 'What do you mean?'

She hesitates. 'She's alive.' The woman's dark eyes pierce through me. 'Your baby, Beth, is alive.'

CHAPTER TWO

I stand in the doorway feeling my stomach drop away. I am still holding the door chain. I press my finger against the metal nub until it hurts.

'What?' I say. A car zooms past the house. A man shouts in the distance. The world is going on somewhere else. Here, everything has been turned inside out. '*What* did you say?'

'Oh goodness.' The woman's hands flutter up to her face. They're surprisingly delicate for her size. 'Oh, Mrs Loxley, please may I come in?'

I tense, all my instincts shrieking a warning through my head.

Whatever this woman has to say, she can say out here. I'm not letting her into my home. I hold the door steady, in case the woman tries to barge past me, but she just shuffles from side to side, looking increasingly awkward.

'Why did you say . . . what you said?' I stammer. 'Who are you? How do you know my name?'

'Mrs Loxley . . .' She coughs, a dry, nervous cough. 'I'm Lucy O'Donnell. My sister was Mary Duncan. She died last year.'

I shake my head. 'I don't understand.'

'My sister is . . . was . . . a nurse. She was there with you at the Fair Angel hospital when you had your baby. She told me that your baby was born alive and well.' The woman puts her hand to her cheek. 'The doctor who delivered her took her away from you while you were still under the general anaesthetic. He lied to you.'

'No.' This is all ridiculous. What the hell does this woman think she's doing? Anger bubbles inside me.

'Yes,' Lucy insists.

'No. My baby died.' As I force the words out, my anger boils over. I push the door shut, but Lucy O'Donnell's scuffed shoe blocks it.

'I know this is a shock,' she says. 'I'll wait down the road. There's a café . . . Sam's something . . .? I'll be there until eleven o'clock. That's one hour from now.' She casts me a final glance of appeal, then shifts her shoe.

I slam the door and turn away, shaking.

How can this be happening? And *why*? I don't understand.

I can't stand still. I pace the hall. Then I stop and lean against the wall. The paint on the door jamb opposite is peeling. I stare at the line of exposed wood. We had the whole house painted when we moved in six years ago. It needs doing again. My pulse is racing. I close my eyes.

Lucy O'Donnell. Mary Duncan. These names mean nothing to me.

I get out my phone but even as I'm dialling I'm remembering that Art's in a meeting in Brussels. The call goes to voicemail. I leave a breathless message telling him to ring back urgently and slump against the wall.

Why would anyone turn up on the doorstep to tell such a monstrous lie? For a joke? As a dare? Though Lucy O'Donnell didn't look like she was enjoying herself very much. Who would put her up to this?

Doubt and fear swirl around my head. A thought seizes me and I fly up the stairs. Mary Duncan's name should be easy

20

enough to check. Surely we must have hung onto some paper-work from the maternity hospital? The Fair Angel was a private, state-of-the-art facility; Art will have a file on it somewhere. I race into his office on the second floor, a large, light room with lots of storage and shelving. I scan the file names in the cabinet: it's all accounts and clients. Nothing personal.

I walk to the window and peer out. There's no sign of Lucy on the street. Where had she said she was going? Sam's Deli – the café at the top of the road. I glance at the clock on Art's desk. 10.15.

I try to focus on what she said . . . that her sister was one of the nurses present when Beth was delivered. That the doctor only pretended Beth was dead.

It's insane. Inconceivable. I might not remember the nurse, but I certainly recall Dr Rodriguez, the god of an obstetrician I was assigned at the Fair Angel. He was tanned and handsome and oozing calm bedside manner – there's no way he would have done *anything* unprofessional, let alone lie about our baby and take her away from us.

I lean my head against the cold glass of the window pane. It's been so long since I've let myself relive the time leading up to the C-section. Art and I spent the last month of my pregnancy at a rented house just outside Oxford. We went there to be close to Fair Angel, which I chose, like so many before me, because of its amazing natural-birth pod – a unit which I never, of course, got to experience. In the end, my thirty-seven-week scan showed Beth was dead and I had a C-section under general anaesthetic straightaway. At the time I thought that Dr Rodriguez agreed to move so fast out of compassion. Could that decision really have been part of a plan to take Beth away from me?

I look out over the roofs and chimneys of our Victorian neighbourhood. Back in Oxford, our rented house near the Fair

Angel hospital was the perfect place to be heavily, dreamily pregnant. It overlooked the river Cherwell: beautiful and peaceful, with a small wood in the grounds and a long stone path leading down to the water's edge. Being there suited my mood. I'd slowed right down by that last month and drifted through my days, all the exhaustion and sickness of the first trimester long behind me.

Art worked the whole way through our time there, although, to be fair, he only disappeared off to London a couple of times each week. We had a few visitors: my mum came, as did some of our friends. Art's sister, Morgan, visited twice, on whirlwind stopovers as she jet-setted between her main home in Edinburgh and her offices in New York and Geneva. Even though her visits were short, she was incredibly thoughtful, organizing a driver to take me to the birthing centre for check-ups; a daily supply of the fresh, organic grapes that I craved throughout the last three months; and sending a steady stream of flowers plus a hugely expensive cut-glass vase to put them in. During our time in Oxford I saw Dr Rodriguez every few days and never once did he make me feel uncomfortable or suspicious that he had anything other than my best interests at heart.

The rumble of the rubbish-collection truck outside stirs me from my memories. I watch the truck stop and the men inside get out and stride over to my neighbour's wheelie bin. I give myself a shake. Nothing that Lucy O'Donnell has told me can possibly be true. It's just some cruel trick.

I go back downstairs, find my mobile and call Hen. Crazy and flaky, but fiercely loyal, she's been my best friend since sixth form. We used to introduce ourselves together, grinning, like a double act: Gen and Hen.

She answers on the second ring.

'Hey, how are you?'

I hesitate. Now that I'm faced with communicating what Lucy O'Donnell has told me, it sounds almost too ludicrous to say out loud. I must be mad even to have considered it might be true.

'You're not going to believe this.' I plunge right in. 'A woman just turned up on my doorstep and told me Beth is still alive.'

'*What*? No way.' Hen gasps. I can hear the outrage in her voice and instantly feel better.

I explain exactly what O'Donnell said.

'Oh my God, I can't believe anyone would *do* that.'

'She is just some nutter, isn't she?' As I speak I realize how much I'm looking to Hen to reassure me.

'Or worse,' Hen says darkly. 'Sounds like she could be just trying to get you out of the house for a few minutes or something.'

'Why?'

'Probably so she – or whoever she's working with – can sneak into the house to burgle it while it's empty.'

I think of the plump, anxious woman who stood on my doorstep.

'I don't think that's it,' I say uncertainly.

'Then what the hell is she playing at?' Hen's voice rises. 'Why would anyone make up such a terrible story? Why would anyone want to hurt you like that?'

'You don't think I should go down the road and . . . and find out more?'

'Jesus Christ, Gen, no *way*.' I can just picture Hen's expression as she speaks, her pale eyes wide with shock, her frizzy hair wild around her face. 'Don't give the mad cow the satisfaction of thinking she's got to you.'

I'm chewing at the skin around my fingernail. I tear a tiny strip of skin away with my teeth.

Hen's son, Nathan, is yelling in the background, 'Mum! Mum!'

'Sorry, Gen.' Hen sucks in her breath. 'I'm gonna have to go. Nat's off school with a cold. Hey, d'you want me to bring anything for Art's party on Friday?'

Oh, shit. I take my finger away from my mouth. *That's* what I was going to do today: Art's fortieth was last weekend, but the party is planned for the end of the week. I was going to make a shopping list.

'No,' I say. 'Just bring yourself and Rob.' Nathan's shouts rise in volume. 'Speak later.'

I put down my phone. Talking to Hen hasn't helped as much as I hoped it would. I don't believe Lucy O'Donnell was trying to lure me out of my house. She wanted to come in.

With a jolt, it strikes me: maybe she really believes Dr Rodriguez *did* steal Beth away from us.

I wander from room to room. The house feels oppressively silent. I check the time again. It's almost 10.30. Art will still be in his meeting. I want to tell him what's happened. I want him to tell me that Lucy O'Donnell is wrong. A con artist, like Hen said.

But they didn't see her; the nervous look in her eye, the trembling hands, the attempt to look smart in her cheap suit with the sweat patches under the armpits.

I'm certain she believed what she said.

I sit on the bottom step of the stairs, my head in my hands. A minute passes. Then another. Soon it will be eleven o'clock. Soon my opportunity to find out what O'Donnell was talking about will be over. I'm almost completely certain she's wrong, but that tiny sliver of doubt fractures inside me, shooting poison through every vein.

I stand up. I fetch my keys and my purse. I don't have a choice. I have to find out what she believes. And why.

Sam's Deli is one of my favourite local shops. It always smells of cheese and smoked meats, while its dark wooden shelves groan with pickles and preserves. I walk through the deli section, past a shelf of chilli jam and pickled okra and into the café at the back.

Lucy O'Donnell is sitting at a small round table well apart from the only other people in the room – a gaggle of mums and toddlers by the far wall. A cup of white coffee stands in front of her. It looks cold and untouched. She looks up and sees me watching her. She blinks rapidly as I walk over. The floor is bare, the tables and chairs are wooden and functional. Pictures of Italian-American film stars are dotted around the walls. I sit down under Al Pacino and fold my hands in my lap. My heart is racing and my throat feels so dry I'm not sure I can speak.

Lucy reaches across the table and touches my arm. I pull back.

'Would you like some coffee?' she asks, as a waiter walks over.

'Just water, thanks,' I croak.

The waiter leaves and I look at Lucy. Her eyes are still full of embarrassment and fear.

'Mrs Loxley . . .' She coughs. 'Thank you for coming. I'm sorry I didn't explain properly before. Let me start again.' Lucy heaves her fake-leather handbag onto the table between us and rummages inside it for a second. She pulls out a photo of herself and another middle-aged black woman, both smiling at the camera. The second woman is wearing a nurse's uniform. 'That's my sister, Mary,' Lucy says, handing me the picture. 'She attended the birth of your baby eight years ago . . . Eight years ago this June.'

I stare at the photo. The second woman is vaguely familiar, but I can't place her for certain. The time just before the emergency C-section is such a blur. I'd met Dr Rodriguez many times, of course. But my normal midwife was on holiday when I had the operation and I only met the theatre team as I was being prepared for the anaesthetic. There were five or six people at least, but I was in such a daze I don't remember any of them properly.

Lucy's brow creases with concern. 'Don't you recognize her?'

For a second I wonder if the woman is simply insane.

'I'm not sure,' I say. My voice is hoarse. Barely a whisper.

'But she was with you at the Fair Angel when you had your baby.'

I stare again at the photograph, trying to remember.

One of the theatre nurses *was* a black woman. I remember her holding my hand as the anaesthetist put me under for the emergency caesarean. I can't recall her face clearly, though, and certainly not her name.

'I can't be sure this is her,' I say, handing back the photograph.

Lucy takes it and tucks it absently into her coat pocket. She gives that nervous little cough again. 'Mary was there. The doctor – Dr Rodriguez – he hired her from an agency . . . he paid for her to travel from Birmingham, where we live . . .'

The waiter returns and places my glass of water on the table. A tiny drop splashes onto the wood.

'But there were a lot of other people in the operating theatre,' I insist. 'Are you seriously saying they *all* witnessed a baby being born alive then pretended it was dead?'

'Just the anaesthetist, and Mary,' Lucy says. 'Dr Rodriguez got the junior doctor and the other nurses out of the room before the baby was born.'

'How?' I shake my head. It all sounds ridiculously far-fetched.

Lucy shrugs. 'I'm not sure . . . Mary was so ill when she told me . . . but I think he might have given them something . . . made it look like food poisoning.'

What? I stare at her, my mind in overdrive. What she is describing would have taken such elaborate planning. 'Why?'

'I don't know. I just know that Dr Rodriguez took your baby to give to someone else,' Lucy goes on. Her voice is low, but filled with emotion. 'Mary saw, because she helped Dr Rodriguez with the delivery. The doctor paid her ten years' wages for that one birth. The only condition was that she keep quiet.'

My head feels like a million tiny bombs are exploding inside it. Could Dr Rodriguez really have pretended Beth had died, then paid his staff to keep quiet about it? My mind shrieks that these are lies and yet, as I look into Lucy O'Donnell's eyes, my instinct tells me she is sincere.

I try to focus, to force myself to form a coherent question, a challenge . . .

What about Beth's chromosomal abnormality? What about the fact that I saw a picture of our poor dead baby, and Art saw her in the flesh? What about the fact that reputable doctors don't risk being struck off to steal babies from healthy, wealthy women?

The question I ask, however, is not any of these.

'Why are you telling me this?' My voice is shaking. My whole body is trembling, whether with shock or anger I don't know. I fix my gaze on Lucy's anxious, worn face. 'Why now?'

'I only just found out,' Lucy says. Her eyes fill with tears as she speaks. 'My sister . . . Mary . . . she passed away just last month. Cancer. Cancer of the colon. Caught late, it took her fast, but just before she . . . before the end, she told me what happened . . . what really happened.' She pauses. I stare at her intently.

'And?' I say.

'Mary and I were brought up Catholic,' Lucy goes on, her voice falling to a whisper. 'Mary said she knew what she'd done was wrong and she couldn't go to her grave with such a wicked sin on her conscience. I don't see why she'd lie to me, and what she told me made sense of so much . . . you know, where the money came for her and Ronnie to pay for their new place and . . . and . . . that's what she told me, Mrs Loxley, just that. "Her baby was born alive." Those were her exact words. She said: "I feel so bad, Lucy, so bad for that poor lady because they took her baby away and told her the little thing was dead."'

My heart is thumping so hard the whole café must be able to hear it. It can't be true. And yet I want it to be true. I want and I don't want . . .

'So if . . . if you're right . . .' It's an effort to form the words, to speak them. 'If what you're saying is really true, then where is . . . where's my . . . my baby now?'

Lucy's face creases with sympathy. 'I don't know,' she says. 'I'm so sorry but I don't know any more than what I just told you. Mary was close to the end when she told me. She didn't say much after but, to be honest with you, I don't think she knew anything else about your baby.'

'But . . .?' I stop, trying to work out what I'm asking. 'Why would Dr Rodriguez steal my baby away from me? It doesn't make any sense. I mean, if someone else wanted a baby, and they couldn't have their own, why not adopt or use a surrogate? Why not steal a baby from someone very poor or very young, with no resources?'

'I don't know.' Lucy offers me a hopeless shrug. 'Mary said there was just her and the doctor and the anaesthetist in the know, that the doctor handed her the baby while he sewed you up.'

My mouth is dry. I take a sip of my water.

'So you're saying the anaesthetist knew about this as well?' I try to remember what he looked like, but all I can picture is a pair of bushy eyebrows above a surgical mask. 'Do you know *his* name?'

'No,' she says. 'I don't.'

I shake my head. 'Okay ...' I hesitate, trying to marshal my thoughts, to get the words right. 'Okay, I understand why your sister told you, but why are *you* here, telling me this?'

Lucy's cheeks redden. 'Well, I didn't want it on my conscience any more than Mary wanted it on hers and ... and then ... Bernard ... that's my husband ... he's recently out of work and well, anyway ... it just seemed like the right thing to do.' She stops and looks away.

My heart sinks. So Bernard has lost his job. *Of course.* That's what this is about: money.

'Was it a good job?' I ask, lightly.

'Yes, well, it was a regular salary. Bernard worked for a construction company, but he's getting older and they're always looking for ways of getting rid of the union guys before they get too close to their pensions.' She shakes her head, lost for the moment in her own problems. 'When Bernard came home and told me, it was too much on top of knowing how sick poor Mary was getting, but then, after she died and I told him what she told me about your baby he said that it wasn't a coincidence, that the Lord had taken Mary so that she would tell us about your baby. And he went on the internet and found out all your details – about how you'd called the baby Beth and you being a writer and your husband appearing on that TV show.'

Lucy picks up her cup of coffee. It suddenly all clicks into place. She's only here because of Art's involvement in *The Trials*. The series – a reality TV show that's a cross between *Dragon's Den* and *The Apprentice* – was shown over four weeks earlier in the year; Art was one of the three panellists. It's not like the show has made him a household name. And – apart from once or twice during the weeks when the show was broadcast – he hasn't been recognized in the street either. But in business circles, Art's reputation has definitely been enhanced. And he's developed a small but devoted fan-base of female admirers too. Any internet search on Art would quickly reveal he is successful and wealthy – just as any attempt to find out about me online would identify me firstly as his wife and mother of his stillborn baby girl and, secondly, as a writer, albeit one who hasn't published a book in eight years.

Lucy puts down her cup. It rattles in the saucer. 'So it was easy to find you, Mrs Loxley. And . . . oh, goodness, Bernard and I knew this would be a shock for you but we hoped that in coming here . . .'

'We?' I look around. The only man in the café is the young waiter. 'Is Bernard here too?'

'He's outside in our hire car, waiting for me.' Lucy looks embarrassed. She pushes across the table a scrap of paper on which a mobile phone number is neatly printed. 'We didn't want to overwhelm you. Here's my number for when you've had a chance to think about what I've said.'

The reality of the situation settles inside me as I pick up the piece of paper and shove it into my coat pocket. A couple with vague connections to the hospital in which I lost my baby have seen an opportunity to make money out of my grief by selling me false information. The cruelty of it almost blinds me and, now that the terrible hope is dashed, I realize just how huge a part of me craved that Beth was, truly, alive.

This hope, of course, is the very emotion that Lucy and Bernard have been counting on. In seconds, my hurt turns to humiliation and my humiliation to rage.

'So how much do you want?' I snap.

Lucy looks shocked. 'That isn't what we . . . it's not like that . . .'

Christ, they're not even good extortionists.

'So do you have anything else to sell apart from your sister's deathbed confession?'

Lucy frowns. 'I don't understand.'

I lean forward, spitting out the words. 'Do you have anything else to tell me?' I say, not expecting an answer.

She frowns, then bites her lip. Hesitating.

So she has held something back, some other bargaining chip. I steel myself. 'You want the money first? Is that it?' I'm seething now, my fists clenched, barely able to contain the fury that roils inside me.

'No, Mrs Loxley, it's just this last thing is hard to tell you . . .' she tails off.

'Harder than telling me my daughter's stillbirth was a con? That a perfectly reputable doctor risked being sent to prison?'

A couple of the mums sitting across the room glance over. Lucy looks desperate. 'I don't know why the doc—'

'So what *do* you know?' I say, struggling to keep my voice down. 'Apart from everything you've already told me and the fact that my husband and I are relatively well off?'

'Please don't be angry.' Lucy pushes her cup across the table. 'I can't say that Bernard and I weren't hoping for a reward for this news when we saw about your husband's success. I mean, to Bernard it isn't right that Mary and Ronnie had so much with us having nothing. They haven't even got children, while Bernard and me, we have four. And our youngest two are still living at home. I would have emailed you, but . . . but Bernard said you needed to see my face when I told you. That otherwise you might not believe me. But it's true, Mrs Loxley. And no matter what you think, I'm not here for the money. I'm here to be true to Mary. I know it's what she wanted. Else why would she have told me?'

31

I stare into Lucy's eyes. For a second I falter . . . Every instinct tells me she's telling the truth. And yet she *can't* be.

'Tell me the final thing,' I snarl. 'Then we'll see about a reward.'

Lucy swallows. 'It's just this.' She hesitates again. A fly crawls across the table between us.

'Yes?' I look up.

'It's your husband,' Lucy says, her voice barely audible. 'According to Mary, he knew. He knew what Dr Rodriguez was doing.'

It's the last straw. Shock sucks all the air out of me. I'm on my feet before I've even registered standing up.

'Lies,' I hiss. 'Liar.'

Moments later I'm outside, running down the road, desperate to get away.

Desperate to get home.

This was the day Ginger Tall and Broken Tooth happened. I was in the playground but I knew where there was a rip in the fence and when the teacher wasn't looking I crawled under because there was a big conker on the other side but it was really belonging to us because it had fallen from the tree on our side. I didn't think anyone would notice but they did before I even got to the conker.

There were two of them.

'Hey, Pig Face,' said the tall one with ginger hair. 'Why are you in our playground?'

'Yeah, why?' The one with the chipped front tooth was short and skinny with glasses on, but still bigger than me.

I pushed my hair back, trying not to look like I was scared. But I was. And they could see it. Ginger Tall smiled – a mean, thin smile, all glinting from metal braces.

'You shouldn't be here.'

'Yeah,' Broken Tooth added.

The rain was like someone throwing pencils on my face. I turned to leave, but Ginger Tall ran in front of me. 'Where are you going, Pig Face?'

I said nothing. Tried to pass.

Ginger Tall grabbed my arm with nasty fingers. They dug in so hard they hurt. 'You deaf now, too?'

I opened my mouth, but there was a tight feeling in my throat,

33

stopping my words. I was so scared that I could feel a little bit of wee coming out.

Help, let me go. *That was what I wanted to shout, but my voice wasn't working.*

And then Ginger Tall made his hand into a fist.

CHAPTER THREE

Art's phone is still going to voicemail, so I speak to Hen again, ranting down the phone at her as I pick apart everything Lucy O'Donnell said. To her credit, Hen refrains from pointing out she told me not to go and meet the woman.

I come away from the call exhausted and wound up. It's not quite midday but I pour myself a glass of wine and sit down in front of my computer. I need to sort out a lesson plan for later in the week and check my emails. Hopefully that will take my mind off what's just happened.

There're a couple of messages from the Art & Media Institute, just admin stuff. One from my agent, inviting me to a drinks party in May. I squirm as I read it – all friendly and chatty but with a rather barbed 'Do hope you will have some news for us soon' at the end. She's referring to my writing, of course. I was starting to plan a fourth book when Beth died. I haven't written a word since. I've checked my contract and there's nothing to say I have to send her my next idea by a certain date. Still, after producing nothing and working on nothing for eight years, I can't help but wonder when she's finally going to get fed up and chuck me back on the slush pile where she found me.

The last email I open is from Morgan, Art's sister. I've left this one to the end, because virtually all communication with

Morgan leaves me feeling inadequate. It's not really her fault – she's just so groomed and ultra-organized. She and Art didn't know each other for most of their childhoods, which were spent at opposite ends of the social spectrum. Morgan was born into privilege and privately educated splendour, growing up in Edinburgh. Art, meanwhile, was the illegitimate son of Morgan's father and a pretty London waitress, and grew up in single-parent poverty in Archway.

I force myself to read Morgan's email. Sure enough, she's asking what the arrangements are for Art's fortieth-birthday party which, as Hen reminded me earlier, is *this Friday*. I take a breath. It's not really a problem. I've already told our friends and was just planning to pop to M&S at some point to stock up on party food. We have a well-loaded iPod and plenty of booze – Art buys wine and beer in bulk as part of some business deal, and our entire dining room is basically a large drinks cupboard.

My meagre arrangements, however, clearly won't satisfy Morgan. I read through her email with a growing sense of guilt – and resentment.

Hey Gen!!! How are things? I'm planning to be with you Friday lunchtime (I'm flying in on the Red Eye from a conference in New York). Hope that's okay? Is there anything you'd like me to bring for Art's party? I'm dying to hear all about it – when did you send invites? I guess mine's waiting for me at home – or did you leave me off the list?! Only kidding. Who is your caterer? What music are you planning? Will you be working from a theme for the decorations or just going with something traditional? What kind of cake have you ordered? Is there any surprise element I should know to keep quiet about?

Etc., etc. I start to email back but am soon overwhelmed by the impossibility of explaining to Morgan in writing that her idea of party arranging is a far cry from the low-key efforts that pass muster in our corner of north London.

Feeling irritated, I simply reply that I'll see her in two days' time, then crawl onto the sofa, determined to spend the next ten minutes making a shopping list in my head. *Hummus, olives, pitta ... maybe I could introduce some sort of camp, seventies theme with prawn cocktail canapés or cheese and pineapple on sticks ...* But my mind keeps going over what Lucy O'Donnell told me.

Her words swim around my head.

Beth is alive. Your husband knew.

It's bright and crisp and clear outside. The sort of early spring day I normally love. But today it doesn't touch me. Today, I can't think straight. Can't think at all. The woman was lying ... it was a scam ... that's the only explanation. Art would never, *could* never, have colluded in such a lie.

And yet doubt crawls through my mind. Could any part of what O'Donnell told me be true?

The phone rings. And though I've been expecting the call, the sound makes me jump. I reach for the handset beside the sofa.

'Gen?' Art's voice is full of concern. 'Are you okay?'

'Oh, Art.' I can feel the tears welling up just at the sound of his voice.

'Hen just called me,' Art says. 'She told me about ... that woman ...' He spits out the words. 'I can't bloody believe it.'

'Oh.' I'm slightly thrown. Hen knows Art well, of course, but I didn't expect him to hear this intimate piece of information from anyone other than me.

'So tell me exactly what this woman said to you?' he says.

I go through the whole thing again. I hesitate when I get to the part about O'Donnell's conviction that Art himself was involved, then I rush in and tell him that too. He makes a noise that's halfway between a growl and a groan.

'I can't believe they would do this,' he says.

'Who?' I sit straight up on the sofa. 'Art, do you know who . . . who that woman is?'

He sighs. 'Not for sure, but I'm guessing John Vaizey from Associated Software sent her. We totally crushed them on a pitch last week.'

My head spins. 'Why would one of your business rivals pretend that . . .?'

'Vaizey threatened me after the pitch, called me a "media tart" and said I'd better not take the account if I wanted to stay in business.'

'Why didn't you tell me?' I say.

'I thought it was just a meaningless threat but . . .' Art's breathing is shallow. 'I never thought he'd do something so cruel . . . or . . . or aimed at you.'

I think it through. Fourteen years of listening to Art talk about his business dealings have left me with no illusions; the apparently sedate world of corporate investments often produces unbelievably destructive and underhand tactics. 'But . . . but how would he know the sister of the theatre nurse at the hospital?' I say. 'It doesn't make sense.'

'It's a con, Gen,' Art says bitterly. 'You don't even know this woman *was* the nurse's sister. You said yourself you couldn't even be sure the woman in the photo she showed you was *really* the nurse from the hospital.'

This is true. For the first time in hours the horror of O'Donnell's claims slides into a context I can cope with. Everything she said was designed to hurt me and – through me – Art.

'Anyway, who else could it be?' Art goes on. 'You don't have any enemies. You don't even have a proper job.'

There's a pause while I register what he's said. It's true, of course – I only work at the college eight hours a week – but it's blunt, even for Art, who never sugar-coats anything. He obviously realizes this and softens his voice.

'The point is, everyone loves you. It's *got* to be a business thing.'

I'm nodding on the other end of the phone, desperately wanting to believe him. And yet Lucy O'Donnell's anxious face is still in my mind's eye.

'It's just . . . she seemed so sincere, like . . . even if the whole thing was made up, she genuinely thinks it's true.'

'That's stupid.' Art's voice has the force of a hurricane. 'Don't start imagining things. I was there too, remember? Beth died inside you.'

I flinch.

'How could anyone think she's alive?' Art persists. 'There was a whole team of people in the operating theatre who said she was dead.'

'Lucy O'Donnell said Dr Rodriguez got most of them out of the room before the baby was born; that he gave them food poisoning or something so they wouldn't be there when—'

'Can you hear how far-fetched all this sounds?' Art demands. 'What about the scan that *showed* she was dead? No movement, no heartbeat. What about the tests on her they did later?'

'You can manipulate images and turn off sounds and substitute bodies,' I say stubbornly.

'For goodness' sake,' Art says. 'The doctor took her out of you. He *saw* her.'

'*I* didn't see her,' I say, remembering how Beth had been born so disfigured that the doctor had advised against it when I came round after the anaesthetic. The phone feels hot against my ear.

'No.' Art hesitates. 'But I did.'

A woman's voice sounds in the background. She has a slight French accent. She's asking Art to go with her. Art muffles the receiver.

'Okay, Sandrine, sure.' He sounds self-conscious. Unlike himself. Then he's back. 'Sorry, Gen, I have to go. I was supposed to be in my next meeting ten minutes ago.'

'It's fine,' I say.

'Are you sure you're okay? Why don't you call Hen to come over, or Sue, or—'

'I'm *fine*, Art, honest.'

We say goodbye and I curl up on the sofa. The memories that I keep walled up are flooding back. How I got pregnant with Beth so easily – within a couple of months of coming off the Pill. How happy Art was when I told him: his eyes lit up with a boyish grin. How tired I felt and how it didn't feel real until I saw Beth sucking her thumb on the scan. Not that I knew she was a girl then; I asked, but they said the position she was in made it impossible to tell. How I sang to her songs that my dad used to sing to me. How she would kick when I was in the bath and how Art and I would watch my belly moving, entranced and – we laughingly admitted to each other – ever so slightly freaked out.

The day we travelled to Oxford to stay in our rented house for the last month, I was all hormonal, crying at the change of scene, worried I wouldn't settle and that we should never have left the security of London and our local hospital. But the house was so lovely and Dr Rodriguez was so reassuring that I felt right at home within hours of arriving.

My mind skips to the day itself: 11 June. I'd been feeling light-headed and groggy all day and hadn't felt the baby move for hours. At first, I wasn't particularly bothered by this – at 37 weeks her movements had slowed right down. But Art was anxious. Jittery. He was trying not to show how concerned he felt, but he kept suggesting I went to the hospital for a proper check. I hadn't had a scan for weeks but Dr Rodriguez said they could fit me in late afternoon. We got there early, so took a stroll around the natural-birth pod, which wasn't being used that day The pod was – is – an amazing creation. A womb-shaped environment designed to replicate whatever natural scene you choose: at the flick of a button, the walls show a film of the sea, or woods or open countryside – or even, at an extra cost, the client's own footage – with sounds and smells to match. There's a birthing pool, a soft, padded floor that can be sloped at various gradients, and pillows and cushions in a range of sizes and textures. I was still, at that point, hopeful I'd be able to give birth there. I remember Art and I agreeing that the pool with the film of the ocean all around and a starlit sky above would be our first choice – both of us loving the swish and drag of the waves and the scent of salt in the warm air.

Still feeling lightheaded, and increasingly worried that I hadn't felt the baby move for hours now, I walked with Art across to the main building for my check-up. Dr Rodriguez asked me to wait: there was some problem with the ultrasound scanner in his usual room. We waited nearly two hours until another was free. It grew overcast outside. Art was fidgeting, anxious. And then Dr Rodriguez was with us. The radiographer had gone, so the doctor did the scan himself. I remember him peering at the screen, the concern on his face. And then him turning to us, saying that he was so terribly sorry. He had to say the words three times before I heard them: our baby had died in the womb.

Art and I were distraught. Then Art insisted the hospital did the C-section to remove Beth as soon as possible. I hadn't eaten for hours, he argued, there was no reason not to go ahead straightaway. The doctor insisted I should have a few hours

– maybe even a few days to get over the shock of the news. Art refused to listen. I don't remember having an opinion myself. I was too numb, swept along by Art's fury and determination.

Then the doctor suggested I should give birth naturally, and both Art *and* I insisted that we wanted a C-section. Art was a whirlwind on this. At the time I felt grateful to have someone fighting my corner for me.

Now, I can't help but look back and wonder why he was so insistent.

We left the soft surroundings of the consulting rooms to enter the steel-and-antiseptic world of the operating theatre. I was so scared before the general anaesthetic, my hands were shaking. I remember Art's warm fingers curling over mine, covering the raw torn skin around my nails, his eyes gleaming wet.

'I'm here, Gen,' he'd said. 'Everything's going to be all right.'

And then the silence in the recovery room as I came round. My eyes so heavy, struggling to open. Trying to focus on the clock on the wall, wondering where I was for a split second, then catching a glimpse of a nurse scurrying past outside the room, her face turned away. Shifting my gaze a fraction. Seeing Art sitting beside me, leaning forward, his face lined with pain. No baby. No baby. Dr Rodriguez walking over . . . a shadowy figure behind Art . . .

'I'm so sorry we lost her,' Art said. And his words sent me spinning and falling into darkness.

After that it's a blur: I remember the view from my window – a willow tree sweeping across a patch of grass with the curving glass roof of the birthing pod in the distance, a harsh reminder of the labour I had hoped for. I stared at the tree and the grass and the glass roof for hours on end, trying to take in what had happened. Dr Rodriguez explained his suspicions – later confirmed by the tests into Beth's DNA – that she had a defective chromosome. We got the details weeks later. Full Trisomy 18, a random genetic condition that isn't hereditary and which can be suffered to varying degrees. It killed my Beth before she could live.

I was numb for days, way past Beth's funeral, way past the test results. And then, slowly, stealthily, Grief crept up on me. A monster, fighting me inside my head, where no one, not even Art or Hen or my mum, could reach me. And with the grief, the anger. The unreasonable fury at perfectly nice people with babies and well-meaning women who tried to empathize by telling me about their miscarriages.

Unthinkable, uncontrollable, this pain seeped through me, gradually becoming a part of my life, absorbed into its reality. Wanting to move on and yet not wanting to leave Beth behind. No baby. No writing. Just drifting. For the past eight years.

I get up from the sofa. It's still early afternoon. Art won't be back until the evening. I wander listlessly into the kitchen, but have no appetite, so I wander out again. As the afternoon wears on, doubt creeps over me again.

I meander around the house, unable to settle to anything. In the end I find myself at the top of the house, in Art's office again. I don't want to look but I have to. If there's any paperwork on my stay at the Fair Angel still in our possession, it will surely be in this room.

I stand in the doorway, looking around at the large desk and the rows of shelves and filing cabinets. Light strikes the wooden floor in stripes. I have no idea what I'm even looking for. Immediately after the stillbirth Art took charge, making all the arrangements, signing whatever needed to be signed. I was glad at the time but, looking back, it's like that set the tone for the years that have followed, with Art increasingly in control of who and what he wants to be and me floundering. It's ironic that the differences that brought us together – me drawn to Art's energy and sense of purpose, and Art attracted to my creativity and, as he saw it, unpredictability – are the very things that have driven us down parallel paths since Beth.

The floorboards creak as I cross the office floor. They need to be re-laid – have done since we bought the house. I promised this year I would finally get around to sorting them out, but it hasn't happened yet. Art, bless him, has never complained about this or any other of my administrative failings.

I don't know where to begin, so I start opening drawers at random. Art's filing system is highly organized, but unlabelled. He has a phenomenal memory and knows – or claims to know – exactly where everything is. Apart from the cupboard in the corner, which is locked, everything is accessible, so there's a lot to get through. I could, of course, call him again and ask where the Fair Angel info is, but he won't understand why I want to look. Anyway, he'll still be in his meeting, not to mention in another country.

After a while I work out the logic to the layout. Everything to do with his personal tax affairs in one cabinet, personal investments in another, household stuff, contractors . . . I stop at a section of the cabinet that seems more haphazard than the rest. I pull out a few papers. Certificates. Licences. Diplomas.

Half an hour later, I've been through every official document Art has stored here, from his childhood swimming certificate for 50 metres ('You have now achieved Flipper level!'), through various school reports from City of London Boys – to which he won a scholarship – to his degree cert. in Economics, finding nothing relevant to Beth.

I start again and work systematically through every single file in each of the four cabinets. There are business records going back years and letters from various financial advisers too. I flick through a sheaf of paperwork from one of Art's old accountants . . . business loans . . . overdrafts . . . VAT . . . It's overwhelming and largely incomprehensible.

I come to a folder marked: 'Personal'. Inside there's a small sheaf of bank statements for an account I didn't know Art had. The account covers the year after Beth died and is in the name of 'L. B. Plus'. As far as I know, this isn't a Loxley Benson trading name, though Dan, the finance director, has set up various business accounts for the company. But the folder says 'personal'. I can't stop myself from looking down the list of transactions, a slightly sick feeling in my stomach. I know Art loves me. I know he is devoted and faithful, and yet I can't help but wonder what I might find here. The suggestions shriek inside my head: Evidence of meals in romantic restaurants? Payments to prostitutes? I tell myself not to be stupid.

And there's nothing that looks out of the ordinary. The running balance on the account is high – it never seems to drop below £10,000 – and there are several outgoings in the thousands: a few online payments to the wine store that Art uses for the office, deposits for business trips to the places Art regularly visits . . .

And then I notice a lump sum . . . £50,000 paid in on 16 June eight years ago, one week after Beth died, and paid out again a few days later.

What was that for? The payee is named as 'MDO'. I don't recognize the initials. I think back. Eight years ago, Loxley Benson was already well-established and generating a decent income, with hundreds of thousands of pounds going through the books every month. Art and I were planning to buy a bigger house soon after Beth was born – a plan that ended up being shelved for two years. It is entirely possible Art could have spent 50k from the business that I didn't know about, though I can't believe he wouldn't have told me if the money was used for something personal.

I flick through more bank statements, searching for additional payments to MDO. But there isn't anything.

I sit back on my heels, my heart thudding. *Stop it, Gen, you're being stupid, paranoid, crazy.* This money could be for anything. It certainly isn't enough to pay a doctor to fake a baby's death.

Another couple of hours pass and I'm exhausted. There's info here on holidays and business trip, plus copies of both Art's and my birth certificates. But there is *nothing* here on Beth or my time in the Fair Angel hospital.

I rub my eyes. They're sore from staring at all the fine print and my head is aching too, so I put all the files back and, after a quick look to check nothing appears too obviously disturbed, I go downstairs, get into the car and drive to M&S. I spend an hour shopping in a daze, stocking up on party snacks and mixers. I'm so preoccupied with my thoughts I almost walk out of the store with my unpaid trolley of goods, realizing my mistake just inches from the door.

I drive home, eat several cocktail sausages and a handful of salad leaves straight from the bag, then switch off the phone and go to bed. I don't normally nap in the daytime, but today I feel utterly exhausted. Our bedroom is a mix of our tastes. Simple, uncluttered and plain for me, with splashes of the strong, bold colours that Art loves.

I lie under the duvet, but sleep doesn't come. Instead, memories wash over me like the sea crashing over the shore – unstoppable.

My dad died long ago, when I was a little girl. I don't remember him well – just snatches out of time – but from what people tell me he and Art had a lot in common. Like Art, my dad was charming, driven and talented. And in a sense he was equally successful.

But Art is on top of his life in a way my dad never was.

My dad was a musician – a brilliant guitarist who played with every major seventies band from Pink Floyd to The Rolling Stones. He was away from home a lot, but when he was around he made everything a party. He would always bring me exotic presents and greet me with a huge smile and some silly song he'd made up for me. *My Queen*, he called me, all mock serious – or *Queenie* when he *really* wanted to tease me. He had long, dark hair that fell over his face when he played his guitar, and hands that always shook in the morning.

I hold out my hands in front of me. Mum says they are like his – slim, with long, tapered fingers. And my mouth. That's like his, too. Bottom lip thin, top lip full. I think Beth would have had our mouth. I wonder what Dad would have been like as a granddad.

I close my eyes, remembering how his breath smelled sweet when he kissed me goodnight. I didn't realize until I was older that the sweetness came from vodka. He had bottles hidden all over the house. I tried some once, when I was about six – a bottle I found under some towels in the bathroom cupboard. Just a little sip. It made me feel sick, like a liquid version of the way Mum's hairspray smelled.

They called me Geniver after a character in a movie they'd watched during the trip they made to India together before I was born. I can't imagine Mum – even the young, hippyish version I know from photos – enjoying the rough freedom of India, but I loved Dad's stories of how they wandered together through village festivals and markets, the scents of cardamom and cumin heavy in the humid air.

Dad drank himself to death just before my ninth birthday. He was on tour – back in India, ironically – with a now long-forgotten group called Star Fire. You can hear Dad's guitar solo on their only hit: 'Fire in the Hole'. Apparently, the day he died, he recorded the song then argued with the band's manager. That was the start of a ten-hour drinking session that ended with him choking to death on his own vomit in an alley-way outside a nightclub.

They found a little salwar kameez he'd bought for me in his hotel room. I still have it.

On an impulse I get out of bed and head for the large walk-in closet that leads off our bedroom. Art's stuff takes up less than a third of the space in here. The rest is crammed with my own clothes, mostly things I no longer wear – or that no longer fit.

I rummage along the bottom shelf, looking for the pile of old clothes I brought from Mum's house when we moved here. I find my Brownie uniform, covered in badges, then my school tie with its blue-and-maroon stripes. The salwar kameez lies underneath. It's red silk. I never wore it. It only fitted me for a few months after Dad died, when the idea of actually putting it on was too painful. Suppose I tore it? Or spilt something on it? I kept it pristine, a treasure, a precious memory. And then one day I went to dress up in it in front of my bedroom mirror and had grown too big for it. I wept then, thinking about Dad dying alone, missing him.

It's funny, I have no memory of him ever being drunk around me. Sometimes I even wonder if he was really as bad as Mum likes to say. After all, musicians are allowed a little licence. Partying goes with the territory.

One of the things that drew me to Art was that his father wasn't around when he was a child either. He understands what it's like to be without a parent when you're young and to idolize them while somehow, somewhere, thinking you must be to blame for their absence.

I reach under the salwar kameez and take out what I know is there: a small, white babygro. It's the only item of Beth's baby clothing that I kept. I let Hen have everything else – it seemed only fair, she had so little money for Nathan back then.

I take the babygro and hold it to my face. After Beth, I carried it with me everywhere for a year, I even slept with it. I packed it away the day we scattered Beth's ashes. It's years since I've seen it and, as I feel its softness against my cheek, I realize that it no longer has any power over me. It's just a piece of cloth. Never worn, never used. That I invested it with the significance I did seems amazing to me now.

Could Art have lied to me about Beth?

The question ricochets around my head.

Ridiculous. Impossible. Even if he were capable of such dishonesty, what possible reason could he have for colluding in a plot to take our child – our first and only, much-wanted baby – away from us?

I put the babygro and the salwar kameez away, run a bath and soak in it.

I strain my memory, trying to bring back the moment Art told me Beth was dead. *We lost her.* Suddenly the words sound ambiguous. Lost her to whom?

I close my eyes, remembering how Art had cried in my arms and how I'd wept in his. How each day brought a new reminder that, although we had no baby, no one had informed my body, so that my belly sagged and ached under the long purple gash of the fresh C-section scar, while unneeded milk leaked from my nipples. Art walked every morning along the river, hands in his pockets, shoulders hunched. I saw him from my window and everything in his body spoke of his despair. He went to pieces at the funeral, too. I watched him from behind the numb wall of my own grief as his legs gave way under him and Morgan helped him stumble red-eyed out of the crematorium.

It's impossible to believe that anything Lucy O'Donnell said is true. And yet my gut tells me she wasn't lying. I sink lower into the bath, letting the water lap over my stomach, over the place where Beth once danced inside me.

I fall asleep at last in the warm water. In my dream I'm back in the house where I grew up. I'm hiding under the bed, a child, holding my dad's guitar like a security blanket, and then a voice calls me out and it's the young doctor from the first clinic where Art and I were tested following nine months of trying to get pregnant again after Beth. I'm not anxious about it – not really. After all, I got pregnant easily enough the first time. The doctor turns to me. She smiles. 'We can find nothing wrong,' she says. 'You are both still young. It just takes time.' She shakes my arm. 'Listen to me. It is just a matter of time. The baby should come. Just give it time.' She shakes my arm. 'Geniver. Give it time. Time. Gen . . .'

'Gen.'

I wake, disoriented. Art is gently shaking my arm. It is dusk outside and I am lying on the bed covered in just a towel . . . Cold.

'Are you all right?' Art's eyes are tender in the twilight. He sits on the bed beside me.

I tug at the towel, drawing it up over my shoulders. I don't even remember getting out of the bath and onto the bed. I stare into Art's face and realize how crazy I was to let some stranger make me doubt him for a second.

'You must be exhausted,' I mumble. 'What's the time?'

'Almost seven.' He grimaces. 'I didn't have a minute all day and the flight home was packed.' He pauses, leaning lower and letting his lips graze my forehead. 'It's you I'm worried about, though,' he whispers. 'How are you doing?'

I stroke his face, running my finger over the lines that crease the skin around his eyes. They weren't there a year ago. Art is getting older. And so am I. There's nothing stronger than the bond created by time and suffering.

'I'm sorry about this morning, Art, that woman really got to me.'

'I know.' Art tucks the towel around me as I shiver. 'I put in a call to Vaizey. He wouldn't speak to me, but I left a message.' He pauses. 'Bastard.'

I raise my eyebrows.

'Don't worry, I didn't actually threaten him, just made it clear that if he was trying to stir anything up between us, he might as well stop now. It wasn't going to work.'

'No.' I squeeze his hand. 'So how was your meeting?'

'Good.' Art grins. 'Hey, d'you want to hear something amazing?'

I sit up. 'What?'

'*Two* things actually.' He laughs. 'Count 'em. One, today's pitch went well. *Really* well. The client more or less said the job was ours.'

'Fantastic.' I smile, trying to look like I know which client he's talking about. This one has totally passed me by. All I know is that the company is based in Brussels. To be honest, since Art appeared in *The Trials* there have been too many pitches to keep track of.

'The second amazing thing that happened today is that the woman I was with, Sandrine – she's on a policy committee at Number Ten,' Art pauses for breath. '*Ten Downing Street,* Gen. She'd already said she wanted to talk to me about an "initiative", remember? Well, apparently the PM saw me on *The Trials* and he wants *me* on the same committee that she's on. It's not window dressing either. I got into the weeds with Sandrine about it. She says the PM is really impressed with me, wants me in the "loop", this particular "loop" being a top-level, big-bloody-deal of a weekly session that the Prime Minister is *always* at. Me, him, her and three other people, max. Just think, Gen. Me and the bloody

PM in a meeting together. Starting tomorrow.' He shucks his jacket off with a flourish.

'That's brilliant,' I say.

'Bloody right.' Art laughs. He sits back and loosens his tie. 'And the best bit is the influence on policy I'll have. D'you get it, Gen? They're going to listen to me, because I've grown the company so much – against all the odds – and I've walked the line while I've done it. Everything ethical, sustainable . . . They see me up here on this high moral ground and they want to jump up and join me.' He beams at me. 'This is so much bigger than the company, than just Loxley Benson; it feels like everything's opening up: me getting to make a difference on policy, you trying to get pregnant again . . . Hey, maybe we should celebrate, buy that recycled dance sculpture from Being Green that you liked?'

I stare at him. 'That cost nearly fifty grand.'

An image of the £50,000 payment to MDO on the bank statement flashes up inside my head. My pulse races, my mind suddenly alert and working at a million miles an hour. I *have* to ask Art. It will drive me insane otherwise.

Art laughs. 'Okay then, how about an environmentally friendly barbecue?'

'Actually . . .' I try to sound casual. 'I was looking for something earlier and I came across an odd payment. The folder was marked "personal", but the file was an account for L. B. Plus.'

Art shrugs. 'That's probably just one of Dan's trading names for Loxley Benson, you know he uses loads of them . . .' He pauses. 'What was the payment for?'

'I don't know, but it was fifty grand,' I pause, watching his face carefully. 'The payee's name was MDO.'

'Right.' Art's expression is impassive. 'When was this?'

'Nearly eight years ago. Just after . . . you know . . .'

The atmosphere immediately grows tense. Art sucks in his

breath. 'Has this got something to do with that stupid bitch who came here this morning?'

'No, of course not.' I touch his arm, to emphasize that there's no accusation in my question. 'Honest, Art, it's just made me think about that time and I realized I didn't know where any of the old paperwork is stored and then I came across this weird account . . .' I tail off, hoping Art can't see through me, to the mistrustful heart of my suspicions.

Art takes a step away from me. His face is guarded. 'I can't remember what that payment was for,' he says. 'But it probably got filed in a personal folder by accident. I'll look into it.'

My heart sinks at the distance that's just opened up between us. 'I'm sorry, Art, that woman really upset me. It's hard when a total stranger looks you in the eyes and—'

'And makes an outrageous accusation against your own husband that you can't be one hundred percent sure isn't true?' Art's voice is carefully light, but I can hear the tension underneath.

'No.' I smile. 'I know it's not true. It's just . . .' My voice shrinks to a whisper. 'It's just . . . our baby . . . I never saw her, Art. Suppose . . .'

He stares at me. 'Yes, but *God,* Gen.' His voice is gentler than before. He squats down beside me and reaches across the bed for my hand. 'You *know* why you didn't, but *I* saw her.'

I look away. I didn't see Beth because she was so deformed that Dr Rodriguez advised me not to. Her defective chromosome, Trisomy 18, had caused damage to the heart and kidneys, with massive disfiguration to the head.

Art said at the time he wished he hadn't seen her. I didn't understand why, until I demanded to see the pictures in Dr Rodriguez's file during our visit to hear the results of his post-mortem tests. The photos were clipped to a report on the birth.

I wish I hadn't seen them – but I did. I saw everything, including the way her face was twisted like melted wax.

So I didn't see Beth herself, but I did see the proof that she was dead.

And Art, poor Art, he saw her for real.

'What did she look like, Art?' I say, keeping my gaze fixed on his face. 'Our baby . . . you saw her . . . what . . . how did she look?'

I hold my breath. We've never talked about Beth's specific appearance. I mean, Dr Rodriguez told me about her disfigurement and I saw that picture of her afterwards. But Art's always refused to tell me exactly how our baby looked – the essence of her. I watch his face harden, and even before he opens his mouth I know he's got no intention of talking about it now, either.

'I'm not going there, Gen.' Art stands up, paces to the door then stops, his fingers clenched tightly round the handle. 'Maybe you should call Hen again. Or Sue. Or your mum. See what they say about all of this.'

I shake my head. I already know what Hen thinks. Hen never hides her feelings. My friend, Sue, on the other hand, will be soothing and sympathetic, then try and make me laugh. But she won't really understand, either. Mum will dismiss my fears out of hand, even before I tell her what they're about. She makes no attempt to hide her belief that I've inherited my dad's neurotic, compulsive tendencies, 'though at least you don't appear to be looking for the answers to life at the bottom of a bottle.' Plus she adores Art.

Not that it matters. I know it's crazy for me to doubt the past like this.

'Mum's in Australia.' My voice breaks as I speak.

'So? They have phones there, don't they?' Art's tone is suddenly harsh, his breathing jagged. He strides back to the bed. His jaw is clenched. 'Jesus Christ, I hope John Vaizey, or whoever sent that woman to lie to you, rots in hell for giving you false hope.' He slams his hand, flat, against the wall above the bed.

I jump, my breath catching in my throat. Art *never* loses his cool. He's always absolutely in control. I stare at him, my whole body tensed. I've never seen him so angry. And then, as I watch – half-terrified, half-astonished – Art sinks down beside me on the bed.

'I'm sorry, Gen.' He puts his head in his hands and, when he looks up, there are tears in his eyes. 'I'm so sorry but you have to let this go now because . . . because . . . the hardest thing I've ever had to do was walk into that room and face you after our baby had died. And I'm not – do you hear me? – I'm not letting that moment destroy our future like it destroyed the past.'

He stops, his chest heaving. For a moment I feel guilty. I have to keep remembering that Art lost Beth too.

'I know,' I say. 'Any chance of a cup of tea?'

A beat passes.

Then Art nods, 'Not tea though, champagne,' he insists. I can hear him making himself sound cheerful again. 'We've got things to celebrate.'

Champagne is the last thing I want, but Art is back in ebullient mode and I know from experience it's easier not to resist. 'Okay, you get the bottle and some glasses,' I say, smiling back. 'I'll get dressed.'

Art raises his eyebrows, a flicker of lust in his expression. 'No need for that,' he says, tracing his finger across my bare shoulder.

'Maybe later . . .' I smile and pull away from him. 'Go on downstairs. I'll be there in a sec.'

Art leaves. I hurry into jeans and a sweatshirt and follow him down to the kitchen. I feel disoriented from sleeping the whole afternoon away. Art has already set two champagne flutes on the table. As I stand there he pops the bottle he's fetched and pours two glasses. He hands one to me, then raises his own.

'To the future,' he says. '*Our* future.'

I smile again and take a tiny sip of the chilled fizz. I sit down and Art comes up behind me, sets his glass down, and starts massaging my shoulders. 'Listen, Gen,' he says. 'I know it's hard, but you have to put all the rubbish that woman said out of your mind. Let's make today the day we start again.'

The fading light coming through the kitchen window catches the smudges around the rims of the two champagne flutes on the table.

Art picks up his glass again.

'Do you think we should report her to the police?' I ask.

'What for?' Art dismisses my suggestion with a flick of his hand. 'There's no proof. We don't even know her real name, or where she lives.'

I think of the scrap of paper with Lucy's mobile number scrunched up in my coat pocket. 'Right,' I say.

Art strokes my hair. 'I think what we should do is forget she ever existed. We'll do ICSI and you *will* get pregnant and we *will* have a baby.' He holds his glass out towards me and grins. 'To hope.'

I hesitate. I know Art's is the logical way forward but I *want* to believe the impossible. I *want* to believe that Beth is out there somewhere, waiting for me to find her. I touch my glass against his.

'To hope,' I say.

CHAPTER FOUR

I wake with a start from a bad dream. Anxiety clutches at my chest. Something's gone ... something's missing ... Beth ... always Beth ...

As the sensation fades, I grope for the clock beside my bed: 4.15 a.m. *Crap.* Art is snoring gently beside me. He never wakes early. He never has trouble sleeping. Most annoyingly, he never takes longer than a few minutes to fall asleep.

I get out of bed and pad downstairs to the kitchen. I know from experience that once I'm awake at this time, I might as well get up. I switch on the kettle and fetch a mug, a tea bag and some milk.

I've dreamed about Beth many times in the past few years and though I can never remember the details, I know that she grows older each time, so that she's always the age she would have been if she'd lived.

Maybe the age she *is* ... The thought strikes me so hard I actually drop the mug I'm holding. It bounces onto the counter-top with a thud that echoes loudly in the early morning air. Could I be dreaming of a *real* person?

Is such a thing even possible?

I sit down at the table, listening as the rush and hiss of the kettle coming to the boil fills the room. I rarely remember anything specific from the dreams, just a vague and fading sense of her face: once a rosy-cheeked baby, then a chubby, smiling toddler and now, almost eight years old, an olive-skinned little girl with soft brown curls, like I had when I was younger, with Art's huge brown eyes.

In my dreams she's alive and she's perfect.

I drink my tea, go back to bed and refuse to let myself think about either Beth or Lucy O'Donnell. After a while I fall asleep again. When I wake up it's almost nine-thirty. I can hear Lilia singing along to her iPod as she vacuums downstairs. I turn over. There's no sign of Art. Which isn't surprising. He's always out the door by seven. There is a note on his pillow, however. I reach over, groggily, and pull it closer.

Wish this was flowers. Love you, Ax

I teach today's class in a bit of a daze. I take four two-hour adult-education classes here at the Art & Media Institute each week – all on aspects of creative writing. It's not well paid and, as Art pointed out the other day, it's so part-time it's not even really 'a proper job.' I'm waiting for a lift when one of the women from the class corners me. It's Charlotte West, all designer jeans, sleek blonde ponytail and pushy sense of entitlement.

'Geniver?' Charlotte's voice is wheedling, her accent pure Home Counties. 'I wonder if I might have a word?'

I scan the lifts. All three of them seem to be stuck on the first floor so I force my mouth into a welcoming smile. 'Sure,' I say.

Charlotte moves closer and I have to stop myself taking a step away from her. She's in her early forties, I'd guess – a little older than me, though roughly the same age as most of my writing classes. She looks good for her age – slim and groomed. Today she's teamed her trademark Calvin Klein jeans with an emerald-green boat-neck top that brings out the colour of her eyes.

'How can I help?' I continue.

'I re-read *Rain Heart* again,' Charlotte says, her eyes shining. 'It's *so* brilliant. *Such* an inspiring book.'

'Thank you.' I feel awkward and not just because Charlotte is gushing. Of my three published books, I actually think *Rain Heart* is the weakest. The plot – about a woman whose husband has an affair with the wife of his business partner – has more than a couple of holes, and the characters seem wooden and unconvincing to me now. Ironically, it sold better than the others. In fact, it's the only one still in print.

I edge away. Charlotte follows, backing me into the corner between the wall and the first lift. I get a whiff of her perfume – one of those dark, sweet, cloying scents meant for velvet dresses and expensive restaurants.

'I was wondering where you got the idea from?' Charlotte goes on.

I sigh inwardly. This is the most common question writers get asked and, to my mind, one of the hardest to answer.

'I thought perhaps the story came from real life?' she adds.

'No.' I hesitate, wondering what to tell her. I could offer up the truth as far as I know it, that *Rain Heart* came from my imagination: a blend of half-thoughts and ideas filtered through a couple of newspaper articles, five minutes of overheard gossip at a bus stop and the inside track on two friends' heartbreaks.

And yet there's something unsettling about the intensity of her gaze that holds me back from confiding any of this information. 'I'm sorry, Charlotte . . .' I glance pointedly at my watch.

'Oh, right . . .' She sounds a little injured now. 'I'm in a hurry too. If I miss my train from Paddington . . .'

'I know.' I offer her a sympathetic grimace. Charlotte has mentioned her *long* journey from the West Country to my creative-writing class several times before. She definitely gives off 'the smell of burning martyr', as Hen would say. Other members of the group are now appearing behind her. Out of the corner of my eye I can see the lift furthest away from me has reached the second floor.

'Like I say, I was just curious . . .' Charlotte pauses. She shifts her bag up onto her shoulder and I notice it's an Orla Kiely, identical to the one Hen bought me for my last birthday.

Across the lobby, the furthest lift away from me is opening. Students surge inside. There won't be enough room for all of them, let alone me as well.

'Okay, well, I really have to go.'

Charlotte stares at me intently but says nothing. Her green eyes are impossible to read. For a second she seems almost angry. The lift doors close, leaving several people still outside. I glance at the two remaining lifts. The one nearest me is moving now. *Third floor . . . fourth floor . . .*

'I'm just so fascinated by your work, Geniver,' Charlotte says. There's a fawning tone to her voice that sets my teeth on edge. I take a step towards the lift as it pings its arrival.

'Bye, then,' I say brightly.

Charlotte's face falls. She tosses her head and her blonde ponytail swishes from side to side. I feel guilty, then irritated. People are crowding around, angling for a spot in the lift as it opens. If I don't move now I'll miss this one too. I step inside.

As people pile in after me, I can hear Charlotte, still outside the lift, sniff loudly.

'Well, good luck with your *next* book,' she says evenly.

My face burns as two women I don't know stare at me.

I press the button for the ground floor. As the door closes, I wonder if Charlotte knows what she's saying. If she knows I haven't written anything for nearly eight years.

Since Beth.

I try to push this thought away and head off to meet Hen for lunch. As I reach the restaurant I pass a little girl. She's smiling and skipping along beside her mother in a stripy school uniform, with short dark hair in two stiff bunches. I stop and turn, staring after her. A fear rises inside me. In the same way that you notice lovers in the street after you yourself have suffered a break-up, for years I'd see babies in prams and toddlers in buggies and think: 'That's what my Beth would look like now.'

But I never wondered before if any of the children I notice could *be* my Beth.

The fear increases inside me. I actually take a step after the little girl before trampling on my panicky thoughts. *Don't be stupid. Beth is gone.* Except . . . my panic rears up again. *Maybe she isn't gone. She could be out there somewhere and you would never know, Gen.*

Oh God. I force myself to go into the restaurant. I sit down, feeling hot even though it's cool and calm and the room is only a quarter full. I push thoughts of the little girl with her bunches out of my mind and start puzzling over that £50,000 Art paid to 'MDO'. Who or what is MDO?

The restaurant is starting to fill up when Hen arrives, nearly fifteen minutes late. She flies in through the door of the restaurant, her wild hair streaming behind her, her scarf trailing on the floor. She beams at the maître'd, who smiles indulgently at her and escorts her to our table.

That's Hen all over. Pretty and dizzy. On the surface. Underneath, she's as sharp as a pick.

'Sorry, Gen,' Hen gasps. 'I got held up in Cath Kidston.'

I can't help but smile. If there's one sentence that sums Hen up, that's it. Always late, and with a penchant for girly knick-knacks. Until she married Rob last year, Hen never had any money yet never seemed to stop spending. I've lost track of the number of times we've been in shops and she's had her cards cut up in front of her. She frittered away most of her twenties in a succession of short-lived jobs which she only managed to hang on to for as long as she did because of her charm and her smarts. Unsuitable boyfriends were also a specialty – penniless drifters with endearing smiles and severe commitment issues. No one who knew Hen was surprised when she fell pregnant with Nat or that the father ran away as soon as he found out.

Rob *was* a surprise. He's ten years older than her, and a banker – a breed that the younger Hen would have had put up against a wall and shot. Rob is as grounded as Hen is flighty and, while I believe Hen genuinely loves him, I'm sure she enjoys his money too.

Still, as my mother never tires of reminding me, you can never really understand anyone else's relationship. And the truth is that Hen's been far easier to be around for the past eighteen months, now she's able to indulge her extravagant tastes without worrying about paying her bills.

Hen is on top form. She doesn't mention Lucy O'Donnell's visit for at least half an hour. She's full of the funny shop assistant at Cath Kidston and some quirky expressions Nathan has come up with. I try to put O'Donnell out of my mind too, though her words lurk like a shadow behind everything I think and say.

'Are you okay, Gen?' Hen asks at last, smoothing down her top. It looks expensively cut, with a low neckline and tiny seed-pearl buttons. She casts a glance at my chewed fingernails and the torn, red skin around them and I smile, knowing this is how Hen gauges my well-being.

I tell her how upset Art got last night and then I tell her about the payment to MDO. I feel disloyal bringing it up, but it's on my mind and I can't hide my anxiety from Hen – she's too sharp-eyed for that.

'It was fifty thousand pounds, Hen. I mean, that's a *huge* amount to go out of a personal account.'

Hen shrugs. 'But Art says it *wasn't* personal,' she insists. 'Fifty grand isn't that much in company terms. Rob's always shifting money around different accounts. And I'm not surprised poor Art was upset after that woman coming round. Bringing all the old stuff up – it's going to be stressful for both of you.'

I fall silent. Beth is the one thing I've always found it hard to talk to Hen about. We were pregnant at the same time, though under very different circumstances, and full of plans for how we would be mums together. Nathan was born just a week before Beth. Hen missed the funeral as a result. I know she felt bad about that, but she didn't want to leave her baby and I couldn't cope with seeing a newborn just then. It was hard for both of us to be apart at the very moment we needed each other the most. During the twelve months that followed we spent less time together than we had in years. Hen tried, to be fair. But I couldn't face her and Nathan for a long time. I felt bad about that, but I know Hen understood. She certainly never held it against me.

And yet, though it's never been said, we both know that it's still difficult for me to see her as a mother – or be reminded of what my own life as a mother would have been like. At least Hen understood why I needed to call myself a mum after Beth died. Most people seemed to think that made no sense – as if I didn't really qualify for motherhood. But, to me, Beth was as real as any other baby and not to be allowed to call myself a mother seemed to deny her very existence. Stillbirth grief is like that – full of stupid little heartaches that leave you isolated and floundering. There are no memories to hold on to, no known individual with a distinctive personality to mourn, only a sense of something lost, always out of reach.

Hen puts her hand on my arm. 'I know it's difficult even without some stupid woman making ludicrous claims.' She rests her gaze on me, her normally lively, darting eyes full of sympathy. 'Maybe it would help to look at the certificates and stuff again. Maybe you need to see them all once more to let it go.'

I think about this on the way home. Hen's right, maybe it would help to see all the official documents. The trouble is, I have no idea where Art put everything. Despite my search, I didn't find anything in his office.

It takes me ages to get home. My bus crawls along Seven Sisters Road – there has obviously been some kind of accident and all the cars are stopping to have a gawp. Once I'm back, I check out the obvious places – the cupboards in the hall and the bedroom and, of course, Art's office, though I already know there's nothing about Beth in there unless it's in that locked cupboard.

I find nothing.

Art walks in at ten that evening. I can hear him on his iPhone as he trudges up the stairs. 'But is that volume or value, Dan? We gotta be clear.'

Art ends his call as he enters our bedroom. There are dark shadows under his eyes and his shirt is creased. He looks exhausted, but happy. I lie back against the pillow and watch him cross the room.

'Hey,' he says, sitting down on the bed beside me.

'Hey.' I ask about his day and Art talks for a while about the meeting at 10 Downing Street.

'. . . and then the PM came in. He's much shorter than he looks on TV and he's *definitely* had botox or whatever. No lines on his forehead at *all*. He made a special point of thanking me for being there. Sandrine and I got the policy wonks to talk about their Work Incentives programme, especially the stuff about increasing productivity through demonstrating ethical decision-making. The PM couldn't believe the Loxley Benson figures.' Art grins. 'He *listened*, Gen, he really did.'

'Sounds brilliant,' I say. I mean it, but at the same time my mind is running obsessively over everything I've been thinking about all day. I wait for him to stop talking, then I take a deep breath. 'Art?'

He looks up. 'What?'

I meet his gaze. 'I'm really honestly not saying I believe anything that mad woman said yesterday, but like I told you, it did bring everything up again. It ... it made me want to see Beth's death certificate, but I don't know where it, where anything is ...'

'Gen ...' Art shakes his head, his body visibly tensing. 'What's the point in going over all this again? You're just torturing yourself.'

I shrug. 'Sometimes I need to go back to go forward.'

Art shoots me a tired smile. 'You're crazy,' he says affectionately.

'Sure, I'm crazy.' I try to smile too. 'So where are all the papers from back then?'

I'm so expecting him to tell me that they've been lost or that he can't remember, that it comes as a complete shock when Art swings his legs off the bed and stands to face me, a look of weary concern on his face.

'They're in the locked cupboard in my office,' he says. 'I put them there because I don't like looking at them. I'll get them now.'

And before I can respond, he's walked out.

I sit on the bed, my stomach in knots. Am I being cruel to Art over this? I think back to that first week after the stillbirth ... I can't remember much at all. Just a few random snatches of conversation. I do remember Art talking about the funeral – he

65

wanted a cremation, but insisted it should be a joint decision. At the time it seemed like the most insignificant detail in the world. But now it means there is no body to dig up. No proof of death.

I shiver. I'm being morbid.

Upstairs the floorboards creak violently as Art walks around his office. I lie back on the pillows.

We scattered Beth's ashes the following April. I'd been seeing a therapist, at Art and Hen's suggestion, for several months and felt like I was starting to emerge from the dark sea of my grief, tipping my face at last to the spring sunshine. Of course what I didn't realize then is that grief, like the seasons, is cyclical. I would just start to feel open to life again, then find myself thrust back under the water, drowning in loss. Perhaps if I had fallen pregnant that year it would have been different, but I didn't. And every attempt at IVF pushed me deeper and deeper back beneath the waves.

There's a final creak from Art's office floorboards, the sound of his footsteps thundering down the stairs, and he's back, a red shoebox under his arm. He sets it down on the bed.

'Everything's in here.' He doesn't meet my gaze. 'I'm going to take a shower.'

He disappears into the bathroom. I know he's hurt, that he doesn't want me upsetting myself by raking it up . . .

But I have to face the truth.

Heart racing, I lift the lid off the red box. The first paper I pick up is the death certificate. I stare at Beth's name – chosen in the first flush of our grief because it sounded so delicate and fragile, a soft, simple, sigh of a name. *Beth Loxley*. It's strange seeing it written down. I trace my finger over the words – the name of a person who was never properly a person. There's no word for what Beth is, just as there's no word for the mother of a stillborn baby. I don't mind the lack of a label, but it makes what happened harder to talk about. Of course, talking isn't easy either. When strangers ask if I have children I have to choose whether to explain about Beth, which feels too intimate, or simply say 'no', which feels like I'm denying her again.

I sift through the papers. I'm not any sadder for seeing these, I realize. They're mostly official forms, just facts and figures. Underneath the Registrar's death certificate is the medical certificate of stillbirth, signed by Dr Rodriguez. I remember Art explaining to me that he had to take this to the Registrar to get the death certificate. I examine it closely, then filter through the rest of the papers – most of them to do with the funeral arrangements. There's a leaflet – subtle and understated – for Tapps Funeral Services and a letter from Mr Tapps himself, offering his sympathy for our loss and outlining various practicalities such as the booking of the crematorium and the date of the funeral.

I don't want to think about the funeral right now but, even so, Beth's tiny coffin forces its way into my head . . . The two white lilies Art and I placed on top of it and the numb whisper of my soul as I stared at them.

Inside the bathroom I can hear the shower running.

I close my eyes. What am I doing? Art was *stricken* at that funeral. He could barely walk. How can I make him go through all this again?

Enough.

I pick up the bundle of papers. As I place everything back in the box, a business card floats out onto the bed. It's Dr Rodriguez's card, with the number and address for the Fair Angel. In the bathroom the water stops running. I hesitate for a second, then for reasons that I refuse to articulate to myself, I slide the Tapps letter and the business card under the mattress beneath me. I put everything else back into the red box, replace the lid and push it away across the bed.

A minute later and Art's out of the shower. He walks towards the bed, a towel wrapped around his waist. He still works out at weekends sometimes, but the muscles in his arms aren't defined like they used to be – and there's definitely the beginning of a slight paunch around his middle. We're both getting older. Sometimes I can almost sense time as a force of nature, racing relentlessly into the future, with Art at the heart of the ride and me watching from the sidelines, unable to join in.

'Found what you were looking for?' He still sounds hurt.

'Yes.' I hesitate. 'Did you check out what that MDO payment was for?'

'No,' he groans. 'I forgot, but I know it was some sort of business loan. I just can't remember the details.'

'Right.' I'm wondering if that is really true. Art never forgets anyone he's done business with.

'Right, okay, well when you get a moment . . .' I say, vaguely. 'Thanks for getting everything out for me.'

Art nods, then whisks the box away. He takes it upstairs, back to his office, then comes back and flops into bed.

'I'm knackered.' He sighs, then picks up his phone and starts scrolling through emails. With all the international business Loxley Benson is involved in, there's not an hour of the day when people don't try and contact him.

I get up. The house is cold, the heating has gone off. I pull on a pair of thick socks and pad downstairs. Lucy O'Donnell's phone number is still in my coat pocket. I take it out and creep into the kitchen. I stop at the door and listen. No noises from upstairs. Art must still be busy with his emails.

I unfurl the scrap of paper and stare at Lucy's neat handwriting. The carefully printed numbers look more like the work of a primary school teacher than a con artist. I hesitate. I don't know why I need to speak to her again. I don't even know what I'm going to say. I just know that I can't let it go, like Art wants me to. If I'm going to take things any further then I need as much information as I can get. I mean, suppose just *some* of Lucy's story is true? Not the part about Art being involved, of course, but babies can be stolen, can't they? And once an idea has been planted in your head, you can't just toss it out again. You have to follow it through to the end.

I move silently through the kitchen without turning on the light and into the utility room. Hands shaking, I take a deep breath and call Lucy O'Donnell's number. It's unobtainable. I don't even get the chance to leave a message. I wait a couple of minutes, then try again, just in case. Still nothing. Maybe it's just as well. Surely this is all the proof I needed that the woman was a flake. Crazy. Deluded.

I save the phone number on my mobile, then throw the scrap of paper in the bin. As I come back out into the hall I hear the creak of the office floorboards on the second floor. I stop, my heart racing. Is Art up there again? Did he somehow hear me down here making a call? Why did that make him go back up to his office?

I wait a few seconds. There are no more floorboard noises. Then I go up the stairs to our bedroom. Art is lying on the bed, just where I left him. He looks over as I walk in. 'What is it?' he asks.

'Nothing.' I glance around. I'm all on edge. 'Did you go upstairs again, to your office?'

Art shakes his head, going back to his phone. 'Nope.'

'Oh.' My pulse is skipping about. Why on earth would he lie about that? 'I thought I heard the floorboards creaking.'

'Those things?' Art raises a disdainful eyebrow. 'Those bloody things have got a mind of their own. In fact, didn't you say you were going to get them sorted this year?' He grins at my recalcitrance and pats the duvet. 'Are you coming to bed?'

I get in and take off my thick socks. Maybe I imagined hearing the floorboards. I am certainly jittery enough.

Art turns out the light and lies back on the pillow with a sigh.

'Art?'

'Mmm?'

I've been thinking about the day, a few months into the pregnancy, when after obsessive research into alternative birth options, I found the Fair Angel private maternity hospital and we went to meet the obstetrician who would oversee my pregnancy and labour.

'Did you ever do any background checks on Dr Rodriguez – you know, basic research on where he came from, or his qualifications or his circumstances?'

'No,' Art says after a second. 'Why?'

'Well, I guess I'm thinking how much did we really know about him?'

Art snorts with derision and turns over so his back is towards me. 'Rodriguez had an impressive CV and recommendations coming out of his backside, Gen. He showed us that stuff *and* a bunch of personal thank you letters the first time we met him. Fair Angel had a brilliant reputation, too.'

'But—'

'Gen, don't go there.' Art pauses, then turns over again to plant a swift kiss on my cheek. 'Goodnight.'

''Night.'

Seconds later Art's breathing evens and deepens, but it's a long time before I fall asleep myself.

I stared at Ginger Tall's fist. A bit more wee came out of me. It felt warm at first, then cold. I couldn't stop it.

I looked down. The rain jabbed at the back of my neck. Run, I thought. Run away. But they were blocking my way back to the fence.

'You're a loser, Pig Face.' Ginger Tall's fingers on the hand that wasn't a fist hurt my arm.

Broken Tooth took my other arm, pressing and twisting the skin.

I wanted to yell them away but my yells were stuck in my throat. Ginger Tall moved so close I could feel warm breath in my ear. 'You're an ugly, pig-faced loser.'

'A fucking loser,' Broken Tooth added.

I knew that was a bad word. I stared at the wet stones by my feet, waiting for it to be over. The fist punched into my tummy. It hurt. I closed my eyes. Another punch. Another. Then it stopped.

I held my breath. Ginger Tall's shoes turned. Broken Tooth's shoes turned. Then there were just my shoes. I stared at them so hard my eyes burned. I looked at my trousers. There was a small dark patch right in the front of them so if anyone looked they would know I had done a bad wee.

Down there felt damp and sticky and cold.

I put my hand over so no one would see. Then I crawled back under the fence.

CHAPTER FIVE

I'm still asleep when Morgan arrives the next morning. Her brisk, sharp rings on the doorbell rouse me from my bed. I grab a cardigan from the chair, pull it on over my pyjamas and stagger downstairs wiping the sleep from my eyes.

I can see Morgan's slender outline through the glass in the front door. Instinctively I glance at the hall mirror. My hair is sticking up in different directions and yesterday's make-up is smudged under my eyes. I hesitate, making a half-hearted effort to wipe my face with my fingers and run my hand through my hair, trying to smooth it down.

The doorbell rings again.

It's hopeless. Whatever I do, I'm never going to match up to her. With a sigh I open the door.

Considering she's just arrived off a transatlantic flight, Morgan looks amazing. She's dressed in a fitted black suit with a real-fur trim, black-and-cream kitten heels and a leather clutch bag. The bottom of her sleek dark hair forms a perfect line. Two huge suitcases stand beside her on the front door step.

'Gen, honey,' Morgan coos, looking me up and down. 'You look fabulous.'

She's not a great liar. Even as she's speaking I can see her eyes widening with the horror of my appearance. That's Morgan all over, though. She can't help but come across as condescending, even when she's trying to be warm and friendly. It's an unsettling personality trait and one which I'm certain partially explains why, at nearly forty-two, the woman has never had a boyfriend for longer than three months.

'I just woke up,' I explain. 'I didn't sleep well last night.'

'Oh, no.' Morgan's voice softens into concern. 'I'm so sorry but I did say what time I was arriving and . . .' She checks her elegant, diamond-studded watch, 'it is after ten.'

'I know,' I say, tugging the cardigan more tightly around me. There's an egg stain on the lapel. Great.

'So how are the party plans going?' Morgan says brightly, stepping into the hallway. She glances back at her suitcases, still standing on the doorstep.

In Morgan's home in Edinburgh, her holiday homes in Martha's Vineyard and Tuscany or in any of the fancy hotels she normally stays at there would be men to help carry in the bags.

'Party plans are going fine.' I reach over the threshold and drag Morgan's two suitcases into the hall. Art can lug them upstairs later.

There's an anxious knot in my chest all day, but I have no time to think about any of the stuff that was keeping me awake last night. Morgan – though she claims only to want to help – is full of demands: 'Do you have any juice *without* the pulp?' . . . 'I don't want to interfere but do you really think you've bought enough canapés?' . . . 'I can't see any bags of ice in your freezer, should we order some in?' . . . 'Do you mind showing me where you keep the towels? I'm so sorry but I need to change the one you've given me, my skin's *terribly* sensitive . . .'

On top of this, the phone doesn't stop ringing. Most of the calls are from friends, checking on details of the party, asking what time to arrive or whether they can bring anything. I drift from the kitchen to the dining room, where bottles of wine are stacked floor-to-ceiling, trying to work out what to do and which order to do it in.

Morgan disappears upstairs at about three, shortly after which Hen pops over. Nat is on a play date with a friend, giving Hen an hour or two to help me prepare for the party. While I'm searching for the fairy lights from last Christmas that I want to drape over the living-room mirror, Hen obligingly goes to fetch a bumper pack of crisps from the stash in the garage. She doesn't reappear. After ten minutes I start to worry she's tripped over the garden furniture or something else stored in the garage and hurt herself, so I go looking for her.

I hear her before I see her. She's just inside the utility room, talking on the phone. Her voice is low and conspiratorial.

'I *know* she's my best friend,' she is saying. 'But she's *not* letting it go.' I freeze. Hen's voice is a mix of pity and irritation. 'I *have* tried talking to her.' Another pause. 'No, not yet.'

Confusion turns to anger and shame in my head. I can't bear to hear any more. 'Hen?' I call out.

There's a muffled whisper from inside the utility room, then Hen reappears. 'Sorry.' She rolls her eyes. 'Got sidetracked.'

I open my mouth ready to challenge her, then close it again. Who she was talking to? Art? I don't want to think about it.

I'm withdrawn as she comes into the kitchen, but Hen chatters away, all breezy like there's nothing wrong. We put the crisps she brought from the garage into bowls then string up the fairy lights together. After that, I retreat to the kitchen while Hen spends an hour setting out candles and reorganizing the furniture in the living room to allow more space 'for dancing'.

I can't help but laugh when I see what she's done. I point out that Art hates dancing.

Hen rolls her eyes. 'Don't be so negative,' she says, and though

74

her tone is light, there's a cutting edge to her voice. 'I'm sure he'd dance if you asked him.'

I feel uneasy. Does she think I'm being unfair on Art? Is her caustic tone connected to what I just overheard her say about me 'not letting it go'?

Hen obviously catches my discomfort. 'Sorry, Gen,' she says, waving her hand, as if to direct the tension between us into the next room. 'Is there anything else I can do?'

I look around. It's almost five now and, to be honest, I'd rather get on with sorting out the rest of the food by myself. Hen has brought a quiche and several of the other guests will come bearing dishes, so I've really only got a pavlova and a Black Forest gateau to finish off – the seventies theme proved irresistible in the end. Anyway, Hen always makes a mess in the kitchen and I'm still feeling a distance between us that hasn't been there since the first year after Beth.

'I'm fine,' I say. 'Just a few dips to do really . . . Morgan can give me a hand if anything major needs doing.'

'Yeah, right.' Hen rolls her eyes. 'Careful she doesn't chip a nail.'

'Sshh!' I grin.

'Aw, you know I love Morgan,' Hen says, heading for the door. As if to prove the point she calls up the stairs. 'Bye, Morgan.' But there's no reply.

'I think she's in the bathroom,' I explain.

'Can't wait to see what she's wearing,' Hen says in a catty whisper. She points to the fur trim on Morgan's black suit jacket, which is still lying over the larger of her two suitcases. 'How many animals died to make that?'

'Sssh!' I scold again, ushering her out of the front door.

I head back to the kitchen and get busy with the gateau. Before I know it, it's gone six and I'm just laying prosciutto and olives on a plate, feeling frazzled and desperate for a bath, when

Morgan appears. She stares at my ragged fingernails. I catch my reflection in the fridge door. God, I look even more of a mess than I did when she arrived. I'm still in the sweatpants and T-shirt I threw on this morning, my hair is messily piled on top of my head – and there's a smear of cherry jam across my cheek.

'So how's the latest IVF going?' Morgan asks, her hands behind her back. 'I'm so pleased you're considering trying again.'

I'm taken aback, but I try not to show it. This isn't the first time that Morgan has known more about my life than I expect her to. Art has always talked to his sister about our relationship; she was certainly the first person he told that we were engaged, and I know he confided in her years ago, over the failure of our previous IVF treatments. I used to mind but not any longer. The older I get, the more I realize how much family matters and, after his mum died, Morgan and her brothers were all the family Art had. Anyway, while Morgan always knows the facts of our relationship, I'm certain Art rarely confides his feelings.

'We're still thinking about the IVF,' I say vaguely and with what I hope is an air of finality.

'Right.' Morgan hesitates a second, then holds out one hand. A small, silver package nestles in her palm. She crosses the room and hands it to me. 'I know it's Art who had the birthday, but I wanted to give you this.' She half-blushes as she speaks, her shoulders hunching slightly as she takes several steps back.

'Er, thank you,' I stammer. The silver package is a box, expertly wrapped with a small silver ribbon. I pull the end of the ribbon and it unfurls in my fingers. I glance at Morgan as I prise the lid off the box. She seems uncharacteristically uncertain, anxious almost.

Inside the box is a silver butterfly on a chain. I lift it out. It's as simple as it is beautiful. The letters 'a' and 'g' entwined sparkle on one wing.

'It's white gold and diamonds,' Morgan says. 'I had it done for you and Art.'

'It's lovely,' I breathe, examining the bracelet again. 'Oh, Morgan.'

I'm overwhelmed. How like my sister-in-law, so brusque and supercilious on the outside, to show such hidden depths of thoughtfulness. I look up. Morgan is blushing again, her face half turned away. For a second she looks utterly vulnerable.

'The butterfly is the symbol of change. I thought it might help you...' She pauses. 'I don't mean to patronize you, Geniver, but I know what its like to feel stuck and I thought this might help you to move on, to let things be different. Maybe even to write again.'

It's not easy to hear Morgan's insight into my life, but I am truly touched and genuinely grateful for her kindness. I rush across the short distance between us and hug her tightly.

'Thank you.' Tears spring to my eyes.

'You're welcome.' The sharp quality returns to Morgan's voice, her momentary vulnerability fading.

She disentangles herself from me and I draw back, aware that Morgan needs to retreat into her shell again. I fasten the bracelet around my wrist and turn it so the diamond 'a' and 'g' catch in the light.

'I won't forget this,' I say.

Morgan shrugs. Her gaze flickers over the dips, mostly still in their packaging, that are spread out across the kitchen counter-tops. Even though I know there are some delicious dishes in the fridge and the larder, I can't help but feel hopeless and disorganized. I experience a stab of self-loathing.

Morgan is so together, jetting around the world to meeting after meeting, with never a hair out of place. And yet she still finds time to come up with a thoughtful gift like this while I can barely make it downstairs by midday without an egg stain on my lapel. Morgan must look at this house and wonder what on earth I do all day.

Hell, I wonder myself.

'If there's nothing I can do here, I'm going to take a shower,' she says.

My jaw drops. What on earth has she been doing for the past three hours if she hasn't showered yet? But Morgan has already vanished. By the time she gets back downstairs, with her hair artfully teased into large, dark curls and a satin robe over her clothes to protect them, the food is all on plates and back in the fridge. The living room and the kitchen are in a reasonable state of tidiness so I start up the music and light the candles Hen set out earlier.

Art's due back any second, there are only twenty minutes before we're expecting guests to arrive, and I'm now truly desperate to get upstairs to wash and change. Of course, Mum chooses exactly this moment to call from Australia.

'How are you, sweetheart?' she coos.

'Great, Mum, how's the holiday going?'

'Super, sweetheart,' she says. 'Though Doug's IBS has been playing up for the past few days and my golf game has gone to pot. I totally fell apart on the back nine yesterday . . .' She rambles on for a few more minutes. I try to listen, but my mind's on a million different things. The truth is, I have hardly anything in common with Mum. She's all into golf and her bridge games and what colour pelmets will go with her new three-piece suite. She never reads a book and thinks it's bad manners to discuss anything even vaguely connected with politics or philosophy or religion. She doesn't understand why I wrote my novels – or, for that matter, why I stopped.

Though she's never said so, I'm sure that privately she thinks I'm lucky Art puts up with me. Maybe if I'd given her grandchildren, our relationship would have been different but, as things stand, the gulf between us feels unbridgeable.

Art arrives home as Mum is telling me about Ayers Rock and the nice couple she and Doug had dinner with yesterday evening. I watch Morgan waft towards him. Her satin robe slips from her shoulder, revealing the thin red strap of whatever she's wearing underneath. There's something possessive about the way she opens her arms to let him hug her. No, not possessive. Controlling. It's not surprising coming from Morgan, and maybe it's often like that with an older sister and a younger brother. As an only child, I find sibling relationships both strange and fascinating. I spent much of my childhood before Dad died wandering around our garden making up imaginary families for myself. Dad loved me to tell him about my made-up brothers and sisters. Mum just found it plain odd.

Art pecks Morgan on the cheek but holds back from her hug.

I realize I'm watching some kind of power struggle in play. Well, that makes sense. Art wouldn't want to feel owned by anyone. Perhaps it explains why I've never properly understood his relationship with his sister. They're less than two years apart, and while anyone can see how close they are, Art's always seemed slightly wary around her. He's never admitted this, of course. In fact, he looks at me like I'm mad whenever I bring it up. *Morgan's just Morgan, Gen,* he said once. *A bit spiky, but she means well.*

They talk in low voices in the hall. At one point Art looks up at me and half smiles. It's a sad smile. He looks exhausted. Morgan touches his arm, to get his attention back, but instead of looking at her, Art takes a step away. I can't see Morgan's face but her back stiffens. She tosses back her dark hair and stalks off, into the living room.

'So is Art looking forward to his party?' Mum chirrups down the line.

'Yeah, I think so. Hey, speaking of which, I'd better go and get ready,' I say.

'Well, make sure you look nice for Art,' Mum says meaningfully. 'He works so hard. You should make more effort, darling, so he feels special.'

What's she saying, that I'm some hopeless, loser wife, just along for the spending money, not really good enough for my golden husband? Thanks to her, and Morgan and Hen earlier, I'm feeling more than a little bruised; not the best start for a party.

'Okay, Mum.' I'm itching to snap at her but she's thousands of miles away and the last thing I want is to start an argument, so I just get off the phone, wave at Art and head upstairs for my shower.

When I come down again I can hear Morgan and Art talking in the living room. I can't make out what they are saying. They're sitting side by side on the sofa and look up as I enter. Art smiles with unmistakable relief. In contrast, Morgan looks annoyed. Still in her robe, she holds up two almost-identical black shoes. Both are narrow and elegant with high, spiky heels. They make my feet hurt just looking at them.

'What d'you think, Gen?' she says. 'I can't decide.'

I glance at Art who, very subtly, rolls his eyes. I suppress a grin.

'They're both gorgeous,' I say, honestly.

'These are Manolos.' Morgan holds one shoe higher than the other. 'But I'm thinking of wearing these.' She raises the other shoe. 'They're from a new designer I found in New York. You wouldn't have heard of her but she's really building a reputation stateside.'

I stare at the shoes more closely. The second shoe is slightly sleeker than the first, with a marginally more pointed toe and thinner stiletto heels.

'Like I say, they're both lovely.' I glance at Art again. He gazes up at me, appealing to be rescued. He's still in his suit from work.

'Hey, darling, you should go and change,' I say, wandering over and resting my hand on his shoulder.

'You're right.' Art smiles gratefully at me. He stands and leaves.

For a second, Morgan looks exasperated, though whether with me, Art or herself I can't tell. Then she smiles and follows Art out of the room.

I take a breath and study myself in the mirror.

My hair is brushed now, curling over my shoulders. My fringe is still too long and there are still shadows under my eyes but, thanks to Bobbi Brown and Urban Decay, I don't look as haggard as I did earlier. The top I'm wearing is semi-fitted and suits my curves, though I'm sure Morgan thinks I could have chosen something more glamorous than a pair of GAP jeans to go with them.

I turn sideways, eyeing the slight roll of my stomach. Before I was pregnant I had a flat tummy. Now I'm just like all the mums out there with stretch marks and bulges. Only without the baby, of course. There'll be here soon, some of those mums, full of chat about their kids. I'll probably end up talking to the guys about their work; at least they won't pity me. I glance at my watch. This is always the worst moment before a party, when there's nothing more to prepare but nobody's here yet.

Will enough people turn up? Now I'm standing, waiting for our friends to arrive, I can't help but feel a twinge of nerves. I make a face at myself in the mirror. It's no big deal. Just thirty-odd people coming round for snacks and a few beers. As with work, so with home: Art hates anything that looks or feels elitist.

I can hear Art humping the second of Morgan's cases up the stairs. Looking in the mirror again, I can't help but wonder what she really thinks of me. On the surface she's all smiles and appreciative noises, but underneath I suspect she thinks Art could have done better. In so many ways Art is echoing the career of their father – but when it comes to women, he's made very different choices.

Brandon Ryan was born in Glasgow towards the end of the Second World War. He never spoke much about his childhood, at least not in public, but from what I've picked up from the articles and occasional hints dropped by Morgan, it was a pretty brutal upbringing. As a boy, Brandon was beaten by his father and regularly went hungry. He cut all ties with his family at the age of eighteen and travelled to London in the early 1960s, determined to make his fortune. He was a born entrepreneur – a millionaire within five years and a billionaire before he died. He fathered three children – Morgan and her two younger brothers – with his wife, a beautiful socialite called Fay Langham. I've never met Fay. She and Art don't exactly get along.

Brandon and Fay moved to Edinburgh when the children were little, but Brandon still spent much of his working week in London, which is where he met Anna, Art's mum. Brandon was, as far as I can gather, as ruthless about the affair as he was in his business dealings. At the time, Morgan was not yet two and the first of her younger brothers had just been born, and – I'm guessing here, obviously – maybe he felt like he wasn't getting enough attention at home. He met Anna at some fancy club where she was working as a waitress. At the time, Anna apparently had ambitions to be an actress and, according to Art, Brandon hinted he would help with her career. He was in his prime then – a good-looking man with piercing eyes. Even in the photos you can see he exuded power. Fragile, naive Anna didn't stand a chance. When I met her, over twenty years later, she still had 'victim' stamped on her forehead.

Anyway, Fay found out about the affair after Anna became pregnant with Art. Brandon gave Anna money for the abortion, but Anna refused to have one – about the only moment in her life when she stood up to anyone. I suspect Anna could have got quite a lot of money out of Brandon if she'd handled the situation more cannily but, in the end, Brandon gave her nothing and the whole story was hushed up. Fay stood by her man, on condition that Brandon cut all ties with both mother and child.

When Art tracked him down, aged eighteen, Brandon was cold and uninterested. Art hates talking about their meeting. In fact it's only thanks to Morgan that I heard about it at all. Apparently when Art arrived on the doorstep Brandon refused to let him into the house. There was a big scene, which Morgan witnessed from the landing. Art left, having been completely humiliated. Morgan ran out of the house after him and they talked on the street. I've asked Art about this showdown with his father several times but he's only ever talked about it once – shortly before our wedding – saying it was the worst moment of his life.

When Brandon died soon after their only meeting, Art was, unsurprisingly, left out of his will. Fay refused to entertain the idea that Art was entitled to any money, despite Morgan's pleadings. However, Art has told me, often, that even if he'd been offered an inheritance, he wouldn't have taken a penny; that he 'wouldn't give the cold-blooded bastard the satisfaction'. It doesn't take a psychiatrist to see the root of Art's drive and ambition in Brandon's rejection, but Art always dismisses such notions. He doesn't like to feel his father has had any influence over him whatsoever.

'Gen?' Art calls from upstairs. 'Gen, have you seen my black shirt?'

With a sigh, I turn away from the mirror as the doorbell rings with the first guest. What with Morgan all brittle and exasperated and Art exhausted from work, it feels like it's going to be a long night.

CHAPTER SIX

The Prodigy followed by an old Basement Jaxx song followed by my favourite disco track of all time: 'Disco Inferno'. I smile to myself, watching the party's hardcore dancers – Tris and Boris and Art's PA, Siena, plus Dan and Perry with their wives.

The party is in full swing. The majority of Art's colleagues are here. I haven't seen most of them for a while, though I know practically all the Loxley Benson staff well: Art doesn't stand on ceremony and runs his office with something I once heard Tris describe as a 'flat hierarchy'.

The room is also full of the friends who were once mine and are now ours: Sue and Hen and their husbands among them. Hen squeezes my hand when she arrives.

'Sorry I was on edge before,' she whispers. 'I need to talk when you get a moment.'

I nod, wondering what on earth she has to tell me that she couldn't have said earlier. For a second I wonder if it's something to do with Beth, but before I can ask, Hen has moved into the middle of the living room, and half the guys from Art's work have surrounded her. She's in her element, though poor Rob looks a little stiff and awkward. He has followed her over and is sticking to her like she's going to save his life, which, socially, I imagine she often does. I watch, fascinated, as Hen flirts and charms her way around the group, while Rob gazes at her in adoration.

Art's working the room, chatting and smiling to everyone. I should have known that no matter how tired he feels, he wouldn't let it show in public. He's easily as charming as Hen, but there's something commanding about him too – a way he has of making everyone he speaks to feel like the only person in the room. Right now he's with a couple I don't recognize. Must be clients. Personally, I wouldn't have invited business contacts, but Art likes to mix business and pleasure. Well, to Art, business *is* pleasure.

I don't mind, but it does mean Art and his colleagues have to watch how outrageous they get. And I do too, I suppose. Not that anyone's likely to get that out of control.

'Hey, Gen, come and dance!'

It's Boris, one of the Loxley Benson directors and a good friend of Art's. The whole board are here: Boris, Dan, Perry, Leo, Tristan and, of course, Kyle.

I let Boris drag me over to where the others are dancing. Dan and Perry both got married last year and they're with their new wives. Two tall, dark, handsome men with two petite, pretty, blonde women. I start moving to the music – George Michael, 'Outside', which I don't remember being on my iPod. I glance over at the stereo . . . a different iPod is in the slot.

Tris – very posh, very gay, very camp – grabs me around the waist and starts twirling me round. He's tall and smells lightly of something vaguely musky and hugely expensive. He sings the chorus in my ear, then laughs. 'You look gooorgeous, darling. I love that bracelet.'

I glance down at Morgan's gift which has been getting admiring comments all evening.

'Is this yours?' I shout over the music, pointing at the iPod.

Tris makes a mock-penitent face. 'What could I do, darling? George was just begging to be played.'

I grin. Tris throws his hands flamboyantly up in the air. I try to give myself up to the dance, letting Tris twirl me around. I don't want to think about IVF and Beth and all my unanswered questions right now, and yet, despite the music and the chatter and the general organized chaos of the party, my doubts cling to me, refusing to be put down.

After a minute or two, Boris drags me away. He's half Tris's height, but built like a brick – solid and ruddy-faced. I've always suspected he had a bit of a crush on me.

'She's mine, you ridiculous queen,' he says.

I glance over at Boris's wife, standing in the corner. Like Boris she's Russian; unlike him, she has never fitted in. At this moment, she's staring at me as if she'd like to kill me.

I disentangle myself from Boris and back away, into Kyle.

'Gen? How're you doing?'

I smile up at him. Kyle Benson's a sweetheart. A big, lumbering bear of a man and Art's partner at Loxley Benson. He's fiercely protective of Art. Morgan might know the facts of our session at the IVF clinic, but if Art's told anyone about our argument over whether or not to go ahead – and how he feels about it – it will have been Kyle.

They met when Art was fourteen and his mum wasn't coping with either her life or her teenage son. Art, by his own admission, was out of control – in trouble at school and getting into petty crime: joyriding and shoplifting beers, that kind of small-scale stuff that social workers with serious faces warn can easily escalate.

Anna was working as a receptionist at a beauty salon at the time and one of the beauticians knew someone who knew someone who took in troubled boys for weekly, informal fostering. It could have been a disaster, unpoliced and unregulated as it was, but it turned out to be the best thing that ever happened to Art. The couple who fostered him on and off over the next couple of years already had a teenage son, Kyle, and the two boys became firm friends.

'I'm good, Kyle, thanks,' I say. 'How about you?'

Kyle shrugs. 'Fine. Work's been manic though. Has Art told you about meeting the PM?'

'Yeah,' I say to Kyle with a grin. 'Once or twice.'

'I bet.' Kyle's solid, jowl-heavy face splits into a huge smile. 'It's good to see him happy about something. That is . . .' The grin vanishes and he groans. 'I mean . . . shit, Gen, I didn't mean he isn't happy . . . it's just he told me you were thinking about the IVF again and I know how hard that is on both of you . . .' He blushes, his face weighed down by embarrassment.

'It's okay.' I smile, trying to make him feel better. He's kind and dependable and has stood by Art all their lives. At Loxley Benson he pads around in the background, and while Art's the dynamo coming up with creative ideas and driving them through, I sometimes wonder if it isn't Kyle who holds everything together. 'So what impact do you think *The Trials* has had on business?' I say, changing the subject. 'Art seems to think it's all positive – better name-recognition, that sort of thing. D'you think there are any downsides?'

Kyle grins. 'Only the bunny boilers, and they're tailing off now it's not on the air any more.'

I smile back. Art has shown me a selection of the emails sent to him at Loxley Benson. They range from the sweetly admiring to the blatantly sexual. Several women even attached topless pics of themselves.

'If I Were a Boy' comes on Tris's iPod and he starts writhing about, performing what looks like some sort of pole dance using Hen as the pole. Almost everyone in the room is watching and laughing.

87

A thought strikes me. 'Does Art ever talk about . . . about other stuff from the past . . . from when we had our baby?'

I look closely at Kyle. He's reddening again, looking awkward, then he shakes his head. Does he know something about Beth? Surely not. Kyle is so open and honest, I'm sure I would be able to tell if he was keeping secrets. He's just embarrassed.

I look through the window towards the dark street beyond. The reflections from the fairy lights Hen strung up earlier twinkle in the glass.

'Are you okay, Gen?' Kyle's kindly face creases with a frown.

'I'm fine.' I give myself a shake. 'Tell me about the meetings with the PM Art's been having. Don't they take a lot of his time away from Loxley Benson?'

'Not as much as you'd think.' Kyle looks relieved. 'At the moment I think they're focusing on the Work Incentives programme. It's great publicity for the company. In some ways it's even better than *The Trials*. Our clients are *seriously* impressed.'

'Sounds brilliant,' I say.

'It *is* . . .' Kyle pauses. He lowers his voice, so I can barely hear him over the music. 'I know how Art can be, and he's even more sure of himself since *The Trials*, but Vicky and I . . . well, we just want you to know that we think this should be *your* decision . . . whether you try IVF again, I mean.'

'Thanks.' I squeeze Kyle's arm, genuinely touched.

'No, seriously, it's unbelievable what you've gone through. Vicky and I can't imagine . . .'

Vicky is Kyle's wife of fifteen years and the mother of their four children. Like him, she's solid and kind.

'Thanks.' I look around, realizing I haven't seen Vicky yet this evening. 'Where *is* Vicks?'

'Babysitter let us down.' Kyle makes a face. 'Shame, she'd love to be here.'

I wonder if he means that. I've always felt Vicky is a bit intimidated by Art and the other directors and their wives . . . by how slick and sophisticated they are. Maybe she couldn't face a party full of slim, attractive, designer-clad women. I know how she feels.

As if to illustrate my point, Morgan chooses this moment to make her entrance. She looks amazing: the savage stilettos have been teamed with a deep red dress that fits Morgan like a sheath. It finishes just below the knee and is off-the-shoulder and slash-necked, with thin straps – kind of fifties-looking, like something out of a Grace Kelly movie or early *Mad Men*.

All the men stare. In fact, so do the women. Art's PA, Siena, a posh, slightly plump twenty-something with creamy skin and over-plucked eyebrows, actually drops her jaw.

Morgan stands in the doorway, looking around. I'm willing to bet her dress alone cost more than every other item of clothing in the room combined. She looks amazing – but totally unapproachable. There's something self-contained in the way she's gazing at the rest of us which, combined with her ultra-groomed look, sets her apart. She's so shiny she almost gleams. No wonder the poor woman can't get a man. You'd need nuclear levels of confidence to walk up to her.

The music is still blaring out – some trance track I don't know – but the dancers have stopped moving. As hostess, I should go over and claim Morgan – she has met the Loxley Benson board on a couple of occasions and knows Hen, of course, but underneath the poise she's looking a bit self-conscious right now. Luckily Tris saves the day. He trips towards her.

'Morgan, honey,' he says, 'I bring fabulous news. I've got the perfect man for you.'

'Really?' Morgan raises an expertly manicured hand to brush back an invisible wisp of hair. 'So when does he arrive?'

'Lorcan Byrne,' Tris goes on. 'Irish guy from way back. Maybe you met him with Art when you were younger? They were, like, best friends. And Lorcan is *gorgeous*. Remember?'

Morgan wrinkles her nose disdainfully. 'Hmmmn . . .'

I move closer, arriving at Morgan's side at the same time as Art. Behind us the dancers have started up again.

'Isn't Lorcan the guy you were with that time in the States?' Morgan turns to Art. 'Kind of a wild guy?'

'Er, yeah.' Art makes a face. 'You didn't really hit it off. Lorcan isn't everyone's cup of tea.'

Morgan looks like she wants to talk some more, but Tris whisks her off to join the knot of dancers. She's only a few years older than they are – and could easily pass for younger with her skinny hips and suspiciously smooth skin – but there's a sedate, middle-aged quality to Morgan that makes her look out of place. She can't dance, either – and those spiky shoes certainly don't help.

For a second I experience a mean stab of pleasure, then I think what a cow I am and turn to Art.

'Who's this Lorcan?'

'No one, really,' Art says, watching the dancers. 'He was in at the start of Loxley Benson, but . . . it didn't work out . . .'

A vague memory stirs in the recesses of my brain. Art has mentioned Lorcan before.

'You were good friends,' I say. 'I remember you telling me. The Irish guy who went to drama school? He's an actor now – he's been in some Irish soap for years.'

Art nods. 'When I knew him he wasn't an actor. We hung out a lot together. He encouraged me to set up my business but . . .' Art tails off.

'You fell out, didn't you?' I'm frowning, trying to remember the story.

Art shrugs. 'Lorcan let me down. He let the company down.'

I wait for him to expand on this but he doesn't.

'Anyway,' he carries on, 'he left and became an actor and went home to Ireland for a TV show and I haven't seen him since. He's not an easy guy. Fun, though. At least he used to be.'

I consider this. 'How come he's coming here tonight?'

'You'll have to ask Tris. They bumped into each other at some PR thing last week and Tris invited him.' Art raises his eyebrows. 'Typical Tris, eh?'

I grin. 'So is he right for Morgan?'

Art snorts. 'No way,' he says.

I want to ask him why, but at that minute Art gets called away to talk to another couple I don't recognize.

Morgan has stopped dancing, I notice, and is in deep conversation with Camilla, one of Loxley Benson's longer-serving receptionists. Hen wanders over and she and Morgan hug enthusiastically. I watch the three of them. It's always so weird to see people from different parts of your life getting on. Of course, Hen and Morgan have always hit it off. Everyone likes Hen.

The party's divided along friendship lines. Most of the people in this room know me through Art. The ones who were *my* friends originally are in the kitchen. Hen's the exception to this, of course. She straddles both groups, thanks to her university friendship with Tris. She's just started dancing again and looks amazing – as natural and appealing as Morgan is stiff and unapproachable. It strikes me that, apart from Art and me, Hen is the only person at the party who knows about Lucy O'Donnell. I gaze around the room. Does anyone here know what really happened to Beth? Could any of our friends somehow be involved?

I shudder. I can't let myself think like that.

Tris wanders up to Hen and spins her around while Rob just watches. He's smiling, but I get the impression he's feeling a bit out of place standing there while his wife gyrates away. I'm just thinking of heading in his direction when Kyle wanders over with a fresh drink. He looks lost without Vicky, so I ask after his kids then search for something else to say.

'So d'you know this Lorcan Byrne who's coming?' I ask.

Kyle's eyes widen. He looks completely shocked. '*Lorcan*'s coming here? *Tonight*?'

'Yes, Tris asked him. What's the—?'

'Gen, babe, what a great party!' Tris bounces over, his pupils suspiciously dilated. 'Are you still talking about Lorcan? He definitely said he was coming.' He pauses for dramatic effect. 'Maybe he's here already.'

'I don't think so.' Kyle raises his eyebrows. 'We'd all know if he was. Tris, I can't believe you invited him.'

'What d'you mean?' I'm really curious now. Kyle isn't the kind of person who normally makes a fuss. 'What did he do?'

'It doesn't matter now.' Kyle turns to the shelf beside him and reaches for a crisp. Tris and I exchange a look.

'So do you know Lorcan through Art?' I persist, trying another tack.

'Actually Art met Lorcan through me,' Kyle says, munching on his crisp.

'Really?' I stand back to let Siena move past us. 'I don't know anything about him. At least, Art hasn't mentioned him for years.'

'He did some building work on our house when Art was still at school.' Kyle looks uncomfortable. 'We went out drinking a couple of times. Art came along. They became friends.'

'A builder?' I stare at him. 'I thought Lorcan was an actor?'

Tris laughs. 'He's whatever you want him to be, baby.'

CLOSE MY EYES

'He's an arsehole,' Kyle snaps. 'He nearly destroyed Loxley Benson.'

My mouth falls open. I've never heard Kyle sound so bitter.

Tris frowns. 'That's a bit harsh, after all this time.'

'What the hell did he do?' I ask.

'I told you, it doesn't matter now.' Kyle plonks his drink down on the shelf so firmly the bowl of crisps shudders.

'For God's sake, Kyle,' I say. 'If you don't tell me I'm only going to ask Art.'

'Go on, Kyle,' Tris urges. 'Tell her.'

Kyle gives a defeated sigh. 'Okay, it was at the start of Loxley Benson,' he says. 'Literally, the first few months, before Art met you. We only had two clients and debts everywhere. Basically, the main client was keeping us afloat. Without him we'd have gone under within weeks. The bank . . . the wages . . .' He pauses.

'And?' I say.

'This client . . .' Kyle shudders. 'Lorcan slept with his wife. That's why Art fired him. It was the only way to keep the contract. Lorcan's an irresponsible bastard.'

'He's a player,' Tris says philosophically.

'Shut up, Tris,' Kyle grunts. 'You just fancy him.'

Tris grins. 'Busted.' He turns to me. 'I bet Art never talks about that time.'

He's right. The only thing Art hates more than almost failing at something is telling people about it. He has certainly never told me what Kyle has just confided.

'Lorcan's *hot*,' Tris goes on, in a stage whisper.

'Jesus Christ, Tristan.' Kyle shudders.

'Oh, don't be such a big fag-nag, Kyle.' Tris turns to me. 'And tell Morgan not to worry. Lorcan's *definitely* straight.'

'Gen.' Art appears and pulls me away from Tris. 'Come and meet John and Sandrine.'

I follow him across the room and allow myself to be introduced to a woman with a Cleopatra bob and sparkling eyes, and her husband – shy and immaculately dressed in a suit and tie.

'Sandrine's my main ally on the PM's committee,' Art says with a classic Art smile – slightly flirtatious but also deeply sincere. 'She was with me in Brussels the other day. I told you about her, remember?'

I nod, recalling the woman I heard in the background when Art and I were on the phone. I take a closer look at Sandrine. She's very pretty – as groomed and elegant as Morgan but with an animated smile that makes her look a whole lot more fun.

'We've been focusing their minds on how to present an ethical stance on investments, haven't we, Sandrine?' Art says with a chuckle.

Sandrine smiles back, revealing a dimple in her cheek. 'If we can just get them to understand the principle of negative screening instead of all that preference bullshit . . .' She laughs and it strikes me that she is just Art's type – bubbling over with personality and sexy as hell thanks to her curves in that simple silk dress and her French accent. I suddenly feel terribly scruffy and unglamorous in my high street jeans and split ends.

'I know.' Art gives a mock groan. He glances at Sandrine's husband, whose name I've already forgotten but whose jacket pocket contains a perfect triangle of red handkerchief. 'What d'you think, John? It would help if we could agree on an SIP but getting everyone to even define the terms looks like it's going to take about ten bloody years.'

'Well, that's politicians for you,' John says smugly, removing an invisible speck of dust off his lapel.

'What's your view, Geniver?' Sandrine says.

'I guess politicians have a lot to juggle,' I say noncommittally, not having properly understood the subject under discussion.

What I *do* want to say is that I think her husband is quite possibly the most anal-looking man I've ever met in my life and I have no idea what the vivacious Sandrine sees in him; but I do my best to nod in all the right places as the three of them carry on their conversation.

After five minutes or so I murmur something about having to check on the food and scuttle away. I stop at the door, taking stock of the room. People are dancing and chatting. Everyone has a full glass. So far, so good. I'm almost ready to feel relieved. The party's working.

Art catches my eye and smiles. He looks more relaxed than I've seen him in weeks, clearly enjoying his conversation with Sandrine and her husband. I turn away. I can handle Art's business contacts for a while, but right now I need time with some of my own friends. All my anxieties about Beth are still there, but the party has pushed them into the background, and what I want right now is to let off some steam, to find some relief from the stress of the past few days.

Hen and Morgan have withdrawn to the kitchen. They're chatting with a group of women, including Sue and a couple of old uni friends of mine. Morgan smiles at me as she leaves to use the bathroom, but the others are so deep in conversation they don't even notice as I approach, eager to join in.

'It's bloody ridiculous having to put their names down at three.' Sue jabs her finger as she speaks.

A couple of the other women nod. I'm right next to them now but they still haven't noticed me.

'I know, but that would have been better than going through a transfer at this stage.' Hen sighs, her forehead furrowed with a deep crease. 'Meadway has *got* to be better than the school he's at now. It's a total sink – the class sizes are ridiculous . . .'

My enthusiasm for the conversation is fading fast. It's not that I don't care, but I can't be anything other than a spectator on this topic.

'It's not just the class sizes,' Sue says confidentially. 'The teachers have such low expectations. When we went to Alfie's last parents' evening she actually said "There's no problem with Alfie so there's nothing to talk about," as if so long as he wasn't falling behind and messing up their league tables it didn't matter about him.'

'I know.' Hen shakes her head. 'It's just so expensive to go private, though, especially now there'll be two of them.'

Two?

I take a step away.

Hen spots me and blinks. 'Oh, Gen, hi . . . are you okay?'

I stare at her face. It's flooding red with guilt and embarrassment. My chest tightens as I realize exactly what she was saying.

'I'm fine.' I try to smile.

'I've only just found out,' Hen says quickly. 'I was going to tell you – that's what I wanted to talk to you about.'

I look around. All the others share Hen's guilty look. They all knew she was pregnant, then. *All* of them.

'Hey, that's great news,' I say, trying to hide my embarrassment. 'When are you due?'

'Ages.' Hen rubs her nose. 'September. *Late* September.'

I nod, working it out. Roughly three months gone, then. Which means, even allowing for how scatty Hen is, that she *must* have known for at least a month. She certainly must have known earlier today, when she helped me get ready for the party. A little voice inside my head reminds me that I have been full of my own concerns lately, that it would have been hard for Hen to tell me about having a second baby when I was being forced to relive the trauma of losing my first. Even so, the hurt of being left out of what I know is great news for my best friend still stings.

I can't help remembering when she found out about Nat. She told me before anyone else, just as I'd confided in her first about being pregnant with Beth. We kept each other's secret for over a month. She didn't even tell her mum.

And now I'm among the last to know.

The music is pounding away in my ears. Everyone is watching Hen and me, looking concerned. No one says anything.

I finally force a smile onto my face. I'm not being fair on Hen and, anyway, I'm genuinely pleased for her. I am. I kiss her cheek. 'That's really fantastic. So what were you guys talking about? Schools?'

'Yeah, but that's so boring.' Sue grins. 'Hey, great party. The Black Forest gateau is *amazing*. My mum used to make those, though she used grapes instead of cherries.'

'Thanks.' I keep smiling but I know it must look rigid. Truth is, I can't bear this being treated like an invalid around the topic of children. I look at Hen again and she looks away.

Suddenly I'm overwhelmed with anger. Before, Hen and I were pregnant at the same time. But now she's a proper mother and I'm just the ghost of one, and the fact that our babies were due at the same time makes the whole thing so much worse. Nat's birthday six days before Beth's reminds me of her every year. Except Beth didn't have a birthday. Not one single one. Ever.

My eyes fill with tears. *Shit*.

'Oh, Gen, I'm so sorry.' Hen's touches my arm. 'I didn't mean to upset you.'

'You didn't,' I say, more fiercely than I mean to. 'For God's sake, it's fine.'

There's an awkward pause. I look down at the floor and the anger fades and I feel overwhelmed by the future. By my future

– in which everyone else gets to talk about their kids and schools and exams and universities and unsuitable boyfriends and then, in twenty or thirty years' time, about their grandchildren and *their* schools and exams and so on . . . and I'll be left out of the whole bloody conversation.

Forever.

I look up and force another smile onto my face at the sight of the pity on Hen's. I back away from her and Sue. 'I'm good. I'm great, in fact. I just need to check on some stuff.'

I turn and fight my way through the room to the hallway. Various people try to talk to me as I pass, but I ignore them. I think of going out into the front garden, but then the doorbell rings and the front door is instantly blocked by bodies moving to open it.

I turn, ignoring the whoops behind me as the door is opened and head the long way around to the kitchen, intending to shut myself in the utility room for a couple of minutes. I hate feeling this sorry for myself . . . if I could just sit still for a few minutes I'm sure I'd be able to let it go. I reach the utility room and open the door, only to find Art's PA inside. Siena is deeply immersed in a snog with one of the young guys from the office. They jump apart when they see me and I'm so embarrassed I just say sorry and walk out again.

I wander back to the living room. *Bloody hell, how many people are here?* The house is crammed full. Five minutes ago I was having fun and now I just want everyone to leave so I can get back to missing Beth and worrying over Lucy O'Donnell's claims and all the other pathetic elements of my miserable, non-writing life.

Feeling furious and upset, I walk into the living room and look up, just in time to see Art shaking hands with a man I don't know in a black jumper and jeans.

The whole of the Loxley Benson board are standing around

them and, though the dance music is still playing, everyone in the room is watching Art and the stranger. I glance at Kyle's face. He's not smiling.

This has to be Lorcan Byrne.

CHAPTER SEVEN

Lorcan Byrne is tall, a couple of inches taller than Art, so about six-two-ish. He has broad shoulders and dark auburn hair that curls onto his neck.

Art stands back and the man turns round. He's as good-looking as Tris promised, with even features and a square jaw. He's grinning, apparently undaunted by the effect his entrance has made.

Art beckons me over.

'Gen, this is Lorcan Byrne.' He sounds as relaxed as usual on the surface, but underneath I can hear the ice in Art's voice.

'Hi.' I smile.

'Hi.' A soft Irish accent. Lorcan shakes my hand. 'I can't believe we've never met.'

'I'd like to say "I've heard so much about you".' I raise my eyebrows. 'But I'm afraid I haven't.'

'Thank Christ for that.' Lorcan laughs. I'm struck by the way it's his whole face laughing and laugh myself.

Then Tris wafts up and Lorcan's negotiating the hug. Kyle turns away but Boris and Perry wander over, and suddenly the party's back on track, the tense atmosphere evaporated.

After a few minutes I manage to get Art alone for a second.

'Having fun?' I put my arms around him.

He smiles and leans down to kiss me on the lips. 'It's great, Gen. Thanks so much.'

We look at each other and, for a moment, it's as if it's just him and me in the room. Over the years I've learned marriage is like this – a lot of mundane jogging along and compromise, punctuated by times when you're almost ready to walk away, and then those rare, lovely moments where the power of the bond between you puts everything else in the shadows.

'Hey,' I say, looking deep into his dark eyes. 'Kyle just told me about Lorcan and why he left the company. How come you never mentioned it?'

Art shrugs. 'Like I told you, Lorcan let the company down. Why talk about it?'

'So Kyle said you were, like, really close . . . best friends even?'

Art shrugs. 'I don't think in terms of best friends.'

I roll my eyes. It's true, of course. Art's friends with everyone, but that doesn't really answer my question.

'Look, it's complicated.' Art sighs. 'I just don't trust him. He isn't all bad. In fact he's smart and creative and he was the first person who suggested I should set up my own company.'

'Really?' I'm genuinely surprised. 'I thought Loxley Benson was your idea?'

'It was. I mean, specifically I came up with Loxley Benson itself, but long before then Lorcan focused my head on the idea of running my own business. I was a kid, sixteen or something, and he was doing carpentry work. He built Kyle's parents' conservatory. That's how we all met. I'd never come across anyone even vaguely entrepreneurial before. You know what Mum was like, and Kyle's parents. They all had – or wanted – steady jobs, like working for the local council, with sick pay and paid holidays and all that. I'd dreamed about being rich and successful, but Lorcan was the first person who made me believe I could actually set up my own business one day.'

'Hey, Gen, where's the corkscrew?'

It's Sue, very smiley and a bit slurry. I want to ask Art more, but I hurry off to the kitchen. Morgan is in there again chatting with some of my old friends, while Boris's wife is deep in conversation with Lorcan. To my amazement Boris's wife is actually smiling. Lorcan has wandered off by the time I've found the missing corkscrew and given it to Sue. She asks if I'm okay after Hen's pregnancy revelation. I reassure her that I'm fine. And then Hen herself comes up, all tearful about not telling me before, and we spend about half an hour clearing that up again.

'It's great,' I keep telling her. 'I'm thrilled for you.'

'Really?' Hen sniffs. 'I was going to tell you tonight, Gen. Honest.'

Eventually Rob comes up and I congratulate him on the baby and he blushes, which makes me laugh and then Hen laughs too, at last, and drags him off to dance.

By the time I get back into the living room it's gone midnight and half the couples are thinking about getting back to babysitters. Rob is talking to Boris and his wife, and Art is chatting and laughing with Hen, who is clearly trying to persuade him to dance. There's no chance of that – Art wouldn't dance if you paid him. I smile to myself. Hen might have Art's ear when it comes to me, but she doesn't really understand him.

He beckons me towards them but before I can head over, Tris grabs me and spins me around. We dance together for a bit. My iPod is back in the dock and the party playlist is still going strong – the Motown section never fails. I take some photos of Art with Hen, then with a bunch of other people: Sandrine and John; Siena, who's emerged from the utility room without the young guy; and Boris and Dan and their wives. Art is smiling in them all.

In the end I collapse onto the sofa. Plenty of people are still dancing, though the party's definitely thinning out. Art's saying goodbye to Sandrine and John.

'Enjoying your party?'

I look up. Lorcan's smiling. He sits down beside me and runs his hand through his hair.

'Course.' I smile back.

Lorcan raises an eyebrow. 'Yeah? I wasn't sure.'

We stare at each other. There's something knowing about his look . . . an edge . . . a challenge. I can certainly see how he could have ended up sleeping with a client's wife.

'I'm fine,' I insist. 'Anyway, it's Art's party really.'

We both look over at Art, still chatting away.

'Art says you're a writer.'

'Did he?' I'm honestly surprised to hear that. After urging me to write for over two years after Beth's death, Art finally stopped talking about it. I can't remember the last time he even mentioned the subject.

'What are you working on now?' Lorcan asks.

'Nothing specific.' God, I haven't had to do this – talk about my writing with anyone outside my tutor groups – for ages. Everybody else stopped asking me years ago. I stare at the floor for a moment, trying to think of a way of changing the subject.

'Why's that?'

I look up. Lorcan is watching my face, his eyes intent on my answer. His skin is fair and there are faint lines on his forehead. He has soft blue eyes and stubble on his chin. I take all this in without really noticing it. I'm trying to work out what to say. And then, without any warning at all, I tell the truth.

'I haven't been able to write since my baby died.'

Lorcan nods slowly. 'I'm sorry, I didn't know,' he says. 'Art and I haven't spoken in a long time.' He pauses. 'I can understand why it stopped you writing.'

'Can you?'

He nods. 'Sure. Something like that changes who you are, so you have to work out who you are all over again.'

'Which is more than enough creativity to be going on with, you mean?' I laugh gently. 'I guess so. Though, for me, it was also that I just spent so much time thinking about her.'

'What was her name?'

'Hey, Gen, we're going.' Sue and Paul loom up in front of us. I jump, slightly. I'd forgotten about the party still going on around us. I stand up and kiss them goodbye. Then more people come over. Sue and Paul have started a second wave of couples leaving amid yet more explanations about late nights and waiting babysitters. By the time I return to the sofa, it's half past one and there're only about twelve of us left. Tris and Boris – clearly off their faces – are now dancing to 'Vogue' in the middle of the living room. Morgan and Art are chatting by the door with a group of people from Art's office. Lorcan's still on the sofa, a bottle of beer in hand, talking to Boris's wife. She scowls at me as I sit down.

'Are you alright, Tanya?'

'Yes, except for shoes which are hurting feet.' She looks over at Boris and sighs. 'We must go.'

'Really?' I say. 'That's a shame.'

I catch Lorcan's eye. I can see he knows I'm not that bothered Tanya is going. I sip at my wine, trying not to grin.

'Yes.' Tanya sweeps off to get their coats and I let myself smile.

Lorcan sits up. 'It's kind of strange seeing everyone again.'

I'm curious. I can't help it.

'I heard you left Loxley Benson under a cloud?'

Lorcan wrinkles his nose. 'I thought maybe after all this time they might have forgotten, but . . .'

'Art never forgets.' I hesitate. That sounded kind of disloyal. 'I'm kidding. It's all water under the bridge. I mean, I think Kyle might still be a bit upset, but that's just because he's so devoted to Art. The others looked really pleased to see you.'

A beat passes. Lorcan is still looking at me.

'I don't think Art wants me here,' he says. His tone is neither angry, nor self-pitying. He's just stating a fact.

'Of course he does,' I bluster, my face growing hot.

'Mmmn . . .' Lorcan looks away.

'Tell me . . .' I say, desperate to change the subject. 'Art says you're an actor. But you also apparently built Kyle's conservatory. *And* you were part of Art's business at the beginning, which has got nothing to do with either acting or building.'

Lorcan laughs. 'Yeah, all those things are true, I guess. I am an actor, but I didn't get into it until I was in my mid-twenties.' He pauses, as if deliberating whether to say more. Then he runs his hand through his hair, pushing it off his face, smoothing it back. 'I did carpentry work back then to earn money.'

I'm held by his look, which is somehow open and yet enigmatic at the same time. 'Art says you were the one who suggested he set up his business.'

'I was only stating the obvious,' Lorcan says. 'You could see there was something about Art, even back then. He was this restless kid with masses of energy and far cleverer than everyone around him. If he wasn't going to end up a gangster he'd become a businessman. He had entrepreneur written all over him, he just needed the time to work out what to "entrepreneur" about.'

'But not you?'

'No way. I mean, I thought it was great Art was setting up a business, but I wasn't cut out to be a part of it. I'd never had a job or a boss. The only thing I was good at then was acting the bollix, as my dad used to say.' He laughs again. 'Art and me used to go out drinking when I was bumming around doing occasional carpentry work and he'd say to me: "This isn't right for you, Lorcan, mate. This isn't enough. There's good money out there, you know? If you're prepared to go after it."' As Lorcan quotes Art, he changes his voice, imitating Art's North London accent and the eager, intense way Art sometimes speaks.

I grin. It's a good likeness.

'You see I thought I could hack it . . .' Lorcan looks down. He's talking in his natural voice again now. I like the way he speaks, the laidback way he rolls his words around his mouth. 'At the time, before Loxley Benson, Art was working in some financial consultancy, and with his help and a lot –' he grins – 'a *lot* of bullshit on my part, I talked my way into this public relations company, because I was tired of labouring and I wanted more money. And it was good. I mean, it suited me in lots of ways. Then when Art set up Loxley Benson I thought I could handle the PR side no problem.' He sighs, and swigs at his beer. 'But actually I hated it. And . . . and there was loads of other shit going on in my life. So getting out of the business was the best decision I ever made.'

'I thought . . .' I hesitate, wondering if what I'm about to say will sound rude. I decide to say it anyway. There's something about Lorcan that tells me he prefers people to be direct. 'I thought Art fired you.'

'Right.' Lorcan sighs. 'Yes, I would have gone anyway, but yes.' There's an awkward pause.

'So what was the other shit you mentioned?' I say, hoping to smooth the moment over.

Lorcan widens his eyes dramatically. 'Woman shit.' He laughs. 'Yeah?'

'Yeah. I became a dad, which wasn't planned. At *all*.'

I glance at his left hand. There's no wedding ring.

'So who is that?' Lorcan points to a photo on the shelf to the right of the sofa. It's one of my favourite pictures of my dad as a boy – a close-up of his face: dark floppy hair falling over his forehead, soulful eyes and that expressive mouth, with the top lip fuller than the bottom, pressed into a determined smile.

'That's my dad,' I say. 'He died when I was a kid.'

'So did my mum,' Lorcan confides. 'Well, I was seventeen. Cancer.'

We look at each other for a second, bonded by that invisible tie that exists between all children who lose their parents too young.

Lorcan sits back. 'So what do you do, if you're not writing?'

I hate that question. I don't want to answer it. I want to ask Lorcan about his kid and what happened with the woman shit. And about whether he's with anyone right now. Instead I shrug, feeling stupid. As I speak, I pour myself another glass of wine.

'There isn't anything else I want to do. God, that sounds so pathetic. I mean I do a bit of creative writing teaching and I know how lucky I am that Art . . . that I don't have to earn a living . . . it's just . . . writing's the only thing that I've ever done that felt authentic. You know, "real". The right thing. The thing I'm meant to be doing.'

How pretentious does that sound? I gulp my wine, embarrassed.

But Lorcan is nodding. 'I get that,' he says.

The sound of glass smashing rises above the music. I turn in time to see Morgan staring at her skirt, a glass of red wine on the floor at her feet. Miraculously the glass is only broken into two pieces, at the stem. The man next to her is swaying slightly, looking guilty. I recognize him as one of Art's clients. He's in his fifties, with a red face and pissed eyes.

'Sorry,' he's slurring. 'Sorry 'bout that. Oops – did I get your dress?' He reaches forward and tries to brush wine off Morgan's skirt.

She backs away.

'No problem.' Morgan's voice is even more clipped than usual.

I glance over at Art. He rolls his eyes. 'I'll get a cloth.'

As Art and Morgan head for the kitchen, it crosses my mind that I should probably go over and talk to the drunk client. In a second, maybe. Instead, I sip some more wine and turn back to Lorcan. He's watching Morgan and Art leave the room.

'Morgan's amazing,' I say. 'She's been working the room all night.'

Lorcan shrugs. 'She doesn't like me. Didn't when we met the time before, either.'

I don't know what to say to that.

Lorcan grins. 'Hey, I'm not everyone's cup of tea.'

'That's what Art said about you earlier.' I smile. 'So what did you do to piss Morgan off?'

'She thought I was a bad influence on Art,' Lorcan says. 'Which, to be fair, I probably was.'

'She cares about him. They're really close. Art and Morgan are alike in lots of ways.'

'You think?'

'Yes.' I try to work out what I mean. Art and Morgan are both forceful and confident, like I imagine their dad must have been. I'd say the resemblance to Brandon Ryan is strongest in Morgan's case. Not surprising I suppose. She's more imperious than Art by nature and, since their father died, she's taken over the running of one of his core businesses: Ryan Insurance Services. Now she jet sets around the world just like Brandon once did.

Lorcan runs his hand through his hair again. 'Maybe they're both used to getting their own way, but Morgan's much more materialistic. She's like a personification of the Brandon Ryan legend – all about making money. Whereas Art ... well, he doesn't really care about money so much.'

I stare at him. Few people who know Art well would describe him as a man who doesn't care about money, and yet it's true. Art has never wanted to build up riches for the sake of it or accumulate material stuff. He has a Mercedes, sure, but he rarely drives it. And we have this house – but it's hardly crammed full of status-bestowing possessions.

'You're right,' I say. 'Sometimes I wonder why Art's so driven when he's not bothered about being rich.'

Art rushes through the door as I speak, a tea towel in his hand. Morgan trails behind, her lips pressed together in irritation. She smoothes her skirt down. I experience a tiny prick of guilt that I haven't gone to help her. Still, the wine stain is barely noticeable on that dark red dress.

'Control.'

'What?' I turn to Lorcan.

'Control,' he repeats. 'That's why Art's driven. He wants total power over his environment. No boss to tell him what to do. No problem he can't solve. No aspect of his life he isn't in complete control over.'

I stare at him. That's exactly how Art is.

'And Morgan's much the same in her own way,' Lorcan goes on. 'Except she's more complicated.'

'And very beautiful.' I look at Morgan. She's chatting to the people from Art's office again, while Art, the broken wine glass now wrapped in the tea towel, steers the drunk client towards the front door.

From the back, Morgan makes an elegant outline, with her

dark, glossy hair snaking over that beautifully fitted couture dress. She's still wearing her high, thin heels. If I'd been wearing them I'd have kicked them off hours ago.

'I don't know about beautiful.' Lorcan wrinkles his nose. 'She's certainly not sexy.'

'No?' Something inside me is pleased he doesn't think Morgan is sexy.

Lorcan shakes his head. 'No arse.'

I stare at Morgan. Her dress goes in at the waist a little, then curves out very slightly, over narrow hips, but Lorcan's right. Her bum underneath is flat.

I pour myself some more wine. I feel relaxed now that the party's almost over and perhaps even a little bit drunk myself.

'So you're into arses then?' I giggle at my own boldness.

Lorcan grins, clearly completely unashamed. 'Oh, yeah,' he says.

Hen and Rob appear, saying they are already late getting back to Nat's babysitter and I realize, with a jolt, that I haven't thought about Beth the whole time Lorcan and I have been chatting. I give Hen a big hug, kiss Rob on the cheek, then turn back to Lorcan. He seems to understand me so instinctively that, for a second, I'm filled with an urge to tell him about Lucy O'Donnell and her claims. But then common sense kicks in and I realize how ridiculous it would be to speak about something so private to a total stranger, so I keep my mouth shut. A moment later, Art's standing there in front of us.

'Everyone's going, Gen,' he says.

He looks tired again. Like he's done the party and now he just wants to go to bed. I get up, feeling guilty I haven't networked with his clients as much as I should, and put my arm around his waist. He kisses my cheek.

Lorcan stands up and glugs down the remainder of his beer. 'I should go too.'

110

Art shakes his head. 'I didn't mean . . .'

'Hey, I've got to pick up Cal first thing tomorrow.' Lorcan grins at me. 'That's my son,' he explains. 'But maybe I'll come and visit you guys again?'

'Sure.' I glance at Art. He says nothing. Embarrassed, I chatter on. 'Are you here for a while, Lorcan?'

'Couple of months.' Lorcan is answering me, but he's looking expectantly at Art.

There's a pause.

'Great.' Art forces a smile onto his face. 'Like you say, we should meet up.'

Lorcan nods, then goes. I realize I have no idea where he's living at the moment, or what he's doing for work, or any of the small talk details of his life.

There's a flurry of people leaving and the house is, finally, empty. Art disappears straight up to bed leaving just me and Morgan.

We look round the living room. It's not too bad, considering, though there are glasses everywhere and plates piled up on most of the available surfaces. I half-heartedly peel a slice of salami off a silk cushion. The rest will have to wait till tomorrow.

'What time does your cleaner arrive in the morning?' Morgan asks, stifling a yawn. 'Not too early, I hope?'

I swallow. I've made no arrangement with Lilia at all, which means the clearing up will fall to me and Art.

'Oh, we left things a bit vague,' I say, not wanting to explain all this to Morgan.

Her make-up is still perfect and she's still wearing those bloody shoes.

It's a relief to reach the peace of our bedroom. Art's asleep already: face-down, naked and sprawled across the bed. Before I pull the duvet out from under his body and get in beside him, I shove my hand under the mattress. The Tapps Funeral Services letter is still there. So is Dr Rodriguez's card from the Fair Angel hospital.

The next day passes in a whirl of activity. There are lots of thank you phone calls and texts and, in the end, I don't get a second alone to make my call to Dr Rodriguez. Morgan insists we have dinner at a rather formal restaurant in Mayfair that evening. Her treat. It's nice, though we spend most of the evening listening to Morgan reminiscing about her peripatetic childhood. Art doesn't mind. He claims not to care about his dad, but it's obvious to me that he's still hungry for inside information – and Brandon Ryan was undoubtedly an extraordinary man. Morgan tells one story I can't get out of my head: how, one Christmas, aged about six or seven, she declared that she couldn't live without her favourite toy – a doll she'd named Maisie – and how Brandon took the doll and threw it on the living-room fire, telling her she should never become so fond of anything that she couldn't bear to lose it.

'Of course Daddy was right,' Morgan says with a breezy air of resignation. 'But it was a harsh lesson.'

She glances at Art who shakes his head. I wonder, not for the first time, why Art doesn't speak up at times like this. It's surely as obvious to him as it is to me that it wasn't only Brandon's life lessons that were harsh, but also the man himself. And yet I've never heard Art criticize him to Morgan, who behaves most of the time as if their father had just been a little eccentric, rather than a vicious, arrogant tyrant who ruled his home like his business empire – solely for the power and the glory.

I think back to my own father. In all my memories of him he is laughing.

'But what Brandon did was horrible,' I say quietly. 'I mean, you say it was right, but what a cruel thing to do . . . to destroy a child's favourite toy. And what a cruel outlook, too: never rely on anyone or anything.'

Morgan freezes in her seat. I can sense Art beside me, stiffening, but I keep my gaze on Morgan. Her lips tighten and her eyes darken with resentment. For a moment she looks as if she'd like to hit me, then she draws back and sneers.

'Daddy was right to teach self-reliance,' she spits. 'It's only blood family you can count on. And even then not everyone.' She looks at Art – a challenging look, almost a question – as if *he* had disagreed with her rather than me.

Art meets her gaze. 'Brandon was tough. You're right, Morgan, he had to be.' He pauses. 'But you have to remember that Gen can't possibly understand his world.'

I stare at him, irritated by the way he makes Brandon Ryan sound like a difficult subject that's almost entirely beyond me.

Art sighs. 'And there has to be some trust in business or there's only chaos.'

Silence falls across the table. I still feel miffed that Art weighed in to make an excuse for me. Morgan, meanwhile, is pointedly looking across the room, ignoring him. No one speaks, but I sense that any attempt I might make to ease the atmosphere will be viewed as an interference. Maybe that's normal for brothers and sisters – a display of some baffling private code that outsiders, even loved ones, will never completely understand.

Morgan buries herself in the dessert menu, which I know she has absolutely no intention of ordering from. Art squeezes my hand, then disappears to the toilet. When he comes back, he's all smiles and full of a funny story about Siena and the guy from the office she got together with at our party.

I remember bursting in on them in the utility room and tell Art, who thinks it's all very amusing. Morgan remains outside the conversation for a while, unyielding. I don't understand why she's upset, but I let Art handle her. He wins her round as he wins everyone round: at first with occasional glances, then smiles, then with requests for information. He listens so well and so intently to what she says that, after a while, she thaws and balance is restored. I've seen Art do this before and it always intrigues me, particularly because all this emotional fluency is unconscious and instinctive. So much so that, later, when I ask, I'm sure he'll say he didn't even notice Morgan was rattled . . .

Morgan has to fly to Geneva for a week-long conference the next morning, Sunday. After she's gone we meet Kyle and Vicky for brunch at Banner's with all their kids. Art takes a phone call while we're eating, then looks distracted for the rest of the afternoon. I ask what's wrong and he mutters something about the Prime Minister's advisory committee. I tell him to call Sandrine – rather more waspishly than I mean to – and he snaps at me that I don't understand how important it is.

We come out of the café to find a dusting of snow on the rooftops. Back home, the TV is full of how exceptional the weather is for March. Transport chaos is predicted for Monday but Art is certain everyone will make it in to Loxley Benson. He spends an hour or two researching ICSI. I feel guilty that he's doing this – during the only part of the weekend he has to himself – when I feel so far from agreeing to another round of fertility treatment. Art comes off his computer full of stats and research data that he's eager to impart, but I plead a headache and disappear upstairs to lie down.

I fall asleep for half an hour, waking with a start when Lorcan calls Art's mobile to suggest a drink in The Railway Tavern. Art's tired and though he doesn't say so directly, I'm sure he doesn't really want to go. Still, he agrees to meet Lorcan.

'What's up?' I say, as he gets off the phone. 'Normally you

only go out on a Sunday if there's a big business deal at stake. Is it . . . to talk about what Lorcan did in the past?'

'Of course it isn't,' Art snaps. 'It's just a quick drink. No big deal. Why don't you come too, if you're so interested?'

I shake my head, wondering if he's just being irritable because he's tired, or because he's stressed about something. I'd like to see Lorcan again, but there was definitely some kind of awkwardness between him and Art. I should leave them alone to sort it out. Anyway, I feel like I haven't had a moment to myself for days, and even though it's Sunday afternoon I don't want to put off my call to Dr Rodriguez any longer.

It takes me several minutes after Art leaves to pluck up the courage to dial the number for Rodriguez's office at the Fair Angel hospital. I have no idea what I'm going to say when I speak to him but, in the end, it all comes to nothing. My call goes straight to the hospital's main switchboard, where a temp answers. She clearly doesn't know any of the doctors. She pores over the list in front of her, but Rodriguez isn't named as either an attending physician or one of the weekend doctors on call. I ring off and check the Fair Angel website. I can't find any reference to Rodriguez on that either. Has he left? Was he fired? A quick Google search turns up nothing. In the end, feeling frustrated, I try calling Lucy O'Donnell again, but her number is still unobtainable.

Art is gone for a couple of hours; then, shortly before 7.30 p.m., he and Lorcan roll in with a takeaway. Art shoots me an apologetic look. I can tell coming back here wasn't his idea and, again, I wonder why he hasn't just made some excuse.

Lorcan looks as laidback as he did at the party. He walks into the living room and greets me with a kiss on the cheek, like we're old friends now too.

'How was your day?' His accent makes his voice gentle. Yet it has an edge too, something unsettling behind the softness.

'Good.' I shrug, suddenly embarrassed by my lack of activity. All I've done since the party, it seems, is eat out. No wonder Morgan looked at me so disdainfully; I never seem to get anywhere with anything.

I fetch some beers while Art takes the curry into the kitchen to unload the cartons onto a tray.

Lorcan sits on the sofa in exactly the same place as when we talked at the party. He pulls a Swiss Army knife from his pocket and flicks out the bottle opener attachment. He opens one of the beers, pushes it towards me, then puts the knife on the table in front of him. Intrigued by its compact design, I reach over and pick it up.

'Careful!' Lorcan's too late. The blade of the knife is sticking out just under the bottle opener. It slices my skin. I drop the knife onto the table and stare at my finger. A globe of blood rises up at me.

'That's lethal,' I say, sucking at the wound.

'I know, sorry.' Lorcan coughs. 'I wouldn't . . . it's just Cal, my son, gave it to me. He sharpens the knife whenever he gets a chance. Are you all right?'

'Sure.' I examine the cut. A fresh drop of blood is oozing up to take the place of the previous one. I press it against my thumb. 'Only a scratch.'

Lorcan picks up the knife again. I notice how carefully he holds it as he concentrates on prising the top off the second bottle. He's wearing dark blue jeans, slightly faded. He has taken his jacket off and his jumper is charcoal grey. Loose round the neck. There is red in the dark of his stubble. It catches in the light as a curl of hair falls over his forehead.

He glances up at me. 'Tired?' He smiles as he puts my bottle in front of me.

I shake my head, feeling myself blushing. 'No, it's nice you're here.'

Lorcan laughs. 'I meant were you tired from the party. You sounded fed up just now when I asked about your day.'

'Did I?' I squirm. 'No, today's been fine, I just haven't done much.'

'Hey, I'm not getting at you.' He laughs again and holds up his bottle. '*Sláinte.*'

'Cheers.'

Lorcan grins. 'Beer is my only remaining vice. How about you?'

'Alcohol generally, I'd say, though beer and wine more than anything else.'

'Grand.' Lorcan reaches for a third bottle, for Art. 'No other vices?'

I shrug. 'Nah, I'm very boring.'

Lorcan looks up. 'I don't believe that for a moment.' He pauses. 'So how are you, really?'

'Today wasn't great, I guess.' I hesitate, not sure what or how much to say. 'I guess I'm a bit tired from the party, and Morgan, as you know, can be full-on, but we saw Kyle and Vicky earlier which was nice. There's just something . . . something on my mind . . .' I tail off.

Lorcan raises his eyes. 'Sounds complicated.'

'It is.' I look away.

'So,' Lorcan lowers his voice. 'Is the thing on your mind something you don't want Art to know about?'

I stare at him, my heart thudding.

How does he know I'm keeping secrets from Art?

I open my mouth to ask him what he means, but just at that moment Art walks back in the room.

CHAPTER EIGHT

I look away, embarrassed that Lorcan has seen through me.

'We bought far too much food.' Art's hands are clamped around a large tray laden with cartons of curry. He clearly hasn't heard what Lorcan just said, but one look at my face will give me away.

'I'll get the plates.' My voice is too high. I scurry off to the kitchen, feeling unsettled. Lorcan can't possibly know that I'm obsessing over what Lucy O'Donnell told me. He's just fishing.

I reach into the cupboard and pull out three plates.

'Hey, you all right?' It's him. His fingers rest on my arm for a moment. 'Thought you might like a hand.'

'Thanks.' I give him the plates, then walk over to the cutlery drawer.

'I'm sorry,' he says. 'I didn't mean to upset you.'

'You didn't.' I open the drawer and grab a handful of spoons and forks.

'I was only asking because I know how hard it is keeping a secret,' Lorcan says in a low voice. 'You don't have to tell me anything, I'm just saying I get it.'

'Right, thanks.' I tuck a roll of kitchen towel under my arm and head back to the living room. Lorcan follows.

We sit and chat over the food. I don't eat much. I still feel too troubled. It's not just Lorcan's intuition, I realize. It's my own inaction. The weekend is almost over, it's been almost a week since I saw Lucy O'Donnell and I've done nothing except rifle through Art's bank statements, fail to track down Dr Rodriguez and worry a lot.

The worst thing is that I don't know what else to do, just that I have to do something.

'You okay, Gen?' Art asks. ''Cause normally you're a pig for the chana masala.' He's trying to sound light-hearted but there's a harsh edge to his voice. I get the sense he's still uncomfortable in Lorcan's presence, just like he was at the party.

'I'm fine.' I dig my spoon into the dish of chickpeas and haul out a second helping. I force myself to eat another mouthful.

Lorcan starts reminiscing about the trip he and Art made to America in their early twenties, a Greyhound bus tour of the East Coast, punctuated by a short stay at Morgan's holiday home in Martha's Vineyard.

'Was Morgan there?' I ask, trying to remember what Art has told me about the trip.

'She was,' Art said. 'I'd only met her that once before, but we'd kept in touch, as you know. And when she knew I was coming on holiday to the States she offered us use of the house.' As he speaks, he looks down at the table. I'm sure he's remembering how, unlike Morgan, their father had rejected him.

I catch Lorcan's eye. He senses my concern and gives me a swift nod. 'We had a laugh all right, didn't we, man?' He punches Art's arm playfully.

But Art seems lost in thought. 'We didn't expect Morgan to be there, but you know Morgan – even then she was jet-setting about, working for her . . . our dad. She was at some conference in New York and flew down for a couple of days.'

119

'It was good of her to put us up, considering the state we were in.' Lorcan turns to me, chuckling. 'We were off our tits most of the time we were there.'

Art nods. He looks uncharacteristically awkward.

'D'you remember that weird guy we met in that bar near Morgan's house?' Lorcan asks. 'The one who sold us that E mixed with acid?'

I stare at Art. In all the time I've known him, he's never taken so much as a single puff on a spliff. He'd mentioned vaguely being a little bit more experimental with drugs when he was younger, but I'd kind of assumed he'd meant trying out cannabis, not getting high on class As.

'Sort of.' Art's avoiding my gaze.

Lorcan shakes his head, his whole face expressing manic delight. 'That was crazy.' He turns to me. 'We were so out of it we built an entire imaginary wall in the middle of this fancy bar.'

Art nods again, but says nothing. Lorcan chuckles. 'You were yelling instructions at me like a sergeant major: "Set that brick straight, you fucker"; "Spread that cement smooth, you piece of shit". I had no idea what I was doing.'

'It was a long time ago,' Art says. He still hasn't looked at me.

'Then your sister turned up and tried to get us out of the bar and you swore at her.' Lorcan turns to me. 'I've never seen anyone look so angry. There were death rays coming out of her eyes, man.'

I suddenly remember what Lorcan said about Morgan not liking him. Well, that makes more sense now. I grin to myself, imagining Morgan's fury when faced with a brother she hardly knew, under the influence of hardcore substances, and a big, swearing Irishman in a smart East Coast bar.

'D'you still do that stuff?' I ask.

Lorcan shakes his head. 'No . . . well, maybe the occasional toke on a joint, but nothing major. Not for years. What about you, Art?'

'No.' Art rubs his temple.

Lorcan grins. 'Fair play. You're a wise man.'

I get up to fetch more beers. Art's bent over his plate, shovelling in a mouthful of curry, but Lorcan watches me as I walk to the door. I turn and meet his gaze – it's full of curiosity and . . . and recognition. *I know you.*

I'm transfixed. Then Lorcan looks away and I hurry into the kitchen. Hands suddenly trembling, I take three more beers from the fridge. As I come back into the living room, Lorcan is laughing. He glances up at me, just for a split second, without meeting my eyes properly. Then he turns back to Art, all cheery and chatty again.

I sit with them for a few more minutes. I didn't imagine that look of Lorcan's. It was the kind of look you only get from someone who's interested in you. *Properly* interested. My hands are still shaking. I sit on them and try to calm myself. *Jesus, Gen, get a grip.* It was only a bloody glance. It didn't mean anything. It's just been a long time since someone looked at me like that.

Lorcan's talking about his acting job – a long-running TV drama set in Cork. The show is broadcast exclusively in Ireland, so I don't know anything about it. Neither does Art, though he claims to have caught Lorcan in a few episodes on various business visits to Dublin.

Lorcan is charmingly self-deprecating about both the show and his own role in it. 'I play this troubled ex-rock star who's been in and out of rehab since series one,' he explains. 'The lead is my son and I pop up every now and then to offer him advice based on my years of therapy . . .'

'So you're there to provide the show with a bit of psychoanalytical depth?' I say.

'Yeah, except when I fall off the wagon when I'm there to provide a drunken man getting into a fist-fight.'

I laugh. 'So d'you like the part?'

'It pays the bills.' Lorcan shrugs. 'It's not exactly what I imagined I'd be doing when I gave up everything to go to drama school. Still, most actors don't even manage to make a living from acting so I shouldn't moan.'

Art snorts. He seems more relaxed now that Lorcan – rather than their shared past – is the subject of the conversation. 'You're lucky to be working at all, you ginger bastard.'

Lorcan tips his head back and laughs. I'm transfixed again by the way his smile fills his whole face.

'He's not ginger,' I protest. 'It's auburn. Chestnut.'

'Well, whatever you call it, Art's right. My hair made a difference when I was younger,' Lorcan says.

'No way.' I take a swig of my beer.

'No?' Lorcan eyes me. 'How many leading men with red hair can you name?'

I nod, taking his point. 'Not many,' I say. 'Ginger. The last taboo.'

'Oh, yeah,' Lorcan says. 'Way bigger than incest . . .'

'Or paedophiles,' I add.

We both laugh. I glance at Art. He's smiling but the smile seems a little forced again.

'So when's your next job?' I ask Lorcan.

'I don't have to be back in Cork till June. I'm hoping something will come up here; I've got a meeting in a couple of days, actually.'

'You don't fancy another stint at Loxley Benson, then?'

Shit. I wish the words back as soon as I've said them.

Art glowers, while Lorcan utters a sardonic 'not really.'

I look out of the window. The thin layer of white has vanished from the roof of the house opposite.

'Maybe it won't snow tomorrow, after all,' I say, then flush at how obvious I sound, trying to change the subject by talking about the weather.

'What?' Art sounds rankled.

'She's embarrassed at her inner Englishness,' Lorcan says with an easy chuckle.

I get up without looking at him. 'I'm going to bed,' I say. 'Nice to see you again, Lorcan.'

He holds his hand up in a wave.

Art yawns. ''Night, Gen. I won't be long.'

A shiver snakes down my spine as I walk away. Why do I find Lorcan so unsettling? I can't believe I was on the verge of confiding in him at the party. I climb the stairs, still feeling uneasy. Then I reach the bedroom and remember Dr Rodriguez's business card tucked under the mattress and all my focus turns to one thing: how on earth am I going to track him down?

Monday morning brings with it no sign of the threatened snow. In fact it's a beautiful day, cold but clear and brilliantly sunny. I call Fair Angel again. I can't think what else to do. Dr Rodriguez isn't registered on any medical directory I can find, nor is his name on the electoral roll. At least the office manager is in today. I start by saying that I'd like to make an appointment with the doctor but she cuts in impatiently with the news that Dr Rodriguez left the hospital several years ago. And 'no', she has 'no idea where he works now'.

'What about where he lives?'

'I'm afraid I can't give out personal information,' she says.

There's no point in pushing her, I can hear it in her voice.

The whole thing is still on my mind when the doorbell rings a couple of hours later. It's Lorcan on the sun-drenched step outside.

'Hi.' A dark red curl falls over one eye. He brushes it back off his face.

'Hi.' I step away, conscious that my breath must smell garlicky from the leftover curry I just had for lunch.

'Hi.' Lorcan pauses. 'Look, I'm sorry to just turn up like this, but I've only got Art's mobile number and ...' He stops and I know, without any doubt, he'd been going to say that he hadn't wanted to speak to Art.

I back away into the hall, now horribly aware that I'm wearing sweatpants and that the line of my knickers is probably showing.

'I left that lethal Swiss Army knife here.' Lorcan strides ahead of me, towards the living room. 'I wouldn't be bothered but Cal gave it to me.' He glances at me over his shoulder. 'My son. Did I tell you about him?'

'No, not really.' I scuttle after him, quickly pulling on a long cardigan.

'He's fourteen and a total computer geek. Doesn't have all that much to say to me at the moment but the Swiss Army knife was the first present he bought me without his mum involved and I'm always giving out to him when he loses stuff, so ...'

'No problem.'

We're in the living room now. Lorcan is pulling at the sofa cushions, sliding his hands down the sides. 'I'm sorry.' He glances up at me again. 'I'll be out of your hair in a minute.'

'It's fine,' I say. Now I've got over the surprise it's actually quite nice to have him here. It might take my mind off my failed attempts to find Dr Rodriguez. 'Would you like a cup of tea?'

'Sure.' Lorcan flops onto the sofa. 'Man, maybe it isn't here.'

I feel down the back of the sofa where Lorcan was sitting and find the knife immediately. As I hand it to Lorcan, I can't help but wonder whether he really lost it, or whether he deliberately left it here so he would have an excuse to come back.

I push this thought out of my head and wander into the kitchen. As the kettle boils, I bend down and check my reflection in the steel. My nose is shiny and I'm wearing only a trace of eyeliner, but at least it hasn't smudged. I make a face at my reflection. Why on earth would Lorcan be interested in me?

'Geniver?' His voice is close.

I jerk upright, startled, and clutch at the wooden countertop. He's standing in the doorway, watching me. 'Jesus.'

'Sorry.' There's a preoccupied look on his face. The Swiss Army knife is in his hand. As he speaks he absently flicks out the blade. The lethal metal glints in the overhead light.

I take an instinctive step away, remembering how easily it cut my hand yesterday.

'Sorry,' Lorcan says again, noticing my alarm. 'Habit.' He strokes the blade carefully back into place. 'Look, I'm not just here for my knife. I mean, I did, obviously, leave it behind last night, but that's not the only reason I came back.'

'Oh?' It comes out slightly strangled-sounding. I fold my arms and lean against the counter, trying to appear relaxed.

Lorcan grins. 'We were talking. Last night, I mean. And I know there was something you wanted to talk about. And, well, sometimes it's easier to speak to someone you don't know.'

'So you came round to listen?' I raise my eyebrows.

'To help, if I can.' He doesn't take his eyes off mine. 'I wanted to be a priest when I was a kid.'

I laugh, as relief and disappointment spread through me in equal measures. 'I've got plenty of friends, you know.' I reach for two mugs.

'Sure you do, yeah.' He moves over to the fridge and pulls out the carton of milk. 'But they all have children, don't they?'

I shake my head, opening the cupboard and rootling around for tea bags. 'What's that got to do—?'

'I saw you talking to one of them in the kitchen.' He offers me the carton of milk. 'Couldn't help hearing some of it. How happy you were she was pregnant. Reassuring her you were all okay with it, which was obviously bollocks, but . . .'

'You don't know me.' I grab the milk and turn away.

There's a pause. The kettle boils and hisses away into silence again. I look up, wondering if I sounded rude.

Lorcan grins. 'Never said I did. But tell me I'm wrong.' He points to my bitten fingernails, clutching the milk carton. 'Those nails don't lie.'

I shake my head. I can't think what to say. My head feels like the kettle has just boiled inside it.

'Okay, look, I'm sorry.' Lorcan shrugs. 'I only wanted to help.'

I roll my eyes. 'I don't need any help.'

He stares at me. I glare back. I should feel furious at his interference. But there's real kindness in the way he's looking at me.

'I just want her.' My voice is tiny. Like a child's. Small and vulnerable. I look down, humiliated.

'Your daughter?'

I nod, unable to speak.

'You never told me her name.'

'Beth.' It comes out like a sigh, so soft I think he won't have heard it.

But he has. 'Beth? That's a beautiful name.'

I nod again. It's all I have of her. Her name. I wipe my eyes. 'Sorry, I'm not upset. I'm not.'

Lorcan chuckles. 'Look, let me make the tea. You go and sit down.'

I walk past him, back to the living room. I sit on the sofa and wait. I can't tell him. I can't. It'll sound mad and I don't want to cry in front of him again.

He walks in with the tea and sets both mugs down on the

table. He settles into the opposite corner of the sofa, right by the photo of my dad as a boy, and smiles. 'I know it's not the same, but I miss my son very much. He's here in London and I spend nine months of the year in Cork . . .' He tails off. 'Look, I'll just drink this and go.'

I nod. That's the best thing. He should go. Just drink his tea and go.

The phone rings shrilly.

'Gen?' It's Hen. Her voice is all wavery, like she's been crying. 'I've been thinking about you all morning. Please can we talk? I need to talk to you.'

'What's wrong?' My mind immediately flashes back to her revelation at the party. 'Is it the baby?'

'What?' She sniffs loudly. 'No, yes, no . . . no, there's nothing wrong. I just still feel so bad I didn't tell you about . . .'

'About being pregnant?' I sigh. My chest constricts. For a second I feel the unfairness of having to deal with Hen's guilt, then I push away the resentment. It's not Hen's fault things turned out the way they did. 'It's fine, Hen, we went over this at the party. I'm happy for you.'

'I know but I'm really beating myself up that I didn't tell you.'

Lorcan is on his feet across the room. I look up. He takes a long swig from his mug then sets it down on the table. He points to the door, indicating he's going to leave.

'Hang on, Hen.' I put the phone down on the side table and walk over. 'You don't have to go,' I say quietly.

He shrugs and holds up his Swiss Army knife. 'I've got what I came for.' He stares at me, his dark blue eyes heavy with meaning. A shiver snakes through me – somehow both terrifying and intriguing at the same time.

'Right.' I step back, letting him pass. As we reach the front door Lorcan takes out his phone.

'I'm sorry about this,' I say. 'You really don't have to—'

'It's not a problem.' Lorcan checks the time on his phone. 'I'm seeing Cal for lunch in half an hour anyway.' He hesitates. 'Would you like my mobile number? In case . . . if you want to talk, if there's anything I can do?'

I nod. I can't help but feel there's something illicit about me taking his number. Like it should have happened through Art, if it was going to happen at all.

We swap numbers and Lorcan leaves. I go back into the living room and it's not until I see the phone on the side table that I remember Hen. I spend the next ten minutes reassuring her. She doesn't mention Lucy O'Donnell's claims – or refer to the money Art paid to MDO until the last part of our conversation. Then she asks if I'm still worrying about it all.

'A bit,' I confess.

I hear Hen draw in her breath. 'Oh, Gen,' she says. 'I'm so sorry to go on while you're having to deal with all of that.'

'It's okay, I—'

'But I'm sure it's nothing,' she says. 'I mean, it would be crazy to get obsessed over some random madwoman and a bit of money going out of one of Art's accounts.'

'Fifty grand isn't a "bit" of money,' I say.

'Okay, but Gen, even if it was a million pounds it wouldn't prove anything except . . . God, except how much you want it to be true that Beth is still alive.'

I suddenly see myself from Hen's perspective: childless and obsessed and clinging to a pipe dream. I remember overhearing her on the phone the other day, her voice pitying and exasperated.

'Honestly,' I insist. 'I'm not obsessing about any of it.' Right now I've had enough of Hen. I love her dearly, but she's demanding and I don't have the energy to manage all her emotions as well as my own.

Soothed, Hen finishes the conversation by making me laugh at an encounter she had in Harvey Nichols on Saturday with a shop assistant who once cut up her credit card.

'She was all over me like she couldn't do enough for me,' Hen says, with a grin in her voice. 'Just goes to show. She was snooty as hell five years ago when I didn't have any money.'

One hour later and I'm all set to head into town to teach my Monday afternoon class. It still hasn't snowed but when I step outside there's a bone-freezing chill in the crisp, dry air. I go back into the house and dig a blue wool beanie out of the hall cupboard. I tug it down over my ears and wander along the road enjoying the combination of cold and sunshine. I'm almost in a good mood when I reach the Art & Media Institute.

Plenty of today's students are keen to talk to me after class. I have a quick chat with a couple of them, then slip out of the building and head to the bus stop. I'm feeling remarkably positive until I get off the bus at the other end and realize that it's now late Monday afternoon and, despite my promise to myself, I'm no closer to tracking down Rodriguez than I was last week. I'm so lost in my unhappy thoughts that I walk into someone as I turn the corner, two streets from home.

'Oh, excuse me,' I say, all flustered. Then I look up.

The woman I've walked into is Charlotte West from my Thursday tutor group.

'Geniver,' she says, as if we're old friends. 'Fancy seeing you here.' She runs her hand over her blonde hair, letting her fingers trail down to that Orla Kiely bag, identical to the one Hen bought me. With a jolt I realize she has had her hair shortened and styled into a shaggy bob with a long, wispy fringe. It's like a mirror image of my own hair, only fair.

'I live here,' I say, utterly thrown. 'How come you're here? I thought you only came up to London for your writing class . . .' For a second my mind goes blank. Should Charlotte have been in today's class after all? Have I got completely muddled up? No, Charlotte definitely comes on Thursdays.

'I have lots of friends in London actually.' Charlotte smiles again.

'Of course,' I stammer.

'Before we moved to Somerset we lived quite near here. Then after the divorce . . .' She pauses. 'Well, I'm on my way to visit a friend now, in fact.'

I have the strong sense she's lying about that last statement. But why? 'I'm just back from today's class,' I say, trying to pull myself together.

'Did you come on the bus?' Charlotte asks smoothly.

'Er, yes.' My eyes drift down to the book in her hand. *Oh goodness.* She's holding *my* novel – *Rain Heart* – the one she was talking about at the end of our last class.

Charlotte follows my gaze. 'As I say, I'm visiting a friend.' Charlotte's smile deepens. She touches her fringe self-consciously. 'And I was reading your book again. It really is very good. Will you sign it for me?'

'Thank you, sure.' I take the book and pen Charlotte offers and scribble her name, 'Best wishes' and my signature on the title page. I hand the book back, still feeling awkward. This is just such a weird coincidence . . . Charlotte being near my house, carrying my book and my bag and with her new hair style.

'So where are you . . .?' Charlotte waves her hand, taking in the surrounding roads.

'A couple of roads up there.' I point, vaguely, in the direction of home. Maybe I'm overreacting, but there's something about the way Charlotte's looking at me that is making me feel increasingly uncomfortable. She's trying to sound casual, but there's an insistence in those hard green eyes.

'What, Burnham Street? That's the next one on from where my friend lives.'

'Er, yes . . .'

'Just you and . . . your husband?' Charlotte raises her eyebrows.

Again, I feel the pressure behind her question. Still, it's no secret that I'm married. I wear a platinum band on my ring finger. Art has a matching one. 'Yes,' I say. 'Oh, well, it's nice to see you.'

'I'd love to be able to write like you,' Charlotte says. 'I was going to ask, actually, if there was any chance of private tuition after the end of term. Maybe I could buy you a coffee? Discuss it?'

'Sorry,' I say, taking a step back. 'I don't do private classes. Look, I really have to go now, Charlotte. I'll see you on Thursday.'

Charlotte says nothing for a moment, as if she's waiting for something to happen. Then she nods with a sigh. 'Bye, then, Geniver.'

'Bye.' I turn and walk away. I can't help but feel spooked. I stop at the corner and look around, half-expecting Charlotte to still be standing where I left her, watching me, but she's gone.

I get home and switch on all the downstairs lights. Art hates it when I do this, but thanks to Charlotte I feel unsettled and the house is big and dark and empty. Another huge mound of junk mail is spread out over the doormat. I pick everything up, check there's nothing important or personal and carry the whole lot to the recycling pile in the corner of the kitchen.

I'm about to drop my armful of brochures and envelopes onto the rest, when I catch sight of the story on the front page of the local free paper. There's a small picture of a middle-aged black woman.

Lucy O'Donnell.

I scan the caption underneath the picture. My blood turns to ice.

She is dead.

CHAPTER NINE

I snatch up the paper and read the full story:

> Police are appealing for witnesses to a fatal hit-and-run
> accident that took place last Thursday afternoon at the junc-
> tion of Seven Sisters and Berriman Roads. The victim is a
> black woman in her forties. Anyone who thinks they may be
> able to identify this woman should contact . . .

My heart thumps in my chest. I stare at the words, as the terrible
realization settles over me. Lucy O'Donnell has been killed. The
woman at the very centre of the truth about Beth has died under
– I glance over the news story again – under what *have* to be
suspicious circumstances. If it was just an accident, why haven't
the police identified her? The image they've used is from the
photo Lucy showed me, only with her sister, Mary, cut out of the
picture. I remember her shoving it into her coat pocket. But
what about her handbag? Why didn't she have that with her too
– or her purse or her phone? And what about her husband,
Bernard? She said he was here in London too, so why hasn't he
gone to the police?

I'm clutching the newspaper so hard the sides of it are crumpled in my fists. I remember coming home from my lunch with

Hen last Thursday afternoon and the police lights flashing up ahead as my bus crawled along Seven Sisters Road. That must have been for Lucy.

I sink into a chair at the kitchen table and carefully pore over the story again, looking for more clues about what might have happened. Is Lucy's death a coincidence? Could it have something to do with what she told me? I feel sick, my mind running over the sequence of events. Lucy turned up on my doorstep on Wednesday morning. I told Art about her soon after. The newspaper says she died on Thursday afternoon, the very next day – and just a few hours before I tried to call her that night.

No, surely I'm being ridiculous to think there's any connection between what Lucy told me, my telling Art, and her death. Disconnected thoughts clutch wildly at my mind. I go upstairs and I crawl into bed and all my limbs feel heavy and I'm exhausted but my brain is whirring and won't be still and I lie there and everything I've been told is crowding in on me.

Art paid MDO money just after Beth's stillbirth. But Beth was alive.

Dr Rodriguez stole Beth.

Art knew.

Somehow these accusations are all mixed up with each other. But I don't know how – or if – any them are true. It's like an itch I can't scratch. It's driving me mad. I force myself to focus. Other people were involved – not just Dr Rodriguez and Lucy's sister, Mary. What about the funeral home that buried my baby? If Beth wasn't really dead then who *did* they bury? I get up and fetch the letter from Tapps Funeral Services.

I make the call with trembling fingers. But I'm too late. It's gone six and all I access is the answerphone. I leave a message for Mr Tapps to call me on my mobile as soon as he can.

Art arrives home just after eight, from some long, out-of-office meeting. I'm waiting in the kitchen. He looks exhausted and I know the last thing he needs is an interrogation from me. But I have to talk to him. Not about Lucy O'Donnell dying in a hit-and-run. I've agonized over that and I'm not going to mention it. Art will just see how upset I am and say I'm being neurotic. He'll say it's a sad accident bearing no relation to the lies she told me. Instead I'm going to push him on MDO. If Art is somehow involved in all this then that money, paid so soon after Beth was born and hidden away in a mysterious file, is surely significant. Anyway, it's the only concrete lead I have to follow.

I pour him a beer, then sit down beside him at the table and take a deep breath. 'Did you find out about that loan?' I ask, trying to sound as offhand as possible. 'The one to MDO from L B Plus from years back?'

'No, I told you.' Art sighs. 'I don't remember. It was just some business thing.'

'Come on, Art.' I say, still trying to make my voice light. 'You never forget your business deals.'

'Well, I've forgotten this one.' He looks directly at me. 'I asked Dan. He said he'd have to check but it was probably a client payment.'

'But why would *you* be paying a client?' I persist.

Art rubs his eyes. 'No, I mean it was probably client money we were passing through another company . . . this MDO of yours. Dan offered to check it all out for me, but I told him not to bother. We're really busy at the moment, Gen. I don't want him tied up looking into ancient transactions on a whim.'

'It's not a whim.'

Art's head shoots up. 'So what *is* it, Gen?' His voice is sharp. 'What the hell is all this about, because all I can see is you over-reacting and getting obsessed—' He stops with the word 'again' on his lips, but not quite out of his mouth.

135

'I don't think it's unreasonable to ask,' I say, hating the injured tone of my voice. 'It's a lot of money.'

Art rolls his eyes. 'Loads of money goes through our books every day.'

'But the timing . . . it just looks . . . weird. I mean, so much cash, just after Beth . . .' I tail off, floored by Art's stony glare.

'It's a coincidence, Gen.' Art sits back in his chair, pushing his glass of beer across the table.

A dull weight settles in my chest. I know from years of living with him that he has withdrawn. Pushing him further will get me nowhere.

And yet I can't stop.

'Please, Art,' I persist. 'You're making me feel like I'm totally overreacting but—'

'You *are* totally overreacting,' he says coldly. 'It's horrible not being trusted.'

'I do trust you,' I insist.

'Right.' Art gets up and walks out.

Feeling weary, I sit for a while, listening to Art move around upstairs. He sounds like he's in the spare room, just down the corridor from our bedroom. The last time I can remember him spending the night in there was two years ago, after we'd had a massive row over a holiday he couldn't go on at the last minute because of work. It's not fair for him to be so angry now. Just as it wasn't fair of Hen to be irritated with me before. I know I'm being mistrustful, but why can't either of them understand just how devastating it is to be told my baby might be alive?

I switch on the TV and attempt to distract myself with the news. There's an item about the Irish economy. For a second the commentator's accent makes me think of Lorcan, then I'm back to wondering about Art and that MDO payment. It's the uncertainty that's killing me. Is Art really hurt because he thinks I don't trust him? Or is he hiding something?

After twenty minutes or so, I follow him upstairs. As I thought, he's in the spare room. I creep past the door. He's on his side on the bed, fast asleep. Frustration fills me. And irritation that he can sleep so easily when I am in such turmoil. I'm going round in circles wondering what to do. Getting nowhere. It's time for action.

Without thinking about it any further I go up the stairs to Art's office. If Art is hiding anything, it's going to be inside the cupboard where he said he kept the paperwork on Beth. The floorboards creak louder than usual in the evening silence. I march over to the cupboard. Just as before it's locked, so I grab a pair of scissors from the nearest desk and insert the slim blades between the doors. With a single fierce thrust I snap the lock. It gives more easily than I expect. The doors swing open. I see the red shoebox immediately, on the middle shelf, surrounded by files labelled 'Personal Tax'. Another look at its contents feels like a good place to start. I hesitate, listening out for any sounds from downstairs. Art will discover what I've done in the morning of course, but right now I'm too angry to care. I take the shoebox and lift the lid.

The box is empty.

I stare into it, unbelieving. For a moment I think I've actually gone mad. I doubt everything: that this was the box Art showed me before; that it contained all the paperwork on Beth's still-birth and funeral; that my eyes are working properly. Then the shock passes and the realization sinks through me. This *is* the box. But all the papers are gone. Where are they?

I look around, scanning the other shelves and the nearby desk. A few slivers of coloured paper lie beside the shredder. I pick up a handful of red and blue. I'm sure these are the colours of the Tapps Funeral Services logo. I recognize it from the letterhead.

'What the fuck are you doing?'

I spin around. Art is standing in the doorway, bleary-eyed, his hair tousled. He's looking at the open cupboard and the broken lock.

I hold out my hand, palm open, revealing the scraps of shredded paper.

'Did you shred all Beth's papers?'

Art walks across the office towards me. The floorboards creak loudly. His eyes are fixed on the splinters of wood that stick out from the cupboard door. 'Why did you break this open?' He stares at me in horror. 'Gen, what is the matter with you?'

'Answer my question.'

Art reaches the door and touches the broken lock.

'Art,' I insist. 'What did you do to everything in the box?'

His face is pale. 'Gen, I'm seriously worried about you. If you wanted to look inside this cupboard, why didn't you just ask me for the key? This isn't normal behaviour.'

Frustration surges inside me. 'Neither is shredding a death certificate.'

'I didn't. The death certificate is in with all our other legal papers,' Art says. 'I only got rid of the brochures and the letters.'

'But they were all we had of her.'

'No they weren't. They were *admin*. They were *nothing* to do with her. Anyway, until that bloody woman turned up on the doorstep you hadn't looked at them for years. You didn't even know most of them existed.' He reaches out to touch my face, his eyes desperate with tender concern, but I lean back, away from him.

'Come on, Gen. I don't want it to get like it did with that babygro.'

I catch my breath. Art never understood why I wanted to keep the little white babygro. He thought it was morbid.

'I don't think it's healthy for you to be going over everything again,' Art says sadly. 'I'm *worried* about you, Gen. You're becoming obsessed. First that stupid payment, then all of the paperwork . . .'

'I just want to know the truth,' I insist.

Art shakes his head. He reaches for me again. I back up against the desk. I feel trapped, penned in. Art's fingers stroke my cheek. 'Gen, darling, I've been talking with Hen and we both think you should go back to that therapist.'

I push his hand away. So it *was* Art on the phone to Hen the other day. Or, if not then, another time. I feel sick. It's not just the idea that Art's been confiding in Hen again. Therapy is the last thing I need right now. The counsellor I saw for a while after Beth died helped a little, but in the end I got sick of the sound of my own voice going over the same old ground. The support group I tried was just as bad. All those mothers had other children already – or got pregnant again during the course of our meetings.

'When did you destroy all the papers?' I demand.

'I don't know.' Art frowns. 'Just after you looked at them last week.'

I remember how, that evening, I'd gone downstairs to call Lucy O'Donnell and heard the office floorboards creaking as I crossed the hall, and how Art had denied he'd been up here.

'You said you didn't come up here again.' My mind is careering around now. 'What is this? Are you trying to make me think I'm going insane?'

Art shakes his head. There's a terrible sadness in his eyes. 'Oh, Gen, *listen* to yourself, will you? I don't think I did come up straightaway. I think it was later, so I *didn't* lie. And I'm not suggesting you should go back to therapy because there's anything properly wrong with you. It's just because I care about you and you've obviously not been coping since that stupid woman and her lies.'

'Her name was Lucy O'Donnell and she's *dead*, Art.' Despite my earlier intentions, the words shoot out of me. 'The woman who told me about Beth is *dead*. She died last week, the day after I saw her, in a hit-and-run accident.' I gasp, a sob welling inside me. Because I don't think it was an accident, but I know Art will be as dismissive as he was earlier if I suggest Lucy was deliberately killed. I turn away from him, not wanting him to see my tears. I don't think I've ever felt so alone in my life.

'That's terrible,' Art says, his hand stroking my arm. 'But it's got nothing to do with this, and you have to admit breaking into my cupboard is irrational, Gen. I'm only trying to help. *Please*.'

I turn around and look into his eyes. He seems genuinely worried for me. I falter, seeing myself from his perspective.

'I understand that it seems extreme,' I say, as calmly as I can, 'but I'm not being obsessive. I'm just trying to find out what really happened to Beth.'

Art's expression clouds, a terrible bitterness sweeping over his face. It's in the hurt in his eyes and the curl of his lip, and in his voice as he speaks.

'Beth *died*, Gen. You need to move on or—' He stops, rubs his hand over his forehead.

'Or what?'

'Or it will kill us too. *Us*. Our relationship. Our marriage. *Us*.' Art holds my gaze for a second. 'Don't you see what's happening? Can you just stop for one second and think about how *I* feel. Beth was my daughter too.'

I nod, suddenly ashamed of being selfish.

Art pulls me towards him but I'm not quite ready to surrender entirely. I hold up the shredded bits of brochure between us. 'You still shouldn't have destroyed all the papers.'

'Maybe so,' Art acknowledges. 'I'm sorry, Gen . . .' His voice cracks. 'I just don't know how to help you any more.'

I let him hold me. I feel numb. I can see how I look – spun out of control because of one woman's outrageous claims. And yet I didn't imagine the look of sincerity in Lucy O'Donnell's eyes. And I haven't imagined her death either.

'Let's go to bed.'

I let Art lead me down to our bedroom. He fetches his things from the spare room, waits while I brush my teeth and get into the long T-shirt I wear at night, then he spoons me into his arms and holds me as he falls asleep.

I lie awake for a while, listening to Art's steady breathing, feeling the dead weight of his arm on my ribs. I'm hyper-aware of the Tapps letter and Rodriguez's business card under the mattress below me. What would Art say if he knew I'd been calling both the funeral home and the Fair Angel private maternity hospital?

Thinking about that empty shoebox upstairs keeps me wide awake. Art shouldn't have shredded its entire contents. He says I'm being obsessive but what he did was extreme too. As I lie there, unsleeping, my anger builds. How dare Art make that decision to destroy everything? It was up to *both* of us to decide what to do.

I lift his arm up and wriggle out from under the duvet. I stand, watching him breathing for a moment.

If Art can act unilaterally, then so can I.

His phone is on the bedside table. Without thinking, I snatch it up and go into the bathroom at the end of the corridor. I sit cross-legged on the edge of the bath, the phone in my trembling hand. I know the password. I also know that using it – and checking Art's calls and emails – crosses a line I've never dreamed of crossing before, in all the years I've known him.

I hesitate for a few long, silent seconds. I have no idea what I'm doing, just that, for all Art's sincerity, there's something, some shadow that lurks in the background, stopping me from being able to dismiss Lucy O'Donnell's claim that Art let the doctor take Beth away.

A dustbin lid clattering to the ground outside startles me. I can't wait any longer. I *have* to find out what I can. I enter the password and click on the email icon. I flick through the entries – all work stuff. I turn to his texts but they're all deleted. So are the voicemails. What about the call log? I have no idea what I'm looking for, but I scroll through the list of callers anyway. Most of them are identified . . . Kyle several times, Tris and Dan . . . other work people . . . Art's accountant . . . plus names I recognize as clients. Interspersed with these are a few numbers without names attached. I scroll back further. There are calls from Morgan and Hen from last weekend, and from Hen the week before – the week when Lucy O'Donnell first turned up. More unrecognized callers. I take out my own phone and look at both Lorcan's and Lucy O'Donnell's numbers. Lorcan's is on Art's phone – just once, on the Sunday afternoon after the party. Well, that's no surprise; I knew he called Art to go out for that drink. Lucy's number is not showing on Art's phone. Neither, when I check, are the numbers for the Fair Angel hospital or Tapps Funeral Services. I stop for a second, registering what this means: Art has not been in touch with anyone from the past – at least not on this phone.

A dog barks outside. I glance into the corridor, straining my ears for the sound of Art getting out of bed, but the house is silent. Sweat beads on my forehead. I keep scrolling down the list, panic rising, swelling my throat. What am I doing? What if

Art wakes up and finds me? What do I hope to find? What will it prove?

I have no answers, but I keep looking anyway. It's no good, these numbers mean nothing. They're all just random, single callers that—*Wait*. There's one number that keeps coming up. It's a mobile number ending 865. Whoever owns that number has called Art every day for the past week. Yesterday they called twelve times.

I quickly scribble the number down. Palms sweating, I tiptoe into the bedroom and put Art's phone back where I found it. He's still lying exactly as I left him, breathing steadily.

I stare at the number. Who is calling Art so obsessively? For a second I want to wake him up and demand an answer, but that would mean confessing I'd snooped.

If I ask Art he will make some excuse . . . find some way of making me look ridiculous for asking. I take a deep breath. There are three possibilities.

Option one: the caller is an annoying client/someone trying to sell him something/a nut-job. I'm sure this is what Art would claim if I forced an answer out of him, though why he wouldn't just block their number I don't understand.

Option two: Art's having an affair and the caller is a woman entirely unrelated to Beth. Apart from the fact that I can't seriously believe Art would be unfaithful, all the calls are *from* this number. Art has never called it back. Not once.

Option three: the caller *is* connected with Beth. Perhaps he or she even knows where Beth is. No . . . *no* . . . This is total madness.

Gritting my teeth, I snatch up my own phone. I make sure the call will be anonymous, then dial the number. I have no idea what I'm going to say if someone answers but I can't bear not knowing any more.

My palm feels clammy on the handset as the number rings.

Oh, God, what am I doing?

A recorded message, asking the caller to leave a message. Generic, giving only the phone number as identification. I hesitate for a second then switch off the phone just before the beep.

I feel sick as I tear up the piece of paper with the number on and flush it down the toilet. I shove my own phone in my handbag and get into bed again. I lie under the covers, Art now gently snoring beside me.

I try to take stock. Lucy O'Donnell has died under suspicious circumstances. Art paid someone fifty grand just after Beth was stillborn. Someone is calling him repeatedly and he hasn't told me about it. He and Hen think I'm becoming obsessed with finding Beth.

There's nothing concrete. Nothing solid to tell me what to think, one way or the other. None of my questions and enquiries and phone calls has led anywhere. In fact, everywhere I turn is a dead end. Which means I'm going to have to go further. Action has to be better than this, this vortex of suspicion and not-knowing.

Next morning the telephone rouses me with a start. I can't see the time but it's light outside and Art is long gone.

'Mrs Loxley? This is Mr Tapps.' The man's voice is formal, his accent slightly affected. It's the voice of a man not entirely comfortable in his own skin. 'You left a message for me yesterday.'

'Hi, er, thanks for calling back.' I sit up in bed, trying to focus. I explain about Beth, about the cremation eight years ago. 'It would have been just after June the eleventh. I just wanted to speak to whoever was involved. I mean whoever dealt with . . . our baby . . .' As I speak, I get out of bed and wander to the window to draw back the curtains.

'Ah.' Mr Tapps pauses and, when he continues speaking, his voice is softer. 'I'm so sorry, Mrs Loxley, but I'm afraid I can't help. I thought it might be this . . . sometimes, after the event, it seems to help people to speak to those involved.'

'Do you remember . . .?' I say. I'm still not properly awake so I push the window open and breathe the crisp morning air.

'Of course,' Mr Tapps says, and his voice is full of compassion. 'I checked the records when my assistant said you were a client and . . . well, as I say, I'm terribly sorry, but for some reason there's no record of who laid out your daughter's body.'

'No record?' I'm wide awake now. A freezing cold wind whips into the room, rattling the window. It whistles in my ears. 'But you remember her; you have records of the funeral?'

'We have records of everything,' Mr Tapps says smoothly. 'When the body was received, when it was prepared . . . the funeral itself was carried out very quickly after that. All the dates and times are recorded, but not which of my staff was involved.'

'I see.'

'I'm really very sorry, Mrs Loxley. I've asked everyone who worked here then. No one remembers handling this particular . . . child. It was a long time ago.'

'I see,' I say again. Then an idea occurs. 'What about the payment for the funeral? Do you have a record of who covered the costs?' I'm hoping, for some reason, he's going to say Dr Rodriguez, though it's far more likely, and logical, that it was Art who handled the funeral payments.

'We don't charge for stillbirth funerals, Mrs Loxley,' Mr Tapps says, a note of confusion creeping into his voice. 'Standard practice.'

'Oh, right, sorry.' It's another reminder of how disconnected from the real world I was at the time. 'Well, thank you for your time.'

I hang up, then close the window. I go back to bed and sit cross-legged on the covers, lost in my thoughts. Tapps is another blind alley. I put my head in my hands. The doctor who handled my C-section has vanished, the attending nurse has died and there's no way of finding out who dealt with my supposedly still-born baby.

Is all that really a coincidence?

I take out my phone. I can't do this alone, but there's no point calling Art . . . or Hen. She's made it quite clear she doesn't believe there's any truth in Lucy O'Donnell's claims. I could try one of my other friends, but when I imagine their faces as I explain my anxieties, all I can see is puzzlement and concern that I'm letting desperation take me over . . . that crazed hope is making me mad . . . that I've lost all sense of perspective. And then I think of Lorcan, that steady gaze. The way he empathized with my feelings over Beth. The way he sensed that my troubles were in some way connected with Art. I scroll to his number and call him.

'Gen?' He answers on the first ring. His voice is warm. 'What's up?'

'Hi.' My voice cracks as I speak. 'Before, you offered . . .' I hesitate. Now I'm speaking to him, it seems too much to ask.

'And I meant it,' Lorcan says. 'How can I help?'

Lorcan arrives within the hour. I lead him into the kitchen, feeling guilty that I'm going behind Art's back. Still, I'm not planning on telling Lorcan all my suspicions . . . and certainly not the ones about Art himself. So far, all he knows is that I need his help.

He sits down opposite me at the kitchen table and fixes me with that intense look of his. There's stubble on his chin and a tiny scar above one eye. He's still gazing at me. Does he look this intently at everyone?

I hope not. The thought is out before I can snatch it back.

'This isn't easy.' I blow out my breath.

Lorcan leans forward and smiles. 'Relax,' he says. 'You don't have to tell me anything you don't want to.'

'I know.' I hesitate again. 'This woman came to see me,' I stammer. 'She says my baby was born alive . . . that the doctor stole her away . . .'

'Jesus Christ.' Lorcan looks genuinely shocked. 'But how could that happen? Is that even *possible*?'

'It is, just about . . . I had a C-section and I was under general anaesthetic.' I go on, explaining everything I've done and discovered in detail. The only thing I don't mention is Lucy O'Donnell's claim that Art was involved.

He shakes his head, but more in wonderment than disbelief. 'So do you really think that your baby could still be alive?'

'Yes . . . well, I believe Lucy O'Donnell *thought* she was. But she can't be, can she? I mean it's ridiculous.'

'Have you told the police?'

'No . . . I don't have any proof.'

'What does Art say?'

I fall silent.

Outside a police siren screeches in the distance. Lorcan is still watching me intently.

'Ah,' he says. 'Art thinks the whole thing's mad.'

'It probably is.' I stare down at the raw, bitten skin around my fingernails. 'I can't go back to Lucy O'Donnell because she just died in a hit-and-run accident.'

'Christ.'

'I know. *I* think it looks really suspicious but there's no proof of that, either.' I show him the newspaper cutting. 'I don't know what to believe. I don't know what to do. It all seems impossible. I mean, why would a doctor fake a baby's death? Part of me wants to go to the hospital in Oxford where it all happened.

147

I know my doctor doesn't work there any more, but it's the best place to start tracking him down. Then the next minute I'm thinking it all sounds so ridiculous . . .' I sigh.

'Well, you're right about that.' Lorcan leans back in his chair. He's still staring at me. 'And most people would say you're only even considering that what you've been told might be true because you *want* it to be true – you *want* Beth to be alive.'

I nod, held by his gaze.

'Which is hell for you, because now you're torn between doing something and worrying you're crazy, and doing nothing and missing an opportunity – however slight – that your daughter might be out there somewhere.' He pauses. 'Right?'

'Right,' I say.

'Okay.' Lorcan gets up. 'Then let's go.'

'What?' I stand up too.

'Let's go to the hospital.'

'Go to the . . .? Now? But it's in Oxford,' I say, shocked.

'So?'

'We can't just turn up.'

'Why not?' Lorcan asks. 'Whatever that office manager said, the hospital is bound to have a forwarding address for your Dr Rodriguez. It'll be easier to get it off them if we talk to them in person. More persuasive.'

'But what will we say?'

'We can work it out on the way. My car's outside. We can be there in an hour if we get going now.'

I stare at him. My heart's racing. 'But . . . but I have to teach this afternoon.'

Lorcan raises his eyebrows. 'Then cancel,' he says. 'Tell them you're sick.'

I hesitate. I don't like to do that – it's dishonest and it leaves the Institute in the lurch, but the temptation is strong. Anyway, with my mind all over the place like it is, I wouldn't be much use to my students.

'Why are you helping me like this?'

'Why shouldn't I?' Lorcan shakes his head impatiently. 'I'm not seeing Cal again until tomorrow. I've got no work . . . no auditions . . .' He pauses. 'Unless you don't want me to come?'

I stare at him. I feel almost delirious; scarily out of control.

'It'll take a bit of effort,' Lorcan goes on. 'And we'll need a cover story. But we can sort that out on the way too. Come on.' He's already halfway to the door.

'Wait.'

He stops and turns. There's something so powerful about his determination, so overwhelming, I can't think straight for a second. Then my head clears.

'D'you think it could be true, that Beth's alive?' There's a sick feeling in my stomach. 'Isn't this all a bit reckless?'

'So? I'm an actor. I'm allowed to do reckless things. And, yes, of course it's possible. You never saw her body, did you?'

'No, but, everything is stacked against it being true. It *feels* impossible.'

'So what? You need to know, one way or the other.' Lorcan smiles. 'Anyway, sometimes I believe as many as six impossible things before breakfast.'

'Okay, Alice in Wonderland.' I can't help but smile too. Lorcan's face and voice are so utterly intent.

He holds out his hands in an expansive gesture. 'So, come on then,' he says. 'You and me. What do we have to lose?'

With a jolt I realize I feel alive. I can't remember when I last felt like this.

'Okay.' I walk towards him. 'Let's go.'

When I got back to my form room after Ginger Tall and Broken Tooth happened, Miss Evans saw my trousers. I pretended I had an accident and Miss Evans was nice and gave me trousers from the lost property box. But when I got home Mummy saw I was upset and made me tell her the truth. After, she was angry and shouting. She said that Ginger Tall and Broken Tooth were Bad People. She said that I am better than they are. She said I must get them back. That it would be good training because of the grown-up Bad People who might tell me lies and try to hurt me.

Mummy said she didn't mean things like kicking and fighting (or yelling 'Stranger Danger' if it was a grown-up Bad Person, though that was good too) and she didn't mean telling the teacher either. At first I didn't understand because I was so little. But then I realized she meant clever fighting, like when someone hurts you, you have to hurt them worse.

Mummy said that just because you are smaller than the people you are fighting against it doesn't mean you can't get them back. She said doing sneaky fighting against Ginger Tall and Broken Tooth was a good place to start and that I should think about a special way to pay them back.

So I did.

CHAPTER TEN

Before we set off for Oxford I call the Institute and tell Sami I've got a terrible migraine and can't teach this afternoon. I feel guilty as I speak to her, but once I'm off the phone Lorcan distracts me with questions about which route to take. We spend the first part of the journey simply negotiating our way out of London, but once we're on the motorway I sit back and steal a look at him.

He exudes a quiet determination that I really like. Whereas Art is dynamic and forceful, all energy and purpose, Lorcan's manner is far more relaxed. He's managed to make haring off to Oxford to snoop round a hospital sound like the most normal thing in the world, a day trip to the countryside. And yet, in his own way, he's just as focused as Art.

'So tell me . . .' I say. 'You hardly know me, why are you help-ing me like this?'

Lorcan glances around. His eyes hold mine. 'I understand this, Gen. When Elaine and I split up she was mad as hell, threatened to stop me seeing Cal. We fought over access, everything. It wasn't sorted out when I had to go back to Ireland for the show. It ate away at me. I honestly didn't know what she would do: take Cal out of the country? Tell lies about me to the police? Tell lies about me to my son? He was only tiny at the time – he wouldn't even have remembered me. I nearly went mad not knowing if I'd ever see him again, whether we would sort it out or whether she'd find a way of keeping him from me. Until you know for sure, one way or the other, you can't stop yourself going over and over it. Maybe this will happen ... maybe something else ... maybe whatever ... So – I understand – you *have* to know.'

I nod, slowly. *It's the hope that kills.* Art has never really understood that. Thinking this reminds me of Art himself.

'What am I going to say to Art later? You know, if I'm not home?'

Lorcan pauses. 'Maybe you won't need to say anything. What time does he usually get in?'

'Eight or nine-ish,' I say.

'The guy's a machine.' Lorcan mutters, rolling his eyes.

There's a moment when neither of us speak. Something shifts between us, something to do with whatever is behind Lorcan's offer of help. I can't put my finger on it yet, but I know Lorcan's history with Art is at the root of it.

'You resent Art firing you from Loxley Benson, don't you?'

Lorcan's gaze is part-embarrassed, part-defiant. 'It's not that simple.'

Another silence stretches out between us. I want to ask him what he means, but something tells me he will change the subject if I do

I settle back in my seat. I can send Art a text later, telling him I'm meeting a friend in town this evening. The chances are high I'll be back before he gets in from work anyway.

I gaze out of the window at the blur of trees speeding past. I know that I should feel guilty, that trying to track down Dr Rodriguez means I don't really trust Art ... that, whichever way you look at it, lying to the Institute and planning on lying to Art about it is wrong. But I don't feel guilty any longer.

It's not just because of all the doubts and suspicions crowding my head. There's also a part of me I don't want to acknowledge that really likes the idea of spending time with Lorcan. It's the way his presence makes me feel anything's possible. Freeing me up. Not weighing me down. I even feel the once-familiar desire to write, itching under my skin. Maybe that, too, will be possible when I know the truth.

Once we reach Oxford, it's easy to find the Fair Angel maternity hospital. The building – part Victorian gothic, part New Age glass and brick – looks exactly as I remember it. The sight of the shiny brass handle on the front door sends a shiver through me.

In this place my daughter died.

Or was stolen from me.

It's not as cold as it was earlier – despite the continued snow warnings – but I shiver again. Lorcan puts his hand on the small of my back. It feels warm and strong, his fingers pressing into me. Part of me wants to move away – the touch is too intimate. But I like it. The comfort of it. The strength it gives me.

I glance sideways at him.

'You ready to do this?' he says. 'You know what to say?'

I nod. Lorcan reaches past me and presses the buzzer. I catch a whiff of his smell – a mix of wood-shavings and soap and something sharp and lemony.

A prim, female voice comes through the intercom. 'May I help you?'

I give the false name Lorcan and I agreed on earlier. 'I have an appointment to see Dr Rodriguez.'

'I don't . . . wait a minute . . .'

Lorcan and I exchange a look. A second later, the prim voice is back.

'I'm afraid there's been a mistake, Dr Rodriguez no longer works here.'

'But I've come all the way from London.' I let my voice fill with emotion. 'Please . . . I *have* to speak to someone.'

There's a short pause then the door buzzes.

Lorcan grins as he steps back to let me through. All this is his idea, the plan we worked out as we drove here in his smart black Audi. He still seems so relaxed and confident, a million miles from how I'm feeling. I'm deeply grateful. There's no way I could handle this visit alone or with someone less assured.

Inside it's hard to get my bearings for a second or two. Everything's been redecorated and remodelled. The reception desk is now to the left of the entrance and manned by a fifty-something woman in designer glasses, whom I don't recognize. Her gaze shifts from me to Lorcan. He stares back at her, a beat more than is necessary.

I gulp as the woman turns to me. 'What did you say your name was?'

I give my false name again. We've decided to keep everything other than my name the same as in real life. Lorcan insists that lies work best when they are as close to the truth as possible.

'I was a patient here eight years ago,' I say. 'Under Dr Rodriguez. I made an appointment to see him here today.'

The woman looks up from her appointments book, a frown creasing her forehead. 'I don't understand. Dr Rodriguez left here ages ago, before I started. I don't know who gave you this appointment. There must have been some misunderstanding.'

'Oh.' My heart's pounding so loudly I think she will hear it. There's no need to fake the vulnerability I'm supposed to display here. Tears prick at my eyes. 'But we've driven all the way from London.' I turn away, fishing for a tissue in my bag.

As I take one out and dab at my eyes I hear Lorcan's voice in the background. He's speaking very softly so I can only pick up the occasional word . . . *stillborn* . . . *friend* . . . *closure* . . .

As he speaks I glance over. The receptionist's face is softening, but I can see she's not about to give way. When Lorcan's finished, she speaks in a low, firm voice. 'I'm very sorry but there's nothing I can do—'

'But I made an appointment,' I sob. 'How could anyone have booked me in to see him if he doesn't work here?'

The receptionist pushes her glasses higher on her nose. She's looking flustered now.

'I'm really sorry if there's been a mistake.' She's running her finger down the open page of the appointments book. 'I can't see your name down here, but I could ask one of the other doctors if they could speak to you when they have a spare moment.'

'But it's Dr Rodriguez she needs to see.' Lorcan's voice is a perfect blend of firmness and courtesy. 'Could you tell us how we can get hold of him?'

'Yes,' I add. 'I'm sure he wouldn't mind me getting in touch. He always said he'd be happy to see me if I needed to talk.'

The receptionist smiles sympathetically. 'I'm really, really sorry but I'm afraid it's against our policy to give out home addresses.'

Lorcan lays his hand on the desk beside hers. 'Isn't there anything you can do?' he says softly. 'We'd really appreciate it.'

The receptionist gazes at him. 'Look . . .' She hesitates. 'I'll go and speak to the office manager. Maybe there's a way we can get in touch with him . . . pass on *your* details so he can contact you.' She smiles at Lorcan, then trots away out of sight.

'We don't want Rodriguez knowing I'm trying to track him down,' I hiss.

'It'll be okay, we didn't give your real name.'

I nod, then wander across the room. Through the glass doors at the back I can just make out the weeping willow tree I spent hours staring at during the hours immediately after Beth's birth.

The birthing pod lies just beyond. It's so strange to be back here, among sights that are so familiar and yet feel like they belong to another lifetime.

A moment later and the receptionist is back. Another woman – older and hard-faced – is beside her.

'Hello?' The office manager stares at me without smiling.

Oh, God, it's the woman I spoke to yesterday on the phone.

'Hi,' I say. 'I'm so sorry to bother you, but—'

'And *I'm* sorry, but it's simply against our policy to pass on personal information.' She pauses, her eyebrows raised. 'It was you who called here yesterday, wasn't it?'

'No,' I lie, shame at being caught out flushing my neck.

'Really?' The raised eyebrows arch higher. 'Of course, if it *was* you who called, you'd know Dr Rodriguez doesn't work here any more and you most definitely would *not* have an appointment him, would you?'

My whole face is burning.

The office manager offers me a contemptuous sniff. 'Dr Rodriguez moved house soon after he left here,' she says with a stony finality. 'There was no forwarding address.'

Is that true? I stare at her pursed lips, the lipstick running into the lines around her mouth. There's absolutely no warmth in her eyes at all. The receptionist, standing beside her, looks mortified. She keeps shooting apologetic glances at Lorcan.

'I can only assume that if Dr Rodriguez had wanted anyone to be able to find him, he would have left some way for us to reach him,' the office manager says. 'But he hasn't.' She draws herself up to her full height.

We stare at each other. I can't tell whether the woman is simply breathtakingly officious, or whether she has been primed by Dr Rodriguez to fend off all enquiries. Then I realize Lorcan is tugging at my arm.

'Thanks very much for your help.' He nods at both the receptionist, whose face is still shrouded in embarrassment, and the office manager. Then he gently steers me outside.

The wind is up suddenly, cold against my face. I tug on my blue beanie as we walk down the steps in silence, back to the car.

'Guess we'll just have to track down Rodriguez some other way,' Lorcan says with a sigh.

I nod, my mind running over the possible options. I've already Googled Rodriguez and he's not listed in Yell.com or on Facebook or LinkedIn or the General Medical Council's register of doctors. What other ways of finding the man are there?

We reach Lorcan's car and I walk round to the passenger side.

'Wait!' A faint cry echoes down the street towards us.

It's the receptionist from the hospital, scuttling along the pavement. She reaches Lorcan and says, breathlessly, 'Oh thank goodness I caught you. I'm so sorry about that, inside.' She glances sideways at me and I sense she wants to speak to Lorcan alone.

I duck inside the car and pull the door to. Outside, Lorcan leads the receptionist a few steps away. They speak quietly together. A couple of minutes later, Lorcan gets into the car beside me.

'What was that about?'

'She was very sorry for you; wanted to help.' Lorcan sits back in his seat, a slow smile creeping across his face.

'But how?'

'She had a quick word with one of the nurses who's been at the hospital for years. Knew Rodriguez well, apparently. They're pretty sure he stayed local.' He raises his eyebrows. 'Came into some money, the nurse said.'

'So did she give you his address?' My heart's beating against my throat.

157

'Not exactly, but she told me the place he moved to. A Cotswold village called Mendelbury. Very pretty, apparently. Won a regional garden show last year.'

I stare at him in wonder.

Lorcan pulls a scrap of paper out of his pocket. 'She even gave me her phone number,' he says mischievously, 'in case I can think of any other way she might be able to help me . . . us.'

I raise my eyebrows. 'I bet she did.' For a single, ridiculous second I feel jealous. Then it passes. Lorcan is still grinning. The heat fades from my body. Truth is, I don't like the fact that he's capable of being so manipulative. Which is crazy. The man is only trying to help me.

Lorcan pockets the scrap of paper and switches on the engine. 'Mendelbury?'

I glance at the clock on the dashboard. It's almost two. 'Sure, but how are we going to find Dr Rodriguez if all we know is the village he lives in . . .'

Lorcan shrugs. 'Guess we'll just have to knock on every door until we find him – or someone who knows where he lives.' He pulls out onto the empty road.

I laugh. 'You're mad.'

He glances at me. 'Yeah,' he acknowledges, changing gear. 'I'm a bag of spanners. But don't think I'm doing you any favours. I'm enjoying spending the afternoon with you.'

I look out of the window, feeling simultaneously embarrassed and pleased. A row of terraced houses gives way to a line of shops. I point to the sign for Mendelbury, Lorcan takes the turning and we drive on in silence.

'Jesus, how many more houses are there?' Lorcan groans as we slump onto a bench opposite Mendelbury's village green. The place isn't large – my mobile Google search says the population is just over 2000 – and most of it is concentrated around this central patch of grass. A beautiful sandstone church – centuries old – stands to our left. The surrounding houses are made from the same local sandstone, with small windows and ivy-clad walls.

We've checked every house on the green to see if the occupants know Dr Rodriguez. So far, we've drawn a blank, but then half the houses appear to be empty – I'm guessing they're weekend homes that lie unoccupied Monday to Friday.

We spun our cover story to the customers in the pub opposite the church but, again, nobody knew Dr Rodriguez. Lorcan insisted on ordering a sandwich each for us, but mine stuck in my throat. I can't shake this terrible feeling of anxiety – it's partly fear that, after all this effort, we still won't track down Rodriguez. But I'm also scared because the more I look, the more I hope. And suppose Beth isn't alive? Worse, what if whoever took her still has her, and realizes I'm on their tail; what if they take steps to make sure I never find her?

We set off again, each taking a street that leads off from the green. More residents are at home in these houses, but no one knows the doctor. I wish I had a picture of him – my description of him as tall and dark-haired with even features and a long, sloping nose sounds ridiculously Mills & Boon. We meet up again at the green to swap notes.

'Nothing,' Lorcan says with a sigh.

'You'd think the fact that he has a Spanish name would make him stand out,' I grumble.

'Only if you've heard of him in the first place.' Lorcan sighs again.

I hug my knees. The sky above us is bright blue, the sun fierce on our faces. The day is growing crisper and colder. 'I'm sorry.'

Lorcan pats me on the back. 'Don't apologize. It's fine. I'm just having a moan.'

I'm suddenly conscious of how close we're sitting, and get to my feet. 'I'll carry on. Why don't you sit here for a bit?'

'No.' Lorcan pushes himself up. 'I'll come with you. Let's try down there.' He points to a leafy street leading away from the church at the end of the green.

We walk over to the first house on the street. I look around the front garden of the cottage we're standing in – neatly trimmed bushes around a square patch of pebbles – as he leans forward to press the bell.

I turn back and face the door. It creaks, starting to open, and I imagine whoever is on the other side, wondering who we are. It's a youngish mum with a couple of toddlers playing around her legs. Lorcan launches into our story. He's a good actor. Each time he tells our fake tale he makes it sound fresh and genuine.

'I'm so sorry to bother you.' He flashes her that big smile that spreads across his whole face. 'We're looking for a Doctor Martin Rodriguez. About sixty; olive-skinned, dark hair, dark eyes . . . an old family friend we lost touch with . . . moved to Mendelbury last year . . . we've stupidly lost his address and phone number . . .'

The young mum shakes her head and retreats. 'Sorry, no.'

Lorcan and I silently turn and walk to the next house. And the next. Neither of us suggests splitting up again to cover more houses. And then, five doors down, we get our first break.

A middle-aged woman answers. She blinks as soon as Lorcan mentions Rodriguez's name.

Lorcan stops. I know he's seen the recognition in her eyes too.

'D'you know him?' I say. 'Doctor Rodriguez?'

The woman stares at me.

'Please.' I meet her gaze. 'When we said he was an old friend, well, the truth is I was his patient a few years ago. I lost my baby and . . . and he always said that if I needed to speak to him he'd make the time. I *know* he'd want me to find him. It broke his heart too when I lost her . . . he was so kind to me and we've come all this way and I can't believe we've lost all the contact details and . . . *please* . . .' I run out of breath, my voice cracking with emotion.

Lorcan puts his arm around my shoulders. His fingers absently stroke the top of my arm. My shoulder breaks out in goose bumps.

'Any help you can give us would be very gratefully received.' Lorcan hugs me to him. 'My wife and I have been through a lot, as I'm sure you can imagine. We're hoping to get some closure, that's all.'

My face reddens at the lie. I can't meet the woman's gaze any more, so I stare at the ground, watching her out of the corner of my eye.

The woman gazes thoughtfully at Lorcan. 'Well,' she says, 'I'm not sure, but I think I've seen him in the pub.'

I glance over my shoulder, towards the pub across the green, where our enquiries drew a total blank.

'Not that pub,' the woman says. 'The Star. It's a couple of minutes away.'

She points up the long road that leads away from the green in the opposite direction to the streets we've already searched. 'The Star's up the road. Other end of the village.'

'Thank you,' I say gratefully.

The woman nods and, as she shuts her front door, Lorcan slowly takes his arm from around my shoulders.

I button up my jacket and adjust my beanie hat. The anxiety that's been circling inside my stomach for the past few hours tightens into a knot. This, at last, is a proper lead.

I sip, slowly, at my second mineral water. It's well past 6 p.m. and Lorcan and I are sitting alone in a corner of The Star, looking out over the rest of the pub. Right now there's only one person tending bar – a grumpy old guy who shook his head when we asked if he'd seen Dr Rodriguez recently. A few people have trickled in and out but no one, so far, who has heard of the doctor.

Art rang earlier. I didn't answer. He left a message saying he was going to try and get home early tonight. I felt guilty doing it, but I sent a text saying not to worry, that I was meeting up with 'the girls' in town and that I'd see him later. I carefully didn't specify which 'girls', in case one of my friends randomly decides to phone the house later.

In the pub, the clock above the fireplace ticks slowly on. Another thirty minutes pass and the light fades from the day outside. Lorcan and I read the newspapers left out on the bar in companionable silence. An older woman turns up and, from the way they speak to each other, I'm certain she's married to Mr Grumpy who served us earlier. The woman serves a pint then bends over the sink, rinsing glasses. Mr Grumpy grunts something at her and disappears out the back. I catch Lorcan's eye and we stroll over.

'Quiet night?' Lorcan says.

The woman looks up. She's got short, dyed brown hair with an inch of grey roots showing. There's a fixed smile on her face but I can see the sadness of a stale marriage behind her eyes.

'This is a great place,' Lorcan says, leaning against the bar. 'I'd expect it to be busier.'

The woman raises her eyebrows. 'It's always quiet first half of the week,' she says, then glances across at me. 'Would you two like some food? I've done chilli pots tonight.' She smiles, a warmer, more genuine smile than before. 'That's what brings in the punters, to be honest. We don't offer choice but we do offer quality.'

'Maybe later,' I say.

Beside me Lorcan nods. 'I'll take one.'

'We were hoping we might bump into Martin Rodriguez,' I said. 'We drove up from London to see him but I stupidly left all his contact details at home and he's ex-directory, so . . .'

'Oh, Martin'll be in later all right,' the woman says with another smile.

My heart skips a beat, but I just smile back.

'Yes?' I say enquiringly,

'Oh, yes,' the woman says. 'He eats here most nights. I reckon he gets lonely rattling around that big house of his. Told me once I saved him a fortune on housekeepers. I thought he was joking, but you never know with Martin.' She lets out a throaty giggle, which transforms her face, softening her features and taking at least ten years off her age. I have a flashback to my first meeting with Dr Rodriguez – and how impressed I was by the charismatic authority he exuded.

'So how do you know Martin?' the woman asks.

The question is innocent enough, but I can hear the hint of ownership at its edges.

'He used to be my doctor,' I say. 'A long time ago. We knew he lived around here and . . .' I dry up, unsure which fibs about Rodriguez, if any, I've already told in this particular pub.

'I think he's mentioned you actually.' Lorcan comes to my rescue. 'Don't you remember? Martin told us about the excellent food here once.'

I find myself nodding in acquiescence. The woman behind the bar looks pleased and I supposed I should be pleased too. Lorcan's help is making this very easy for me. And yet the lies he's told trip off his tongue astoundingly easily and, at the back of my mind, I'm aware that this is not exactly a reassuring personality trait.

163

'So is Martin's house near here?' I ask, trying to sound as casual as possible. 'I've got absolutely no sense of direction.'

'Sure,' she says. 'Just a few minutes up the hill.' She smiles. 'I guess you heard about the fuss the local council made about those lion statues of his. Personally they're not my kind of thing, but it's his land so we backed his bid to keep them.'

I nod, wondering what on earth she's talking about.

'I'll order a chilli pot for you, sir.'

We watch her disappear into the back room then Lorcan places his hand on my arm.

'She's totally assumed that we're married,' he says in a low voice. 'Play along with it.'

I can feel myself blushing, but before I can respond the door behind us bangs open and a familiar voice drifts towards us on the sliver of cold air from outside.

'Cold tonight, no?' It's Dr Rodriguez.

I freeze. After all this time, all this effort, to track him down, he's finally here.

CHAPTER ELEVEN

The sound of Dr Rodriguez's voice brings it all back – the excitement of my initial appointment . . . the tension as I got ready for the emergency C-section . . . the clock on the wall that was the first thing I saw when I came round, all woozy still from the general anaesthetic, then Art's sad eyes as he spoke to me: *I'm so sorry, we lost her.*

I feel Lorcan tense up beside me. I turn slowly. Rodriguez is greeting someone in the corner of the pub. Taking off his coat.

I walk over in a daze. Lorcan and I rehearsed what we were going to say in the car, but I suddenly can't remember a word. My heart is pounding as I reach the doctor. He's still chatting to some old guy in a pork-pie hat. The old guy's seen us, but Rodriguez is folding up his coat and laying it carefully on a seat. His fingers are long and brown and manicured.

I'm standing inches away from him. He straightens up. Senses me. Turns.

He's as tall and lean as I remember, but that handsome, angular face is less tired-looking. His eyes register shock, then concerned recognition. Is that concern coming from guilt? Shame? Or just bewilderment?

'Mrs Loxley, isn't it?' His voice is carefully light as he offers his hand for me to shake. 'What . . . what are you doing here?' His eyes drift to Lorcan, standing to my right.

I keep my own gaze locked on Rodriguez's face. He has a moustache now – a thin pencil line – and a tiny goatee. They make him look even more dashing and authoritative than he did when I first met him.

'I was hoping I'd find you,' I say, trying to stop my voice from shaking. 'I . . . I'd like to talk to you about Beth.'

Rodriguez nods slowly. His mouth trembles – just a fraction, but it gives away how shocked he is to see me. He moves his coat off the seat and indicates I should sit down. Lorcan is already sitting on the chair on the other side of the table. The old guy in the pork-pie hat has vanished.

Rodriguez is still staring at me. 'Is Mr Loxley . . .?' He clears his throat. 'Does Mr Loxley know you're here?'

I shake my head. Rodriguez looks at Lorcan: a long, full look. Then he turns back to me. This time the question is only in his eyes: *who the hell is he?*

I choose to ignore it. My throat is dry. I swallow and take a deep breath.

'I wonder if you would tell me what happened that day . . .'

Rodriguez looks down and runs his hand along the table between us.

'Mrs Loxley, you know how terribly sorry I was . . . I *am* . . . for your loss, but this is not the time or the place to . . .'

'Please, I just want to hear what happened. The sequence of events.'

'There's not much to say that we haven't said . . .'

'Please,' I insist.

Rodriguez shifts in his seat. He looks uncomfortable.

'Okay,' he sighs. 'You came in for a routine check. I did the scan myself because we had to wait for a machine and by the time one came free the radiographer had gone. I saw straight-away that the baby had died *in utero* so we decided to perform an

166

emergency C-section. We acted immediately, which was at your and your husband's insistence. I know how much you suffered but I can assure you the whole experience was also horrible for me and for the theatre staff involved.'

'But most of them left,' I interrupt. 'Most of them came down with food poisoning while they were inside the operating theatre.'

Rodriguez looks momentarily taken aback. Then he nods. 'Three people out of the entire team were taken ill, that's true, but there was only a short gap before substitute medical staff replaced them. My memory on the exact timing of that is hazy, but it was only a few minutes and I definitely had assistance when I worked on you after the C-section. You were in no danger at any time. And there was nothing that could have been done for your baby anyway.'

'Why didn't you tell us that staff were missing when you delivered my baby? Did you even tell the hospital directors?'

Rodriguez clears his throat. 'As I said, nothing untoward happened as a result of their absence. After the C-section was complete I went outside and spoke to your husband. He insisted on seeing your baby though I advised against it. Afterwards, we both agreed you should not see her yourself. Then we waited for you to come round in the recovery room.' Rodriguez wipes his hand across his forehead. He is sweating despite the fact that we are on the other side of the room from the open fire. 'That's it. There is simply nothing else to say other than how sorry I am for your loss.'

I glance at Lorcan. His gaze is fixed on Rodriguez.

I turn back, my heart sinking. All this way and I've learned nothing. What did I expect? That Rodriguez was going to crumble and admit he faked my daughter's death? That he let Art sell her on somewhere?

I push my chair back and stand up as the woman from behind the bar appears with a pot of steaming chilli and a basket of bread on a tray.

She sets the tray down in front of Lorcan.

'I see you found Martin,' she says pleasantly. 'Martin, are you eating?'

'No, thank you.' Rodriguez rises. His face is impassive. The woman wanders back to the bar. Rodriguez gathers his coat. 'I'm afraid I've just remembered I'm . . . I have to be somewhere.'

'Did anyone ever offer you money to lie to me about my baby?' The words shoot out of my mouth like bullets.

For a split second Rodriguez's eyes fill with panic. 'Money? *Lie* to you? No,' he says. 'No, of course not. I don't know what you're talking about. Excuse me, I really do have to go.'

He heads to the door. He's walking fast, but the man in the pork-pie hat has blocked his way, his face wreathed in a cheerful, drunken smile.

'Did you see how shaken he was?' I whisper.

Lorcan nods. He glances down at his bowl of chilli, picks up a hunk of bread and tears off a strip. 'And now look,' he whispers back. 'He can't wait to get out of here. Although . . .' He pauses. 'You did virtually accuse him of lying to you, so . . .'

I bite my lip. Rodriguez is, indeed, shuffling from foot to foot at the door, but the pork-pie-hat man is still standing in his way, urging him to stay.

'We have to do something,' I hiss.

Lorcan raises his eyebrows, a strip of chilli-smothered bread halfway to his mouth. 'Like what?'

'Follow him.' My heart beats fast. 'Rodriguez knows something. You saw his face.'

As I finish speaking, Rodriguez walks out of the pub at last.

I stand up.

Lorcan stares at me. 'Are you serious?'

'Yes.'

The shock on Lorcan's face gives way to grim determination. 'Okay.' He stands up.

I grab my coat and head for the door. It's dark outside; the cold air slices at my cheeks. It must have dropped five degrees since we came into the pub.

Rodriguez is clearly visible, pacing briskly up the hill away from us, shoulders hunched against the cold. I glance around. Where is Lorcan? I hesitate, buttoning my coat up to the neck. He still hasn't emerged from the pub. Rodriguez is halfway up the hill. What on earth is Lorcan doing? Gritting my teeth, I set off. I can't risk losing Rodriguez. A moment later he vanishes over the brow of the hill. I speed up. Footsteps sound behind me.

'Gen?' Lorcan calls softly.

I glance over my shoulder as he runs up. A smear of chilli to the left of his mouth glistens in the light of the street lamp.

'Where were you?' I whisper.

'Paying for the chilli,' he pants, wiping his mouth. 'Where's Rodriguez?'

I point over the hill. We're still not close enough to the top to see over to the other side. Rodriguez might have taken a turning by now. My heart lurches into my mouth and I break into a run.

A few strides and Rodriguez comes into view again. He's still on the same road, halfway down the hill now.

'Where d'you think he's going?' Lorcan asks.

'I don't know.' My breath mists into the air.

'What's the plan when we get there?'

'I don't know.'

'Excellent.' Lorcan offers up a mirthless chuckle.

Rodriguez turns down a side street. I speed up, determined

not to lose him. As Lorcan and I reach the corner ourselves he is disappearing into a driveway.

'Come on.' I hurry across the road, Lorcan at my side.

Two huge, ugly stone lions stand on either side of an imposing gate. Rodriguez has already disappeared inside a large, two-storey detached house. Privet hedges criss-cross a front lawn. Beyond these a sleek BMW is parked on a gravel drive. I get a sense of highly manicured flower beds, dark curtains hanging at the windows. The house is ornate, expensive . . .

I look back at the lion statues. 'This is his home,' I say.

'Now what?' Lorcan stares at me.

I hesitate. Ringing Rodriguez's doorbell is clearly not an option. The pub landlady implied that he lived alone, but suppose there's someone else in the house? What will trying to talk to him again achieve anyway? And yet, if I don't challenge him, then he'll be free to get rid of anything that links him to Beth.

'Let's just wait a minute,' I say. A light comes on in an upstairs room to the left of the house.

We shelter behind the gates watching Rodriguez cross the room. He's looking at something in his hand. I strain my eyes, but it's impossible to see what he's holding. He bends over for a second then straightens up. A moment later he has crossed the room again and the light is switched off.

I pass through the gates, Lorcan right behind me. My heart is pounding in my chest. I still have no idea what I'm going to do. The front door of the house opens. Lorcan grabs my arm and we duck behind the privet hedge that intersects the front lawn as Rodriguez emerges from the house.

He crunches across the gravel to his car. A phone is clamped to his ear, his voice carrying easily across the still, cold, night air.

'Yes, she found me here, that's what I am telling you. She's with someone.'

I freeze, Lorcan's hand still on my arm.

'It's not her husband. I don't think he knows she is here.' Rodriguez is hissing into his phone now. 'But she knows about the money.'

My legs threaten to buckle under me.

Rodriguez opens the car door and gets inside.

'No, it's safe, I just locked it away, so ...' The rest of Rodriguez's sentence is lost as he slams shut the car door. I huddle behind the hedge as the engine starts and the car roars out of the gravel drive.

I straighten up and Lorcan lets go of my arm.

'Jesus Christ,' he says, peering down the road after Rodriguez's car.

I'm in shock, trying to process what I heard. It's too big to take in. *She knows about the money.*

Does this mean Rodriguez *did* steal Beth away?

Does this mean Lucy O'Donnell was right and my baby *is* alive?

'*Gen?*' Lorcan frowns, as if he's already said my name and I haven't heard him.

'Oh, God, Lorcan ...'

'Rodriguez was talking about money.' His frown deepens. 'Just like you asked him about in the pub. Money to keep quiet, that's what you said to him, wasn't it?'

I nod. I can see from the look of shock on Lorcan's face that this is the last thing he expected. Despite his calm and encouraging words of support, I realize, with a jolt, that he has only been humouring me.

Until now.

'I don't understand,' Lorcan goes on. 'Who would pay him to keep quiet about a baby not being dead?'

I stand in the freezing air, letting it all sink in. 'I don't know ...' I say. It's hard to say the words out loud. But all the

171

evidence seems to point in this direction. 'Oh, Lorcan, I think it's possible Art paid him . . .'

'*What?*'

I tell him that Lucy O'Donnell claimed Art was part of the plan to steal Beth and about the £50,000 MDO money I found in an account marked 'Personal'. The words tumble out of me like I'm vomiting them up. *This can't be true. Please, surely, this can't be true.* 'Art denies it all, but he couldn't explain what the fifty grand was for. He said it was just a business thing, but it's the only big amount that went out of an account that didn't use one of the normal Loxley Benson trading names, *and* the money was paid out *just after* Beth.'

'Okay, but . . . but . . .' Lorcan frowns. 'It just doesn't make sense. The fifty thousand . . . surely that's nowhere near enough to make a private doctor tell such a massive lie.'

'I wondered about that myself.' I hesitate. 'But suppose it was just the first of several payments . . . suppose there were other lump sums paid through other accounts . . . or even cash . . . that could add up to hundreds of thousands of—'

'Did Art have that kind of money back then?'

'Not personally. And someone would notice if he was taking money out of investment accounts, wouldn't they?'

'That depends. He was . . . *is* the MD,' Lorcan says. 'At least we know Rodriguez wasn't talking *to* Art just now. He said quite clearly: "She's with someone. Not her husband." That means there has to be someone else involved.'

He's right. 'But who?'

I follow Lorcan's gaze as he turns to look at Rodriguez's house. Ground floor. First floor. A small light above the front door gives off a dim glow, casting shadows across the brick wall of the house. There are no lights on anywhere else.

'Looks pretty deserted,' Lorcan says.

I nod, suddenly feeling desolate as the adrenalin that's been coursing through me for the past half-hour drains away. I'm certain now that Rodriguez lied about Beth . . . that he knows what really happened to her. And yet I have nothing concrete to go on . . . nothing more than suspicions to take to the police . . . nothing to counteract the huge and overwhelming evidence that Beth was stillborn.

Lorcan moves closer to the house, then points to a window at the far end of the ground floor. It's shrouded in darkness but, even so, I can just make out that the bottom sash isn't entirely closed.

'What?' I say, though I know already what he's thinking.

'No one's here.' Lorcan's voice drops to a whisper. 'We could sneak inside . . . go up to that room . . . find whatever Rodriguez said he locked away . . .'

'We can't.' Even as I say the words I know they're not true. I breathe out a mist of cloudy air then shiver as a gust of icy wind whips around my face.

'We can.' Lorcan's voice is low. Intense. 'If we're careful he won't ever know we've been here.'

'This is insane.'

'Yes.' Lorcan looks at me. He's waiting for me to decide.

The heavy, depressed feeling of the past minute lifts. Adrenalin courses through me again. Can I do this? It's a chance to find out what Rodriguez was doing in that room upstairs . . . what he was referring to when he said 'It's safe'. On the other hand, it's a terrifying risk . . . it's breaking the law . . . it's . . .

A new determination grips me. I *have* to find out what I can.

'Would this be burglary or house-breaking?' I set off towards the house.

Lorcan says nothing. Just follows me to the window. Our feet grind noisily in the gravel. We reach the glass pane and Lorcan grips the wooden base. I watch his strong fingers press against the sill. Force it upwards. It moves a fraction then jams hard.

Lorcan steps back with a sigh. 'Locked,' he says.

'That's it, then.' But even as I'm saying the words I know I can't stop now. A cold fury fills me and I look around for something solid and heavy, something that will break glass.

'Gen?' Lorcan asks. 'What are you doing?'

My eyes light on a group of three plant pots standing against the far wall of the house. I walk over. I have every right to break into this man's home. He lied to me. I pick up the smallest of the pots and return to Lorcan. I hand him the pot and point to the window. Lorcan blinks rapidly. For the first time since I've met him he's lost his laidback air.

'If we do this,' Lorcan says, 'Rodriguez'll know we've been here.'

'He's knows we're on to him anyway.' The logic of this sinks into my brain. I am fiercely rational. Aware, with one part of my brain, that what I'm about to do is lunacy, and yet coldly sure that if I want to know what happened to my daughter this is my only option. 'If we don't act now, if we just walk away, then Rodriguez will be able to move whatever he's hiding here – or destroy it. I can't risk losing this chance to find out.'

Lorcan blows out his breath. 'Right.' A second later he slams the pot against the glass. The sound shatters the silence. Glass shards smash to the ground – such a pretty sound for such a violent act.

I stand, stock still, waiting for a response. Nothing comes. No lights. No voices. I glance around. The house is well-secluded from its nearest neighbour. There are no signs that anyone has heard us.

Lorcan has taken off his jacket and wrapped it around his arm. He reaches through the broken pane of glass, punching out a large shard that pokes out from the side. With a swift click he undoes the window lock. A moment later he lifts the sash window.

'I'll go through here.' Lorcan has already hoisted one knee up onto the sill. 'Let you in the front door.'

I nod. 'Go.'

Lorcan disappears into the gloom of the room. I can't see any furniture clearly, just a few dark shapes along the far wall that could be armchairs or cupboards or even a low bookcase.

A minute later the front door opens. I scurry across the gravel and join Lorcan inside. Lorcan flicks a switch beside me, and the room floods with light. We're in an entry hall – very middle England, with textured wallpaper leading down to a smooth, cream dado rail, cream carpet and elegant, over-ornate, antique wooden furniture. Several oil paintings in muted tones hang on the wall.

'God, this stuff must be worth a fortune,' Lorcan says, looking around. 'It's like a set for *Antiques Roadshow* in here. Whatever else he is, your man is definitely loaded.'

I think back to Rodriguez's professional manner on the day that I met him. He was kind and charming and totally reassuring. Fury wells up inside me. My charismatic doctor was a conman and I fell for his act. Completely.

A polished wooden table stands to the left of the door below a gilt-framed mirror. I catch sight of myself as I pass and barely recognize the intense eyes and pale face of my reflection.

Lorcan is just behind me. The features of his face are composed and relaxed but in the silence of the house I can hear the anxiety in his rushed, shallow breathing. I turn to him, overwhelmed that he is here, risking everything.

'Thank you so much,' I say. 'I couldn't have done any of this without you.'

'We'd better make it count, then.'

I turn off the hall light and follow him up the stairs.

Up on the first-floor landing, Lorcan checks off the rooms,

counting past windows until we reach the room we saw Rodriguez in just minutes earlier.

It's an office. Small, with similar décor to the hall downstairs, and heavy brocade curtains at the window. A large oak desk stands against one wall alongside a matching bookcase. Piles of papers are ranged neatly on the top of an elegant antique cabinet that runs under the window.

As I gaze around, Lorcan strides over to the desk, sits down and switches on the computer. It hums into life and Lorcan starts tapping away at the keyboard.

'What are you doing?' I say.

'Checking to see if Rodriguez has got any files under your name,' Lorcan says without turning round. 'Why don't you look inside that cabinet? But hurry, he could come back any moment.'

I pull the curtains shut in case anyone notices the flickering computer light, then squat on the floor and flick through the papers on top of the cabinet. I make my phone a torch so I can see what I'm looking at. Nothing but recent bills and invoices. I tug at the cabinet handles. The door is locked, but I can tell the lock isn't solid. It would be easy enough to snap the catch. Again I hesitate for a second. Lorcan is still bent over the computer.

I grit my teeth, then I grab the handles with both hands and wrench the doors open. The wood splinters easily.

'Easy,' Lorcan murmurs from the desk. 'We still need to keep the noise down.'

'I know.' Trying not to think about the vandalism I've inflicted, I gaze inside. Stacks of box files meet my eyes. My heart sinks. It would take all night to go through this lot properly.

I pull out the first file and flick through the contents. Mostly household bills, as far as I can see. I move on to the next box file. Conveyancing information on the purchase of the house. The property cost £1.3 million. Rodriguez exchanged contracts about ten months after Beth.

I shove the papers back in the box. That proves nothing.

The next box file is full of family photos. Mostly showing Rodriguez as a young man surrounded by parents, aunts, uncles and cousins.

I move on to the next. It contains a selection of newspaper clippings and articles torn from magazines.

I look up at Lorcan. He is concentrating hard on the PC in front of him. He pushes back a curl.

'How're you doing?'

He grunts. 'Can't get past the password. I'm going to check the drawers of this desk. Maybe Rodriguez wrote it down somewhere. Lots of people do.'

I nod and turn back to my file. Most of these cuttings concern medical breakthroughs to do with IVF treatments. They are almost all dated from the early nineties, before the internet made paper files less essential. I reach the bottom of the file and am about to shove it to one side when an entirely different cutting catches my eye.

It's much more recent than the rest – dated nearly eight years ago – and is a small report from what looks like a local Oxford newspaper about a hit-and-run accident on the outskirts of the city. A man was killed. I peer at his photo and at the name in the caption.

Gary Bloode, anaesthetist at Fair Angel maternity hospital.

It's like a slap round the face.

I remember him now quite clearly – the way he chatted to me before he put me under, explaining how the injection would feel cold, asking me to count backwards from ten. He made a joke of his name: 'Bloode . . . yeah, patients tend to pass out at the sight of me.' I didn't see him afterwards. Didn't think about him.

And now it seems he was killed in a mysterious hit-and-run accident, just a few weeks after taking part in Beth's delivery. Exactly the same manner of death as Lucy O'Donnell. Surely *that* can't be a coincidence?

A soft, rattling sound from across the room makes me look up. Lorcan has prised open the top drawer of the desk and is shaking a small metal box he's found inside. I watch as Lorcan opens the box and picks out a memory stick.

'This has a date written on the side.'

'Tell me.' I scramble to my feet, shoving the newspaper cutting into my bag.

'June the eleventh.'

The room spins around me.

'That was Beth's birth date,' I say.

Lorcan's eyes meet mine. Without speaking, he pulls the top off the stick and turns back to the computer to insert it in the USB port.

My guts twist into a sickening knot.

And then, from downstairs, comes the sound of the front door opening. Lorcan turns to me in horror. I hold my breath, as the distinct sound of footsteps cross the hall and climb the stairs towards us.

CHAPTER TWELVE

I stand frozen to the spot as the footsteps reach the landing. For a second I brace myself, ready for Rodriguez to burst in and confront us. And then I realize that the footsteps are fading slightly. He must be heading *away* from this room, walking along the corridor in the opposite direction. My heart leaps. I'd assumed he'd noticed the broken window downstairs but maybe he hasn't seen it.

Does that give us a chance to get away?

I catch Lorcan's eye. He looks as desperate as I feel. He takes the memory stick out of the computer. With a single, soft stride he's at the door, peering outside.

I close my eyes, my heart drumming against my throat. I can't believe I'm in this situation. I'm nearly forty – a married and respectable sometime author and tutor – and I'm about to be caught red-handed having broken into someone's house with a man who is not my husband.

For some reason Morgan's face appears in my mind's eye, complete with the shocked expression she would almost certainly be wearing if she could see me now. A throb of nervous laughter threatens to burst out of me.

'Gen!' Lorcan's fierce whisper jolts me back into the moment. 'Come here!'

I race to the door and stand beside him. The corridor leading off the landing is empty. I peer into the shadows, my heart pounding.

'Where is he?' I hiss, all the humour of the situation evaporating.

'Must have gone into one of the other rooms,' Lorcan whispers. 'Let's go.' He grabs my hand and leads me out.

We creep silently along the corridor. I can hear Rodriguez now. He sounds like he's moving furniture . . . pulling open doors. A series of dull thuds echo towards us, as if he's dropping piles of books on the floor.

Lorcan drops my hand as we reach the top of the stairs. I scurry down, trying to tread as lightly as possible. Lorcan speeds down behind me. Across the hall, I reach the front door first. There's something wrong with the way it's hanging on its hinges but there's no time to examine it properly. Holding my breath I push it open. The door creaks noisily. I freeze, a trickle of sweat running down my neck, even as the cold air outside sweeps over my face.

Upstairs, the thudding noises stop. Footsteps sound along the corridor.

'Run!' Lorcan hisses in my ear.

I tear through the door and across the drive. Lorcan pounds after me. The gravel churns under our feet, the noise huge and harsh in the still night air. I reach the gate, panting, and glance back to see if Rodriguez has seen us . . . if he's following. As I scan the first-floor windows, my eyes are drawn to the office we just ran away from. The curtains are open and the light is on. A male figure stands at the window, staring out at us.

'*What?*' Lorcan says, his mouth dropping open in shock.

Because the light in the room is glinting off the man's blond hair and, even though his pale face is in shadow, he is most definitely not Dr Rodriguez.

*   *   *

'Who the hell was that?' Lorcan grips the steering wheel, manoeuvring onto the main road.

Ten minutes have passed but, inside the warmth of his car, with Oxford vanishing in a blur of buildings and street lamps, it feels more like ten hours.

I sit back in the passenger seat and close my eyes. I can hardly believe what we just did . . . the risk of it . . . the illegality.

'I don't know but he must have broken into the house after us,' I say. 'We didn't leave the front door like that.' For a second I feel like bursting into tears. And then another thought strikes me. 'Oh God, do you think we left fingerprints?' My eyes are wide open with horror.

'Hundreds,' Lorcan says grimly. He glances over at me and I suddenly remember the memory stick, marked with Beth's birth date, that he found in Rodriguez's desk.

'Do you still have—?'

'Oh, yeah.' Lorcan pats his pocket, then draws out the stick. 'My laptop's on the back seat. Do you want to take a look at what's on this?'

I reach round and drag the rucksack on the back seat towards me. A white MacBook is inside – an oldish model with dirt in a crack that runs along the casing. I open the computer and insert the memory stick.

A line of code flashes up, then the message that the contents are encrypted.

'I can't read it,' I say. 'I mean, it *won't* read.'

Lorcan glances across at the computer which is propped open on my lap.

'Shit,' he says.

I look out of the window. We're passing fields and trees. I'm reminded, as I often am outside London, how quickly cities turn to countryside. There's a misty glow over the

181

treetops. In fact . . . I strain my eyes, certain I can see snow in the distance.

'What do we do now?' My voice reflects how I feel after all the energy and excitement of the past few hours: flat and lifeless.

'You need to see whatever's on that stick,' Lorcan says, changing gear. 'I'll get Cal to take a look. That's my son – he's an IT geek, remember, I told you? He's genius with stuff like that.'

'Really?' Hope fills me again.

'Sure.' Lorcan shrugs, his voice gruff. 'Might as well get some use out of that expensive education Elaine insisted on.' He hesitates. 'Cal's really smart when it comes to computers, maths . . .'

He tails off, sounding awkward. I sense he's just embarrassed, self-conscious about showing pride in his boy.

'Was that something you and Elaine disagreed on, the private education?'

'Not really, it's just she can be a bit . . .' Lorcan pauses, clearly trying to choose his words carefully, '. . . a bit insistent and . . . well, I don't like being told what to do.'

I raise my eyebrows, noticing for the first time how his face in profile is perfectly proportioned. 'Nobody likes being told what to do.'

'I guess that's true,' Lorcan replies with a smile.

He falls silent and I stare out of the window again. Snow is drifting down now . . . just the lightest of flakes, swirling in the headlights of the car.

'Are you sure about all this? About helping me?' I say, realizing as I speak how much I'm hoping Lorcan will reassure me. How important it feels to have his support.

For a second he says nothing, just checks the wing mirror, then he clears his throat.

'I told you before,' he says. 'I get it.' He glances over. 'I get you.'

The atmosphere in the car tenses. The freezing world zooms past, outside.

A shudder runs through my body. Nothing feels steady or safe any more. Even sitting inside this warm car while the snow blows outside doesn't feel properly real. I'm alone with my thoughts and fears and yet I have to talk ... I have to tell someone.

'I dream about her,' I say, my voice so low it's almost a whisper. 'I've been dreaming about Beth since she was born. I ... I never told anyone but ... now I'm wondering ...' I hesitate. It's so hard to let myself speak this terrifying, crazy thought out loud. 'Lorcan, do you think I could be dreaming of a real person?'

A long pause. 'Anything's possible.' Lorcan's voice is as soft as mine.

The lights gradually brighten around us and I realize we are already on the Westway, about to drive onto Euston Road. I press my hand against the window. Light flakes swirl outside the window.

'When do you next see Cal?'

'Tomorrow. I'll call him when I get home ... see if he can come over earlier than we planned, for breakfast,' Lorcan says. 'I can't promise he'll be round first thing, but he'll definitely come if I offer to cook him all his favourites.'

'Which are?' I smile, pleased Lorcan is talking about his son.

'Bacon, mushrooms, grilled tomatoes, scrambled eggs.' Lorcan slows at a T-junction and takes the left turn.

'That your party piece?' I ask. 'Or can you cook anything?'

'You should try my Thai green curry.' He grins. 'I like cooking. Anyway, I'm better at it than his mum, so he won't turn down the offer of a meal. Elaine's into all that macrobiotic shite.'

'How long were you two together?' I ask, trying to sound casual.

'We were barely together at all.' Lorcan glances in the rear-view mirror. 'She runs a health centre now, but when I met her she wanted to be an actress. We were at drama school together. I . . . well, we tried to make it work for a while after Cal, but it was never going to happen long term. She's crazy, though I'm sure she'd say the same about me.'

'Not true love, then?' I ask lightly.

'With Elaine? I thought it was at the time, but . . .' He tails off. 'There were people afterwards, off and on, there's someone in Ireland, actually, but . . .' He shrugs. 'I don't know . . . that's not serious . . .'

'No?' It doesn't surprise me to hear Lorcan is seeing someone. Serious or not, the news leaves me feeling a bit disappointed. 'You don't like letting people in much, do you?'

He glances sideways at me. 'Neither do you,' he says with a smile.

We turn off the Euston Road and drive in silence up through Camden and Kentish Town. Lorcan drops me at the corner of my street. Outside, the snow is falling more heavily than it was in Oxford, though it doesn't appear to be settling.

'I'll call you in the morning, yeah?' he says. 'See if there are any more houses you'd like me to break into with you.'

'Sure.' I get out of the car.

'Bye.' He leans across the seat to peer up at me. I hold his gaze for a moment then stride off down the street. As I walk up my front path, I try to shake off the sense that I'm more connected to Lorcan, back in his car, than I am to my own home and my husband inside it.

I let myself in through the front door. The house feels quiet. Maybe Art isn't in. The thought fills me with relief. After the rollercoaster of my day I don't want to have to deal with any more stress. As I stand in the hall, the silence buzzing in my ears, the thought creeps into my mind: could Dr Rodriguez have tipped off Art that I've been to Mendelbury trying to track him down?

'Gen?' Art appears from the kitchen, his iPhone in his hand. He smiles at me and suddenly all my fears about him being involved and the drama of everything that happened earlier with Lorcan feel like a dream.

This is my reality. My home. My husband. There is no way Art knows where I've been. It would show in his eyes if he did.

Art puts his phone down on the hall table and strides towards me. 'I was worried you'd get stuck in town,' he says. 'Apparently the snow's starting to settle and they're predicting transport chaos. As bloody usual.' Art envelops me in a hug. 'Jesus you're *freezing*.' He keeps his arm around my shoulders, walking me into the kitchen. He sits me down at the table and puts the kettle on, eager to warm me up with a cup of tea, then sits down beside me. 'I'm so sorry we had that row last night, Gen.' His voice drops to a whisper. 'It's just really hard when you don't trust me.'

'I know.' And in that moment I do, absolutely, see how unfair I've been on Art. Whatever Dr Rodriguez did, I can't believe Art knew, because it's impossible to get my head around the idea that he could have colluded in keeping Beth from me all those years ago and through all the years since. In that moment I decide that I can't yet tell him I tracked Rodriguez down. He will only take it as another sign of mistrust, not to mention reinforce his belief that I'm obsessed with chasing a dream. After all, I'm still operating on the basis of hunches and overheard conversations.

Okay, so Rodriguez mentioned having been paid money, but he didn't say for what. And yes, both the others involved in the delivery – Mary Duncan, the nurse, and Gary Bloode, the anaesthetist – have since died, as has Lucy O'Donnell. And Lorcan and I were not the only ones to break into Rodriguez's house.

But none of it proves Beth is alive. And Art surely doesn't have anything to do with any of it. Even if he was capable of sustaining such a lie, *why* would he do so? After all, what possible reason could my husband, who so badly wants a child, have for pretending that our daughter died?

I feel guilty, not telling him where I've been and what I've done, but it's easier than opening the can of worms my trip to Oxford would become. Maybe the memory stick Lorcan and I found will provide some sort of proof of what Rodriguez has done. Now that I'm back at home, I half-wish I hadn't let it out of my sight. I try to tell myself a few hours won't make any difference. I'll talk to Art when I've seen what's on the memory stick . . . when, hopefully, there's something more concrete to show him.

Art asks about my evening out and I answer as vaguely as I can.

Lovely to see the girls . . . took ages to get back.

Art swallows it all – which leaves me feeling even more guilty. While he makes my cup of tea he tells me about the ICSI stats, just the topline findings. He thinks we should definitely give it a go. Not wanting to argue, I say I'll think about it. I give him a hug as he sits down again. He smells of the office and himself – his own particular Art smell that's as comforting to me as home.

'What's that for?' he says, pleased.

'Nothing, just glad we're not arguing. How was your day?'

He tells me about today's meeting at 10 Downing Street. 'The PM was really impressed with our model for incentivizing profit-making.' Art beams like a little boy. 'We talked about a couple of their policies. He was *pumping* me for information, Gen. Practical stuff he can use in draft legislation. Afterwards Sandrine told me he *never* reacts like that ... that I should seriously consider a career in politics myself.'

'Wow.' In spite of all the anxieties swirling around my head, I'm genuinely impressed. 'I can't imagine you as a politician.'

'Me neither.' Art grins. 'All that "having to please the electorate".'

His mobile sounds and he takes the call. I head upstairs and run a bath. I'm going over everything I've found out today. Rodriguez has definitely covered something up. But what?

I'm out of my clothes, about to step into the steamy water, when the doorbell rings. I hesitate, my foot poised above the side of the bath, wondering who the caller is. Could it be Lorcan? Maybe he's already seen his son and found out what's on the memory stick. Maybe it contains some kind of confession from Rodriguez ... or perhaps copies of falsified documents? If Rodriguez passed Beth on to another couple, there might even be a fake birth certificate. My heart thuds as I drag on my long T-shirt and open the bathroom door. I can hear Art talking downstairs, but his voice is too low to make out what he is saying.

A woman's voice answers. Thoughts of Lorcan fly out of my head. Who is at the door? I'm at the top of the stairs now. Art hasn't let the woman inside the house, but she's still speaking. His body hides her from view. His back is tensed, like he's angry. My stomach twists into knots as I pad softly down the stairs.

Art is talking again, his voice a fierce, low hiss. I can't hear what he's saying. Who on earth is he talking to?

I'm almost down and the stairs creak under my feet.

Art turns, half-shutting the door on the woman on the other side. Why doesn't he want me to see who it is?

'Art?' I scuttle down the rest of the stairs, the knots in my guts turning and twisting. 'Who's there?'

A flash of anger crosses Art's features, then his face settles with a practised calm. Panic rises inside me. And then Art steps back.

Charlotte West is on the doorstep. I stare at her, too shocked to speak. She stares back, her expression both guilty and resentful. In less than a second I've registered that she's still got that fringe *and* the Orla Kiely bag. And that she's also wearing a soft blue wool hat, almost identical in colour to the beanie I was wearing when I bumped into her the other day. A chill snakes down my spine.

'Charlotte?' I say. 'What are you doing here?' I glance at Art. His face is thunderous.

'I was just passing . . .' Charlotte's voice is high and fake. 'Remember when I saw you around here before? I'm visiting that same friend again.'

'How did you know where I live?' I walk to the front door, tugging my T-shirt further down my thighs, self-conscious.

Charlotte shrugs. 'You mentioned it the other day,' she says, 'when I bumped into you around the corner.'

I search my memory. I might have given her a street name, but surely I never told her a house number.

'I recognized the car.' Charlotte points to Art's Mercedes parked outside. 'I've seen Art pick you up from the Art and Media Institute in it.'

'Oh.' It's true Art has, once or twice in the past few months, come to meet me from work in the car, but I can't believe Charlotte would have seen us *and* remembered the car's make and licence number.

'This, er, lady, says she's one of your students,' Art says, tight-lipped.

188

'Your husband is even better-looking than on TV.' Charlotte's carefully made-up face softens as she smiles at me. Her hand flutters over her fringe and her blue wool hat. 'Gosh, I'm so sorry to have bothered you. I wasn't thinking how late it is.' She steps away from the door.

I'm still staring at her. She's lying. She knew *exactly* what time it was. She glances at Art and I see the look of adoration in her eyes. What the hell is going on here?

Charlotte turns away and heads down the front path. Art shuts the door before she's even reached the pavement.

'Bloody woman,' he says.

'I don't understand,' I say, struggling to make sense of what has just happened. 'Do you know her?'

Art shakes his head. 'No, but it's obvious, isn't it? She's seen me on *The Trials*. Tracked me down. I can't believe she's one of your students . . .' He shakes his head again. 'God, the lengths some people will go to . . .' Muttering, he marches off to the kitchen.

I stare after him. Is that true? Is Charlotte West mimicking my hair and my accessories simply in order to get close to Art? I know Art has female admirers who've seen him on TV, but if Charlotte was only interested in my husband, why come to my writing class – does she think she can somehow get to him *through* me? And, if Art has really never met her before, why did he sound so angry when he was talking to her on the doorstep? I head slowly back upstairs to the bathroom. Surely there's no way Charlotte West is somehow involved in all this, is there?

My mind goes back to the memory stick. I'm close now to finding out the truth, I know I am. I step into the bath, the water now lukewarm. As I turn on the hot tap, a new panic rises. Suppose Lorcan loses the stick? Suppose his son damages it while attempting to decrypt it? I force myself to calm down, taking deep breaths as fear threatens to consume me. I can't allow myself to imagine endless disasters. Tomorrow there will be answers. I have to believe that.

My phone beeps while I'm in the bath. It's Lorcan. His text contains his Hampstead address and reads:

Cal coming over tomorrow morning. See you for lunch? Lx

I text back that I'll come round after teaching my class.

Tomorrow, there will be answers.

The next morning Art's gone when I wake again. It's all I can do not to cancel today's class. The last thing I want to do right now is stand up in front of people and bang on about character development. But that would mean leaving Sami and the others trying to find a replacement teacher two days running – plus the Wednesday class was cancelled last week by the Institute – so I drag myself out of bed and go into town. I sleepwalk through it, relying on the fact that I've led this session a million times before. We're looking at characterization. I bring in a passage from Vikram Seth's *An Equal Music* and ask the class in groups to identify the core traits of the main characters as they are introduced to the reader. I leave them for a while after this to write biographies for their own characters. The whole time my mind is on the memory stick, wondering about the information it holds.

As I'm leaving the college my phone beeps. It's Lorcan.

File decrypted. Come asap.

Anxiety twists in my stomach. Why doesn't he say what the file contains?

I'm on the verge of calling him, then I realize I can't have that conversation in public.

I send a text back saying I'll be with him in half an hour. The wait is agonizing, and yet part of me doesn't want it to end. What on earth has he found? For once, I reject the bus as too slow and head for the nearest underground station. I hate the stale smell on the platform, the way the tunnel seems to press in on all sides. I feel spooked, too, startled by the rustling of a discarded plastic bag behind me as I wait for my train. I keep imagining I'm being watched, but when I turn to look over my shoulder there's no one there. I try and shake off the sensation, but it persists throughout the tube ride, and is still with me, oppressive and unsettling, as I come out of Hampstead station, walk down the high street and turn onto a quiet Victorian terrace.

I look around again. There's no one in sight. Just a couple of giggling schoolgirls in short skirts, hunched over a phone.

A minute later I'm ringing Lorcan's doorbell. He's already told me that he has leased out his own house for the duration of his Ireland contract and is living in a rented flat – one of the many Victorian conversions in the area.

He looks serious as he opens the door, but turns away immediately and leads me inside without speaking. I follow him up the stairs to his first-floor flat. I get a brief glimpse of cream walls and grey carpets as he leads me into a smartly furnished living room complete with squashy couch, brown leather armchair and glass-top coffee table.

A gangly teenage boy is standing by the table. His gaze is fixed on the large-screen TV in the corner, which is playing BBC News with the sound muted.

He turns around as I walk in and offers me a shy smile. He doesn't look much like Lorcan. Darker in colouring, and with a thinner face and close-set brown eyes. He shifts awkwardly from foot to foot.

'Geniver, this is Cal,' Lorcan says.

'Hi.' I smile and raise my hand in a half-wave.

'Hi,' he says and blushes.

191

Poor boy. Tall and skinny, with arms and legs that don't quite seem to fit his body, he has that awkward air I remember from my own teenage years, when you know you're supposed to be able to talk with adults, yet you're not quite sure how to do it.

I'm already aware, from our conversation in the car, that Cal is fourteen, but to me he seems far younger. He picks up a rucksack and heads to the door.

'All right, man?' Lorcan says. 'I'll see you later.'

They talk quietly as Cal leaves the room and heads for the stairs. As his footsteps disappear downstairs I spot Lorcan's laptop on the table. It's closed, but the memory stick is inserted.

Heart racing, I walk over and turn the computer around to face me. Lorcan comes back in and stands close as I lift the lid. The screen flickers into life. A small window is open. A Real Player file.

'Is that what was on the memory stick?' I say. 'A video recording?'

'Yes, CCTV footage.' Lorcan's voice cracks as he speaks. 'I can't . . . I haven't taken in what it . . . God, I'm not sure if I . . . well, you better see for yourself.'

He leans across me to press a key on the computer, then steps back as the film begins to play.

As I watch my mouth falls open in horror, and all the blood seems to drain out of me, because here, surely, is the proof I've been waiting for.

The best and the worst news there could be.

CHAPTER THIRTEEN

The film finishes. I'm dimly aware of Lorcan's hand on my shoulder, but it's like he can't really reach me. Like I'm shut up in my head where the world is imploding.

'Play it again.'

Lorcan reaches past me and presses the keyboard. The film fizzes into life once more.

It's in black-and-white, like the CCTV footage you'd see on *Crimewatch*. At first all it shows is an empty concrete corridor with a fire door at one end. And then a man walks into view. Art. He turns, facing the camera, his eyes on whoever is walking towards him. Another second and she appears: a black woman in a nurse's uniform. As soon as I see her, I remember her. Not just from the photo Lucy showed me, but from all those years ago. It's Mary Duncan, the nurse from my C-section. She is holding something wrapped in a blanket. Her mouth moves. She is talking. Art is listening, nodding.

Art takes a step towards the fire door. There's a carpark sign with the Fair Angel logo just below it, then the words 'Parking Restrictions Apply'. Mary follows Art to the fire door. Art is speaking now. Then he looks down, at whatever Mary is holding. And in this moment, before I see her, I know she is there. *Beth.*

Everything inside me pulls towards the screen as Mary turns and offers the bundle in her arms to Art. I'm powerless, watching, following the movement, knowing what I am about to see.

Wrapped tightly in a blanket, just her tiny, perfect face peeking out, is my baby.

Art takes her. He doesn't look at her face but I'm staring at it . . . drinking it in . . . a tiny, scrunched-up oval with big eyes and an unmistakable look of Art about her. She blinks, her mouth opening as if she's about to cry, as Mary reaches for the fire door and opens it into the darkness of the Fair Angel car park.

Art gives a brisk nod, then turns away, still holding our baby. He walks through the fire door and is swallowed up by the darkness. Mary closes the door behind him carefully, then walks away, along the corridor, out of sight.

The film fizzles out.

I stare at the screen. For a second I have this stupid feeling that Beth is trapped inside it and I have to resist the urge to pick up the laptop and hold it.

'Are you all right?'

I've completely forgotten Lorcan standing beside me.

I shake my head, unable to speak. My legs are trembling. I let myself slide into the chair by the table and hug my arms around my chest.

'Gen?' Lorcan puts his hand on my shoulder. I bow my head.

'Gen, please say something.' Lorcan sounds genuinely frightened.

I squeeze my eyes tight shut. My whole being feels like it's in freefall.

'He did it.' My own voice sounds strange – hoarse and forced and somehow not really a part of me. 'Art took our baby. He did it.'

As I speak my voice breaks. A sob so painful I draw my breath in sharply.

Lorcan leans his head close to mine. He runs his hand down my arm. Half of me wants to fall into the security he offers, to give into the raw agony inside me, but the other half senses that if I let go now, I'll lose myself completely. I already have the sense of falling, tumbling over and over in a darkness from which there is no way out.

'It means she might be alive, Gen.' Lorcan's soft whisper becomes a rope to hold onto.

I grasp it eagerly. As I open my eyes, Lorcan releases me. He stands, leaning against the wall of his living room.

Reality floods back and with it a raging fury. Of two things I am sure:

One: Art has betrayed me. He took our little girl and I will never forgive him.

Two: He must know where she is.

I jump up. Adrenalin is pumping through me. The tears, for now, are gone. The pain just a dull, distant ache. All I feel right here, right now, is the need to force the truth out of Art.

'Would you call me a cab, please?'

Lorcan frowns. 'Where to? D'you want me to come?'

I gaze at his concerned face and feel a wave of affection for him. I'm tempted, for a second, to say yes. Then I pull myself together. Right now my business is with my husband. For all his concern, Lorcan isn't a part of that. I barely even know him; I certainly can't let myself start relying on him.

My mind feels clean and clear, like a knife.

'I'm going to see Art,' I say. 'And I need to go on my own.'

'No.' Lorcan shakes his head for emphasis. 'You shouldn't confront him alone.'

It could be dangerous.

The unspoken words hover between us.

Is that true? Up until this moment I would have sworn that Art would never hurt me physically. But now I don't know what to believe. Now, everything is in chaos.

'I'm going to his office. I'll be safe there.'

'Fine, but I'm still coming. I'll drive you . . . wait outside.'

I nod. In truth I'm relieved. Right now I feel about as vulnerable as I've ever felt in my life.

'I'll just get a jumper, then we can go.' Lorcan disappears.

I am so tense I can't stand still. I pace across the room, impatient. He's taking too long. I can vaguely hear Lorcan on the phone. He's speaking softly and I can't make out what he's saying. I wonder who he is talking to. For some reason my mind skips to Hen. She called Art about Lucy O'Donnell's claims before I had a chance to speak to him myself. Was she warning Art then? Is Lorcan warning him now?

I force myself to sit down and take deep breaths. If I mistrust everyone, I will go mad. The image of Art holding Beth flashes in front of my mind's eye.

How can this be happening?

A minute later Lorcan is back in a wool sweater, and we set off. I stare out of the window as we drive through Hampstead and Belsize Park, down the hill towards central London. I barely notice the shops and houses we pass.

Art's business headquarters are near Exmouth Market, just off a trendy street full of boutiques and cafés. It's impossible to park on the road itself, so Lorcan turns down a side street.

He parks and turns to me, his forehead creased with lines of concern. 'Please be careful.'

I look into his eyes, holding his gaze for a few seconds. And then Lorcan reaches over and places his hand gently on the side of my face. His fingers are warm.

'Promise you'll call me if you think . . . if Art does anything that . . .'

'I'll be fine.'

I get out of the car and walk round the corner. As I cross the road and enter the lobby of Art's building, I realize I have no idea what I'm going to say.

It doesn't matter. Once we're face to face, I will work it out.

The security guard knows me and waves me through, into the lifts. I reach the fourth floor and walk into Loxley Benson. Camilla, the receptionist on duty, beams at me.

'Hey, Geniver,' she says. 'Thanks for the party. That New York shop where your sister-in-law got her shoes was wicked. Please tell her massive thanks for the tip. I've ordered a pair off their website. *Gorge*-ous.'

I nod as I pass her, too intent on finding Art to reply. I head for the glass doors that will take me through to the rest of the office.

'Er, Art's in a meeting,' Camilla says, suddenly sounding anxious.

I turn as I reach the doors. 'Which room?'

'Er, the boardroom,' Camilla says breathlessly. 'But let me call Siena.'

She's looking nervous. Is my rage that obvious?

I press my hand against the pad that opens the door out of reception. Like the permanent staff here, I enjoy finger-print privileges. The glass panel slides back and I walk into the corridor.

'Wait, please . . .' Camilla's voice fades as the sliding doors shut behind me. A few people are in the open-plan area from which the boardroom and private offices lead off. They glance over as I pass. I ignore them, head down.

I see him before he sees me. He's standing in front of the large table in the boardroom, holding court. Three men in suits are seated, staring at him in rapt attention. Art in full flow is a mesmerizing sight: all energy and intent. I know how those men watching him are feeling . . . how special he's making them feel.

For a second I hesitate. I have never, in all the fourteen years I have known him, burst in on Art in a business meeting. And then the image of him at the fire door of Fair Angel, holding our baby, erupts in my mind's eye. Fury boils up inside me. I grit my teeth and push the door open.

Art glances round, a look of carefully concealed irritation on his face. It turns to shock as he registers that it's me standing there. The men seated at the table are looking at me too, but I keep my gaze on Art.

'I need to speak to you,' I say calmly. 'Now.'

Art hesitates. Just a beat. I can see him weighing up his options. He clearly decides not to risk the scene that could ensue if he denies me what I want, and turns, smartly, to the waiting men.

'Please excuse me,' he says with effortless charm. 'This is clearly an emergency.'

In a single move, he's across the room, gripping me by the elbow and steering me away from the boardroom. People are staring as Art leads me down the corridor and into his own office. He holds onto my arm until we're inside, then he lets me go and shuts the door firmly.

'What the hell's going on, Gen?'

I swallow hard, trying to put my thoughts into words. 'I need to ask you something . . .'

'Ask me something?' Art blinks rapidly. 'D'you know who those men are?' He points in the direction of the boardroom. 'The PM's special advisers asking me – *me* – for more detail about policy measures that *I* suggested at yesterday's meeting.'

Light from the large window behind him creates a fiery effect around his head. He's almost crackling with fury. It strikes me again that, for all our time together, I have no idea what he's capable of.

'This is important, Art.' I meet his glare head-on.

'*What*'s so bloody important?' he says. 'What do you need to ask me?'

I take a deep breath. 'I know our baby was born alive, Art. I know you took her and lied to me.'

'What?' Art stares at me. His eyes betray nothing but his anger. '*This* again? For God's sake, Gen! How can you do this to me?'

He turns his back and clasps his hands behind his head. I can't work out whether he's buying time or simply trying to restrain his temper. Desolation swamps me. How is it possible I can be standing here, accusing my own husband of such a terrible crime? My stagnant, predictable life has turned into a vortex of misery and suspicion and I'm only just holding on, scarcely able to bear my own feelings.

I wander across the room. Art's large, airy work space is just like his office at home – everything appears organized, and yet nothing is labelled. It strikes me that this is a perfect metaphor for Art himself: all artful organization on the surface; all controlled and hidden underneath. I stare down at the bottle of water and the spearmint chewing gum pack on the desk.

'I have to know the truth.'

He turns to face me. His eyes are hard but his mouth trembles with emotion.

'How dare you?' he spits. 'I know that bloody woman turning up on our doorstep was upsetting, but how can you *possibly* think . . .?' He breaks off.

'I've seen CCTV of you from the Fair Angel.' My voice shakes as I speak. 'I've seen the nurse from Beth's birth handing her over to you in the corridor.'

Art's eyes register horror, then the repressed fury takes over again.

'Impossible.' His voice is hard and cold as steel. 'Or faked.'

'That's ridiculous.' But I stop. *Could* the film I saw have been falsified? I hadn't even considered this possibility. My mind races over the ramifications ... how can I find out? Would an expert be able to tell? Does this mean Art may still, after all, be innocent? Part of me hopes so, even as I'm recognizing that this would also mean the end of my dream of finding Beth. For the first time since I saw the CCTV footage, doubt enters my mind. 'Why would anyone bother to fake film of you with our baby?'

Art holds up three fingers. His eyes bore into me.

'One, to discredit me. Two, to drive a wedge between us. Three, to make you crazy. All of which are bloody happening.' He pauses. 'But that's just off the top of my head. I'm sure if you gave me a few minutes I could come up with another ten reasons. I can think of a million people who'd be happy to see me fail and you not trusting me is a failure for me, for my life ... Jesus, Gen, it's a failure for *us*.' He's suddenly across the room, reaching for my hand, his whole demeanour beseeching. 'Please don't give in to this ... this craziness, Gen. If it's not a fake film, then it must be all the pressure – you're seeing what you *want* to see. It's ... it's just in your head.'

It's so typical of Art to switch from logical reasoning to emotional plea like that. So typical. And so manipulative.

'Stop it, Art. Stop trying to make me feel like it's me ... like I'm going mad.'

He studies me. 'But you know this *is* mad. You *know* it doesn't make any sense,' he says slowly. 'In your heart you *know*.'

For a moment I see him as an outsider would – totally focused, totally sure of himself.

'Okay, so it doesn't make sense,' I say. 'But that doesn't mean it isn't true.'

I walk over to the shelf that runs from the window to the door. A single photo nestles among the row of business awards. It's a silver-framed picture of us on our wedding day. Art is smiling, his haircut preppily short. I'm gazing adoringly up at him. My hair is short too – a gamine crop with a wispy fringe. It makes me look even younger than I was. It breaks my heart how young we both look.

And how innocent.

Art walks round to the other side of the desk. He stands in front of his chair.

'Gen?'

I lower my voice. 'Tell me the truth.'

'I am.'

'What about the money for MDO? I saw Doctor Rodriguez yesterday . . . I heard him talk about the money he was paid . . . was the MDO payment his first instalment?'

'No. I *promise* you, *no*.' Art grips the chair. His knuckles are white but his eyes are steady as they hold my gaze. 'Can't you see you're twisting everything to fit what you want to be true? Ask yourself *why* would I pretend our baby was dead? *Why* would Rodriguez risk being struck off and sent to prison? *Why* would I gamble my entire life on a lie?' His voice cracks. 'Gen, I have never wanted anything as much as I've wanted us to be a family. And . . . and it's not fair that you don't trust me when I suffered just as much as you when we . . . lost her . . .' He turns his face away so I can't see the emotion that is so unbearably obvious in his voice.

I suddenly feel exhausted. Can I really be wrong? Am I seeing links between everything because I can't bear the alternative – that Beth is really dead?

Art turns round. His eyes are beyond miserable. I'm suddenly filled with doubt.

'How did you get hold of this film?' he says. 'Did someone help you?'

I flinch under his accusing gaze. And yet, why shouldn't I tell him . . . we've done nothing wrong.

'Lorcan helped me. We found the film at Rodriguez's house. He offered me a lift, that's all.'

'Really?' Art says sarcastically. 'How many little get-togethers between the two of you is that since the party? If he isn't halfway to seducing you by now then he's losing his touch.'

I've never heard such contempt in his voice. The doubts I was feeling just a few seconds ago vanish.

'That's not fair,' I say, stung. 'Lorcan just wants to help.'

Art lets his breath out with a sigh. He shakes his head. 'So a man you've never met before drops everything to take you wherever you want to go, and you don't even question his motives.'

'It's not like that, I—'

'Whereas I . . . I love you. *I've* known you for fourteen years and been married to you for twelve. But you think *I'm* capable of betraying you without any proof whatsoever.' His voice rises. 'Don't you remember what Lorcan did here . . .' He waves his hand to indicate the Loxley Benson offices.

'You mean having a one-night stand with someone's wife years and years ago?'

Art opens his mouth as if to say more, then clearly thinks better of it. 'Never mind Lorcan,' he says. 'I'm seriously worried about you.'

'I saw you with a baby,' I insist. 'You were at the Fair Angel hospital.'

'Are you sure? *Think* about it,' Art pleads. 'Are you seriously saying I've somehow "got rid" of a perfectly healthy baby that

I wanted as much as you? How could it even happen? Dr Rodriguez pronounced Beth dead. There were other people in the room.'

'Yes, but most of them had to leave before the birth because Rodriguez deliberately gave them food poisoning. And the two who *were* present are both dead.'

'I saw her *body*.' Art carries on as if I hadn't spoken. 'You *know* how much I want a family. It's *me* pushing for the IVF right now. How does me taking our baby away from us make sense? How does *any* of this make sense?'

I don't have any answers. A few moments pass. Through the window of Art's office I can see people peering in at us. There's Kyle and Tris and a couple of the PAs. They're all pretending to talk or work, but they keep glancing in our direction.

'I agree it doesn't make sense,' I say. 'But there're all these things I've found out: I heard Rodriguez talk about the money he got. I saw the baby in your arms the night we had Beth.'

'No.' Art thumps his desk. 'No, Gen. All those things are just coincidences or misunderstandings. You're *making* everything add up to me being guilty because above and beyond anything you want Beth to be alive. You said as much after we saw Mr Tam. You didn't want another baby because you still wanted Beth.'

I back away, my gaze still fixed intently on Art's anguished face. He takes a step towards me.

'Where is this film that supposedly shows me with the baby?'

It's actually in my pocket but I'm not admitting that to Art. If I let him have the film, then he's in control, and I want a chance to check out its authenticity for myself.

'I don't have the film on me,' I say. 'It's somewhere safe.'

'I want to see it,' Art demands. 'Whatever you think it shows it's a fake.' He hesitates. 'I'm going back to my meeting, but I want you to stay here. Afterwards we'll go home and look at this film together. And then I'm taking you to see a therapist.'

'What?'

'Please, Gen. This has got to stop.'

I stare at him. The blood is throbbing at my temples. Art's not going to admit to anything. He's turning it all onto me. I realize, with a terrible, sickening misery that I no longer trust him.

'Fine.' I turn and stare out of the window. The sun is shining in, highlighting a line of smudges across the bottom of the glass. It's a cold, clear day and from here I can see all the way across the river. The light is sharp, the tallest buildings delineated against a bright blue sky.

Behind me the door shuts. Art has gone.

I have to tell the police. Maybe the CCTV film on the memory stick in my pocket *is* a fake, but I need to know for sure. They can check Loxley Benson's books . . . *they* can track the money Art paid to MDO and find out whether it somehow made its way to Rodriguez.

I slip out of Art's office. Avoiding the boardroom, I walk through the open-plan area. The younger guys are there – sharp-suited and slick-haired, hunched over their computers. I have to stop myself from running as I reach the corridor off which the board members all have offices. Tris sees me as I pass and calls out 'hello'. I act like I haven't heard.

Past the reception area. Camilla is on the phone. I shove my hand in my pocket, feeling for the memory stick. My fingers curl round it and its solidity gives me a boost of courage. I glance over my shoulder. Camilla is watching me leave, still talking into her headset. I raise my hand in a wave and force a smile. She waves back, then looks down at her desk.

Heart thudding, I speed up, racing past the Ladies and the lifts and down the stairs. I hurtle down, down to the ground floor. Past the security guard – another quick wave – and outside. I stop for a second on the pavement, feeling the cold air harsh against my face, then look over my shoulder. There's no sign of anyone following me from Art's building.

Lorcan is parked just round the corner. I scurry in that direction. My phone rings. It's Art. He's already seen that I've gone. I switch off the mobile and run. There's no traffic, just a few parked cars. No passers-by. The sun is out yet I'm shivering. I wind my scarf around my neck as I hurry along. I'm intent on reaching Lorcan and going to the police. The road is empty.

I step out without looking.

With a roar, a car speeds past. Every cell in my body freezes as I leap back. The car flies by so close I can almost feel the metal. In a split second it's gone. I stand, staring after it, shocked to the core.

I realize I'm holding my breath. As I open my mouth, a hand grabs my arm. Strong fingers pull me round. Pinching my arm. Pushing me back towards the pavement. It's a man, his face hidden by his hood. I try to scream but my voice won't work. Before I can properly register what's happening, the man shoves me against the wall behind. His hand grips my neck, pressing against my wind pipe.

I gasp, my senses firing, my heart pounding. I can't move. My eyes fix on the man's mouth, his thin lips. He's huge – towering over me. The man leans in close. I can feel his breath against my ear.

'Enough now, Geniver,' he hisses. His free hand delves into one of my jeans pockets. Then the other. I can feel his fingers clawing inside my jeans, pushing against the denim. I strain away from him but his grip around my throat is like a claw. I can't breathe. I want to kick out but my legs won't move.

Inside my pocket, the man's hand bunches, his fingers curling around the memory stick. My heart is thundering in my ears, my whole body frozen. The man withdraws his hand, then leans in close, still clutching my throat. 'Remember what happened to Lucy O'Donnell?' His voice is a low whisper, full of menace.

I nod. Just the tiniest movement.

'Good . . .' The man clutches the memory stick in his fist. 'Then stop raking up ancient history, or the same thing will happen to you.'

This is how I got back at Ginger Tall and Broken Tooth.

Going into school, I hid behind the big tree and took my school sweatshirt and rubbed dirt on the front of it, then pushed my shoe in the earth and trod on the back of it. It was a bit smudgy but you could see it was some of a footprint, like when I was really little and we did finger painting. I put the sweatshirt on again and went inside. I screwed up my face like I was trying not to cry and told Miss Evans that Ginger Tall and Broken Tooth pushed me over and stamped on my back on the way into school.

It was good. Ginger Tall and Broken Tooth got in big trouble. It was specially good when I got home. Mummy said that I was very smart and that it was a good start as practice for dealing with Bad People, though I couldn't expect the teachers to sort out everything and I needed to think of ways of paying back people so they would be hurt too and not just told off. She said that was the only way it was fair because if one person gives an eye, the other person has to as well. I think it was eyes. Anyway, she let me have extra sweets. I liked those fizzy sweets then, in the shape of snakes, but now I think those sweets are for babies, though I would still eat them if I had some.

Mummy said not to eat too many sweets as that can make you sick. I wished I could go back and make Ginger Tall and Broken Tooth eat sweets until they were sick. Then I thought about how Broken Tooth wore glasses and how I would like to get them and smash them up really small and put them in some sweets for them both to eat. I thought how the glass bits would cut your throat and really hurt. It would be so good because they would think it was nice and then they would see it was to make them be ill, ha-ha-ha.

CHAPTER FOURTEEN

The man shoves me away from him and races off, the memory stick in his hand. I want to move, but shock and fear root me to the spot. The man disappears around the corner to the right and I let the air out of me in a gasp. I force myself to focus: Lorcan is just around the corner, waiting for me. I have to get to him. I make myself cross the road. My legs feel like dead weights and I'm trembling as I reach the other side, but I keep walking, one careful step after the other. As I turn the corner on the left, I see Lorcan leaning against his Audi. He sees me and rushes over.

'Gen, what happened?' he says. 'What did Art say?'

I open my mouth but I can't speak.

'Gen?' There's a real urgency in his voice. 'Are you all right?'

I shake my head.

'Get in the car.' He puts his arm around my shoulders and ushers me to the car. As I slip into the passenger seat I realize that my hands are still shaking. I shove them into my pockets.

'Art denied everything,' I explain. 'He wanted to see the film on the memory stick, but I came outside and this man – this huge guy – mugged me.'

Lorcan's fingers tighten on the steering wheel. 'Jesus Christ, are you okay?'

'It wasn't random.' My voice shrinks with fear. 'He knew who I was. He took the memory stick. And he threatened me.'

'What did he say?'

As I tell him, my mind is in overdrive, trying to piece together what I know.

'Gen, this is bad,' Lorcan glances at me. His face is contorted with worry. 'Rodriguez must have sent that man, which means he knew what we took and he's been watching us . . . he must have *followed* you . . . or else . . .'

I'm silent. He means: or else Art sent the man. Would Art have had time to do that? I can't answer. I can barely think.

Lorcan drives off. Outside the car, people are rushing past – a blur of activity through the window. Their lives carry on as normal, while I can't be sure of anything or anyone, any more. I look over at Lorcan. The doubts I had the other day come rushing back. He has bent over backwards for me, even though we've only just met. Have I been incredibly naive to trust him?

I'm sick to my stomach. I can still feel the man's fingers, pressing against my skin. 'It's all true,' I say hoarsely. 'Someone took Beth. And whoever it was killed people to cover it up . . . the anaesthetist . . . Lucy O'Donnell . . .'

Lorcan slows the car as we reach a set of traffic lights. 'Did you see his face, the guy who attacked you?'

'No.' I look out of the car. An old man with a walking stick is struggling to walk past a newsagent. A little girl with sleek dark hair skips by, holding her mother's hand. I stare after her. She's too young to be Beth. Isn't she?

'It happened too fast, I just know he was tall. Big and tall.' I shiver, remembering how the man appeared from nowhere, looming over me . . . a hooded, menacing giant.

'Could it have been that blond guy we saw at Rodriguez's window?'

'I don't think so.' I close my eyes, trying to visualize the blond man. I can just about picture his shape in the window, but that's no help, I didn't see his face properly. I got the impression that he was stocky but – unlike my attacker – only average height. Still, from the angle at which I was looking up at him it's impossible to be sure. 'I don't know.'

There's a long pause. I'm unable to gather my thoughts. And then I remember what I decided in Art's office.

'I have to go to the police.'

Lorcan says nothing for a minute, then he glances over, his expression grave. 'Are you sure that's a good idea, Gen? I'm just asking the question. I know that guy threatened you, but . . . what exactly would you tell the police?'

Suspicion shoots through me. Why on earth would Lorcan object to me turning to the very people who are supposed to protect us?

'I'll tell them what I know, that I've seen film showing Art with Beth . . . that she didn't die.'

'But that film doesn't prove or explain anything. You don't even have it any more.'

He's right. There is nothing whatsoever to back up my story.

'Maybe I can get the police to investigate,' I say, feeling defeated. 'At the very least I could get them to properly investigate Lucy O'Donnell's death. I mean, what else can I do?'

'Okay, then,' Lorcan agrees, reluctantly.

I find the address of the nearest police station on Lorcan's phone and we drive on. As we near our destination fear circles me like a vulture.

What if Art really did all this . . .? Took Beth. Paid Rodriguez. Killed Lucy O'Donnell. Got someone to threaten me.

My guts twist into knots. I can't bear to believe it. 'Art didn't know I had the memory stick before I went into his office,' I say

211

out loud. 'He couldn't possibly have organized that guy to take it so fast.'

'Unless someone rang ahead to warn him. Anyway, it doesn't prove anything.' Lorcan pulls the car over and stops. We're right beside the police station. I stare at the dark blue sign. 'That's my point. Nothing you know proves anything.'

I open the door.

'Shall I come with you?' he asks

'No,' I look him in the eyes. 'I'll be fine by myself.'

Detective Sergeant Gloria Manning gazes at me. She's about thirty-five, with a lined face and lank hair that curls limply onto her shoulders.

'So you don't have this memory stick any more?' she asks gently.

'No, I told you.' My voice rises and I place my hands flat on the table in front of me. I press the palms against the cold steel, trying to stay calm. In the clinical atmosphere of the interview room, with its bare walls and scrubbed floor, my story sounds hysterical. 'I was mugged.'

Manning shoots a swift glance at my handbag, hanging on the back of my chair.

'The memory stick was in my pocket . . .' I explain. 'The man *knew* . . .'

'Okay,' Manning says slowly. 'And you think that the doctor who was present at your daughter's stillbirth may have got this man to steal it. *And* organized the death of the woman in the road traffic accident last week who, you claim, came to you last week and told you your baby was alive?'

I nod, suddenly exhausted. I can see in Manning's pitying eyes that she doesn't believe me. Lorcan was right – without any proof, my whole story sounds ludicrously far-fetched, like some sort of melodramatic soap opera.

DS Manning clears her throat. 'But until a week ago, you believed your baby was stillborn . . .?'

'Yes.' I look down at the table.

DS Manning leans back in her chair. It gives a weary creak that matches the look on her face.

'Look, I know there's no real proof of what I'm saying, but that's why I've come here, so you can *find* the proof,' I insist. 'And find my little girl?'

DS Manning studies me carefully. 'Have you told me everything? I mean, if you think this Doctor Rodriguez really pretended your baby was dead, why would he give you this film showing she was alive.'

I bite my lip. 'He didn't exactly give it to me.'

DS Manning raises her eyebrows. 'What does that mean?'

'We . . . I broke into his house and took it.'

DS Manning sighs. 'Mrs Loxley—'

'I found a newspaper cutting as well.' This, I remember, I still have in my bag. Eagerly I take it out and offer it to the sergeant. 'This is the anaesthetist at my C-section. The one who assisted Doctor Rodriguez.'

DS Manning takes it and holds it gingerly between her finger and thumb. She glances at the headline. 'Killed by a hit-and-run driver,' she says. 'So?'

'Well, don't you think that's suspicious?'

Manning stares at me. 'You're saying you think *this* man's death was a fake too?'

'No.' Frustration wells inside me. 'No, I'm saying that maybe Rodriguez killed him because he was threatening to expose the fact that my baby was born alive. Why would Rodriguez keep the cutting otherwise?'

'Because they were colleagues?' DS Manning offers. 'Because they worked together?'

There is a long silence. 'I'm so sorry for your loss, Mrs Loxley,' she says. She leans forward and pats my arm. 'I had a miscarriage too. Ten weeks. I know it's hard to accept.'

I shake my head. I can't speak, I'm too angry. How dare this woman compare my losing Beth with her own experience? How dare she imply I've been unhinged by my grief?

DS Manning clearly takes my silence for some kind of acquiescence. She pats my arm again and leaves the room.

Ten long minutes later she's back.

'There's no record of a break-in at the house belonging to Doctor Rodriguez in Mendelbury.' There's a flat finality to DS Manning's voice.

I nod, letting this news sink in. Rodriguez hasn't reported the break-in. Of course he hasn't. Why would he want to draw attention to the memory stick I stole? Especially now that he has clearly managed to get it back.

'We'll circulate the description of the man who mugged you and I have the number here of a victim-support unit.' DS Manning pauses. 'As I say, I'm very sorry, Mrs Loxley. Now, is there someone we can call for you? Someone who could take you home?'

The truth sinks into my head like a stone falling through water: the police aren't going to believe me. 'It's fine,' I say. I am numb with shock. 'My friend's outside.' I stand up. My hands are still trembling. If the police don't believe me, I have nowhere to hide.

Nowhere I will be safe.

Tears blur my vision as I walk to the door. Somehow I make it back out to the waiting area, down the steps and onto the pavement. I reach Lorcan's car and get inside.

'Gen?' he says.

'They didn't believe me.'

'Oh, Gen.' There's compassion in his voice. He puts his hand on my shoulder and I lean against him. All the tension of the past few days leaks out of me along with my tears. I rest my head against Lorcan's chest, letting him wrap me in his arms, and a memory hits me from nowhere.

I'm racing out of primary school, a painting of my dad, created *for* my dad, in my hand. And he's *there*, my dad. One of the rare occasions he picked me up after school, and he's *there*, watching for me. And the unexpected and amazing coincidence of this over-whelms me and I hurtle towards him. And he sees me too and he smiles and he opens his arm and I'm almost flying through the air to reach him faster, faster; and then something trips me and the playground rushes up to meet me and I'm smashing onto the tarmac and there's pain in my knee and then his strong arms pick me up and my dad holds me and he's saying: 'Hey, Queenie, don't cry,' and his breath is sweet and comforting and I cling to him like the universe is disappearing all around us. And then he sets me down and I'm still sobbing but they're little jerky sobs now and he takes my hand to lead me away and I remember the painting and I look round and it's on the ground behind me, mud-spattered and trodden into a puddle by the other children. And no one has noticed, and I stare at it over my shoulder, the tears rising again and my dad is walking along, talking to one of the other mums and he is tugging me after him and I want to make him stop so we can go back and fetch the painting but he pulls me after him: 'Come on now, Geniver,' and I stare at the painting and my knee stings but I stop crying because there is no point and in that moment I know the hopelessness of love.

I lift my face, knowing it is tear-stained and that my nose must be red and my make-up must be smudged under my eyes. Lorcan says nothing but I see the tenderness in his eyes as I pull away from our hug.

As he drives off, he glances over.

'Where do you want to go now?' he says.

I look at him. 'I don't know.' I want to say that I just want to be somewhere quiet, where I don't have to answer to anyone or even think about Art lying to me or that Beth may be alive. But the words in my head are trapped there. Too hard to express.

Lorcan reaches out his hand and gives my shoulder a gentle squeeze.

'You can come and stay with me, if you like,' he says.

I shake my head. Lorcan has been brilliant, but sleeping over at his flat feels like too great an intimacy. I run through the options in my head. Hen is the obvious choice – the person I always turn to – and yet I don't want to confide in her. Not after all her conversations with Art, and knowing how unstable she already thinks I am. On the other hand, it doesn't really matter where I go. I don't have to talk. I just don't want to be at home.

'I'll go to Hen's,' I say. 'Would you drop me off?'

'Sure.'

I call to check this is okay with Hen, ignoring the five missed calls from Art that flash up on my phone as soon as I switch it on.

'I won't get in the way,' I say to her. 'I just want to sit and chill.'

'You could never be in the way, Gen.' Hen is speaking with characteristic warmth, but I can also hear the concern in her voice. I feel sure she has already heard about my latest outburst from Art. 'We can talk properly when Nat goes to bed.'

'Okay.' I'm still not sure how much to say to Hen. Part of me can't bear the prospect of opening up, knowing how she and Art have been talking about me. Part of me is desperate to convince her that I'm not imagining that Beth was born alive – that the man who attacked and threatened me is, like the CCTV footage, proof of a terrible crime. As soon as I've finished the call I turn my phone onto silent. On the way to Hen's house, I explain to

Lorcan exactly what the police said. The anger and the despair of my encounter with DS Manning are gone now. I'm strangely calm, in fact. So the police aren't going to help me. At least I know where I stand. I'm on my own . . . wholly responsible for what comes next.

Hen's house is in uproar when I arrive. It sounds like she's set up a crèche in her living room, though, in fact, the noise is emanating from just two kids: Nat and his friend, Josh, who have created a camp with sofas and blankets for tents. The room is one of those knock-through jobs with two fireplaces. Hen has decorated with chunky modern couches, two of which are currently covered with blankets. I'm still not used to her living somewhere so grand. Most of the time I've known her she's survived in a succession of bedsits, getting by on a combination of luck, charm and indulgent landlords.

I glance over at the bookshelves, where Hen's English-degree novels sit side by side with Rob's extensive collection of classic-car magazines. They only moved here last year and the house is still settling around them, their possessions not yet properly merged. Or maybe all Hen's stuff just stands out to me because I've known her for so long.

Right now, she's flushed and harassed. I follow her into the kitchen and listen to her complaints about Josh's manners for five minutes, while she takes two cartons of organic juice out of the fridge and forgets to make the cup of tea she offered me at the front door.

At last she quietens down and puts the kettle on. The kitchen we're sitting in is Hen's dream room, from the mottled granite work surface to the pale green kitchen cupboards. The dying light outside glows off the aquamarine mosaic splash-back, casting shadows across Nat's latest paintings that adorn the walls.

When I close my eyes I can still feel the mugger's grip around my neck. And yet, in Hen's cosy kitchen, it feels like the attack happened years ago.

'I'm sorry about the chaos, Gen,' Hen says with a sigh, sinking into the chair opposite me. Shrieks of laughter drift towards us from the living room. Hen leans forward, her forehead creased with a frown. 'I feel so awkward,' she says. 'Art keeps calling me. He was on the phone just before you rang earlier.' She stops, catching the irritation that must have flickered across my face. 'Gen, *please* don't think we're talking behind your back. He's only calling me because he loves you so much and he's worried about you. He says you're convinced now that he stole Beth away from you just after she was born. Is that really true, Gen? Do you seriously think he's capable of doing that?'

I don't know. I gaze into her eyes and my irritation dissolves. This is just Hen and me and she's my oldest friend. Of course Art has turned to her – he knows that *I* turn to her. And if I can't trust Hen, who can I trust?

I open my mouth to tell her about the CCTV footage and how I was just mugged outside Art's office, when Nat appears in the doorway asking for his and Josh's drinks. Hen shoots me an apologetic look, then crosses the room to retrieve the juice cartons. Nat hovers in the doorway, watching me in that slightly detached way he has. He's a miniature version of Hen in terms of both his pale colouring and the shock of wild, frizzy hair that frames his heart-shaped face. I still can't look at Nat without remembering the darkness of the time surrounding his birth. And yet, the older he gets, the more I have learned to love him. He seems to carry all Hen's best qualities – openness, charm and affection – but with an undertow of kindness and a genuinely sweet nature.

Hen hands over the juice cartons and Nat trots away. If Beth hadn't been taken away from me, then it might have been her

218

and Nat playing camps in the living room. I wonder what Hen would have made of my daughter . . . whether Beth would have been as like me as Nat is like her . . .

Then it strikes me . . . if Beth is still alive, then maybe she already *is* like me.

Hen sits back down in her chair. 'Go on,' she says.

'I found a film,' I say slowly. 'A film that shows Art with our baby.'

Hen frowns. 'How is that possible?'

I explain about the CCTV footage from the Fair Angel hospital.

'Art claims it was faked but—'

'It *must* be,' Hen interrupts. 'There's no other explanation.'

'No, the film shows the nurse at the birth – Mary Duncan – actually handing Beth to Art. He—'

'But you said you couldn't remember what she looked like,' Hen interrupts again. 'When her sister came to see you, you said you couldn't be sure the picture she showed you was the actual nurse from the hospital. I remember you *saying* that.'

'I know,' I concede. 'But when I saw the film I *did* recognize her. And then I was mugged and the man who mugged me *threatened* me. He said I would end up like Lucy O'Donnell if I didn't stop asking questions about Beth.'

I stare into Hen's eyes, hoping to see her look of bewilderment turn to an acknowledgement that this, at last, is proof that I am right – that Beth *was* stolen away from me. But all I see in Hen's expression is fear – and pity.

'Oh, Gen.' She reaches across the table and takes my hand. 'Gen, I'm so sorry, but where is that film now?'

'The man who mugged me *took* it.' I stare at her. Hasn't she understood what I've been saying?

Hen's whole face crumples with concern. 'Oh, Gen . . .'

She squeezes my hand and I suddenly realize what she's thinking. I can't believe it. I stand up, pulling my hand away.

'You think I've imagined all this?' My voice cracks. How can Hen think I am that paranoid? That deluded? That sick?

She doesn't deny my question. She stands too, clasping her hands together – a supplicating gesture. 'Please, Gen, don't be angry. I don't think you're doing any of this deliberately. I just think you've been fragile for a long time and this woman turning up and telling you Beth is alive has tipped you over the edge. It's not your fault, it could happen to anyone. Me and Art are—'

'You and Art.' My voice is hard and brittle. It stops her in her tracks.

'Not like that.' Her eyes widen, appalled. 'It's only because we love you, Gen.'

'Right.' For a second I'm faltering, sucked into the possibility that Art and Hen are right and I am, in fact, insane, imagining everything, from the film to the attack in the street to those threatening words that still echo in my ears.

Stop raking up ancient history, or the same thing will happen to you.

And then I remember that it's not just me who has seen the film.

'Lorcan Byrne saw the CCTV too,' I said. 'His son opened the file for us. He *saw* Art taking Beth away.'

Hen shakes her head sadly. 'How do you know it wasn't Lorcan who faked the CCTV?' she says.

The idea spins like a knife in my head. I have a sudden flashback to a party, the year I met Art, where the two of us were among a group playing 'truth or dare'. I spun the bottle. It pointed at Art.

'Truth or dare?' I'd asked.

'Truth.' He met my eyes, unafraid, and I ran over possible questions in rapid succession, discarding each one in turn as too cheesy or too silly.

'Can I trust you?' The words spilled out of me, unbidden. The atmosphere tightened as everyone looked at Art. We had only been together a few months and I had, I realized, just exposed more of my feelings than I'd meant to.

Art held my gaze, his look so intense that the rest of the room faded away.

'With your life,' he said.

For a second we had stared at each other and, in that moment, I gave up my heart, knowing that he would one day ask me to marry him and that I would say yes.

'Gen?' Hen touches my arm.

I come back to the present. I'm standing in Hen's designer kitchen and she thinks Lorcan Byrne faked the CCTV footage of Art taking Beth away.

'Lorcan's an actor who knows a bit about carpentry,' I say. 'He wouldn't have a clue how to fake a film.'

Hen rolls her eyes. 'He must know people who would – people in the film business.'

I think of Lorcan's son, Cal. He managed to decrypt the file. I guess it's possible he could have faked it.

'Or maybe Lorcan's just humouring you,' Hen goes on gently. 'Maybe he's agreeing that the film shows something it doesn't so that you'll rely on him more.'

I feel sick. 'Why would he bother to do that?' I ask, though I know what she's going to say.

'Gen, you've heard his reputation,' Hen says with a sigh.

I step away from her. I don't want to hear any more. I still feel sick. My head is a battleground of conflicting thoughts and feelings. I came here so I wouldn't have to think, but Hen is making everything worse. I want to turn around and walk out, but I can't bear Hen thinking I'm mentally ill.

'It's not just the film and the attack,' I say, my hands defiantly

221

on my hips. 'What about the money I told you about? The fifty grand Art paid out *just after* Beth?'

'Come on, Gen,' Hen groans. 'That was to Manage Debt Online. It can't have anything to do with Beth.'

I stare at her. *'Manage Debt Online?'* My heart seems to freeze in my chest. 'How do you know that's who he paid?'

Hen meets my gaze. 'You *told* me, Gen.'

'I told you *MDO*,' I say, my voice rising. A new panic swirls in my head. What does Hen know? She spoke just then with assurance, like she was stating a fact. A fact she couldn't have got from me. 'I told you the initials because they were all that was written on the bank statement.'

Hen is now staring at me as if I'm totally crazy. 'But MDO *stands* for Manage Debt Online, doesn't it?' she says.

'No . . . I don't know . . . Hen, what do you know about this?' The sunlight outside the kitchen window is fading. A thin shadow falls across Hen's face. She crosses the room and switches on the lamp on the dresser. I stare down at my cup of tea, cold now, on the kitchen table.

'I don't know anything,' Hen insists. 'I just assumed MDO stood for that loan company.'

'But Art said he couldn't remember . . . that MDO was some business transaction . . . a payment for a client . . .'

'Well, it probably was then,' Hen goes on. 'Clients have debts . . . Manage Debt Online only processes transactions over the internet . . . perhaps this client asked Art to pay the debt through one of the Loxley Benson accounts . . .'

'How do you know about this . . . this Manage Debt Online . . .?'

Hen blushes. 'I heard about them once,' she says vaguely. 'Back when I had big debts, remember?'

'Yes, of course I remember. But still . . .'

'Jesus, Gen, maybe I'm wrong,' Hen says. 'Maybe MDO stands for something else. But I'm certain it's got nothing to do with Art paying anyone to lie about Beth. That makes no sense at all.'

I start to doubt myself, then I remember the mugger's hot breath in my ear. He threatened me. Lucy O'Donnell was murdered. I have seen the film of my baby with Art.

I chew the skin around the nail on my middle finger.

'Gen, please?' Hen's voice wobbles slightly.

How would she know about MDO? She didn't *suggest* MDO was a debt company just now, she was *sure* of it. How is that possible, unless she has been talking to Art about it all behind my back?

I can't trust her. The knowledge settles on my chest. A dead weight.

'It's okay,' I say, more to myself than to Hen. Though it's not okay. I'm living in a nightmare.

Hen nods, apparently reassured, then the doorbell rings. 'That'll be Josh's mum to pick him up.' She hesitates. 'Are you sure you're all right?'

'Of course.' I force a smile. 'Go.'

Hen disappears. I fish out my phone. There are more missed calls and voicemails from Art. I ignore these and Google Manage Debt Online. The company doesn't appear to exist any more, at least under that name, but I find a newspaper article referring to it as a "loan-shark firm". I shake my head. Was Art in debt eight years ago? Is *that* what the payment I found was about? Is that why Art refuses to talk about it? That would explain why the payment was in a file marked 'Personal'.

I rest my head in my hands and close my eyes. I can hear Hen chatting at the door. She's apologizing for not inviting Josh's mum inside. Josh himself is grumbling about having to leave.

Maybe Hen's right . . . maybe it's a coincidence that Art paid money to MDO just after Beth.

My phone, still on silent, lights up. It's a text from Lorcan.

Just checking you're okay.

I hesitate for a second. Out in the hall Josh is continuing to make a fuss about going home. Both kids and both mums are talking. Loudly.

I call Lorcan. 'Hi,' I say softly.

'Are you all right?'

The sound of his voice calms me. I know I'm latching on to him because I'm feeling so vulnerable, but right now I feel safer with him than I do with Art – and more sure that he's not hiding anything from me than I can be with Hen.

'Do you fancy an early dinner?' I whisper, suddenly desperate to get away from Hen's house, from the domesticity and the pity. 'No talk about Beth, tonight, I promise. Just dinner.'

'Sure.' If Lorcan is surprised at my change of heart, he doesn't show it. He says he'll come straight over to pick me up.

'I'll be waiting at the end of the road.' I ring off.

Out in the hall, the front door shuts. I can hear Hen talking, trying to usher Nat upstairs. 'I know, but your hands are *filthy*,' she's saying.

I should go out there and tell her I'm leaving. If she really does think I'm deranged, my running off will only feed her suspicions. But my instincts are telling me that she is hiding something. Which must mean she's somehow involved.

Two sets of footsteps on the stairs indicate Hen has taken Nat up to the bathroom. I grab a pen from the pot on the side and scribble a note on the back of an envelope lying by the toaster.

Had to go. Sorry not to say goodbye. Gen x

Then I rush away. My heart's beating fast as I scuttle along the street. How has my life come to this? It occurs to me in a

224

moment of grim humour that if I wasn't insane before I'm certainly being driven mad now.

Maybe that's what they all want.

I reach the end of Hen's road and turn the corner so I'm out of sight of her house. I'm sure Hen will try and call me. Art too. I switch off my mobile and shove it deep into the bottom of my bag. As I lean against a lamp post, waiting for Lorcan, a single thought settles in my head: *I'm not going to give up until I know about Beth for sure.* However hard this gets, whatever I end up finding out and no matter what it costs, I'm following this through to the end. It's no longer about the past, it's about the future ... it's about tracking my daughter down. It's time to focus on where Beth is now ... to stop trying to find evidence she didn't die, and just find *her*.

I feel better. This, surely, is a plan. I can work from this point, looking at the records of births in the area where I had my baby. If she was adopted by another family, there must be paper-work ... a cover story ... I can check the local press and the internet for tales of babies born in suspicious circumstances. It's not much, but it's a start. It's something to build on.

A few minutes later Lorcan pulls up. It's a relief to sit inside his warm Audi and see his smiling face. 'You okay?' he asks.

'No.' I make a face. 'But I don't want to talk about it now.'

And we don't. I ask Lorcan more about his acting job in Cork while we drive north, to a restaurant he suggests in Finchley. He confesses that it's a limited part, that he feels trapped by the show's success.

As we leave the car, the wind whips up. I lean against Lorcan's arm. I have that sense I experienced before that his presence makes everything possible. I will find Beth. We sit down at a table in the window and I suddenly realize I've barely eaten all day. I order a steak.

'Tell me about your dad,' Lorcan says, as he pours us each a glass of wine.

'He was an alcoholic.' I trace around the base of the salt cellar on the table. 'Vodka mostly. But a functioning, happy drunk. At least in front of me he was.'

I stop, remembering how Dad would turn up and transform my dull, black-and-white world of school lessons and Brownie meetings into glorious technicolour, bursting with opportunity.

'He once just whisked me off to Stonehenge on a school night. "For an adventure," he said. That was what he was like with me. He made everything fun.'

'And yet he killed himself?' Lorcan says.

'No.' I feel a visceral revulsion at the idea. 'He didn't kill himself. He just drank too much.'

Lorcan raises his eyebrows and I have a flashback to my first day at university. Mum had dropped me off and we'd argued, as usual. She'd driven away and I'd sat in my tiny student room, gazing out of the window, watching the other dads hugging their daughters goodbye and hauling their cases and boxes inside their rooms. For a single, terrifying moment it had struck me that by choosing to drink to the point where it killed him, my dad had taken all those ordinary experiences away from us. From me. Not because he was glamorous and exciting and important – as I'd thought for so long – but because he was weak and sad and sick.

I push the hurtful memory out of my head, just like I did when I was eighteen. 'All of the times I spent with my dad were great. When he was around we'd play these wonderful games. Imaginary games. And he'd make up songs for me on his guitar.' I close my eyes, picturing my dad, his dark hair flopping over his forehead as he strummed away: '*This is* your *song, Queenie. All yours.*'

'My mum told me stories,' Lorcan says softly. 'My favourite was "The Children of Lir". D'you know it?'

I shake my head.

'It's an Irish folk tale about a king.' He smiles. 'The king has four children and their stepmother turns them into swans so they can't speak to him. They're apart for hundreds of years.'

I stare out of the window at the busy high street outside. 'Why is it that fairy tales are full of evil stepmothers?'

Is Beth somewhere with another mother right now? The thought shatters in my head. It's unthinkable that my child doesn't know me.

'We'll get her back, Gen.' Lorcan squeezes my hand.

I put my hand over my heart, almost trying to hold my feelings in. This is too hard. Too painful.

'Come on,' he says. We leave the restaurant. As we get back into Lorcan's car, he asks where I'd like him to take me.

I suggest coffee back at his. I've got no intention of staying over, but I can't face Art right now – and I'm not sure I want to see Hen either – though I'm aware both of them will be expecting me to turn up at some point later this evening.

Lorcan nods and drives away. We're soon in Hampstead. Lorcan has to park at the other end of his road from his flat. As we walk along the cold street, I catch a flash of a dark overcoat out of the corner of my eye. I turn, look over my shoulder, but there's no one there. I stare at the tree on the opposite side of the street. Is that a shadow or is someone lurking behind it?

'What?' Lorcan asks.

'Nothing.' I shake myself. But I'm not at all sure it is nothing.

Lorcan takes my hand. 'I don't think coffee's what you need,' he says with a chuckle. 'Maybe some Valium.'

I laugh. 'God, yes, please.'

The spooked feeling I'm experiencing persists. It really feels

227

like we're being watched. I look around again. This time I see him more clearly: dark overcoat tightly buttoned against the cold ... blond head ... pale, square face. I stop at the top of Lorcan's road, frozen with fear.

'What is it?' Lorcan says.

'It's the man we saw in the window at Rodriguez's house.'

'The blond guy?' Lorcan's eyes widen. 'Here?'

'Yes.' I nod. 'He's following us.'

CHAPTER FIFTEEN

We duck around the corner, down the next road. The houses are detached, with high brick walls. We dive along the side of the first house, then peer back round. My fingers are cold against the rough brick. The man following us is attempting to cross Lorcan's road but the traffic is thundering past, forcing him back. He is frowning, clearly desperate to pass.

'Oh, man.' Lorcan is looking now. I can feel him behind me, his chin brushing against the top of my head. 'You're right, that's definitely the guy from Rodriguez's house.'

The traffic is still dense, but the lights are changing up ahead. Soon the man will be able to cross.

'What do we do?' I say.

'Come on.' Lorcan reaches for my hand and pulls me down the street.

I look back, over my shoulder. No sign of the man. He appears at the corner as we reach the next turning. We race down the street.

'He's seen us,' I gasp, hurrying along the road. 'Hurry.'

'No.' Lorcan pulls me back. He indicates a gap between two of the houses. 'Let's wait there for him.'

'*Wait* for him?' I stare at Lorcan. 'Are you out of your mind? He's *following* us.'

'Then let's find out why. Let's stop him and ask him *why* he's following us.'

I open my mouth to argue with him, then I realize he's right. I need to find out what has happened to Beth. And this man must have some answers.

'Okay.' We scurry into the tiny alley between the two houses.

As I peer out, the blond man appears at the corner of the street. He looks up and down, uncertain, then breaks into a jog, heading towards us along the road. Lorcan is watching him, eyes intent. He presses his hand against my arm as the blond man draws nearer.

The blond man reaches the house just before the alley where we're hiding. He's looking round, clearly confused. Lorcan marches out.

'Hey!' he calls.

The blond man's eyes widen as Lorcan strides up.

'Why are you following us?' he demands.

'Where's Geniver Loxley?' The man is panting, trying to catch his breath as he rasps out the question. Now I'm closer to him I realize he's older than I thought – in his fifties at least, with plenty of grey mixed in with that blond, and a weather-beaten face.

Lorcan steps forward and grabs the man by the lapels. 'I asked *you* a question,' he snarls.

The blond man stumbles back. He's overweight and, as he pulls away, the shirt under his jacket strains over his belly. With a grunt he twists and ducks and somehow he's out of Lorcan's grip and lumbering away. Lorcan races after him. Catches him in a couple of steps. He slams the man against the wall.

I run over, panting. My breath spirals up in front of my face.

The man shrinks back, hands up in a gesture of surrender. He's trembling. There are dark shadows under his wide, terrified eyes. Lorcan shoves him in the chest.

'Who are you?' he snarls. 'Why are you following us?'

The man is open-mouthed now.

Across the road, a small knot of teenagers is staring at us. For a second I see the scene through their eyes: three middle-aged people in a fight – then my attention snaps back to Lorcan. He grabs the man's jacket and bunches the material up in his fist. His body radiates anger.

'It's not what you think,' the man says. He is still panting, breathless, but I notice his Midlands accent. He takes out an inhaler and draws a few puffs.

'So what is it then?' I say. 'Why are you here?'

'I'm here for you, Mrs Loxley,' he says. His eyes are watery – a soft, pale blue. He looks terrified and defeated and alone.

I stare at him. 'What do you mean?'

The man blinks rapidly. 'I . . . I have information you want.'

'What information?' Lorcan spits. He tightens his grip on the man's jacket. 'Is this another threat? Like this morning?'

The man cowers away. 'I don't know what you're talking about. I haven't threatened anyone.'

'It wasn't him.' I touch Lorcan's clenched fist. 'Let him go.'

Slowly, Lorcan releases the man's jacket. The teenagers over the road are still watching us.

'How do you know it isn't him?' Lorcan demands. 'You didn't see his face.'

'No, but this man is shorter than you are and the mugger was well over six feet.'

'What mugger?' The man looks horrified.

Lorcan turns to me.

'Are you sure?'

'Yes.' I lean closer and whisper in his ear. 'This *definitely* isn't the guy.' I turn to the man. 'But you *were* at Doctor Rodriguez's house; why did you follow us there?'

'I didn't, ma'am.' The man's forehead creases in an anxious frown. 'I was following Rodriguez. I broke into his house to look for information. I didn't know you were there until you left.'

'Information about what?' Lorcan asks.

'Anything that linked Rodriguez to your husband. A *recent* link.'

'What? Why?' I stare at him. His hair is thinning on top. I can see the pink of his scalp underneath his grey-blond comb-over. A strand of hair has come free. 'Who the hell are you?'

The man looks up, properly meeting my eyes for the first time. He smoothes the stray hair back over his head. 'I'm Bernard O'Donnell. You met my wife last week.'

He pulls his wallet and passport out of his pocket and, with trembling fingers, hands me both. Lorcan takes the passport and studies it.

'This looks real enough,' he says.

I open the wallet and find a picture of Bernard with Lucy O'Donnell.

'Oh.' I look up and see the pain in his watery eyes. 'I'm so sorry for your loss.'

Bernard looks away. 'Thank you.'

There's a silence. I take in the shiny patches on Bernard's suit and the scuff marks on his moccasin shoes. Everything is faded and worn, just as it was with Lucy. The teenagers over the road are moving away. A car squeals past us, its engine fading into the distance.

'I don't understand,' Lorcan says. 'What exactly are you trying to do? Why did you want to speak to Gen?'

Bernard looks up at him and gulps. 'I saw you both leaving Doctor Rodriguez's house.' He turns to me. 'I . . . I followed you here this morning after your class.'

I nod, remembering the spooked feeling I'd had earlier.

'You got in a car and I was on foot so I lost you. I've been waiting for you here ever since.'

'Outside my house?' Lorcan says.

Bernard stares at him. 'Excuse me, sir, but who are—?'

'This is Lorcan Byrne,' I explain quickly. 'He's a friend of mine. He knows what . . . what your wife told me.'

Bernard nods. 'Lucy was telling the truth about your baby, Mrs Loxley,' he says. 'And now she's . . . she's dead and I want to find out who killed her.'

'What do you mean "who killed her"?' What does this man know?

'Her death wasn't an accident.' Bernard's mouth trembles. 'I'm sorry, but I think your husband was involved.'

'Art?' My pulse races. 'What do you mean?'

'Someone murdered her.' Bernard's voice drops. 'Lucy always carried her handbag and yet the police couldn't identify her. Whoever made sure she was knocked down also organized someone to take her things. I think that person was looking for evidence of the baby being born alive. Your husband certainly had a motive to do all of that. So did the doctor.'

'So you think Art or Rodriguez had your wife killed in order to protect themselves?' Lorcan says slowly. 'And now you're looking for proof?'

'Exactly.'

'Why not go to the police yourself?' I ask.

'I did go.' Bernard sags against the wall behind him. 'I was scared to at first, but I couldn't bear the idea of Lucy lying in some police morgue . . .'

'What happened?' I ask.

'I . . . I identified the body, then the police explained they'd just had an anonymous call saying Lucy stepped out in front of a car, that it was an accident.'

'What about her missing bag?'

Bernard shrugs a single shoulder. His shirt under his jacket is creased and crumpled. I'm suddenly aware just how far out of his depth he feels. 'The police seemed to think it was more than likely someone stole it while the ambulance was on its way.' He sighs. 'I tried to suggest maybe it wasn't that straightforward but . . . anyway, if I tell the police everything I suspect, I put myself on the line when . . .' He tails off again.

'When *what*?' I hold my breath.

'When I know for sure if Rodriguez or your husband was involved,' Bernard says quietly. 'I'm sorry, I know this must be hard for you, but I'm not giving up. We were married for thirty-two years.' His voice cracks and he looks away.

A shiver wriggles through me.

'Why are you here now?' Lorcan eyes Bernard suspiciously.

'To tell you something . . . see if you can explain it, if that's okay, Mrs Loxley.' Bernard looks up at me, his eyes pleading with me to listen. 'See, I know you didn't believe Lucy last week, but she was telling you the truth.'

He means it. Like his wife, he sincerely believes Beth was born alive. A painful lump lodges itself in my throat. I sent Lucy away in anger. I dismissed her claims and then told Art. And now she is dead.

'Why don't we talk somewhere inside?' I suggest.

'Thank you,' Bernard says.

Lorcan and I exchange glances.

'Okay, let's go back to my place,' he says.

Five minutes later we're installed in Lorcan's living room. He fetches a bottle of whisky and three glasses. I take mine, but Bernard pushes his away and asks for water.

He listens intently as I explain what I know for sure: that I overheard Rodriguez admit to receiving money, that the anaesthetist present at Beth's birth, Gary Bloode, died mysteriously – and in a similar way to Lucy – and that the funeral home claims to have no record of who dealt with Beth's body.

Bernard nods slowly as I speak, acknowledging each fact in silence. But when I tell him about the memory stick with the CCTV footage, and the way in which it was stolen from me, he actually gasps.

'But surely that's the proof we need,' he says, hope lighting up his eyes. 'The proof Lucy's sister was telling the truth – your husband *and* the doctor *were* involved.'

I shake my head. 'Art says the film must have been faked. Anyway, I don't have it any more and—'

'You *showed* him this film?' Bernard's mouth falls open.

'No,' I explain, 'I just told him about it—'

'And then it was stolen from you?' Bernard wrings his hands. 'Who else knew you *had* the memory stick?'

'Dr Rodriguez.' I hesitate. 'To be honest, I don't see how Art could possibly have had time to organize someone to mug me. He didn't know about the CCTV film until I told him just a few minutes before I was attacked.'

Bernard looks at Lorcan. The two men exchange a knowing glance. With a jolt I realize they think I don't want to admit the truth.

'Art could have known you had that memory stick all along,' Lorcan says gently. 'He could have just pretended he didn't so that you wouldn't suspect him.'

'But we heard Rodriguez phone someone else … someone who definitely *wasn't* Art.' Desperation rises inside me. My instincts and all the evidence point towards Art. Why is it so hard for me to acknowledge his guilt out loud?

'That just proves another person is involved,' Lorcan says. 'It doesn't prove Art *isn't* involved.'

'That's true, Mrs Loxley,' Bernard adds.

'I know.' I feel humiliated by the admission. My voice comes out small and flat. A dull ache spreads across my chest and I look down, Lorcan's carpet blurring at my feet.

Lorcan strokes my cheek with his thumb – an intimate gesture, full of concern and affection. Something inside me shifts and slips – a mix of desire and relief. I'm not alone.

Lorcan drops his hand and I follow his gaze to Bernard. I wonder what he is thinking about us.

'You said you had something to tell Gen,' Lorcan says. 'Something you thought she might be able to make sense of.'

'Yes.' Bernard gulps nervously. 'I was wondering if you knew what it is your husband does when he goes to that little hotel near . . . where was it?' He fumbles in his jacket pocket.

'I don't know about any hotel,' I say. I press my fingertips hard against my palms. I'm not sure how many more revelations I can take.

Bernard fishes a business card out of his pocket. It contains a picture of a pub hotel with the name 'Wardingham Arms, Andover' written across the front.

'It's in Hampshire. I followed your husband there two days ago. He checked in for the afternoon.'

'And?' Lorcan frowns. He turns to me. 'Did you know Art was going here?'

I think back to Monday. 'Art said he was at an out-of-office meeting all day. He got home just after eight.'

Bernard runs a fleshy hand over his blond hair. 'Apparently your husband's a regular visitor to the hotel. This time he arrived at one p.m.,' he says, staring intently at me. 'He left at six that evening and drove back to London.'

'The timing fits,' Lorcan says. 'Two hours to drive back to London's about right.'

'So what did he do at this hotel?' I ask. 'It could have been a business meeting.'

'It's not that kind of place,' Bernard says.

'How do you know he stayed in his room all that time?' Lorcan adds.

'I was in the hotel lobby or the restaurant all afternoon. And they both overlook the front of the hotel, so I was watching the car park almost the whole time too. The hotel is in the middle of nowhere. If Mr Loxley went anywhere he'd have taken his car and I'd have seen.'

'He could have got a taxi,' I suggest.

'No record of any taxis leaving that afternoon,' Bernard says. 'They keep a log and I made some excuse and got them to check. Anyway, I'm certain I'd have seen Mr Loxley if he'd left the building.'

'Well, maybe someone came to him, then.' I blush, my mind racing ahead over the ramifications of what I've just said. There's usually only one reason why men spend anonymous afternoons in out-of-the-way hotel rooms. And yet surely Art can't have been unfaithful to me? Surely, if he had, I would know?

Bernard blushes too. 'I suppose it's possible that someone did slip up to see him when I was in the restaurant, but I don't think it's very likely. It's a small place and definitely no one else checked in the whole time I was there.'

He gets up to go to the bathroom and I lean back on Lorcan's sofa. I can't hide from the evidence any longer. Art was in a hotel when he said he was in a meeting. I press my fingers into my forehead and close my eyes. How can I trust anything he says now? It all adds up . . . all the suspicious behaviour: the fact that someone called him twelve times in one day and he didn't even mention it; the way he shredded all the papers about Beth and made a payment to a debt company just after she was born

– which, for some reason, Hen knows about, but which Art chose to keep from me. In fact, *all* the conversations with Hen. And then, most terrible of all, there's the CCTV footage from the Fair Angel hospital showing Art with our baby. I'm certain, now, that Lorcan and Bernard are right to dismiss Art's claims that the film is a fake. If it could be proved false, why would anyone want to steal it and threaten me?

I remember my resolution to focus only on the future . . . only on finding Beth . . . but the overwhelming feeling in my heart right now is betrayal. How can Art have done any of this?

There's a creak on the floor in front of me. I look up. Lorcan has squatted in front of me. He holds my gaze.

'We will find Beth,' he says.

We look at each other for a long moment.

'I want to go to the hotel,' I say, trying to keep my voice steady. 'I want to find out what Art does there . . . see if it's connected to Beth—' My voice cracks.

Lorcan checks his watch. 'Okay, we'll set off in the morning. It's too late now – we can't arrive in the middle of the night.'

I nod, then look along the corridor to where Bernard is coming back from the bathroom.

'I want to go via my house in the morning.' I lower my voice. 'After Art's gone to work.'

'Why?'

Bernard walks into the living room.

'I'd like to give you something for trying to help me,' I say. 'I know it was on Lucy's mind, about your two kids still at home and . . .' I stammer to a halt, not wanting to embarrass him.

Lorcan tilts his head slightly to one side. I can't tell if he thinks I'm mad to be offering Bernard money. Bernard himself tugs self-consciously at his shirt collar.

'I . . . er, that is Lucy and I . . .' He tails off.

Lorcan gets up and slaps Bernard on the back. 'It's late. Why don't you stay here tonight?'

Bernard shakes his head. 'No, I'll get back to my hotel . . . I'll come over again in the morning.'

Lorcan follows him down to the front door to see him out. I switch on my phone. It's crammed full of voice messages and texts. Most are from Art but there are also several from Hen and even one each from Sue and my mum, whose message begins: *What on earth are you—*

I don't open the rest of her text – or any of the others. I can only imagine that Art and Hen must have contacted Sue and Mum – and I have neither the energy nor the desire to deal with their concern right now. I switch off the mobile, then lean back on the sofa. I close my eyes. The image from the CCTV footage of Art holding the baby . . . our baby . . . drifts in front of my mind's eye.

Exhaustion creeps like a thief through my bones.

In my dream I'm running. Images jumble inside my mind, one after the other, fast. Beth is ahead of me, unseeing. She's eight, with her dark hair in long plaits that fly out behind her as she runs. Then my dad scoops her up and she's much younger, only two or three and he holds her up, high in the air, and she squeals with delight. My dad lowers her and swings her round. Mum is standing on the sidelines, calling out for him to put her down. I'm running towards them but I get no closer. Then all three of them turn to face me. Dad's dark eyes are angry. Have I made him angry? Mum is shouting, 'Grow up, you're pathetic.' Beth starts crying. She's eight again, her mouth trembling with grief. I have to reach her, have to hold her. But the closer I get, the further away she is. She waves at me, helpless. Tears leak down her face. I'm reaching out for her, crying her name. Then she is gone and I'm alone in our living room with Dad. He's looking at the picture I have of him as a boy. 'Where did you get this, Geniver?' he demands, his dark eyes still angry. 'Why isn't Beth here? What have you done with her?'

I wake to sunshine streaming in through a gap in the living-room curtains. There's a crick in my neck but I'm warm and lying on the sofa where I must have fallen asleep. Someone – Lorcan presumably – has removed my shoes, lain me down and covered me with a blanket. His jacket hangs on the side of the sofa. I catch its scent. It smells of him – of wood shavings and lemongrass.

The house is silent for a moment, then I hear water running in the shower. I sit up, massaging my neck as the water is switched off.

Lorcan appears, hair dripping, a towel round his waist. My eyes are drawn to his broad chest matted with damp hair, to the curve of the muscles on his arms. Then I realize I'm staring and abruptly look away.

'Bernard's on his way,' Lorcan says. 'Cup of tea?'

I nod and Lorcan disappears into the kitchen. I pad down to the bathroom, splashing water on my face and rubbing some toothpaste over my teeth with my finger.

When I come back to the kitchen a steaming mug of tea and a plate of toast are waiting for me. I eat hungrily. Lorcan – now dressed in jeans and a plain black jumper – watches me. I'm suddenly aware of my unbrushed hair and creased sweater and squirm self-consciously in my seat.

'I'd like to go home and fetch some clothes,' I say. 'And if I'm going to transfer money to Bernard without Art as co-signatory, I'll need proper ID . . .'

Lorcan raises his eyebrows. 'How much are you planning on giving him?'

I shrug. 'I don't know, but more than I can get unless I use this particular account.'

'You don't have to pay him anything,' Lorcan insists. 'He'll help you without it. He just wants justice for his wife.'

'I know,' I say. 'But his wife died because she told me about Beth. I have to do *something*.'

A few minutes later Bernard appears and a few minutes after that the three of us pile into Lorcan's car and he drives us to Crouch End. As we near my house I check the time. It's 8.30, half an hour before Lilia arrives and well past the time Art usually leaves for work, but I call his iPhone just to make sure. I'm psyched up for Art to answer, steeling myself against the sound of his voice. But the call goes straight to voicemail, so I ring the office number. Siena puts me straight through.

'Gen?' Art's voice is strained to breaking point. 'Gen, thank God, where are you?'

I switch off the phone. 'He's definitely in the office.' Lorcan parks outside the house and I open the car door. 'Wait here, I won't be long.'

I let myself in at the front door and head straight for our bedroom. There are signs of Art's presence everywhere: clothes on the floor, a half-drunk cup of coffee by the bed. A towel lies strewn across the duvet. I pick it up and experience the familiar irritation that it is damp. As I place it back in the bathroom, I'm struck by how natural these intimacies of our marriage still feel. In spite of what I've learned about Beth and how increasingly close I feel to Lorcan, this room and the relationship it represents is still the centre of my life.

I fetch a hold-all and start hauling clothes out of drawers. I fill a small bag with toiletries from the bathroom, where Art's razor lies on its side by the sink, then go downstairs to fetch my passport from the cupboard in the living room. Using it as ID

241

will be the easiest and quickest way for me to get my hands on the money I want to give Bernard O'Donnell.

As I come into the hall again, the sound of a creaking floor-board fills the silence. I freeze. The sound is coming from Art's office on the second floor. Someone is up there. I stand, stock still, holding my breath. Another creak. I've only just spoken to Art, I know it isn't him. So who else could possibly be here? They must have heard me crashing about in the bedroom just below them. Why didn't they make themselves known?

Perhaps it's Lilia. She could be early – and she often cleans with her iPod playing. Maybe she didn't hear me before. I step onto the stairs and peer up towards the first-floor landing. I can't see any part of the second floor from here.

Another creak.

A bead of sweat trickles down the back of my neck. And then I hear the soft brushing sound of footsteps on the carpeted second-floor stairs – the footsteps of someone padding down to the first floor, trying not to make any noise.

I stand for a second, gripping my bag tightly. Silence.

Instinct tells me it's not Lilia. Then who? If it's the guy who mugged me before, then why hasn't he already come to find me?

There's no further sound. My whole body is tensed, waiting. Perhaps I imagined the noises I heard. Like Art once said, those office floorboards have a mind of their own.

'Hello?' I call out. My voice sounds croaky to my ears. 'Is someone there?'

'Geniver?' A familiar voice drifts down the stairs.

And then the last person I expected to see comes into view.

CHAPTER SIXTEEN

I stand at the bottom of the stairs, still clutching my little bag, looking up at Art's sister.

'*Morgan?*' My mouth drops open. 'What are you doing here?'

Morgan stares down at me. She is dressed to perfection, as usual, in a pale grey skirt, tailored blouse and her trademark kitten heels. Her lipstick is a soft pink, to match her nails and the coral chain that hangs around her neck. But there's nothing soft in her expression.

'What the hell is up with you, Geniver?' she demands. 'My brother is going out of his mind.'

Anger wells up inside me. How dare Morgan leap right in like that and judge me?

'You don't know what you're talking about,' I snap.

Morgan picks her way down the stairs and brushes past me. I turn to follow her. The hallway, as always, is cluttered with coats and bags, with a teetering pile of magazines in the corner. We face each other at the foot of the stairs.

'This has to stop,' Morgan says, giving her foot a little stamp. There's a fleck of spittle resting on the lipstick in the corner of her mouth. I get a perverse sense of pleasure from seeing this chink in her armour. 'I spoke to Art last night. He told me what you accused him of and he's *devastated*. I dropped everything and rushed over straightaway.'

She knows about the private things I've said to Art *and* she's been here overnight. *In my house.* I let my bag fall to the ground.

'This isn't any of your business,' I say. 'You don't know the whole story.'

Morgan's thin eyebrows arch dramatically. 'About your baby? Of course I know the whole story. *Everyone* knows the whole story. You and Art lost your daughter. We were all so sad for you both. Art pulled himself together and got on with his life. Brilliantly. You let the whole thing drag you down to the point where you've become a millstone around Art's neck.'

'Shut up.' My hands clench with fury.

'And now this . . . this hysterical nonsense—'

'How dare you talk to me like this? You've got no idea.' But even as I speak, I'm flooding with shame. Morgan's right, though I don't want to face it. I have let what happened drag me down . . . let my life stagnate, while Art's has exploded with colour and opportunity.

I have to get away. I pick up my bag and try to walk past Morgan, but she grabs my arm.

'Listen,' she says. 'I know I'm being hard-assed here, I understand it's hard to move on. I just can't bear to see what you're doing to Art.'

'What about what Art's done to me?' I wrench my arm away.

'Is it that you think he's having an affair?'

I stare at her. Why would she think that? My mind flashes back to the hotel room Art was in on Monday afternoon. What does she know?

'No,' I say, hoping I sound more sure than I feel.

'Good, because he would *never* be unfaithful to you.'

'For God's sake, Morgan. You don't know what Art's capable of.'

'Yes, I do,' Morgan snarls. 'I'm his sister. I know him better than you think, Geniver. Maybe even better than you. Don't you see? He loves you. He's sacrificed *everything* for you.'

'What?' I glare at her. 'Sacrificed *what*?'

'Children for one thing.' Morgan's mouth trembles slightly. 'You won't do IVF. You're making him suffer because you don't have the guts to move on.'

Again, shame floods me. My heart is pounding. I *hate* her. I absolutely *hate* her.

Morgan glances at my bag. 'Where are you going?'

'Get out of my house.' My voice rises.

'Art invited me to stay.' Morgan flicks her dark hair over her shoulder. A gesture of defiance.

'Did he invite you to rummage around in his office too?' I snap, remembering the creaking floorboards that betrayed her presence.

Morgan rolls her eyes. 'He rang me just now to ask me to look something up in a file for him. I'm waiting for my car, then I'm into town for a meeting.' She tilts her head to one side. 'Doesn't Art ever ask *you* to help him like that, Geniver? After all, you're at home all day.' She pauses, a sneer creeping across her lips. 'No, I suppose he doesn't. Not reliable enough.'

I'm so angry I can't speak. In the back of my mind I know that my fury is partly because Morgan has touched a nerve. But she has no right to say any of this.

Morgan sniffs. She looks at my bag again. 'Where were you last night?' she asks. 'Maybe it's *you* having the affair?'

'What? *Jesus*, Morgan . . .'

'You've been with Lorcan Byrne, haven't you?'

I freeze.

'Nothing's happened.' The words are out of my mouth before I realize how guilty they make me sound.

'Between you and Lorcan?' Morgan raises an eyebrow. '*Really?* I've met the man before. I know how he operates.'

What the hell does that mean?

'How do you know I've even *seen* Lorcan?' I say.

'Art told me,' Morgan says. 'And Hen knows all about it too. She called Art after you ran out on her last night. It was obvious to both of them that you'd gone to *him*. Poor Hen was *weeping* down the phone.' Morgan shakes her head. 'You put her in a terrible position, Geniver. It's very selfish.'

'*What?*'

'Oh, come on. Art and Hen know Lorcan's reputation as well as I do.'

'You mean the reason he got fired?' I say. 'That was a long time ago. Lorcan's just been helping me.'

Morgan throws me a contemptuous look. 'I bet he's outside waiting for you in his car right now.'

I say nothing. Fear swirls about my head. And embarrassment, too. It's humiliating to think of Art discussing me and Lorcan with Hen and Morgan.

'I saw the way he looked at you at Art's party. Same old Lorcan. Like a wolf who's picked out a sacrificial lamb.' She pauses, her eyes widening. 'God, is it *him* who's fed you these ridiculous ideas about Art?'

'No. And they're not ridiculous.'

'It *is* him,' Morgan persists. 'And I bet he's denied sleeping with the client's wife at the start of Loxley Benson too.' Morgan snorts.

'We haven't talked about it, Morgan. Like I said, it was all a long time ago.'

I force myself to stop. I should just leave, and yet Morgan's words about Lorcan being a wolf are running circles in my head.

Morgan senses my uncertainty.

'Look, this is really hard for me to tell you, but I want you to

246

know the truth.' She draws closer and I get a whiff of her perfume. A dark, dense, herby smell. 'It's not just that client's wife. When Lorcan and Art travelled round the States there wasn't a drug Lorcan didn't take. And he got Art to try plenty of them too.'

'So what?' Lorcan and Art have already told me about this. 'They were in their early twenties. It was years ago.'

'It's not just the drugs.' Morgan purses her lips. 'Lorcan slept with about twenty women on that trip. Most of them were older and wealthy. He *used* them, Geniver. And it wasn't just on vacation. I know of at least three similar cases back home. And when he was friends with Art he often juggled two women without the other's knowledge. Art told me.' She pauses. 'Did you know Lorcan has got someone in Ireland right now?'

Her self-righteousness is almost funny. And yet, if I'm honest, I don't want to hear that Lorcan has a reputation as some kind of womanizer.

'I know he has a girlfriend,' I say. 'He told me. Anyway, the rest of it is ancient history. You don't know anything about Lorcan now.'

'People don't change. Believe me.'

'Right.' I march past her to the door. I want her out of my house, but Art has asked her here. He has turned to her, like he turned to Hen, because I went away. And everything is such a mess.

I walk out, my eyes full of tears, slamming the door behind me.

Lorcan raises his eyebrows as I get back in the car, but I shoot a warning glance at Bernard, hunched over in the back seat, and Lorcan takes the hint and says nothing.

We go to my bank and I request the transfer of £20,000 from the savings account that Art and I share to Bernard's account. I call the Art & Media Institute and say I'm ill again, too sick to take today's class. I just don't care anymore. Then I phone Jim Ralston, Art's accountant. I can't stop thinking about the money Art paid MDO and Hen's conviction that those initials stand for Manage Debt Online. Could terrible debts that I don't know about have something to do with Art's lies about Beth?

Jim Ralston answers my call straightaway – such is Art's influence these days. I explain I'm going over some old papers and was wondering how long I should keep financial records.

Jim goes into mind-numbing detail on the ins and outs of different types of records and their requirements. I let him talk for a minute or two, then ask if Art has any debts that I should be worried about.

'No.' Jim sounds a bit anxious. 'I don't understand. Why are you asking? Has Art said something?'

'No, it's just me,' I say quickly. 'Probably just being neurotic, not wanting to believe everything's really going as well as it is.'

'Well, you can believe it,' Jim says with a satisfied chuckle. 'Loxley Benson is making money hand over fist . . . bucking all economic trends, in fact. As MD, Art takes an excellent income from the business. But you know that, Geniver.'

'What about debts from the past?' I enquire.

'There was never that much debt, considering,' Jim says thoughtfully. 'Nothing to speak of now. Er, Geniver, if you don't mind my asking, what's all this about?'

'Nothing.' I get off the phone, feeling confused. If Art has never had terrible debts, then Hen must have been wrong about Manage Debt Online. And yet she seemed so sure. Of course, it's entirely possible Jim is lying – he works for Art rather than me, after all. But nothing I've ever seen makes me suspect Art has ever had large debts. He took a huge risk setting up Loxley Benson and the company's fate was certainly touch-and-go at first – but all that was fourteen years ago. Beth wasn't conceived for another six years after that – and Loxley Benson was doing really well by then.

The £20,000 is transferred to Bernard O'Donnell's account. It's a lot of money, but not that much in terms of our annual income. I remember Lucy O'Donnell saying they were struggling, and how I'd thought she was lying to get money out of me. I know this payment to Bernard is partly an attempt to assuage my guilt but it's surely better than doing nothing. After all, if I'd taken Lucy seriously when she came to see me, she might still be alive. The money I'm giving her husband is my apology.

I don't tell Bernard how much I've transferred until it's done, then I walk back to where he and Lorcan are waiting in the Audi and hand Bernard the print-out.

'I hope this is useful,' I say.

Bernard looks down at the paper. His weather-beaten face crumples with shock. He looks up at me, his mouth gaping open.

'I can't believe this,' he stammers. 'I thought you were just going to cover my travel costs. You didn't have to do it, Mrs Loxley. Lucy and me, we always managed okay . . .'

'She told me you had two kids still at home,' I say. 'I just wanted to help a little, especially now . . . now they've lost their mother . . .'

He nods. 'Thank you,' he says, his eyes filling with tears.

'It's nothing,' I say, looking away. 'It's the least I can do.'

We drop Bernard back at Lorcan's so he can pick up his hire car. He's planning to spend the next few hours following Art again, while Lorcan and I check out the Wardingham Arms. I'm aware this is a dangerous tactic. It's risky for Bernard, and if Art has any idea he is being watched he will surely try to cover his tracks, leaving me further away from finding Beth than ever. But Bernard is determined – and confident he can act without detection.

SOPHIE MCKENZIE

I wish him luck, then we exchange numbers and agree to talk again this afternoon.

As we drive off, Lorcan asks me what's wrong ... what happened when I went home earlier. I don't tell him about Morgan – I just say I'm upset about Art deceiving me. And yet Morgan's accusations continue to prey on my mind.

The traffic is bad getting out of London, but once we're on the motorway, the sun comes out and the roads clear. Lorcan and I talk about everything other than Art and Rodriguez. We talk about books and films: what we like, what we've read and seen. And we talk about all the other things in our lives. Our work, our childhoods, our children ... I tell Lorcan more about my dreams of Beth. He listens attentively as I go into all the little details my unconscious has imagined – her thick, dark hair ... the birth mark on her left shoulder ... the open, joyful expression on her face as I dreamed her blowing out the candles on her last birthday cake.

Lorcan tells me more about Cal, how he regrets spending so much time away from him ... how he doesn't feel he knows him or understands him at the moment. He tells me that he'd really love to do more live theatre, but keeping Cal at his private school makes that impossible.

I talk about my writing, about the books I got published and the idea I was working on when Beth's death slammed my brain shut.

'My last book was called *Rain Heart*,' I explain. 'About a woman discovering her husband is having an affair with his business partner's wife.'

'Based on something that really happened?' Lorcan raises his eyebrows.

I shake my head, remembering Charlotte West asking the same question. I gaze out of the car window, wondering if

250

I've been hopelessly naive. What other reason than an affair can there be for Art spending the afternoon in a hotel so far from work?

'Do you think Art's having an affair now?' I ask.

Lorcan shrugs. 'What do you think?'

'I don't know.' It's still hard to believe Art would be unfaithful, but then until a week ago it would have been unthinkable to imagine him faking our baby's death.

Now, anything seems possible.

The journey passes quickly and, soon after midday, we pull up outside the Wardingham Arms. The car park is at the front of the hotel, just as Bernard O'Donnell described.

As we walk inside, my chest tightens. We're close to the truth now. I can feel it. The inn is old and, despite the sunshine outside, the lobby feels dark and cool. A couple of chairs are set around a coffee table made of the same dark wood as the panelled walls. An elderly man wearing a cravat and sporting a comb-over looks up from the reception desk on the far wall. He smiles a slightly stiff, formal welcome.

'May I help you?' he says.

'A friend of ours recommended you. Art Loxley.'

The landlord nods. 'Ah, Mr Loxley. One of our regulars. That's nice to hear.'

My stomach cartwheels. So it really is true.

The landlord opens his book. 'You're in luck, we're pretty quiet at the moment.'

'He really liked the room you gave him last time, on Monday I think?' I press my fingers hard against the reception desk, trying to keep my voice breezy and casual. 'Is there any chance we could have that one?'

The landlord frowns. 'Mmm, well, yes, I suppose as it's free . . .'

251

A few minutes later we're inside room seven – full of the same dark wood furniture as downstairs, including a huge bed with a large, plum-coloured quilt that drapes to the floor. I sit down on the edge of the bed and finger the quilt. Art has been in this very room. But with whom? There's Hen, of course, but Hen and Art live just ten minutes' drive from each other in North London, so it seems unlikely they would conduct secret trysts all the way out here. My mind settles on Sandrine. She's stylish, vivacious and smart and, for all I know, she and Art have been going on "business trips" together for months, if not years.

Lorcan wanders to the window. 'This place isn't huge, someone must have noticed if Art met anyone here.'

I stare at the cream-coloured lamp beside the bed, imagining Sandrine's slender fingers reaching for the light, then Art pulling her towards him, his eyes full of desire. The thought sickens me.

'Gen?'

I hadn't even heard Lorcan speaking. I look up.

'Do you think it's worth searching the room to see if Art left anything behind? I know it's a long shot, but . . .' He tails off without pointing out what is obvious to both of us: we have absolutely nothing else to go on.

I suddenly feel terribly depressed. After the frenetic activity of the past twenty-four hours, we seem to have hit a dead end. So what if Art was here? It doesn't bring me any closer to Beth.

I agree to search the room anyway. What else are we going to do? I follow Lorcan's lead, turning out drawers and searching the nooks and crannies of the wardrobe, desk area and bathroom. I leave the bed to Lorcan. I can't bring myself to pore over the sheets, even though I'm well aware that the linen will have been changed since Art's visit.

An hour passes. We find nothing and learn nothing. I go

downstairs and chat to the landlord. I ask him if the hotel ever hosts functions, which leads me neatly to a mention of Art's birthday party. I refer to Art's "girlfriend" as I talk, but the landlord doesn't pick up on this at all. As far as I can make out, Art checks in alone.

Back upstairs, the window in the room won't open and the air becomes heavy and stuffy. I switch on my phone for the first time since this morning and find yet more texts and messages. I make myself deal with the latest communications – there's a fresh text from Hen, saying she's worried about me and asking me to call her and two new voicemails from Art – both of which are rambling and frantic. '*Please, Gen, call me. This is madness. That film of yours must be a fake. Please, Gen, I'm so worried about you. Call me. I love you more than anything in the world. Please believe me.*' And on and on . . .

I switch off the phone again and look round to find Lorcan gazing thoughtfully at me. 'Let's take a break,' he says.

I stand up. Outside the sun is streaming across the treetops.

'We could go for a drive?' he suggests. 'See if we see anything that might explain what Art's doing here . . . you know, anything connected with the area.'

I nod and we set off. Lorcan drives slowly along the country roads. There's another inn – the Princess Alice – just a couple of hundred yards away from the Wardingham Arms. Otherwise, there's nothing for almost a mile in every direction, save for a couple of farmhouses set back from the road.

We drive on, into a small village where we get out and wander about. We go to a café and order sandwiches. I check my phone again. More messages from Art. This time I don't listen to them. I call Bernard, as arranged. He reports that Art has spent the whole day so far in the office.

I come off the phone and rest my head in my hands.

'What do we do now?' I moan. 'We're not getting anywhere and Art *knows* I think he's lying to me, so if he's got tracks to cover up, he'll be covering them up right now.'

I close my eyes, despair weighing down on me.

'We should go back to the inn and talk to the staff there again,' Lorcan says.

'What's the point?' I sigh. 'I don't think the landlord was lying to us. Art comes on a regular basis. He stays in his room. Period. We don't even know what we're looking for.'

Lorcan looks up from his sandwich.

'So what are you saying?' he says. 'D'you want to give up?'

I fold my arms and look out of the café window. Outside the sky is clouding over. The air – so light and sunny before – now seems grey and oppressive. A few drops of rain spatter the pavement. I feel irritated. I almost itch with it.

'Of course I don't bloody want to give up. What's your problem, only interested when there's some drama to get caught up in?'

'Hey, I'm doing my best to help you here.' Lorcan shoves his plate across the table and sits back in his chair.

There's a tense silence.

'I never asked for your help,' I snap. I know I'm being rude, but I can't stop myself. 'You offered. Anyway, you said you had nothing better to do.'

Lorcan looks up. He half smiles. 'Doesn't sound very chivalrous when you put it like that.'

I shrug, his smile disarming me. 'I'm not looking for chivalry.' The rain is falling harder now, drizzling down the window beside us. For some reason I find this soothing. I reach over and put my hand on Lorcan's arm. 'I'm sorry I snapped. I couldn't do this without you. It's just . . .' My voice wobbles under the swell of my emotions. 'This whole thing . . . I feel like I'm going insane.'

Lorcan nods but he doesn't speak. The silence builds between us. My mind goes back to Hen's suggestion that Lorcan could have faked the CCTV footage, and to Morgan's earlier accusation.

Like a wolf who's picked out a sacrificial lamb.

'So why *are* you helping me?' I keep my voice carefully cool and calm.

Lorcan looks up. We look at each other for a long moment.

'I'm sorry,' he says at last.

'What for?' I hold my breath.

The rain lashes harder against the window. It makes the street outside blurry. I wait, watching him . . .

'There's something I need to tell you.' Lorcan says slowly. 'Two things, actually. The first is that I called the girl I've been seeing in Ireland . . . I did it last night, after you'd gone to sleep. I told her we were over.'

'Oh.' I can feel my face reddening.

He reaches for my hand. His voice is low and intense. 'Okay, listen to me. I finished with Hayley because once I met you I realized that she was never the right person. Not that I ever thought she was . . .' He tails off.

My heart hammers in my chest. What's he saying? That leaving her is something to do with me?

'Christ, I'm shite at this.' Lorcan lets go of my hand. He shifts awkwardly in his seat, looking uncharacteristically unsure of himself. 'I wanted to tell you that before I went on to tell you the other thing.'

'What other thing?' I say, my heart racing.

'You know the information you've been told about me?' Lorcan says. 'The information about what happened at Loxley Benson . . .'

'You mean sleeping with that client's wife?'

He nods. His face is tight with tension.

SOPHIE MCKENZIE

'Look, it was a long time ago. It doesn't matter now.'

'No, it's important,' Lorcan says. 'I want you to know the truth.'

'The truth about what?'

'That night,' he says. 'That night fourteen years ago.'

I wait, watching him.

'I slept with a lot of women in my early twenties but then . . . so do most men, if they get the chance, wouldn't you say?' Lorcan says. 'I'm not trying to justify everything I did. There were quite a few older women, married women who . . . anyway, that doesn't matter now.' He breathes out, a heavy sigh. 'When I met you, the night of the party, I was angry at the way my . . . my history at Loxley Benson was all anyone saw when they looked at me.'

'What d'you mean?' I say. 'Nobody mentioned that, except Kyle and Art, and I *made* them tell me.'

'No.' Lorcan shakes his head slowly. 'Back when it happened, Art told everyone and they haven't forgotten. It was a public disgrace. He made a scapegoat of me just so he could keep that client.'

'But—' I want to tell him it was his own fault for sleeping with someone else's wife. 'But Art said you threatened Loxley Benson's survival. You couldn't seriously expect him to stand by and do nothing. Anyway, you told me you were ready to leave before it happened.'

'No, it's not like you think,' he says. 'It's not like Art said.' He lets out another deep sigh. 'I'm trying to explain . . . why I came back the next day after we had the take-out. The truth is I left that Swiss Army knife behind on purpose. I wanted to annoy Art by turning up out of the blue and seeing you . . . I wanted to get back at him.'

'Get back at him?' I don't understand what he's saying. 'Get

256

back at Art for firing you when you wanted to leave anyway? When Loxley Benson would have gone under if that client had taken his business away?'

Lorcan lowers his voice. 'I did want to leave and Loxley Benson would have gone under. That's all true. But you're missing the point. You see . . .' He pauses, fixing me with his intense gaze. The sights and sounds of the café fade to nothing. 'It wasn't *me* that slept with the client's wife.'

'What?' My head spins.

'It was Art,' Lorcan says.

'*Art?*' I draw in my breath sharply. '*Art* slept with the client's wife.'

'Yes.'

I sit back, trying to absorb this information. It all happened before I met Art, of course. I knew he'd had other girlfriends. There were a few short-term relationships during his teens, then a girl called Emma at university. Art has never said that much about any of them. He's certainly never told me he slept with anyone who was married. I look up at Lorcan, tense with suspicion.

'So what happened?'

Lorcan leans forward, lowering his voice further. 'The four of us were out. The client, his wife, Art and me. She was coming on to both of us whenever her husband went to the bar or the bathroom. I know it sounds bad, but Art and I were both single. All four of us were drunk. It just *happened*.'

'How?'

'You want the details?' Lorcan's eyes widen. 'Okay. We all ended up back at the client's house. The husband fell asleep on the sofa. The wife was all over us. I think she was after some sort of threesome, but I wasn't interested. She was too drunk and too needy . . . plus, no way was I ending up in bed with a man.' He gives a wry, weary laugh. 'So . . . I went home. Art stayed. He left after they shagged, but the husband found Art's watch in the bed later on the next day, when his wife was out.'

My hand flies to my mouth. I'm remembering the first date Art and I ever went on. I'd teased him because he seemed such a focused guy and yet he'd had to keep asking me what the time was. I'd only been joking, but Art was really insistent that he normally had a watch. That he'd lost his just a few weeks earlier and wasn't used to being without it. I remember asking him how he'd lost it and him saying, with a blush, that he'd left it somewhere he should never have gone in the first place. That's why I bought him a new watch for his birthday the following March.

'What happened next?' I say.

'The client called his wife . . . accused her . . . told her to come home. On the way she told Art and Art gave me money to take the rap.'

'Art *paid* you to say it was you? So he could pretend to fire you and make the client believe he'd dealt with you and keep the business?'

'Of course he did. It was ruthless and controlling and very, very Art. He had to grovel to the client, but it worked. I left, and Loxley Benson kept the client and the rest is history.'

I realize I'm chewing on my nail and take my finger out of my mouth. I can so clearly recall Art telling me about Lorcan's betrayal. He'd sounded totally convincing. And yet, it was a lie. *Another* lie. I feel sick at the thought of my past with Art – a past built on deceptions and cover-ups. I thought I could trust him. I thought we were on solid ground. And he has taken all that away from me.

There is nothing left that I can be sure of.

'I didn't let it bother me for a long time,' Lorcan explains. 'As

258

you've pointed out, I wanted to leave the company anyway, but the truth is I should never have let Art make up that story and I should never have taken his money. When I saw him again I could see that, after all this time, he almost believed his own version of events. He certainly didn't feel bad about what happened. I was angry and I wanted to get close to you to get back at him.'

My pulse thuds in my throat as Lorcan curls his fingers over my hand.

'I'm telling you this because I want to be honest,' he says. 'That's how this started – why I offered to help you in the first place. I wasn't humouring you exactly, but I didn't really think there was the slightest chance Beth could still be alive until we heard Rodriguez talking about his money.'

I stare at him.

'But that's not how I feel now. Once I spent some time with you, I . . . it was different . . .'

I nod, feeling numb. Lorcan releases my hand as the waitress bustles over to remove our plates. I gaze out of the window again. It's misty from the rain. Lorcan rubs a patch of glass clear with the back of his hand. We sit in silence together for a few moments. Then Lorcan clears his throat.

'So . . . d'you want anything else to eat or will we go back to the inn?' he says quietly.

'Let's go back.'

We pay, then wander back to the car in silence.

My mind's going over what's just happened . . . what *is* happening. Everything Lorcan has just told me adds up to yet another accusation against Art. And yet that's not why he told me . . . he told me because he cares what I think of him, because . . .

I stare out of the window. I don't want to face this.

259

The rain has slowed to a soft drizzle by the time we pull up at the Wardingham Arms, the clouds darkening the sky so much that I'm startled when I check the time and discover it's only just gone four.

I'm hoping the landlord will have been replaced by another member of staff, but he's still there, smoothing down his comb-over as we approach. We nod at him, but we don't speak until we're inside our room. My heart races as Lorcan stands in front of me.

He puts his hand on my arm. His touch burns.

'Gen?'

I shake my head. I know he's asking how I feel ... what I want ...

'Okay.' He smiles. 'I'll go and book another room.'

A beat passes. I don't know what to think about anything. I'm tired and I'm stressed. Lorcan smiles again and walks out.

I sink onto the bed and look around the room. The inn is old and the floor slopes downwards towards the bathroom. It's clean and it's tasteful. Nothing sleazy. It strikes me again that I am sitting on the bed Art used.

A few minutes later, Lorcan's back.

'I'm booked in two doors down,' he says. 'Want to see?'

Silently, I follow him along to his room. I walk inside. It's similar to mine, but with everything set out in mirror-image reversal.

Lorcan folds me into a hug. I lean my head against his chest. I can feel his heart beating. I look up and he leans down. A soft kiss that brushes my lips. Sweet. My breath catches in my throat. Another kiss. Deeper. This time desire shoots through me.

Desire and fear.

I pull away. 'I can't do this.'

'Okay.' Lorcan breathes out. 'Okay.'

I don't know what to do. My heart is pounding and panic fills my whole body. 'I . . . it just isn't . . . I'm not . . .'

'It's fine.' He says, but his voice isn't entirely steady. 'It's absolutely fine.'

I turn and walk out. I'll go back to my room. I'll sit still until my heart stops hammering. I'll have a drink.

I reach the door of my room. I stop. Look back along the corridor.

I don't want to be on my own. I don't want to calm down.

I don't want a drink.

I walk slowly back along the corridor. Knock on the door.

I can hear him cross the room. He opens the door.

I smile. He raises his eyebrows. I cross to the window, place my hands on the sill and peer out over the back garden. It's raining hard now. One of the lights at the side of the building has switched on and is casting a dim glow over the damp tarmac path.

I turn around.

He's staring at me, hungry and tender.

I turn around again, gazing out at the darkness, the lights. My heart's thudding.

His hand brushes up my arm. I shiver. He takes my hair and pulls it back, holding it away from my neck. Then he bends – I can see his reflection in the window – and he kisses the side of my neck. I feel his tongue and his mouth and his teeth, just light touches, radiating through me, making my breath shudder.

He pulls me round. Kisses my mouth. His hands are stroking my back. There's an urgency and a delicacy and he pulls me onto the bed and we're lying there and he kisses my neck again and now my whole body is trembling. And he takes off his clothes and I peel off mine and we're touching and kissing and

261

the smells and the sounds of us and what we're doing fill my head and there is no guilt and there is no confusion and it's just this moment where I'm somewhere I've never been and I can't think outside that and all I know is this is right this is right this is right.

After what happened with Ginger Tall and Broken Tooth, I dreamed about the Bad People a lot. In my dreams they were big and tall grown-ups with hoods over their faces so all I could see were their smiles except for bits when I would see mean eyes. They would come up behind me and grab me. I would try to cry out but my voice wouldn't work and the Bad People would take me away to a prison far away, like in The Special Child.

One night I remember I thought one of the Bad People was hiding in my bedroom. There was a big shadow from the dressing gown on the door and I thought it was a Bad Lady and I kept getting out of bed to see if she was there. Mummy came home and found me out of bed and she was cross. She said I must toughen up and not be scared and that I must be ready to fight if I had to. She said if I kept imagining the Bad Lady it would make a Bad Lady come in real life. Mummy said being strong is the most important thing and that everyone has to take care of themselves and look after their families and that dogs eat dogs so you have to kill them before they eat you.

She said she didn't mean real dogs.

CHAPTER SEVENTEEN

'Any mustard or mayonnaise with that?' the woman asks.

'Mayo, please.' Lorcan flashes her a smile.

I realize I'm staring and look away. It's nearly midday and we're the only people eating lunch in the restaurant of the inn. The woman wanders away and Lorcan leans back in his chair.

I feel his gaze on me but don't turn straightaway to meet it. The intensity of his presence is delicious but terrifying ... overwhelming ...

'Gen?'

I turn and look at him at last. I'm consumed with self-consciousness. What the hell has happened to me? I can't remember when I last felt this out of control. Images from our love-making burst into my head, all lust and joy. This is nothing like the way it was with Art when I met him. Back then I admired Art before I loved him. I felt attracted to him, sure, but it was his drive and focus that really drew me in.

With Art my feelings grew slowly and steadily. With Lorcan, it's like a bomb has gone off inside me. It's ridiculous – like I'm fourteen years old again. And yet in the cold light of the morning, I am all too aware that Lorcan had his own agenda when he offered to help me. And I still can't be sure I can really trust him.

'Are you all right?' Lorcan asks.

His hand reaches for mine and he smiles as our fingers touch. The woman appears with two plates laden with the tarts and salads we have ordered.

'Everything's going to be fine, Gen,' Lorcan says quietly.

'Here we are.' The woman sets her tray down on the table next to ours and proceeds to place the plates carefully in front of us. She's much the same age as the landlord and equally formal in her manner. Plump, with a carefully blow-dried bob, she's the only other member of staff we've seen apart from a couple of twenty-somethings serving behind the bar last night. We've asked all of them – in roundabout, chatty ways – if they remember seeing Art with anyone and, so far, no one has done so.

I'm hoping we haven't made anyone suspicious, but I know it's too much to expect that Art won't eventually find out we've been asking questions. Meanwhile, we are as much in the dark as ever about why *he* comes *here*. I'm well aware that this hotel could be a complete red herring in terms of finding Beth. Art might simply be having an affair and using this spot as a meeting place. Which would have nothing to do with Beth. Which would mean we are wasting our time . . . and that the truth about my child lies elsewhere.

I go over what I know again. Rodriguez was paid to lie about Beth. Someone else, other than Art, is involved too . . . plus the guy who mugged me. Everyone else present at the birth has died under suspicious circumstances. And no one will talk. Every turn I take, every attempt to find out what happened to my baby, leads to a dead end.

Lorcan is chatting to the woman who served us. I haven't been listening. As she walks away, he tucks into his ham-and-cheese tart. I glance down at my own, picking at the pastry with my fork. I spear a tomato, then realize I have no knife. Lorcan leans over and uses the sharp edge of his Swiss Army knife to cut it in half.

'A million uses,' he says with a smile, and my mind flashes back to last night and his tongue working its way down my body. I flush hot with self-consciousness again.

I tell Lorcan I'm going up to the room while he checks out. We've agreed we'll meet with Bernard O'Donnell back in London. He called us last night to report that Art went nowhere yesterday other than home and office. Bernard hopes that if we get together once more, pooling the information we both have, that something – some clue – will emerge that we haven't seen before.

I have my doubts, but at least we will be doing something.

I leave Lorcan and trudge up the inn's uneven staircase. It strikes me that this kind of hotel really isn't Art's usual choice. And I wonder, for the millionth time, why he chooses to stay here for those mysterious visits. Is he having an affair? Is it Hen? She certainly knows more than she's saying. I'm sure of that. But what? I'm exhausted by the relentless way these questions stalk my mind. And yet I can't seem to stop asking them.

A chambermaid – olive-skinned and dark-haired, with a pretty green scarf trailing down her back – is emerging from the room next to ours. She carries a bucket containing cleaning cloths and sprays and glances shyly at me with a smile. She's young, no more than eighteen or nineteen.

I hesitate. I should ask her about Art and whether she's seen anyone visiting him, but I feel so far from finding the necessary cheery tone that Lorcan and I have deployed with other members of staff that I simply disappear into my room.

I sit on the bed for a second, waves of despair and exhaustion washing over me. And then I force myself up, grab my phone and head out into the corridor again. I can't give up now.

'Excuse me.'

The chambermaid is a little way along the corridor, her hand on another room's door knob. She turns around.

'Please?' Her accent is Eastern European. She reminds me a little of Lilia.

I put a smile on my face and walk over, my phone in my hand.

'I was just going to say thank you; we've had a great stay here.'

'Stay?' She frowns, clearly not understanding the word.

'Visit,' I explain. 'A friend of ours also comes here,' I say, showing her the picture on my phone of Art flanked by Sandrine, her husband and various work colleagues at the party. 'We are happy he told us about this place.'

The lie is so total that it catches in my throat. Tears bubble up behind my eyes. The chambermaid looks at me strangely. 'You are all right?'

'I'm fine.' Tears are now trickling down my face. I try to stop crying but I can't. Misery is oozing out of me. 'Sorry,' I mutter. 'Sorry.'

I turn and walk away. The chambermaid follows.

'Please,' she says. 'Please be you okay.'

The strange construction makes me smile. I turn back. 'Thank you.'

Sympathy shines from her eyes. 'Do not cry,' she says. 'Is it so bad?'

'Yes.' The agony of the past week surges up inside me. I can't hold it back. I indicate the photo on my phone again. 'It's not true this man is a friend. He's my husband. And I think he's been lying to me.'

The chambermaid frowns, then she looks at the picture of Art. 'This man you husband?'

I nod, wiping my face.

'He come . . . he visit this place many times.' She smiles again, a kind, warm smile. 'I not see him with woman, not you worry.'

'Really?' I sniff back my tears.

'Really.' She points along the corridor to the fire door at the end. 'But I see him go through there.'

I follow her gaze. 'Where does that go?'

'Exit out back,' she says. 'I see him use. Before. Many time. Last time Monday.' She unwinds the long silk scarf from around her neck. 'He give me this soon after Christmas. A present to be keep quiet.'

I take the scarf out of her hands and examine it. It's beautiful – a long strip of pale green with just a hint of silver woven through the threads. A tiny tag dangles from the end, easy to miss as the price has been snipped off. Only the shop or brand logo remains: *bibo*.

My heart thuds.

'Do you know where he goes?' I ask.

She draws me to the window beside the end of the corridor. I can see over the yard at the back of the inn. A line of bins marks the path up to a privet hedge, the road lies beyond. The chambermaid points to the left. 'He go that way,' she says with a shrug. 'I am not know where.'

'Thank you.'

I can hear footsteps on the corridor behind me. I turn. It's Lorcan. The chambermaid takes a step away. 'I go now,' she says, gathering up the scarf. 'Please not saying I told.'

I nod, then watch her disappear into a room, then beckon Lorcan into mine.

As I explain what the maid has said, my phone beeps at me. I take a look at the call log. There are eleven missed calls and texts. Not just from Art, Hen and my mum, but also now from Kyle Benson at Art's work. I shove the phone in my pocket.

'But why would Art sneak out the back? And Bernard said Art's car never left the car park. Where would he go on foot?' Lorcan frowns. 'We drove around yesterday, we didn't see anything.'

268

'Maybe we missed something.' I grab my coat. 'Come on, let's dump our bags in the car, then go for a walk ourselves. See what we can find.'

Ten minutes later, we're making our way along the narrow country lane out of the inn. A couple of cars whizz past at high speed. Even though we're keeping to the hedgerow in single file, the passing vehicles feel dangerously close.

'I can't believe Art would just be coming out for a stroll,' I say. 'It's lethal, walking along here.'

'Maybe he turns off somewhere.' Lorcan looks across the fields to the cluster of small buildings in the distance. 'Maybe he heads for one of those farmhouses.'

'But *why*?'

Lorcan shrugs.

I sigh and carry on walking. The sky is grey and gloomy and the air feels heavy with rain, like the pressure in my head. After a couple more minutes we arrive at the hotel down the road. The Princess Alice is also a pub with rooms attached, but it's a far larger establishment than the Wardingham Arms, with a car park off to one side and freshly painted cream walls.

'I guess we should see if anyone's seen him in here,' I say.

We try the front door, but it's shut. As Lorcan rings on the doorbell, I look at his hands, remembering the touch of his fingers. He glances round and meets my eye.

The front door opens into a cool, stone vestibule. A man wearing work overalls and a scowl stands there.

'Sorry to disturb you,' I launch in. 'But we were wondering if you have seen this man?' I hold out the picture of Art.

The man in overalls grunts and shakes his head. 'You police?' he mutters.

'No,' I say quickly. 'No, we're just meeting someone.'

269

A woman bustles into the vestibule. She's about my age, with warm eyes and wispy strawberry blonde curls. 'Hello, can I help?' She glances from me and Lorcan to the man in overalls. 'Thanks, Andy,' she says. 'I'll take it from here.'

Andy slopes off and the woman moves back to allow us inside.

'Sorry about that, I'd just stepped away from reception. Were you looking for a room?'

'No.' I walk into the stone vestibule, Lorcan at my side.

'We're here for a meeting with a Mr Loxley,' Lorcan says. 'We were supposed to meet him in the bar but we're running late and we don't have a number for him.'

I make a face, jumping into the story we've used before. 'It's my fault, I lost the information.'

'Sorry,' the woman says. 'I don't recognize the name you said. There's no one in the bar, though. I'd have seen anyone going through from reception.'

'I've got a picture of him actually.' I'm trying to sound casual but my heart is racing. Lorcan seems to handle our cover stories with ease but each time I have to lie about Art I feel stressed and uncomfortable. I hold out my phone, a picture of Art displayed on the screen. 'I don't suppose you've seen him around?'

The woman takes my phone and tilts it to get a better view. 'Oh, but that's Mr Rafferty,' she says with a frown.

I exchange glances with Lorcan.

'I don't understand,' the woman says, looking up at me. 'Rafferty wasn't the name you said before.'

I think fast. 'Gosh, did I get that wrong too? Head office will have my guts.' I shake my head.

'Total ditz,' Lorcan adds, jerking his thumb in my direction.

'Right.' The woman looks like she's not sure whether to believe us or not. 'Well, I'm pretty sure he's not with us today, though his car's still outside.'

270

'His *car*?' My mind flashes back to the Mercedes parked in our Crouch End driveway.

'Yes.' The woman looks at me, her face now covered in confusion.

I freeze, not knowing what to say. Luckily Lorcan is thinking more quickly than I am.

'Thanks so much for your help,' he says. Then he turns to me. 'I think you're going to have to call head office after all. Track Mr Rafferty down.' He opens the door and shepherds me outside.

I follow Lorcan across the gravel, my mind spinning with what we've just learned. 'Why does Art have a car here?'

'You mean "Mr Rafferty"?' Lorcan shakes his head. 'How are we going to work out which car it is?'

There are five cars parked in the hotel car park. A Mini, an SUV and three mid-range hatchbacks. None of them is the kind of car I'd imagine Art choosing. I glance over my shoulder. The woman is still watching us from the doorway of the hotel. She's looking really suspicious now. I stop walking.

'Go back,' I hiss at Lorcan. 'Go back and say you need the toilet or something. Give me a moment to look around, see if I can see anything that'll tell us which car is Art's.'

Lorcan doubles back to the hotel. I reach the first car, the Mini. It's pristine inside, surely too small and too tidy for Art. And I know he disapproves of big, gas-guzzling cars, so I also only give the SUV a cursory glance. Moving away, I check over my shoulder at the hotel entrance. There's no sign of Lorcan or the landlady.

The next car has a pink teddy bear sporting a heart-shaped 'Be My Valentine' badge on the dashboard. No way. Not unless Art is undergoing some kind of lobotomy every time he comes here.

I stop outside a Volkswagen and peer in through the window. A juice bottle and a sandwich packet – both empty – litter the floor. I look in the back. There's a paper bag on the far end of the seat – pale green – with some sort of greeting card peeking out of the top. I go round the other side of the car, and peer in again. The bag has a tiny logo at the bottom. Written in green swirly lettering, it is instantly familiar from the logo on the chambermaid's scarf: *bibo*.

I'm concentrating so hard on this that I jump when my phone rings. I glance at the caller, expecting to see that it's Art or Hen, but it's a number I don't recognize. Distracted, I put the phone to my ear.

'Hello?'

'Geniver?' The voice is female and familiar but I can't place it. 'Are you all right? I was so worried about you.'

I blink, still staring at the writing – *bibo* – on the paper bag.

'Hello?' I say. 'Who is this?'

The person on the other end draws in her breath sharply. 'It's Charlotte West,' she says. 'You weren't at class . . . they said you were poorly. I was just calling to see how you are.'

Charlotte. I'd completely forgotten about her and the Art & Media Institute. They both seem like they belong to another life.

'Geniver?' Charlotte now sounds anxious. 'Are you okay? Is everything all right with Art?'

With *Art*? She's acting like we're friends, like she has a right to enquire about my marriage. 'I'm fine,' I say, feeling confused and more than a little defensive. 'Er . . . Charlotte, how did you get my number?'

A long pause. 'I was just concerned about you. I know Art is worried too . . .'

Art again. And she's totally avoiding my question. My mind flashes back to Charlotte's appearance on our doorstep, the adoring way she looked at Art and the way Art muttered under his breath when he was speaking to her, angry words I couldn't properly hear.

'You've spoken to my husband?' I try to keep my voice as even as possible.

'It doesn't matter.' Now Charlotte sounds injured, as if I've hurt her feelings. 'I was just trying to be nice. I'm sure Art feels badly that you put your real-life relationship in *Rain Heart*.'

'What? Charlotte, I already told you. *Rain Heart* was made up. I—'

'Fine, I was only calling to see how you were.' Now she sounds really upset. 'I didn't realize it wasn't okay. I'll see you next week. Bye.'

'Wait—'

But she's already rung off. What was she talking about? In *Rain Heart* the husband has an affair with his business partner's wife. Art's business partner is Kyle Benson. What on earth is Charlotte suggesting? That Art is sleeping with Kyle's wife, Vicky? It's ludicrous. How would Charlotte know anyway? And how on earth did she get my phone number?

I look up. Lorcan is striding towards me across the gravel.

'Was that Art?' he says.

I shake my head. 'It was this weird woman from one of the classes I teach. She's says she knows Art's worried about me, that I've written about a real affair in a book . . . I don't know. I don't understand why she thinks she knows anything about us . . . or how she got hold of my mobile number.'

I look down at Charlotte's phone number. Now I'm studying it, it strikes me that there's something vaguely familiar about it . . . about those last three digits:

'D'you think she's somehow involved?' Lorcan asks.

'I don't know.' I'm still staring at the numbers. Where did I see those before? I think back to the way Charlotte gushed over my book, and how she copied my haircut and my handbag, even my blue hat.

'I thought she was a bit odd, but now . . .' As I speak, it hits me. I fish my phone out of my bag to make sure. Flick through the dialled numbers. *There.* I knew I recognized it.

'Look!' I say. 'Charlotte West is the person who's been calling Art. Twelve times on one day. And that's just what I saw on his phone.'

'You looked at his phone?'

'I had to.' I gasp, another realization occurring. 'Oh, Lorcan, there's something else. Charlotte lives in the West Country. I don't know where exactly, but it can't be that far from here.'

'You think *she* could be involved with Art?' Lorcan says.

'Yes. She came to our house the other day and he was angry with her. I heard him whispering. Why would he do that if there wasn't something going on between them?'

Lorcan wrinkles his nose. 'It sounds a bit weird, though. Why would she come to your writing class if she's already involved with Art? I mean, it's asking for trouble, isn't it?'

I shrug. I don't have any answers but there are surely possibilities. Sandrine might look more like the kind of woman Art would sleep with, but Charlotte is obviously interested *and* she lives nearby.

'Art's been lying to me for eight years over Beth.' The words are hard to say, but I have to face them. 'I'd say after that, anything's possible.'

I take a breath, looking around the car park. Lorcan follows my gaze.

'Any idea which car Art might have used?' he asks.

I nod, pointing to the paper bag inside the Volkswagen. 'See that?' I tell Lorcan about the identical *bibo* logo I saw on the chambermaid's scarf. 'She said Art gave that scarf to her to keep her quiet,' I explain. 'And here's a bag using the same design. This *must* be his car.'

Lorcan glances into the Volkswagen. 'But what's it *doing* here? The woman who runs this place made it obvious that Art pays them to leave the car here most of the time. Why *here*, as Mr Rafferty, when he's already driven another car to a hotel just up the road, as himself?'

We look at each other. I can see the same light dawning in Lorcan's eyes that now flares in my own mind.

'This is where he switches over,' I say. 'From one identity to another. He has a separate name and a separate car . . .'

Lorcan nods. 'Because a second identity makes it harder to track him down.' He pauses. 'But why? Where does he go in this car?'

We look inside the Volkswagen again. The sandwich packet and drink are from M&S – and therefore could have been bought anywhere around the country. My eyes fix on the *bibo* logo. 'Let's see what we can find out about that,' I say.

'Good idea.' Lorcan looks up as a few fat drops of rain start to fall.

We huddle under a tree in the car park and Google *bibo* on my phone.

I click on the first link and stare at the screen.

'It's just a gift shop,' Lorcan says.

The *bibo* logo is at the top of a web page that's basically a brochure for a shop. There's an olde-worlde fascia, with the name *Bitsy and Bobs* written across it in an ornate flourish. The page is mostly made up of pictures of handmade vases, colourful notebooks and silk scarves like the one the chambermaid was wearing. There's also a fan-shaped display of greetings cards. I scan the few lines of text, picking out the main words: '*stationery . . . delightful items for the home . . . highest quality . . . gifts . . .*'

'Where's the shop based?'

Lorcan scrolls down the page. The contact address is given as Shepton Longchamp in Somerset.

'It sounds tiny,' I say.

'Could there be any business connection between this Bitsy and Bobs place and Art's company?' Lorcan asks.

'I don't see how, it sells birthday cards and felt-tip pens.' I sigh. 'It's probably just somewhere that Art has bought stuff from. Though I can't imagine why he would want to shop there. The scarf is pretty, for sure, but it's not his kind of place at all.'

The rain falls more heavily around us and I huddle closer to Lorcan under the trees.

'Wanna check it out anyway?' he asks.

'You mean go to Somerset?'

He nods. 'Why not? We're halfway there already. And we don't have anything else to go on.'

I look up at Lorcan's determined face. I still can't be sure if I can trust him, though my instincts tell me he is sincere in wanting to help. But what choice do I have? Art won't give me the answers I need, but he has left a trail. And if I follow it, it will surely, in the end, bring me to Beth.

Either way, I can't turn back now.

CHAPTER EIGHTEEN

It's going to take about an hour and a half to reach Shepton Longchamp. I call Bernard and explain what we've discovered and what we're doing now. Like me, he has never heard of the Bitsy and Bobs shop. He reports that Art has been in his office all morning and that he's going to keep trailing him. He sounds exhausted.

As the countryside flashes past outside, I decide that if today's journey doesn't lead directly to Beth, then I will simply increase the ways in which I look for her. Bernard is doing his best, but he can't watch Art twenty-four hours a day. I will hire a private investigator to follow Art when he next poses as "Mr Rafferty" and I will hire another to access and trawl through birth and adoption records from eight years ago. It's surely impossible to hide a child completely. And I refuse to believe anyone would have wanted to harm Beth. If money changed hands, then her life held value for someone. I just need to find out who . . . and what they did with her.

As we drive, Art calls again. I don't answer. From the look of the call log, he seems to be trying my number on the hour, every hour. I turn my mobile off.

Lorcan and I spend most of the journey discussing how best to approach the owner of Bitsy and Bobs. I'm all for asking directly if they recognize Art. Lorcan thinks we should take a

SOPHIE MCKENZIE

more circuitous approach, pretending that we're looking to match an item a friend bought the other day, and simply showing a photo of Art as a memory jogger.

'We need a reason to show his picture without them getting suspicious. That way they're more likely to fall into the trap of admitting they've seen him,' Lorcan explains. 'If we're convincing enough they won't suspect we have an ulterior motive. The worst that can happen is they say no. If they're innocent of everything Art's done, they won't even realize we've been lying.'

'So you're suggesting we take advantage of them?'

I mean my tone to be lightly sarcastic but, thanks to how stressed I feel, my words sound heavy and accusatory. I glance sideways at Lorcan. He's concentrating on the turning up ahead.

We're both silent for a few, long seconds. Then Lorcan clears his throat.

'I can understand if you think I've been taking advantage of you, but—'

My face burns.

'Listen, Gen. I want to be with you,' Lorcan says in a low voice. 'Here. Now.'

My mind flashes back to the conversation we had last night. As with everything with Lorcan, it felt both strange – and completely natural.

'I know you're in the middle of this terrible situation but . . . we need to see about us . . . where it goes, don't we?'

I gaze out of the window. We're speeding along the motorway. It's still grey and gloomy outside.

'I'm married,' I say.

'To a man who stole your baby . . . who has been lying to you for years.'

'We don't know exactly—'

'Were you happy before?' Lorcan cuts in, his voice calm but

insistent. 'Tell me you were happy with Art before you found out Beth might be alive, and I'll back off.'

I lean against the cold window beside me. Truth is, I haven't been properly happy with Art for a long time. We worked once, when we were younger and Art shared his dreams for his business with me, and when I was writing. But after Beth died, Art's focus turned away from me and when I tried to tell him how much I was hurting he couldn't deal with my pain.

I glance over at Lorcan. He's still driving, his face impassive. In all our years together Art has never really understood me. Lorcan, I realize, gets me without trying. He looks at me and smiles and my stomach does a somersault of the kind it hasn't experienced in a long time.

'I guess . . .' My voice is a whisper. 'I guess I want to know where this goes too.'

Half an hour out of Andover we end up in a traffic jam on the A344. As we crawl along, Stonehenge comes into view. Lorcan nudges me with his elbow.

'Didn't you say your dad brought you here when you were a kid?'

'That's right.' My mind slides over the memory. I haven't thought about it in years, but I remember clearly that I was little – maybe five or six. It was a summer evening and stickily hot and Dad got it into his head that we should have an adventure. Just him and me. I can remember Mum pleading with him not to take me out in the car and the thrill of excitement when Dad whisked me out of the house and bundled me up in the back of our Ford Cortina with a can of Tizer and a packet of salt-and-vinegar crisps.

Lorcan pulls off the main road. I glance over, shaken from my reverie.

'What are you doing?'

'Bathroom break.' He indicates the Stonehenge Visitor Centre up ahead.

We park and Lorcan disappears inside. I gaze over at the stones themselves. You can't get close to them anymore except on private tours. They've been sealed off from the general public for a long time – supposedly inaccessible even back in the late seventies when Dad brought me here. Not that that stopped him. The long-dormant memory surges up: in the dark we stumbled across the field and over the fence. It was spookily silent, but I wasn't scared. I had my dad's hand in mine, and so what if he fell over three times on the way to the stones? He always got up again. I gasp, suddenly realizing how drunk he must have been. No wonder Mum begged him not to take me. I look out towards the stone pillars. I remember Dad and I reaching the first pillar. Dad leaned against the stone, then beckoned me over. I can still see his long fringe falling over his eyes and the fierce gleam of his expression as he spoke solemnly into the night.

'This circle of stones was brought here by magic, Queenie, all the way from Ireland.' He spread his palms against the pillar, swaying a little as he did so. I copied him, feeling the cool roughness under my fingers. He closed his eyes. I followed his lead again. And then he sighed. 'These stones heal the sick, Queenie.'

I opened one eye and glanced up at him. 'Are you sick, Daddy?'

He laughed. I can remember thinking there was something wrong with his laugh, like he had something bitter in his mouth. He didn't answer.

I glance once more at Stonehenge then turn away. All my life, whenever I've remembered that time with my dad, I've remembered it as a special memory, something he did for me. It's only now that I realize that what I had seen as adventure was, for him, something entirely more desperate. What was he looking for?

Salvation? Redemption? Whatever it was, I wasn't with him because he wanted to give me something. He was drunk and just thinking of his own pain. And my only role was as his witness.

'Gen?' Lorcan's voice rouses me again. He's walking towards me from the visitor centre. 'Ready to keep going?'

Shepton Longchamp is a large village, but still very much a village. It's just gone 3 p.m. as we drive along the main road, taking in the few shops – a grocer and a newsagent and a chemist – plus a small pub, the Dog & Duck, a picturesque cliché of a West Country inn, complete with ivy up the walls and flower baskets hanging from iron hooks.

'So where's Bitsy and Bobs?' Lorcan asks, pulling over.

I consult my phone. 'It should definitely be on this road; maybe we passed it already.'

It's as we're driving on, looking for a place where Lorcan can turn the car around, that we find the shop. It would be easy to miss, sandwiched between a rather prim-looking boutique and yet another pub.

From the outside, Bitsy and Bobs looks like any other upmarket gift shop. The window display is different from the one in the shiny picture on the website, but just as expensive-looking. It includes hand made gift cards stuck with glitter and feathers, a row of scarves similar to the one Art gave the chambermaid at the hotel, plus a selection of children's colouring sets and some locally produced pottery, all set against a backdrop of chintzy wrapping paper.

The name of the shop is written in ornate swirls above the window. It's all terribly chi-chi.

'Art would never voluntarily come in here,' I say as we approach the door.

'Let's see, shall we?' Lorcan pushes it open.

Inside the shop I gaze around at the stand of flower-themed cards – *Blank for your own message* – and the shelves stacked with fancy pens and jars of local 'apple-cider flavour' sweets. A girl – young, no more than twenty-one or -two – looks up from behind the counter.

Lorcan smiles and starts talking. My stomach feels heavy as I browse the card stand. This shop can't possibly have anything to do with Art. If he did come inside, it must have been under duress – or because he was out of other options. I can't see either Sandrine or Hen wanting to shop here. Maybe Charlotte West, though.

Lorcan is chatting away behind me. The girl nods as he explains we're on a mission to help a friend replace a missing scarf.

'From what I understand,' Lorcan says, 'it was black silk. He said he bought it here so, as we were passing through, we promised we'd stop off to see if you had a replacement. Sort of a surprise for his birthday.'

I turn around. Lorcan is leaning on the counter. For some reason he has dropped his own way of speaking in favour of a rather upper-class English accent. The young girl behind has pursed her perfect cupid's-bow lips, concentrating on his every word. She has to be less than half his age and yet she's totally caught up in his charm. She points over to the scarf rack, shrugging her shoulders.

'I don't remember a man's scarf in black silk,' she says in the plummiest of accents herself.

Lorcan turns, waving me over.

'Show the young lady the picture,' he says. 'It might help her remember the scarf.'

The upper-class accent he has assumed mirrors perfectly the way the girl speaks. With a jolt I realize it must be a deliberate ploy to make her feel comfortable – and more likely to open up.

Obediently, I scroll to the photo of Art and hand my phone to the girl.

'He only bought the scarf recently,' I say.

To my amazement she nods. 'Oh, yah, he comes here a lot,' she says.

I stare at her, my mouth gaping. 'A *lot*?'

The girl nods again. 'He's a friend of Bitsy and Bobs. Didn't you know?'

'A friend of the *shop*?' Lorcan frowns. 'What d'you mean?'

'Bitsy and Bobs are the owners. Robert and Elizabeth Renner. They're not here right now. Bobs should be in later, though. I'm holding the fort.'

Art is friendly with a couple of shopkeepers who run a bijou gift outlet in the middle of Somerset? It makes no sense.

'So you've seen him recently?' Lorcan points to the picture of Art. 'It's just we didn't know he knew the owners, so . . .'

'Yah, like I don't work every day but, like, I was here the Saturday before last, and he came in then.'

I blink, my mind flashing back to that particular day. The week before Lucy showed up . . . the week before the party. I slept late and when I woke, Art had left a note on my pillow. *Annoying meeting in town. Back by 4.*

He *had* been back by four or so. We'd had a cup of tea and he'd brushed away my question about his meeting with a sigh, saying he didn't want to talk about work tonight. We'd watched some rubbish film on TV while eating an Indian takeaway, then gone to bed. Nothing about that entire day had made me suspect that Art had spent the first part of it in Somerset.

The girl is talking again, in response to something Lorcan has asked that I wasn't listening to. I force my mind back to their conversation.

'I'd say he comes in once a month,' the girl says.

'Alone?' The question sounds inappropriate as it leaves my mouth. *Shit*. I should have left the questions to Lorcan. He asks them far better.

The girl screws up her face. 'No,' she says. 'He's always with his family.'

It's like a punch in the guts. 'His family?' I echo, my legs threatening to give way under me.

The girl looks at me curiously.

'Sorry, I'm not sure exactly what you mean,' Lorcan says quickly.

The girl raises her eyebrows. 'I mean his wife and child, of course.'

The shop seems to spin around me. It was one thing to suspect Art of meeting a woman in a hotel room, but to hear someone talk out loud about a wife and child is beyond shocking.

And yet . . . my mind tries to process what this revelation means.

It surely means Beth *is* alive. *And* Art is having an affair with the woman who he's passing off as her mother. An *affair*. Wasn't this precisely the conclusion Morgan thought I had jumped to? After the chambermaid's insistence that she'd never seen Art with a woman, I'd started to believe that perhaps that part of my suspicions was wrong. But no . . . Art has a double life. He has taken our daughter and put her at the centre of another family.

I lean back against a display cupboard, pressing my hand against the wood to steady myself.

It's unbelievable. And yet it makes sense. If I accept that Art is in love with someone else, then the rest all follows. For her he has been prepared to lie to me and to kill to cover his tracks. For her, he took away my baby. Unless the child is *hers* . . . *theirs* . . . That's possible too. Which means Art took away *our* baby for some other reason that I don't yet understand.

But what if it *is* Beth?

My Beth. And she calls some other woman 'Mummy'.

Fury surges through me. My fingers curl over the cupboard edge, the wood cutting into my palm as the next question explodes like a grenade in my head. Who is this woman?

Who the hell is this woman who has ripped the heart out of my life?

Lorcan is still talking to the girl. I force myself back to their conversation. Before everything else, I *have* to find out if the child Art comes here with is Beth.

'How old?' I demand, striding over to the counter.

The girl stares at me blankly.

Lorcan puts a restraining hand on my arm. I realize I am actually shaking.

'We're just wondering how old the little one is now?' he asks with a smile.

The girl in the shop stares at him quizzically. 'I thought you were all good friends?'

'No, we said *friends* of friends.' Lorcan smiles ruefully. 'When you get to our age it's astonishing how quickly time goes by. One day they're babies. The next they're off to college.'

The girl laughs. 'Yah, well I don't think this one'll be off to uni any time soon. I don't know, about seven or eight, I'd say.'

It *is* Beth. Black shadows flicker in the corner of my eyes. For a second I think I might pass out.

'Hello?' A man stands in the door of the shop. He's in his fifties, with short, thinning dark hair and a Barbour jacket that's glistening with rain. It must have started drizzling outside, but I don't turn and look. I'm transfixed by the man's gaze. He's staring at me as if he's seen a ghost. A second later he recovers with a thin-lipped smile that doesn't reach his eyes.

'Hello there.' The man glances from me to the shop girl. His accent is as posh as hers. 'Are these friends of yours, Franny?'

I stare at him. It's as obvious that he is trying to cover his confusion as it is that he has recognized me from somewhere.

'No.' Franny pouts her perfect lips, flicking her hair back self-consciously. 'But they know of a friend of yours, Bobs. That guy and his wife who come in every few weeks? They buy toys and colouring things for—'

'I can't possibly remember every customer we have.' Bobs rolls his eyes in mock-exasperation, but his face is reddening and there's an undeniable look of panic in his eyes.

He knows who I am. He knows I have a connection to Art. I tense and glance at Lorcan. I can see from his expression he's noticed the recognition in Bobs's eyes too. Lorcan holds out his hand.

'You're the owner?' he says.

Bobs nods. He stares at Lorcan, then shakes his hand. 'I'm sorry, you have me at a disadvantage.'

'We were just trying to track down a black silk scarf,' Lorcan says smoothly.

'Your assistant here . . .' I nod towards Franny then hold my phone out to Bobs. 'She seems to think you know this man quite well, that he's a regular customer.' My heart thumps. I know I'm throwing caution to the wind by being so blatant in my ques-tioning. Lorcan casts me an anxious glance.

Bobs rubs his hands together. He looks nervous. 'I don't think so,' he says.

'You're kidding, Bobs.' Franny's voice from the counter expresses confusion and surprise. 'You *do* know him. So does Bitsy. He comes in with—'

'Would you check the stock delivery in the van, Franny?' Bobs interrupts. 'The schedule is on the front. Last time they sent too many gel-pen sets so we need to make sure this order's correct.'

286

'You want me to check the stock before you've brought it inside?' Franny pouts, looking both put out and surprised.

'Yes.' Bobs stands by the door. The atmosphere grows tenser still.

Franny lopes sulkily across the shop to the front door. Lorcan holds it open for her. 'Will I help you with the stuff in the van?' he says.

'No.' Bobs's head jerks up. His tone verges on the aggressive. He quickly smiles, holding out his arms in a conciliatory gesture. 'Sorry, but if you're not staff, I'm not insured. Health and safety, you know what it's like.'

Lorcan catches my eye. I'm certain he's thinking the same as me: Bobs is lying from his balding head down to his well-polished brogues.

As Franny disappears into the rain, I turn on Bobs.

'How do you know Art?' I say.

Bobs shakes his head. 'I don't.'

I glance at Lorcan. In a second he's across the room, towering over Bobs.

'We know you're lying,' he hisses. 'Why are you protecting him?'

Bobs backs away. 'You have to go,' he says shakily. 'Please leave the shop or . . . or . . .'

'Or what?' I say. 'Or you'll call the police?'

'I don't know what you're talking about,' Bobs insists. 'And yes, if you don't leave I *will* call the police.'

I want to call his bluff but the memory of my recent encounter with Sergeant Manning is still fresh in my head. Lorcan and I don't have any more solid evidence against either Art or Rodriguez than we did two days ago.

I glance out of the window, where Franny is half-visible behind the van doors. Right now she is our best bet.

I dart closer to Lorcan, tugging him away from Bobs. I lean

up and whisper in his ear: 'Keep Bobs here a minute.' Then I walk out of the shop. Behind me I can hear the two men arguing, but I head straight over to Franny. A misty rain shrouds my hair and coat and the air is cold and damp, but I pay this no attention. I'm fixed on Franny. She's still standing at the back of the van, checking the contents of one of the cardboard boxes inside against a list on a clipboard – and looking irritated.

I go up to her. 'Franny?'

She glances over.

'I'm sorry to bother you, but I'd be really grateful if you could tell me everything you remember about the man in the shop and his family. There was just one child, right?'

She nods, looking over my shoulder at Bobs, who is still inside the shop, clearly arguing with Lorcan.

'Yes, but my boss obviously doesn't want me to talk to you about it. Why are you so interested anyway?'

'What about Bitsy?' I say quickly. 'She's your boss too. Maybe she wouldn't mind. Please.'

Franny gives a little snort. 'If Bobs minds a little, then Bitsy will go ballistic.' She looks at me. 'Why is this so important? I thought you said you were just looking for a scarf?'

I look her in the eye. 'I lied,' I say. 'That man in the picture is my husband.'

Franny's eyes widen. 'Your husband?' she says. 'Then who's the woman who comes in with him? They look like a couple and they're definitely the parents. I've heard the—'

'She's *mine*.' As I say the words the reality hits me and my voice cracks. 'The little girl they are with is *my* daughter.'

Franny stares at me. 'Your daughter?'

'Yes.' My heart thumps. 'She's . . . she'd be almost eight, like you said. I don't . . .' I stop, unable to admit that I have no idea exactly what my own child looks like. I say what I think Franny will find easiest to get her head around. 'My husband has taken her . . . my daughter . . .'

Franny shakes her head. 'Then it's not your husband or your child,' she says.

Out of the corner of my eye I can see Bobs trying to get to the door and Lorcan forcing him back. I don't have much time here and I'm struggling to cope with what Franny is saying.

'I don't understand,' I say, feeling sick to my stomach. I shove the phone with the photo of Art under her nose again. 'This is the man you've seen here, yes?'

'Yes.' Franny nods vigorously. 'But the child he was with was a boy.'

CHAPTER NINETEEN

A *boy*.

'No.' I grab Franny's arm. She must be mistaken. 'Maybe it was a little girl with a short haircut . . . young children can look—'

'No way,' Franny insists. 'He was wearing a Woodholme sweatshirt. It's a boys' school.'

I blink rapidly, trying to make sense of what she is saying.

'But you said you saw them the Saturday before last,' I say, shaking her arm. 'Why would he be wearing school uniform at the weekend?'

Franny frowns. 'Woodholme's a private prep school. I've got friends who went there. They do Saturday school.'

I let go of her arm, the sick feeling in my stomach raging up into my throat. My heart is racing so fast I feel like I might keel over. The van has disappeared into a black blur at the edge of my vision. I'm going to be sick, I'm sure of it.

I don't understand . . . it doesn't make sense . . . my baby is a girl . . .

And then the black blur mists up in front of my eyes and I pass out.

'Gen?' It's Lorcan's voice. 'Gen, are you okay?'

Fingers are smoothing damp hair from my wet face. The ground is cold under my body, raindrops falling in a mist.

I open my eyes to find Lorcan gazing anxiously down at me. 'Gen?' he says.

'I made a mistake,' I said. 'It isn't Beth at all, it's some other child.'

'What?' Lorcan frowns. 'What are you talking about?'

I struggle to sit up. The back of my head is sore where I must have banged it and I still feel sick. I lean over my knees, letting the nausea ebb away. I've only fainted once in my life before – at a bar on my hen night. I'd barely eaten anything during the weeks leading up to the wedding and I couldn't cope with all the booze. It was Hen who looked after me then – insisting I went straight home with her in a taxi. My wedding was a few days later. Hen stood with me, my only bridesmaid. It feels like a lifetime ago.

I breathe out slowly, feeling the nausea pass. 'Where're Bobs and the girl from the shop?' I mumble.

'Inside.' Lorcan strokes my back. 'When I saw you faint, I rushed out here and Bobs called Franny in then bolted the door, put the *Closed* sign up and disappeared through to the back.'

I look at him.

'I know.' He grimaces. 'That guy is guilty as hell about something. God, you look pale,' he says, wiping rain off his face. 'Can you stand up? Are you hurt? Let's get you in the car.'

I let him help me to my feet and over to the car. I sit inside, shivering in my damp clothes. Lorcan reaches round and grabs a fleece from the back seat.

'Cover yourself with this,' he orders.

I drape it over my wet coat and lean back against the headrest.

'What did you mean, it was a different child?' Lorcan asks.

I explain what Franny told me. 'So you see, it's a boy. Not Beth. Not my Beth.' I close my eyes, trying to let this revelation

SOPHIE MCKENZIE

sink in. I honestly believed I was getting close to an understanding of what had really happened to her, and now I'm as far away as ever.

'A boy?' Lorcan frowns. 'How does that fit?'

'It doesn't.' I gulp as the shocking enormity of Art's deception rises inside me again. 'Art must have had someone from the beginning . . . from before he even met me. A whole other life . . . family . . .'

My thoughts dart back to Hen. Of all my friends, she has known Art the longest. She has talked to him behind my back and kept things from me and she has a son the same age as Beth would have been. She might be married to Rob now, but is it possible she has some kind of double life with Nat and Art down here? I can't for the life of me see how it could be so, but . . .

'Maybe it's someone I know,' I say. 'Someone I've known for a long time.'

'No.' Lorcan shakes his head. 'I'm sorry, Gen, but that's crazy. Think about it. When you met him Art was completely obsessed with his business, wasn't he? Even if he has a second family now, there's no way he had time for one back then.'

'Then it's *her* child and Art comes to see them *both*. Either way, Art has another family. Maybe it's Charlotte West. She lives near here, after all. And I know she called Art all those times. Jesus, she came to our house and he was pissed off with her. Maybe they were together then it finished and now she's stalking him.' I realize my fists are clenched, and release them.

Lorcan makes a face. 'I don't know, it sounds very convoluted. I mean, if Art really does have someone else, why stay in his marriage?' He spreads his hands on the steering wheel of the car.

'I don't know.' I close my eyes. 'All I know is that the child Art comes here to see isn't Beth.'

292

'Wait a second,' Lorcan says. 'Suppose it *is* "Beth"? Suppose they made it up?'

'Made what up?' I open my eyes. What is he talking about? 'You can't pretend that a girl is really a boy, not all the way to eight years old. The school would know for a start and—'

'I don't mean that Art and the other woman made up Beth was a boy,' Lorcan explains. He runs his hands through his damp hair. 'Suppose they made up Beth was a girl? Suppose, in fact, your baby was a boy all along?'

I think through the list of people who were at the birth. Apart from Art, there's Rodriguez and Mary Duncan and the anaesthetist. I think back to the conversation I had with Mary's sister, Lucy O'Donnell. She definitely referred to "Beth", but then she also said that she'd "found out" my baby's name when she looked me and Art up online. Maybe Mary never specified whether I'd had a boy or girl. She was dying when she confessed, after all. What was it she'd said exactly? I wrack my memory.

'Her baby was born alive . . . I feel . . . so bad for that poor lady because they took her baby away and told her the little thing was dead.'

'Why lie about the sex of a baby you were telling everyone was dead anyway?' I rub my head. It still feels sore.

'To cover their tracks.' Lorcan says. 'It's an extra layer of protection . . . an extra barrier to stop people ever finding the baby. And the child Art has been seen with is the same age as Beth would be now . . .'

I stare at him, a mix of confusion and hope mingling in my head. I can hardly bear to face the idea that the daughter I lost, the Beth I've been dreaming of, is a fiction. It's too much. For the past eight years I've imagined her: my little girl. I've pictured her, I've mourned her, I've even *dreamed* her. She was so real to me. And now I'm being told the very fact of her is an illusion.

'We have to go Woodholme School,' I say. 'I need to see this boy . . . I need to see for myself.'

Half an hour later we're parked outside a high brick wall, softened on either side by banks of oak trees and bearing a brass plaque with the words: *Woodholme School for Boys: Lower and Upper Preparatory.*

From where we're sitting we have a great side-view of a sweeping driveway that leads up to a massive sandstone building. The sound of small children shrieking echoes in the distance. There are two playgrounds separated by a wire fence. One contains a climbing frame, a scattering of animal statues in painted metal and a horse-chestnut tree in the corner. The other playground is bigger and clearly for older kids – just a tarmac square, though the branches of the horse-chestnut tree hang over it.

'We can't wait around here for very long, Gen, if that's what you're thinking.' Lorcan frowns as he looks at me. 'It's too risky. Some nosey do-gooder will call the police and say we're lurking out here.'

'I don't think we'll have to wait too much longer.'

'And what makes you so sure of that?'

'Bobs back at the shop definitely knows Art, yes?' I say.

'I'd bet my life on it.'

'So he'll warn him and Art will send someone to pick up . . . this child.' I want to say *my* child but I still can't get my head around the fact that the baby I've been dreaming of for nearly eight years might be a boy, not a girl. It all feels unreal. I force myself to be logical. 'If Art knows we're on to him, he'll act. He'll know he won't be able to get to the school before we do, but he'll want to get the child out of here. That's if the child goes to this school.' I glance at the sign on the wall. 'If he's eight he could be in the lower or upper prep.'

Lorcan nods slowly. 'You think he might send the woman he's with to take him out of school?'

Fury builds inside me. 'If they're in this together I imagine she'll want to come as soon as she can.'

We sit in silence for what feels like a long time. Several women pass us on the pavement. Others pull up in cars. Then a bell rings – loud and sharp – from inside the school. Seconds later scores of children swarm onto the playground. As their voices fill the air, all the women who haven't already left their cars get out and walk through the school gates. More appear from around the corner, strolling along in pairs and groups, many holding smartly dressed toddlers by the hand.

'The invasion of the yummy mummies,' Lorcan says drily.

'It must be going-home time,' I say, my throat dry.

It couldn't be worse. I'd expected to see a single child being taken out of school early. Now I'm going to have to pick one out of a crowd.

More women pass us, chattering away. They're mostly my age or a bit younger; lots are pushing buggies or prams.

We get out of the car and wander through the school gates. Mothers and nannies and their charges are trickling past. I scan the scene feeling desperate. If my child is here, how will I know? I look for a woman in a hurry . . . someone scared and furtive . . . but everyone around us seems happy and relaxed.

It's hopeless. A new terror fills me. If Art knows I'm here, and this boy is our baby, then Art will move him away from this place, from this school, and I will have to start tracking him down all over again. I think about the mugger and his threat: *Stop looking.* I have gone against his order. I have kept on searching.

My life – and possibly Lorcan's – is in danger. But I need to find this child. I need to know if he's mine. I need something concrete that I can take to the police.

I gaze around. More children are emerging from the younger kids' playground. Most are chattering away, several clutching paper hats with streamers that flutter in the breeze. The sun comes out and some of the women shield their eyes from the glare. I stare from woman to woman. From boy to boy. Each one wears a pale blue Woodholme sweatshirt over long navy shorts. They're a homogenous bunch: almost entirely white, with fresh round faces and high-pitched squeals.

More groups flood out through the school gates now. I can't keep track of them all. I fixate on the hair. Most of these children are blond . . . or blondish . . . but Art and I have always had dark hair. Would our son be dark too? I start walking through them, turning as I stalk the gate area, trying to see every face . . . scanning all the women, all the dark-haired kids.

And then I see him. And everything I've ever known shifts and reframes.

He's racing another little boy across the playground, a look of intense determination on his face. His dark hair is cut short round the back and sides, but hangs in a floppy silky fringe low over his forehead. I stare at his face – at the dark, serious eyes and at the way his bottom lip is thinner than the top – and it's like I'm looking at the photo of my dad as a little boy come to life.

This is, without a doubt, my son.

I stare at him. Lorcan follows my gaze to the little boy. I remember showing him the picture of my dad as a child and wonder if he's noticed the likeness too.

'D'you see it?' I ask, breathless.

'He has Art's colouring,' Lorcan says 'but there's something else too. He looks like you around the mouth, I think.'

'He looks just like my dad.' As I speak the words, the

296

enormity of the moment presses down on me. This is as basic as it gets – it's genes, it's blood, it's family.

A young woman goes over to the boy. *My* boy. She's plumply pretty, with a short, spiky haircut that would suit someone skinny and petite but sits strangely above her round face and rosy, milkmaid cheeks. She's wearing a bright pink tracksuit that is stretched tight over her bum. Is *this* the woman Art took our baby for?

My mind does the maths in my head. Even if she's a bit older than she looks, this girl couldn't have been more than sixteen when the boy was born. *Surely* there's no way Art could have been having an affair with someone that young?

I start walking towards the boy. The plump girl is gesticulating wildly at him, clearly trying to draw him away from his game. As I get nearer I can hear her sharp, nasal whine.

'Come *on*, Daddy said we have to hurry.'

The little boy growls in annoyance, dodging the girl's hand as she lunges to grab him. He sprints away to the point where the playground meets the drive. I keep my eyes on his face. He's grinning now, one eye on the girl as he chats with the little boy next to him. They are pointing to the horse-chestnut tree on the far side of the playground, gearing up for another race.

The grin falls away and the child's mouth sets in a determined line again. As they start running, Lorcan whispers in my ear.

'I'm going to get that girl talking,' he says. 'You speak to the little boy. Find out what you can.'

I nod and head for the racing boys. My son – how strange those words sound – is putting everything he has into the sprint. Despite the other boy's longer legs, for a few moments he is going faster . . . he's going to win. I will him to. And then he trips and slams into the ground.

The other boy reaches the horse-chestnut tree first and punches the air with a whoop.

'I beat you, Ed, you sucker!'

Ed.

I rush over as he picks himself up off the ground. His knee is grazed – red raw.

'Are you all right?' I gasp.

Ed ignores me. His lips are pressed tightly together, like he's trying not to cry. The grim determination on his face has collapsed. For a second, all I can see in his eyes is defeat. And shame. I've seen that look before. A shiver snakes through my entire body as the memory overwhelms me – a man pressing his palms against a rough pillar. *These stones heal the sick.*

It's more than just the set of the features. It's like the ghost of my father has just drifted across the boy's face.

My father. My son.

I glance over my shoulder. Lorcan is talking to the girl who was calling Ed. It doesn't look like she's noticed him fall over.

The other boy runs off and Ed looks up at me.

'Hi.' I squat down so I'm at his eye level, with the horse-chestnut tree behind me. 'You're Ed, aren't you? You're brave not to cry about hurting your knee.'

The boy looks at me with huge, serious, brown eyes. He glances over at the girl who was calling him. She's busy pointing out of the school gates, explaining something to Lorcan.

'I thought you ran very well,' I say. 'You're fast.'

'I'm the fastest in my class.' The way he says it sounds like a fact, not a brag. The same knack of delivery that Art has. My heart beats faster.

'Are you all right?' I say.

The boy sticks his lip out. He's obviously deciding whether it's okay to talk to me. Then he looks around, taking in the other mums and kids and the sunshine. His gaze fixes for a moment on a curling tear in the wire fence that separates the playground we are in from the one next door. I hold my breath, hoping the environment is sufficiently secure for him not to start screaming for help.

Clearly he decides it is. 'I'd have won if I hadn't fallen over,' he says.

'I could see that.' I gulp, desperate for more information. 'So what's your name – Ed *what*?'

The boy stares at me, instantly on his guard. 'I'm not supposed to talk to strangers.'

'Of course.' Out of the corner of my eye I can see that the girl has clocked me. Lorcan's still talking to her, but she's edging towards us. I can hear them both now – Lorcan is talking in an English accent, pretending his kid has just started at the school.

'Is that your mummy?' I ask, my palms sweating.

Ed wrinkles his nose. 'No way, that's just Kelly. She looks after me.'

Well, that's something. At least Art's mystery woman isn't a child herself. My mind skips again through the options. There's Sandrine, of course. And Hen, though I can't see how. Charlotte West is older than I would have expected. Or maybe someone Art knows through work, like Siena, his secretary, or Camilla on reception. Or another client's wife.

Ed gazes up at me.

'Where do you live?' I ask.

'A bit away,' he says solemnly.

'Just one more thing?' Lorcan's voice sounds close now.

Kelly is almost here. I don't have much time.

Ed is gazing up at me. I can't stop staring at him, soaking up his innocent little face and round dark eyes, while my heart surges with emotion. I know I should move away. That I have his name and I know where he goes to school . . . that I'll only frighten the child if I try to say much more . . . that Lorcan can't hold his nanny off for much longer . . . but I can't stop looking. I take out my phone, praying none of the adults notice what I'm doing.

'Say "cheese"!' I say.

Ed frowns. I take the picture fast.

'Thanks.'

Ed just stares at me. This is my child. My baby. It's like a switch has been flicked on in my heart and I realize just how empty and abstract my previous imaginings were. This child who stands before me is real – a flesh-and-blood mix of my body and Art's. Love grabs me like a fist. It holds me prisoner, as real as the child in front of me.

It's a love I would die for.

'We have to go, Ed.' Kelly sails past me, grabbing the little boy by the wrist. She stares at me as she drags him away, her eyes widening in horror. So, like Bobs, she's seen my picture. She knows who I am. She's been warned against me. 'Come *on*, Ed.'

My insides twist with panic. Knowing Ed's name and school isn't enough. Art could take him away from here this afternoon. They could vanish, never to be seen again.

The little boy grumbles, but lets himself be led away. Kelly is practically running now.

I start after them, a brisk, urgent walk. 'We have to follow them,' I say.

The area by the school gate is crowded and I lose sight of them several times, but Lorcan forges a path through the people and we reach the car a few seconds later.

Kelly and Ed are visible, several metres along the road. Ed is clearly making a fuss at being dragged along. After a moment, Kelly opens the door of a large 4x4 car and Ed disappears into the back seat.

I look down at the photo on my phone. The expression is Art's but there's something about the set of the mouth and the curve of the nose that reminds me of my dad again.

This is my son. The words seep through my mind, becoming real as I think them. This is my son.

Now I have found him, I can't lose him again.

CHAPTER TWENTY

Lorcan starts the engine and manoeuvres away from the kerb. We stay behind the 4x4 for a couple of streets. My whole body is tense, desperate not to lose sight of the car.

'What did the nanny say?' I ask.

'Nothing,' Lorcan says. 'She just kept looking over at you. I pretended I had a kid who'd just started at the school, but she wasn't really listening.'

The big car drives on. I'm leaning forward in my seat, trying to catch a glimpse of Ed. After a few minutes, the car stops outside a large, gated house.

I peer through the windscreen, watching as the iron gates to the house open. The 4x4 drives through. As the gates shut behind it, Lorcan drives slowly by.

'Okay, well, we have an address now.' He looks at me. 'Are you all right?'

I nod. I'm trying to convince myself, as much as Lorcan. I could so easily fall to pieces right now, but I mustn't. I have to stay strong for Ed. I gaze up at the house where he lives with the woman he thinks of as his mother . . . with Art visiting when he can. Clearly they have plenty of money. And Ed seemed well-nourished and content. A happy child. That's a consolation, at least.

For the first time it strikes me that this isn't a child desperate to be rescued, but an ordinary boy settled into a normal, comfortable life. The house is three storeys, detached, brick. There's a lawn at the front. There are rose bushes. There are oak trees. And there is the locked, high gate.

I look down at my nail-bitten hands. All my life I've been on the outside. As a child, hiding my dad's long absences; as a teenager, not wanting to admit to his death, which made me different from other kids. And on and on. Always on the outside. And here, now, I'm on the outside of Ed's life. I don't have a part to play. I am not needed.

Maybe, though it hurts like hell to even think it, I will cause him more harm than good by coming into his life.

'Gen?' I realize Lorcan is speaking to me. I turn to him, trying to ignore the hollow feeling in my stomach.

'I think we have enough to go to the police now. All it's going to take to confirm what we already know is some DNA, which they'll *have* to organize once they hear our story. That will just take a few days, then—'

'We can't wait a few days,' I interrupt. 'Art could take Ed out of the country by then.'

Lorcan puts his hand on my arm. 'Easy,' he says. 'The police will be able to stop them leaving the country. We just need to explain what we've found out.'

I glance over at the house again. 'I don't want to leave him.'

'Okay.' Lorcan frowns. 'How about this ... we'll call you a cab. You go to the police. Explain everything. I'll wait here. If someone takes the boy, I'll follow them.'

I think it over. It makes sense. The only alternative is for me to stay and for Lorcan to speak to the police, but this is my story. It should come from me.

'Trust me, Gen,' Lorcan says. 'I know it's hard, but it's your best option right now.'

303

'Okay.' My phone rings. I look at the screen expecting the call to be from Art, but instead I see Hen's name. I hesitate, then take the call.

'Hello?'

'Oh, Gen.' Her voice is at breaking point, teary and strained. 'I've been so worried about you. Art's been on the phone every five minutes. He's frantic. Why have you run away? I keep thinking about your face when I talked about Art and I've been so upset all day that you could even think that we . . . that me and Art . . .' She pauses for breath and I can hear her sniffing. 'Oh, Gen, please tell me you believe me, *please*.'

I stare out of the car window, feeling numb. Part of me wants to tell Hen what I know just to hear her reaction . . . that Ed exists . . . that Art has a double life with some other woman . . . that people have been killed to keep this information hidden . . . But it's hard to say the words.

'Gen?' Hen is clearly on the verge of tears. 'Please talk to me.'

My mind flashes back to her conviction that Art's 'MDO' payment stood for Manage Debt Online. Hen knows more than she's told me. I'm sure of it.

'What do you know, Hen?' I ask. 'If you want me to trust you, you have to be honest. I *know* there's something you haven't told me, so please don't lie. It was about that money, wasn't it? Something about Art being in debt?'

'He isn't . . . it wasn't . . .' Hen sobs. 'Oh, Gen, no.'

'No what?'

'Nothing.' She sniffs again. 'It's nothing.'

She's definitely hiding something. I can hear it in her voice. 'Okay, if you're not going to tell me . . .' I wait.

There's a tense pause, then Hen's voice cracks. 'It was . . . it is, oh Gen, I didn't want you to know . . .'

My stomach twists into knots. 'Know what?'

304

Hen takes a deep breath. 'Art paid that fifty grand for *me*,' Hen explains. 'I was broke, okay? Nat had just been born and I was in terrible debt, worse than I ever admitted to you. I'd signed up with Manage Debt Online because I thought it would all be clean and simple and done over the internet, but they're loan sharks. When I couldn't pay the loan back, they added interest, then they came after me, threatening me . . . and Nat . . .'

I think back. Hen was certainly in debt all the time I knew her, until her marriage to Rob. But could things really have been that bad without her telling me?

'Why didn't you say something?' I said.

'At first because I was embarrassed . . . ashamed, almost . . . I mean you were so sorted about everything. You'd got your books published, you'd found Art . . . I had nothing. No job, no man.' She pauses. 'Then you lost your baby and my worries seemed pathetic next to that, so . . .' She tails off.

'But you told *Art*?' She's surely making this up. '*Art* gave you fifty grand?'

'He *loaned* it to me,' Hen insists. 'He found me crying when I came to see you after Beth . . . I poured it all out to him and he offered to help. God, Gen, I paid him back. Bits here and there for years. And Rob paid off the balance last year, so it's all over, Gen. Finished.'

I still can't believe this is all Art's MDO payment amounts to. 'So why didn't you tell me?'

'Tell you what?'

'That you needed the money? That Art gave it to you? Why didn't *he* tell me?' Terrifying possibilities crowd my head. My husband and my best friend in hushed conversation behind my back. One thing leading to another. Secrets.

More secrets.

'Were you . . . did you . . .?'

'*No*,' Hen wails. 'No, Gen, how can you think that? I just owed a lot of money and Art helped. You *know* I was in debt back then.'

'Why didn't you say something when I asked you last week?'

'I couldn't tell you last week because I didn't tell you eight years ago. And I didn't tell you eight years ago because . . .' She hesitates.

'Why?' I sit up in the passenger seat, trembling. I'm aware of Lorcan beside me. He's staring at me, his eyes filled with concern. 'Give me one good reason why you didn't tell me, your best friend, that your debts were that bad?'

'Isn't it obvious?'

What the hell does that mean? 'I don't—'

'For goodness' sake, Gen; your baby had just bloody died. You couldn't look at mine without crying.'

'But you could have still told me.'

'Could I?' Hen's voice hardens. 'The way I remember it, no one else was really allowed to have anything bad going on in their lives back then.'

I gasp. 'That's not fair.'

'Yes, it is,' Hen snaps. 'D'you have any idea how hard it was for me to be a single mother . . . a first-time mother . . . and have my best friend completely cut off from me?'

'I know I wasn't there for you but—'

'I'm not blaming you! *Jesus*.' Hen sobs, her voice softening again. 'I know how hard it was for you *and* how hard it was for you to see me with Nat. I'm just trying to explain that I was desperate and Art offered to help. That's all there was to it.'

'No.' I won't believe it. Hen has betrayed me, just like Art did. And now there's no way I can trust anything she tells me. It's possible her story is true. But isn't it equally possible that Art paid her the money for some other reason? Could she have found out he took our baby away? Did she know about Art's other family?

'Were you *blackmailing* him?' I demand.

'No, oh, for God's sake, Gen. Eight years ago it was like *you* died. Art was devastated, yes, but he carried on with his life. You . . . you stopped living. To be honest, I don't think you've started living again. Not properly.'

For a moment I feel the truth of what she's said: the weight of the past few years crushing me; not just losing my baby, but everything damaged or destroyed because of that loss.

'I have to go now,' I say. The air in the car feels heavy. Dull. Flat. There's no point talking to Hen. I still can't trust what she tells me.

'Gen?'

'Bye.' I ring off and close my eyes. How has my life come to this? That I'm sitting here, having to face the fact that my husband and my best friend have kept so much hidden from me; that I can't trust a word either of them says; that a man I have known for less than a week should be the one sitting beside me at the most important moment of my life.

'What was that—?'

'It doesn't matter now.' I turn to Lorcan. He's holding his phone in his hand, still looking troubled. 'Have you found the nearest police station?'

'Yes,' he says. 'It's about five miles away, in a town called Enshott. I've called you a cab.'

I stare out of the window at the house where my child lives. I am still so far from the whole truth.

The taxi arrives. I glance over at the house again. There's no sign of anyone coming or going. I lean over and kiss Lorcan on the cheek. 'Stay safe,' I say.

'Gen?'

'I'll call you from the police station.'

As the cab heads off towards Enshott, my phone rings again. I'm anticipating another call from Hen – or maybe Art, but when I glance at the screen I see that the caller is Bernard O'Donnell. We haven't spoken since Lorcan and I set off for Shepton Longchamp hours earlier. Discovering Ed pushed all thoughts of Bernard out of my head.

I snatch the phone to my ear. 'Bernard? I'm sorry I haven't called. We're in Shepton Longchamp and—'

'I'm here too.' Bernard's voice cuts through mine. I stop talking instantly, wondering what new revelation is coming.

'I've been following your husband. He went to the Wardingham Arms again, early this afternoon.'

I gasp. Art must have arrived soon after Lorcan and I left for Somerset.

'This time I waited *outside* and I saw him leave and walk to another hotel . . . the . . . the Princess Alice.' Bernard is speaking so fast the words are tumbling over themselves. 'I saw him get into a VW car. I followed him here, to Shepton Longchamp. He's just parked outside a garage . . . a lock-up on the edge of town. Looks like he's waiting for something.'

My head spins. I look back towards the house as my taxi driver turns the corner. 'Oh God, Bernard.'

'Did you find the shop you were looking for?'

'Yes, and . . .' I lower my voice so the driver can't hear. 'And we found my little boy. Bernard, he's a *boy*, not a girl. Did your wife . . . did Lucy know about that?'

Bernard draws in his breath, clearly shocked. 'No. Mary just told Lucy "baby", but when we looked you up online we saw the references to "Beth" so we assumed the baby was a girl. You're sure it's a boy?'

'Yes.' I try to focus. 'Where exactly is this lock-up?'

'Rushdown Road. It's round the back of some woodland. The place looks pretty beat-up from the outside.' Bernard sucks in his breath. 'Wait, there's a woman – she just got out of a cab. She's going over to Mr Loxley.'

Fear mingles with furious curiosity. 'Who is she? What does she look like?'

'I don't know; she's wearing a blue hat or cap or something. It's pulled low over her face. She's slim. I can see blonde hair. Your husband is just getting out of his car. The cab she came in is driving off. They're talking together.'

I clutch my mobile more tightly. The taxi driver is watching me curiously in the rear-view mirror. I turn away, holding the phone closer to my mouth.

'Is there a child with them?'

'No. Now they're going inside the lock-up.'

My heart races. Is it possible that Art is with this woman he calls his wife – and that Ed is going to be brought to them? Surely Lorcan would have seen if Ed had left the house? Except . . . my thoughts run over each other. Lorcan is waiting outside the front of the house. There could easily be a back door . . . maybe it leads to the woodland . . . maybe Ed has been taken through the woods to the lock-up . . . maybe Art and the woman are waiting for him right now, ready to make their escape . . .

Another thought presses down on me. It's possible that Lorcan is somehow involved. I push this away. I can't let myself doubt him too.

'I'm on my way.' I ring off and give the Rushdown Road address to the cab driver. 'How far from there are we?'

The driver glances over his shoulder at me. 'Just a couple of streets,' he says.

'Go there,' I say. 'As fast as you can.'

As the taxi reaches the woods Bernard described, the cab

slows down. My heart is pounding as I catch sight of the lock-ups. There's a car parked just beyond. It's not Art's VW. Still, I've only been a few minutes. Art and his woman must be here. I've got them at last. Violent images of what I'll do flash into my head. I imagine the burning fury inside me erupting out of my hands . . . my nails clawing at her face . . . my feet trampling her into the ground . . .

And then all of a sudden I see Ed in my mind's eye. My baby is this woman's little boy. At least, that's what he has become after nearly eight years.

It sickens me, but hurting her will hurt him too. The argument rages inside my head as the taxi slows to a stop. When Ed was an idea, it was easy . . . he was my child and I had a right to take him back. But now I've seen his school and his home and his nanny and, most of all, I've seen him. He's a real person with a settled life. It might be the wrong life – but it's *his* life. The one he's used to. And I'm about to explode it into tiny pieces. I grit my teeth. I'll just have to work that out later. I'm his mother. And he has a right to know me . . . to be with me, just as I have a right to be with him.

The driver looks round at me. 'That's four pounds fifty, please.'

'Would you mind just waiting for a minute?' As I speak, I look on the seat for my bag and realize to my horror that I left it on the floor of Lorcan's car. My purse is inside it. I look up to find the cab driver staring at me. He looks furious.

'What, you were going to do a runner?'

'No. It's not that . . . oh, shit . . .' I stammer. 'I'm sorry, look, please wait. I'm meeting someone here. I'm sure they'll help.'

The cab driver indicates the road ahead. 'Where is he then?' he asks aggressively.

I follow his gaze. The row of lock-ups starts just a few metres in front of us, exactly as Bernard described. But there's no sign of Bernard himself. I look around, feeling desperate. Traffic is passing, but there's only one car parked – it's on the other side of the road, but quite clearly empty.

'I don't know where he is . . .' I delve into my pockets, hoping to find some cash, but there's nothing in my jeans apart from a screwed-up paper tissue.

'Get out,' the driver says roughly.

'No, please . . . please wait . . . how am I going to get to the police station? I've got to—'

'Piss off.'

I have no choice but to scramble out of the taxi. I catch sight of my pale, strained face in the wing mirror as I open the cab door. I can hardly blame the driver for not trusting me. I look deranged.

I slam the door shut and the car zooms off. I scuttle along the side of the road, looking around for Bernard. No sign. I reach the lock-ups. There are three of them in a row. Each one has a metal door covered in rust. Half the side wall of the first is missing. It's obvious no one is using them as garages any more.

I stand there, as two cars swoosh by. The sun is out and beating down on my head. Where the hell is Bernard?

I look up and down the road. The parked car must surely be his, so why isn't he waiting for me? And where is Art's VW? I try Bernard's phone. It goes to voicemail.

Shit. I leave a message saying that I'm outside the lock-up, and wait a minute, hoping he'll call back.

My heart is thumping so hard I can hear it over the noise of the next car that passes. I carry on waiting in an agony of indecision. Seconds pass that feel like minutes. Still no sign of Bernard. A succession of possibilities grip me, paralyzing me.

Suppose Bernard has left?

Suppose Art and the woman have left too?

Suppose, in fact, the whole thing was a ruse to get me away from Ed's house so that I wouldn't witness Art collecting him? Or a trap to bring me here?

Except . . . I glance over at the car parked opposite again. It's a hire car. Bernard *must* be here. Maybe he's simply inside one of these lock-ups, checking it out. If Art and the woman *have* left, then Bernard might be snooping about in there. I have to find out. It'll only take a second, then I can go.

Taking a deep breath, I walk on, past the first broken-down lock-up. Thanks to the collapsed wall I can see at a glance that there's no one inside it. I get a glimpse of the woods behind. The trees are densely packed together, surrounding the lock-ups on three sides. Bernard was right – it would be easy to bring some-body in and out through the back. The second lock-up is boarded up. I can't see any way of getting past the padlock chained to the front.

I stop outside the third and final lock-up. The metal door set into the front has been pulled to, but it's not properly shut. A rusting handle hangs limply at waist height. There's a stillness about this place, the only sound the light ruffle of the wind in the branches of the surrounding trees. I push at the door. It creaks halfway open. Holding my breath, I peer into the gloom.

'Bernard?' I whisper.

No reply.

A single car zooms along the road behind me. I hesitate for a second, not wanting to go inside. Christ, maybe I'm being supremely stupid and this *is* a trap . . . with Bernard in on the whole thing, and Art and his bloody woman waiting inside to grab me and . . .

I have to know for sure. I don't have time to work out what's going on. I pick up a large stick that's lying on the ground. It is heavy and feels solid and sturdy in my hands. It's not much of a weapon but it's better than nothing. Heart racing, I push the door open fully and step inside.

It's empty. I'm sure it's empty. There's not much light and I can't see the corners of the room, but the door at the other end is wide open, letting in enough sunshine for me to see stacks of dust-covered crates piled against the walls. Gripping my stick, I tiptoe towards the far door, every nerve in my body tensed, listening for any sounds.

I reach the far door. There's a patch of battered grass straight ahead, bright in the sunlight, then the woods beyond. A shoe lies on the ground, just past the door.

I stare at it, taking a moment to register what I see. My heartbeat thumps in my ears.

It's not just a shoe. It's a foot.

Sweat beads on my forehead. For a moment I'm too terrified to move. Then I take another step to the door. Everything twists and tightens inside me as the body on the grass comes into full view.

It's a man's body: face-down, slightly curled over, with one hand clutching something. I creep towards him, out of the lockup, onto the grass, into the sunshine. Birds are singing in the woods beyond. There is no one around.

Numb, I crouch down and peer at the man's pale face.

It's Bernard O'Donnell. I place my shaking fingers against his neck, feeling for a pulse. Nothing. The fading warmth of his skin and the blank, soulless stare of his open eyes confirm what is already obvious.

Bernard O'Donnell is dead.

I stare at his face for a few moments, then reach out and close his eyes. Strangely, I feel quite calm. My eyes travel slowly down his body. His shirt is strained over his stomach, one of the buttons hanging by a thread. Blood is seeping through a hole in

313

his jacket. I know nothing about such things, but it looks like a bullet hole. My eyes rest on his right hand. The fingers are curled over something small and black. Numbly, carefully, I prise them open and pull out the phone he is holding. I take a step back from the body and try to work out what to do. I'm still strangely calm, but I can't seem to think straight.

Bernard O'Donnell is dead. That's all that my head seems able to take in. Why would he have come inside the lock-up? To follow Art and the woman? I gaze down at the phone in my hand. My own call, made from outside, just a moment ago, will be logged here. A thought strikes me. What if Bernard used his mobile to take a picture of the woman Art was with?

I press at the keys. With trembling fingers I select the images file. The most recent pictures are of Lucy O'Donnell. There's nothing here from today.

A scraping noise – like a crate being pushed across concrete – sounds from inside the lock-up. Someone is there.

I back away, my eyes on the door.

Footsteps cross the lock-up. They're coming towards me.

Terror rises, a noose around my throat. My feet seem to move of their own accord and before I know what I'm doing I've turned and am running, full pelt, into the wood behind the lock-ups.

I crash through the undergrowth. The trees are set close together, the branches hanging low over my head. I pound the twig-strewn earth beneath my feet. It's muddy from the recent rain. I'm panting, listening out for the sound of someone following me. I duck behind a large tree, flattening myself against the trunk.

I listen again. There's no sound in the woods apart from the birds and the wind and the distant hum of the road.

My mind is in freefall – a chaotic whirlwind of thoughts and images. I see Ed being dragged along the road, then Lorcan's smile, then Bernard's body lying twisted on the grass.

Nausea rises inside me, then subsides and, at last I have a clear and coherent thought. I need to call the police. 999. The long-ago-learned emergency number. The national safety net.

I look down. I have dropped not only the stick I was holding but Bernard's phone, which I know was in my hand when I heard the noise from the lock-up. But my own phone is still in my pocket. I reach into my jeans but before I can draw it out, a twig snaps to my right and I look up and he's standing there.

Art.

Mummy always said I should be careful of the Bad People. But that day, when they came, I didn't know they were Bad People so it wasn't fair when I got home and Mummy was cross at me. I tried to tell Mummy I didn't know, but she was shouting too hard to hear me. She said she always told me to watch out for strangers especially when she is not here and that lady was a stranger and so why was I letting her take my photo? And then Daddy came in and told her to stop yelling and then she was shouting at Daddy that he was Hardly Ever Here and it was All His Fault and then they made me go upstairs.

I sat on my bed and looked at the dressing gown I'd imagined before was a Bad Lady and then Mummy came and said what I had already guessed, that the lady outside school was a Bad Lady in real life, which was why Kelly pulled me away all rough and Mummy was upset.

Mummy said Daddy and she would deal with the Bad Lady but if she ever came again I would have to be her brave knight and do really clever fighting. That was a baby way to put it, because knights like that are just in stories, but I was only young then. Mummy said the Bad Lady would tell me lies and try to Poison My Mind against her and that I had to remember she is my real mummy, no matter what anyone says or if they try to trick me.

Then she told me her Special Fighting Plan.

CHAPTER TWENTY-ONE

Art and I stare at each other. His face is pale, his dark eyes appalled.

'Gen?'

He takes a step towards me, through the trees. The twigs on the ground snap under his shoes. He stops and puts his hand against the bark of the tree beside him, just a few feet away.

Bernard's body flashes into my mind's eye.

'You killed him,' I breathe.

'No.' Art shakes his head. 'No, Gen, not that. I didn't do that.'

'Yes, you lied and you took our baby away and now you're a murderer.'

Art stares at me. His eyes are an agony of feeling. 'No, that's not it. Oh, Gen.' He walks closer towards me. The sun vanishes behind his head. My whole body is trembling.

Art stands right in front of me. 'Listen,' he says. 'Please. I know I've lied and it's unforgivable and . . .' He takes a deep breath. 'What matters is now. I'm going to tell you the truth. Just listen.'

I don't believe him. I want to run, but my legs are rooted to the spot.

'Bernard O'Donnell knew what you were doing and you killed him and . . .' Panic whirls up in my head. 'Are you here to kill me? Is that next? Are you going to kill *me*?'

'No, Gen.' Art's eyes are pleading with me to believe him. His desperation is in the lines on his forehead and the hunch of his shoulders. He's wearing a shirt I gave him. It's the one with the tiny hidden rip on the back of the collar. How can I know such a minor detail about Art's life but have no idea whether he might be about to try and kill me?

'What the hell have you done, Art?'

He rubs his temple. It's such a familiar gesture and yet he is now a stranger.

'Please, listen, Gen. It wasn't me. I didn't kill O'Donnell.'

I stare at him. 'But you know who did?'

'Yes.' He must be talking about the woman he's with . . . the evil bitch who has my baby.

'Who is she?' I snarl.

Art shakes his head. 'There's no time.'

'You said you'd tell me the truth.' I feel myself standing straighter. This might be a new Art but it's a new me, too, and I feel strong in the face of his helplessness. 'Tell me who this woman is for whom you have betrayed absolutely everything between us?' My voice rises. I'm almost shouting. I push myself off my tree and fold my arms. The light in the patch of woodland is almost silvery. Clouds are gathering around the sun. I can smell the hint of rain in the air. I steady my gaze.

'You took our baby away,' I yell. 'You paid the doctor and the other staff to say he was a girl and that she was stillborn. You looked me in the eye and you lied to me. All these things are true. And you did it all for some other woman.'

The wind drops and the trees are silent. Art keeps his gaze fixed on my face. His eyes fill with shame. 'Yes,' he says. 'Yes, all these things are true.'

I wait for him to defend himself, for the inevitable 'but' at the end of the sentence. But Art simply hangs his head.

A devastating calm settles inside me. Art has, at last, admitted what he has done. I'm not going insane. And yet there is still no resolution. The enormity of his betrayal is barely conceivable.

'Who is she?' I'm shaking with rage.

'It doesn't matter.' Art rubs his forehead. The first drops of rain fall.

'What?' I shout. 'What d'you mean it doesn't matter? Who is she? Is it Sandrine?'

'Gen, *please*.'

'Charlotte West?'

Art shakes his head. 'I don't even know who that is.'

'The woman from my writing class who called you twelve times in one day just before she came to our house. You said you didn't know her.'

Art frowns. 'I don't. I did get a load of calls, but that's been happening off and on since *The Trials*. If she tried to call me I don't remember it. The only time I spoke to that woman was when she showed up on our doorstep.'

I stare at him. I'm almost certain he's lying again. I'm not going to tell him Charlotte West called me earlier. Responding to him means engaging with him – he'll think I'm starting to buy into what he's telling me. And I won't do that.

'I want to meet her.'

'What?' Art frowns.

'The woman. Charlotte or whoever. *Your* woman.'

'No, Gen. That's crazy.'

'How *dare* you say anything I want is crazy after you made me feel I was going insane about Beth. Losing her. Finding she's a *boy*, for God's sake. I have a right to meet—'

'You can't,' Art says.

'Why?' I demand. 'Do I know her?' My mind ransacks the options. I can't bear to think it, but I have to ask. 'Is it Hen?'

319

'No, *no*.'

'Does Hen *know* who it is?'

'Gen, *please*.'

'So if Hen doesn't know, why did you pay off all her debts and not tell me?'

Art's eyes widen with surprise. 'Because she was desperate and the last thing you needed was to have to deal with her problems on top of everything else. I'd honestly forgotten about it when you asked me that first time.'

I stare at him. I have no idea whether he's telling me the truth or not.

'None of this is like you think, Gen,' Art pleads. 'You don't understand.'

'Then bloody explain it,' I shout. 'Because I think I have a right to know who she is, this woman *my son* calls *Mummy*.'

'I can't tell you who she is, but we're *not*, *it's never* . . . it's . . . *you're* the only one who matters.' Art's chest heaves. 'Oh Gen, I love you *so* much.'

'You lie to me for eight years, you give my baby to another woman and you expect me to believe that you love me?' The contempt in my voice is acid.

Art rubs his temple furiously. 'I don't expect anything,' he says. 'I'm just trying to explain that everything I did was to protect you.'

'What?' It's raining harder now, the pattering on the leaves drowning out the distant hum of the traffic. 'How is any of this to protect me?'

'I can't explain without putting you in more danger,' Art says. 'The Renners – Bitsy and Bobs – when you started digging around, she warned them about you. And Kelly as well.'

'They know I'm your wife?'

Art looks ashamed. He takes a deep breath. 'They think you're mentally unstable, potentially violent.'

'*What?*'

'That's how we explained me being on *The Trials* as Art Loxley, why I have to use a different name down here. They think, *she* told them, that you might be a danger to . . . us . . .' He tails off.

'A danger?' I can't believe what I'm hearing.

'Once we knew you'd seen the Fair Angel CCTV film, *she* was scared you'd find out about Ed,' Art explains. 'She showed Bitsy and Bobs and Kelly your picture and told them to warn her immediately if they saw you snooping around Shepton.'

I stare at him blankly. Why on earth has Art been prepared to go along with all this?

'Don't you see what that means?' Art goes on. 'She *knows* you're *here*. You have to go. Go back to London.'

'Don't be so bloody melodramatic. You can't seriously think I'm just going to walk away?' I shake my head. It's almost impossible to believe the man standing in front of me with rain dripping down his face is my proud, driven, successful husband. I shudder as I look at him. A drop of water trickles down my spine. 'Come on, Art. If you're not going to kill me, what danger am I in?'

There's a pause, then Art glances in the direction of the lockup. 'You're right. She did . . . that . . .'

An image of Bernard's twisted body forces its way into my mind's eye.

We stand in silence for a moment. A car hums in the distance. Rain patters around us.

'You're saying she'll kill *me*?'

'She might, Gen.' Art meets my gaze. His eyes are pleading with me.

Hurt and fury rise up inside me. 'You think she might kill me and you *still* won't tell me who she is.'

'I don't know for sure what she'll do,' Art says. 'But the closer you get to her, the more danger you're in. I saw her kill O'Donnell. She guessed he might follow us. That's why she made me meet her at the lock-up, not the house. But when he turned up she got hysterical because he'd seen her . . . It wasn't done in cold blood, she panicked and the gun was in her hand, so . . . Look, it's simple, Gen. You're just not safe if you keep pushing at this.'

I stare at him.

'Art, you have to go to the police.'

His eyes widen with alarm. 'No.'

'It's not just Bernard O'Donnell, is it? The bitch killed his wife, Lucy, too, and the anaesthetist, Gary Bloode, didn't she? And she sent that guy to mug me . . . to take the memory stick with the CCTV footage?'

'I don't know about Bloode or Lucy O'Donnell.' Art's voice is a whisper. 'But yes, she arranged to get the memory stick back. I didn't know at the time, but Rodriguez told her you'd taken it and—'

'And now you're saying she's going to kill me?'

She's terrified that she'll lose everything . . .

'And she'll do anything to stop me from being with him? With *our son* . . .'

The two words slam into me. *Our son.* It should have been me and Art taking him shopping on Saturdays, holding his hand, walking him home from school. Instead, some other woman has become his mother . . . stolen years of his life from me. I can barely take it in.

'Why have you done this, Art?' My voice breaks as a tidal wave of images washes over me: the lilies at Beth's funeral, arguing with Mum about scattering the ashes – I'd wanted to scatter them on the South Coast, like we did with Dad; she wanted a service at the crematorium – the willow tree through the window of the Fair Angel hospital, the white babygro, soft and empty in my hands. All of it built around an illusion – the lilies for a death that was a birth, the ashes only wood and dust, the pain and the memories. All for nothing. 'How could you do this to me? I don't understand . . . *why* did you give her our baby?'

'I had to,' Art says, his voice barely audible. The rain has stopped now, but our hair is plastered to our heads, our clothes soaked through.

'*Why* did you have to?' I persist. 'What on earth could justify taking a little boy away from his mother?' I pause. 'What could justify destroying my life?'

'I can't explain, Gen, you're safer if you don't know.' Art rubs his arms. He's only wearing a thin jumper over his shirt. It's dirty as well as wet.

'I'm *safer*?' I say. 'If I'm really in this much danger, why can't you stop her? Why can't you just go to the police?'

'That won't work.'

'Art, this is crazy. You're talking about this woman as if she's beyond the law or something. You've admitted to me that you *saw* her murder Bernard O'Donnell. Let's just go to the police and tell them.'

'You don't understand,' Art says. 'My word won't count for anything, not if people find out about Ed and . . . and how I got everyone to lie that he was stillborn.'

'Then you have to *tell* the police about that. *Tell* them how she forced you to give up our baby. Tell *me*.'

There's a long pause as a breeze rustles the branches above us, sending a patter of raindrops onto our heads.

323

'Paying Rodriguez to lie about Ed and paying the others involved to keep quiet about it was the price of your safety,' he says. 'Lying about Ed is *still* the price of your safety.'

'What are you talking about?' I say.

'Back then, when Ed was born . . . she said she would kill you if I didn't do what she said. So I had to choose,' he says slowly. 'A straightforward choice, between you and Ed. I chose you. I chose to keep you alive and to let Ed go, knowing that he would be safe and looked after and I could come here, like I do every couple of weeks, and spend a few hours so I would still get to be his father.'

'But I wouldn't get to be his mother?' I spit the words out.

'I thought, back then, that you and I could have another baby,' Art says. 'I always thought that. I didn't imagine for a second that you wouldn't be pregnant again within months.'

'But I wasn't Art, was I?' Pain twists inside me. 'I didn't get pregnant again. I didn't get to be a mother. Anyway, how did you know this woman of yours – that you were so prepared to give everything to – wouldn't demand the next baby or the one after that?'

'It was atonement,' Art says. 'I owed her. One baby was the payment.'

'You're not making any sense. Payment for *what*?' I take out my phone. 'If *you* won't do it, then *I'm* calling the police.'

'Please don't, Gen. Please think about what I'm saying. If you do that, you won't ever see Ed again.'

I hesitate, my hand over the keypad on my phone. 'That's rubbish. I know where he lives . . . where he goes to school . . .'

'She'll take him away. She'll stop you,' Art insists. 'Look, she and I just argued about it. I said I would try and get you to back off. That if you did, there'd be no need to . . . to take things any further.'

'And what did *she* say?' The words fly furiously out of me.

'She didn't say anything for sure, but I can persuade her to leave you alone. It can end here, if you'll just back away.'

'And if I don't, she's going to kill me?'

'I honestly think that she might. Before, when you started snooping around, I thought I could handle her but now, after O'Donnell . . . *Please*, Gen, Ed is okay. He's looked after. He has a stable life. He's not being abused or unloved. I visit him when I can. Just let it go.'

'Are you listening to what you're asking?' My voice rises, tears choking me. 'You're asking me to forget he's my son . . . to walk away. It's impossible.'

'It's the only way you'll be safe. If you let all this go everything can carry on as before. I'm in this brilliant position with work. I'm advising the Prime Minister on policy and he's listening. I'm in his inner circle, Gen . . .'

'What's your work got to do with this?' I say, disgusted. Is this woman somehow connected with Loxley Benson and Art's government contract? My mind flashes immediately to vivacious Sandrine. 'It *is* her,' I insist. 'Sandrine. She came to our party with her hus—'

'No.' Art shakes his head. 'I didn't mean . . . my work itself doesn't have anything to do with this, but there are reasons . . . I won't be able to work if you carry on pushing this . . .'

'I'm not pushing anything. And I don't care about your bloody work. I've just found out that—'

'You have to go away. Back home or . . . maybe even somewhere abroad. Just for a while, so I can calm things down.'

'You're mad.' I press the '9' on my keypad once. 'I'm calling the police.'

'Let Lorcan help you get away,' Art says.

My finger stops, poised over the '9'. 'Lorcan?' I look up, my heart thudding.

SOPHIE MCKENZIE

'I know you've been with him,' Art growls. 'I know he's helped you already, so let him help you get out of the country.' His expression grows fiercer. 'Though that's all you should let him do, he's not good enough for you any other way.'

'Why? Because of him sleeping with a client's wife?' I snap. 'I know the truth about that now, Art. It was *you* who slept with her.'

Art's face reddens. 'That was a long time ago,' he says.

'That was a lie. *Another* lie. Jesus, Art, I don't know who you are any more.'

There's a long pause.

'Whatever happened in the past, Lorcan still isn't good enough. Christ, I can't bear the thought of you with *anyone* else.' He curls his lip. 'Especially not him. But what matters now is you getting away from here. Just for a couple of weeks ... long enough to prove you've stopped coming after Ed. Please, Gen, because unless you leave right now, I can't guarantee you'll be safe. Or Lorcan for that matter.'

I hesitate. 'You mean she might hurt him too?'

Art nods. 'Lorcan's in danger as long as he knows things ... as long as he's helping you come after Ed.'

I have no idea how much of what Art is telling me is the truth, but I can't take the risk of Lorcan getting hurt. Suppose she's already got to him somehow? I cancel the half-dialled 999 call and scroll to *Contacts*.

Keeping my eyes on Art, I find Lorcan's name and press *Call*. He answers on the first ring.

'Gen? I was just about to call you. Are you at the police station yet?'

'Lorcan? Are you all right?'

Art backs away. 'Go,' he whispers. 'Be safe.'

I press the phone to my ear but my eyes are on Art.

326

'What is it?' Lorcan says. 'Don't they believe you?'

'Are you really okay?' As I speak, the rain starts again – a light drizzle.

Art squints up at the sky and turns away.

'I'm fine.' Lorcan's voice is full of concern. 'What's happened?'

'Are you still at the house?'

Art vanishes behind a tree. I move sideways, trying to keep him in view, but I can't see him.

'Yes,' Lorcan says. 'There's no sign of the boy or the nanny.'

'Okay.' I walk to the edge of the trees, but Art has gone, presumably through the lock-up and out onto the road. 'Bernard called me,' I explain. 'He followed Art to Shepton earlier. He said he'd seen Art and a blonde woman so I came to meet him but Art was here—'

'Art?' Lorcan's voice rises. 'Are you okay?'

'Yes, he admitted everything but, oh, Lorcan. It's Bernard.' As I walk towards the lock-up, the body comes into view. I stop, feeling sick.

'What about Bernard?'

'She killed him. Art said the woman he's with murdered him.'

Lorcan sucks in his breath. 'Where exactly are you?'

I give the address. 'It's just a few minutes away from where you are right now. I'm going to call the police.'

'No,' Lorcan insists. 'Not now. Art and this woman could come back any second.'

'No, that doesn't make sense. Art said it was the *woman* who killed Bernard. And she isn't here any more. Plus Art wants me to leave. He said everything would be okay if I backed off . . . went away for a bit. But I can't leave Ed.'

'Listen to me, Gen.' Lorcan's voice is strained with emotion. 'Think about it logically. If Art came to warn you off, then he and this woman are going to wait to see whether you take the warning, aren't they? They're not going to abandon everything and vanish with your son until they absolutely know they have to. Art has *far* too much to lose. He's not going to leave Loxley Benson behind unless he thinks there's no other choice. So the first thing you need to do is get out of there.'

'Okay.' I start retracing my steps towards Bernard's body and the lock-up entrance. 'You need to be careful too.'

'I can look after myself,' Lorcan says. 'Just get out of there.'

'If he'd wanted to kill me I'd already be dead. He just wants me to walk away.'

'Then *walk away*. Please, Gen, I'm begging you. I'm starting the car now. I'll be there soon.'

'What about Ed?'

'We can come straight back here. You just said it's only a few minutes away.'

'Okay.' As I end the call, I reach Bernard's body. His phone must still be here, where I dropped it when Art startled me earlier. Maybe there will be useful information stored inside it. Bracing myself, I look down. But the phone is nowhere to be seen.

I shiver. Lorcan's right. Art could be hiding nearby, watching to see what I do.

I'm still holding my own phone in my hand. 'Okay,' I say loudly into my mobile. 'No police. I'll see you soon.'

Somehow I make myself walk back through the dark of the lock-up and out the other side. The world is carrying on as normal. A lone car speeds past. The sun has come out and is warming my back through my jacket but my hair is horribly wet and my jeans are clinging damply to my legs.

Two minutes later, Lorcan speeds round the corner. He screeches to a halt, keeping the engine running as I get in. As we roar away, I put the heating on. We drive back to the house. We've only been away a few minutes but I'm still overwhelmed with relief when I see the large car still parked just inside the gates. I strain my eyes, hoping to catch a glimpse of Ed at one of the windows, but there's no sign.

'This house backs onto others,' Lorcan says, parking a few metres along the road. 'I don't think there's a way out to the woods. Anyone leaving would have to go through the gates.'

I sit back and go over what Art told me. It comes down to this: he wants me to act as if nothing has happened. He wants me to go home and pick up the pieces of our life together – or leave him and start again, on my own or with Lorcan.

'How can Art just believe I'll walk away?' I ask.

'From what you say, he sounds desperate, like he's been backed into a corner by something.'

'Or someone.'

I close my eyes. Why does this woman to whom Art has given our child have such power over him? What did he mean when he said it was *atonement*?

Lorcan and I talk some more. I have no idea what we should do next. Part of me wants to break into the house and take Ed. Now.

And yet I know that isn't the right thing to do. If we attempt to remove Ed from his house by force, we will inevitably frighten him. Plus, if even half of Art's warnings are true, then by forcing the issue, I will be putting myself – and Ed, and Lorcan – in severe danger.

'You know, we could just dial 999,' Lorcan suggests. 'You could just report Bernard O'Donnell's body . . . tell the police what Art told you . . .'

'Then the police will start swarming all over that lock-up and Art will know I went to them and he'll take Ed away and *she* will have me "taken care of" before I can give evidence.'

SOPHIE MCKENZIE

I peer along the road, towards Art's house. *Her* house.

'Who the hell is she, Lorcan?'

He shakes his head. 'Did Bernard say what she looked like?'

'He said she was slim and blonde. It sounds like Charlotte West, but Art denied she had anything to do with it.'

'Of course he denied it,' Lorcan says.

I take a deep breath. 'Okay,' I say. 'It's time to go to the police, like you said. We need to tell them everything *and* we need to make sure Art thinks I'm being reasonable and doing what he asked.'

'How are we going to do both those things?' Lorcan asks.

To answer, I pick up my phone and scroll to Art's mobile number. He's there on the first ring.

'Gen, are you all right?' He's whispering. I'm suddenly certain he's with *her* again. I strain my ears, hoping to catch a sound of her voice, but there's no background noise at all, as if Art is speaking in a vacuum. Then I hear a door shutting in the distance.

Fury grips me. A fist inside my guts.

'Meet me again, Art,' I say, trying to keep my voice soft. I glance sideways at Lorcan. He's raising his eyebrows. 'Meet me in that pub along the road . . . the Dog and Duck it was called. Meet me and let's talk it through. I won't ask about her again. It's . . . it's just that I don't understand this, Art. I know you want me to walk away, but I can't go without understanding this better.'

There's a long pause. At last Art speaks.

'Okay,' he says. 'I'll be there in ten minutes.'

'Make it fifteen,' I say. 'I need time to get away from Lorcan. I don't want him to know I'm seeing you.'

Another long pause. 'Okay,' Art says finally. 'But hurry.'

We ring off and I turn to Lorcan, still sitting beside me. Outside the skies are clouding over again. The light is fading from the day.

'That is a *seriously* bad idea.' Lorcan sounds incredulous. 'You can't—'

'I'm not really going to meet him. I just wanted to make sure he thinks there's a chance I'll back off . . . I don't want him to panic and . . . and Ed get taken away.'

Lorcan glances across to the house. 'So he thinks you're doing what you've been told, while in reality we go to the police? What will you say to Art when he rings asking where you are?'

'He won't,' I say. 'Because we're going to get the police to come with me. And they'll arrest him and *make* him talk before he gets a chance to speak to me again.'

'Right,' Lorcan says. 'Then we'd better hurry.' He revs the engine.

It's hard to drive away from the house that contains my son, but I have to trust that the police will help me. Lorcan and I head for Enshott and the nearest police station. The journey only takes ten minutes or so but, once we arrive, it's impossible to find a parking space. The station is in the middle of a busy High Street already jam-packed with parked cars.

I check my watch. I'm supposed to meet Art at the pub in a few minutes. We can't afford to lose any more time.

'Drop me here,' I say. 'I can get the ball rolling while you find somewhere to park.'

Lorcan reluctantly agrees and lets me out of the car. I scurry along to the police station. It's positioned to the left of a shopping centre. I have, this time, remembered my bag, and before I go inside I check myself in my tiny pocket mirror. My hair is still damp and my make-up is smudged. I spend a few seconds fixing this as best I can. I'm determined to make the officers I meet believe me. I need them to see that I'm as sane as they are.

The police station looks exactly how I'd expect. Concrete walls, harsh lighting, with some seats over to the left and a

SOPHIE MCKENZIE

counter to the right. An officer stands behind the counter, speaking softly into the phone. He glances over to let me know he's clocked me.

I walk over and wait for him to finish.

Two uniformed woman come through the door behind him. They're talking to each other in hushed tones. One carries a sheet of paper.

'The call just came through. The body was found in those woods just out of Shepton Longchamp,' says the younger of the two women who is still clutching the piece of paper.

I look up, startled. Are they talking about Bernard O'Donnell?

'And *she's* the prime suspect?' The other woman points to the piece of paper. 'That was quick.'

My heart skips a beat. Could this be the woman Art is involved with?

The younger woman shrugs. 'There was an anonymous tip-off giving her name and placing her at the scene.'

She holds the paper up. It's a colour picture of a woman's face with a few lines of print to the side. She pins it to the notice board at the far end of the counter. From where I'm standing I can't see the detail of the woman's face. The officer I'm waiting to speak to is still on the phone, so I move over to the notice board. As the two women drift away through the swing doors, I catch the younger one's words.

'They'll be trying to trace her now.'

And then I reach the print-out and I stare at the picture and all my insides seem to shrivel and collapse. Because I know the photo well – it's the one from my driving licence.

I stare and stare, forcing the realization to sink in.

The woman wanted by the police for O'Donnell's murder is me.

CHAPTER TWENTY-TWO

I quickly turn away. Head bowed, I tear out of the police station.

I'm almost hyperventilating as I reach the pavement. I don't know which direction Lorcan will appear from so I stand against the wall, glancing furtively up and down the street. I've never known such fear as I'm feeling right now. It's consuming me . . . eating me from the inside.

I force myself to go over what I just heard. The police received a tip-off that I was the murderer, that I was seen at the lock-up. And I *was* there. My fingerprints are on Bernard's things. If they find his mobile phone, they will find my voicemail message saying I'm actually *at* the lock-up and looking for him.

Trying to trace her now.

The female PC's words echo in my head. My mind trips over itself, running on ahead to my being arrested and charged.

Still no sign of Lorcan. *Come on. Come on.*

Panic rises in my throat. I force it down. Lorcan appears, striding round the corner towards the station. I race over to him. Grab his arm.

'We have to get out of here.'

He stares at me. 'What are you talking about?'

I try to turn him around, but he resists. He's too big and tall to force, so I stand in the street, and explain as quickly as I can.

'So Art's set me up,' I finish. 'Or the woman he's with has.'

Lorcan frowns. 'But all you have to do is explain why you went to meet O'Donnell,' he says. 'Give your side of the story.'

I shake my head. 'They'll find my fingerprints all over his stuff . . . I called him from outside the lock-up. God, I must have arrived *minutes* after he died.'

'So?' Lorcan holds out his hands. 'That doesn't make you guilty. How will they even know they're *your* fingerprints?'

'If I go in there they'll take them. Even if I don't, they'll be able to get a set from Loxley Benson,' I explain. 'My fingerprints are on record there . . . the entry system with the doors.'

'But—?'

'They've got a *Wanted* poster of me.' My voice breaks.

'*Jesus*, Art's a lying bastard,' Lorcan growls. 'I knew he was stringing you along with all that "backing off" shite.'

I feel sick. 'I don't know. He said he and that woman had argued . . . that he was trying to convince her to leave me alone if I went away. Maybe he lost the argument. Maybe she's gone behind his back.'

'Or maybe he just lied to you, Gen. Again.'

'Okay.' I take a deep breath. 'Either he was lying to me about giving me a chance to back off – or the woman doesn't want me to have that chance.'

Lorcan hesitates for a second. 'I still think we should go inside and explain everything to the police. When it all comes out it's going to be obvious that Art and this woman are the ones with the motive for killing Bernard O'Donnell . . .'

I glance over at the police station. I'm so overwhelmed with fear that I half expect officers to swarm out of the building towards me. My throat feels swollen. I take a deep breath.

My phone rings. It's Art.

'Where are you?' His voice is desperate. 'You said you'd be here and you're not. I can't stay for long. She doesn't know I've come to meet you. Please, Gen, we don't have time for—'

'You lied to me.' My voice is hoarse. 'You said she was going to kill me. But you've set me up. The police think *I* killed Bernard and—'

'No, Gen. I haven't done *anything*. I don't know anything about that.'

My mind is in freefall. I don't know what to believe.

'Gen, *listen*. I don't have much time. Twenty minutes, max. I *have* to get back to . . . to the house. She thinks I'm there. I . . . I've persuaded her to go out before she leaves for good; see Bitsy, take care of a few things round here. But she'll be back in half an hour and I need to be there, so I can tell her you're doing what needs to be done and . . . and then they're going abroad so there's not much time.'

They.

'She's taking Ed? Abroad?' My voice breaks over his name. *No.* Not after all this. I can't lose my baby again. 'She's leaving with him "for good"? No, Art, *please.*'

'It's the best thing,' Art says. He sounds desperate. 'Please, Gen, it's taken everything for me to get her to agree to leave Shepton and *not* come after you.'

'But she *has* come after me. She's gone to the pol—'

'The police won't be able to make any charges stick, Gen. If we're going to meet it has to be *right now*. If I'm not home for when she gets back in half an hour she'll panic – maybe even change her mind. You have to understand that I'm trying to protect you. I'm trying to keep you safe. Now, where are you? I can only wait another twenty minutes. Then I *have* to go.'

'I'm on my way,' I lie. 'I just need a bit more time to get away from Lorcan. Please wait.'

'Okay, but hurry.'

I switch off the call and turn to Lorcan. 'She's going away. She's taking Ed.'

He stares at me. 'All the more reason to go back in and explain everything to the police.'

'No.' A beat passes. Lorcan is right, of course. We *should* go to the police and tell them everything. But being right isn't the point. 'It will take too long,' I say. 'By the time I've convinced them I didn't have anything to do with Bernard's death – *if* I can convince them – Art's woman could have taken Ed anywhere . . .'

'But—'

'It's happening *now*. Art said they're meeting back at the house in thirty minutes and she's going to take Ed abroad straight-away.' I hesitate. The traffic is still rushing past, the street still full of busy shoppers. It's a noisy, hectic scene but, for the first time since I set off from home yesterday, I see what I have to do.

Lorcan's eyes fix on me. 'So what are you saying?' he asks, uncertainly. 'D'you want to go away too, like Art said?'

'Not if it means me living like a fugitive *and* knowing that Ed is alive and never seeing him.' I close my eyes for a second, imag-ining that future . . . the upheaval of leaving my entire life behind . . . the agony of knowing my child is out there some-where, growing up without me. 'No,' I say. 'No way. I'm not running away.'

'Then . . .?'

'I'm so sorry you're mixed up in all this,' I say. 'I will totally understand if you want to leave right now.'

'Not a chance,' he says. 'Just tell me what you think we should do.'

I give him a quick hug, his stubble brushes, rough, against my cheek. And then we get back in the car and I tell him my plan.

Lorcan drives like a madman back to the house in Shepton

Longchamp. He parks outside and I check the time. Art should still be waiting for me at the Dog & Duck I imagine him pacing up and down by the door looking out for me.

'You sure about this?' Lorcan asks.

I look at the big brick house beyond the gates. It's almost dark now and lights are on in several of the downstairs rooms. Ed is inside. I have to find him and take him with me to the police. It's the only way to make sure he isn't taken away from me forever. Once the police test his DNA and believe he is my son, everything else will fall into place. I know it will be scary for him. But I wouldn't ever forgive myself if I didn't try.

What if one day Ed finds out about me? What if he tracks me down? What if he asks why I didn't fight for him?

'Art should still be in the pub,' I say. 'He said *she* was out too and wouldn't be coming back until after him. If that's true, then Ed will be at home alone with the girl who picked him up from school.'

'But there could be security,' Lorcan protests. 'And for all you know, Art and the woman could both have come back already . . .'

'No, not yet.' I'm trying to convince myself. 'Anyway, they won't be expecting us.'

Lorcan shakes his head. 'Just keep your eyes open, okay?'

'I will. Let's go.'

As we get out of the car, a wry smile sweeps Lorcan's face.

'What?' I say.

'It's nothing. Just that when I saw you for the first time at Art's you looked so lost. Like . . . all confident on the outside but desperately sad too, as if life had beaten you down. And now look at you – it's like you're on fire.'

I smile back. *I am* on fire – determination burns through me to my bones. We approach the gates. I peer through the bars, taking the house in more carefully. It's a clue to the identity of the woman. She must have money, that's for sure. The house is large and old and detached, with stone walls and columns propping up the front porch. There are three floors, with a wide bay window on either side of the front door. The front garden is elegantly laid out, with a patch of lawn to the left of the drive and carefully tended shrubs in the flower beds. Two pretty ficus trees stand on either side of the front porch. It's definitely the kind of house I'd expect Charlotte to live in.

We work our way round the gate. It extends into the trees that form a border between the house and the road. I cut my hand on one of the spikes climbing over. Lorcan rips his shirt. But seconds later we're down on the soft earth in the dark shadow of the trees. I wait under cover of their low branches and watch Lorcan cross the gravel to the front door. My heart is thudding as he rings the doorbell. Seconds tick past. The early evening air is mild. No breeze. A dog barks in the distance.

The door opens. It's on the chain. 'Hello?' It's Kelly, the girl who picked Ed up from school earlier. She sounds suspicious.

'Hi there,' Lorcan says. He's putting on an English accent like he did at the school. 'I'm sorry to bother you; we met in the playground earlier, actually. Er . . . my son brought a DS home with him. I think it belongs to Ed. God, I'm so embarrassed, but I think Sammy might have taken it earlier today. I'm so sorry not to call in advance but we couldn't find the class list and my wife has seen you coming in here with Ed so we knew this was home.'

'I don't think its Ed's,' Kelly says uncertainly.

'Are you sure?' Lorcan says. 'Would you mind asking him?'

'I don't—'

But before Kelly can finish her sentence, Lorcan hurls himself at the door with such force that the chain breaks and in a split second he is over the threshold and inside the house. He grabs Kelly's arm and twists her round, his hand over her mouth. Kelly struggles, she's trying to shout out, but Lorcan is stronger. He pulls her backwards along the hall. I rush across the gravel and slip inside after him. A vase on the hall table catches my eye. It looks vaguely familiar, but there's no time to work out where I've seen it before. As I reach the stairs, Kelly sees me. Her eyes widen with alarm. Heart beating fast, I race up to the first floor.

I'm moving as quietly as I can. There's no sound from any part of the house. I reach the landing at the top of the stairs. It's ultra-modern, excessively neat and expensively decorated. Smart and stylish. Now I'm inside, the decor seems fresher and younger than Charlotte West would choose. I pass a delicate china ornament – abstract, a curving shape like a wave. It suddenly all seems very French. There's definitely an international flavour to the furniture and the paintings. Much more Sandrine than Charlotte.

I tiptoe across the hessian flooring, taking in a row of carved wooden disks on the window ledge overlooking the back garden. I try the first door I come to. A blue-and-white tiled bathroom. I move on. The next room looks like a spare room: with pale yellow curtains at the window to match the yellow-trimmed quilt on the bed. One of Art's jackets has been flung over the quilt. An overnight bag I recognize from home stands next to it. Does that mean Art sleeps here? Or just stows his stuff here? I move on. Another spare room. This one much larger, with an en-suite bathroom. Still no sign of Ed.

I scuttle back across the landing. There are just three more doors to try. I open the first. It's a little office area with a desk and a computer. A few toys – a train and a couple of teddy bears are scattered on the floor. They're the only sign that a child even lives in this house.

I pull the door to and try the next. As soon as I push it open I know that I've found him. It's a kid's room, with a bookcase crammed with books, a huge toy bin and bunk beds against the far wall. The curtains are drawn and a night light spins on the bedside table, sending shadows dancing around the room. Ed is fast asleep on the bottom bunk. I creep towards him, my heart pumping furiously. He looks so peaceful as I approach, a lock of dark hair falling over his small face. I stand over him for a second. Again, I see my father. I try to work out what it is . . . the mouth, yes, but what else? The shape of his chin? The curve of his cheek? And then I see that it's in the space between his features: the set of his eyes and the shape of the gap between his nose and his mouth.

I reach down and touch his arm, which is flung out across the bed. The night light casts enough light for me to see that the duvet contains a picture of some cartoon character. I have no idea who. For some reason, this reminder of how far outside Ed's life I am hurts more than anything.

Ed's skin is soft. I lift his arm – a dead weight. He's deeply asleep. I shake him gently, but he doesn't wake. There's a crash downstairs – the sound of a chair tipping over. I start. Did Lorcan do that? Is Kelly trying to get away?

Or could Art have come back? I check the time. He promised he'd wait twenty minutes for me at the pub and it's only been fifteen so far, so surely he's still there.

Ed sleeps on. I try to haul him up, but he stays asleep. He's heavy. I'm not sure I'll be able to manage him all the way down the stairs on my own. I shake his arm again. No response. There's another sound from downstairs – this time a door slamming.

I lay Ed back on the bed. I need to find Lorcan. He can help me carry Ed. I race out of the room and towards the stairs. Everything's silent on the ground floor.

Reassuring myself as best as I can that there's no one else in the house, I creep along the hallway towards the place I last saw

Lorcan. He was heading for the door at the back of the hallway. He and Kelly must be through here.

I push the door carefully open. A pear-wood table sits in the middle of a large kitchen, which, like the rest of the house, is all very minimalist and uncluttered, with lots of shiny chrome and an eau-de-nil splash back. A chair lies on its side. Apart from that, the room looks undisturbed. There are two doors, one at either end of the room. The door at the far end is wide open. Cold air blasts through it. I feel the chill against my face and hands. I'm guessing it leads to the garage we saw outside. Is that where Lorcan has taken Kelly?

I want to call out, but I'm scared to in case anyone else is here. I tiptoe across the kitchen, towards the open door. I have a sudden flashback to the lock-up and the way I walked through its darkness to the open wasteland on the other side . . . to Bernard's body.

I can hear nothing except the sound of my own heart beating. A bead of sweat trickles down the back of my neck as I reach the open door. The garage beyond is in darkness. I can just make out a line of shelves and a cardboard box of wine bottles. I reach for a light switch, but it's not where I expect it to be. I step into the garage, letting my eyes adjust to the gloom.

Across the room, past a shelf lined with tools, a figure is slumped in a chair. It's Lorcan. For a second I can't take it in. He appears to be bound with a rope; there's a gag around his mouth. As I stare at him, he looks up. His face is bruised – two red marks on his chin and his cheek – and there's a trickle of dried blood from a cut on his lip. His eyes, however, blaze with fury. He starts shouting as soon as he sees me, but the yells are muffled.

I freeze. The tall, broad man who mugged me is here too. He's standing behind Lorcan. I notice him as he steps forward and places a restraining hand on Lorcan's shoulder. He's wearing a dark overcoat with a hood pulled low over his face. He looks up at me too and I see him properly for the first time: flat, Slavic cheeks and closely cropped hair. He really is huge. Broad as well as tall. He holds up a gun. I stare at the metal barrel. Is he going to shoot me? The thought filters through my head with absolute clarity.

'Who are you?' I say.

The giant waves the gun, beckoning me towards him. 'Over here,' he grunts.

I don't have a choice. Shivering with cold and fear, I walk over. Lorcan stamps his feet as I draw near. He's making muffled shouts from behind the gag, but I can't tell what he's trying to say.

'Give me your phone.' The giant's voice is a low, threatening growl. I don't want to hand over my only contact with the outside world but, again, I don't have a choice. Eyes fixed on the gun, I pass him my mobile. He removes the sim card and pockets it separately from the phone, then he pushes past me. He walks over to the door and disappears into the kitchen. I stare after him. He's leaving us alone? I look around, remembering Kelly. There's no sign of her.

'Hnn?' Lorcan's voice is still muffled, but I think he's saying my name. It sounds like a warning.

I rush behind him, my fingers feeling for the knot that ties him to the chair. Lorcan glances from me to the far corner of the garage. Again, he seems to be signalling a warning but I can't see anything in the darkness. 'Come *on*.' My hands fumble as I fail to unpick the knot.

The light tap of a footstep makes me look up. The sound came from the darkness opposite. I peer into the shadows. A figure is standing beside the garage doors. All I can see are her smart, cream kitten heels.

'Who's there?' My voice falters.

And then she takes another step out of the shadows.

CHAPTER TWENTY-THREE

Morgan.

My mouth falls open as she emerges into the pool of light cast from the kitchen. A slow smile creeps over my sister-in-law's face. She's elegantly dressed, as always, in a long cream coat that fits her perfectly and a cap made of soft, pale blue leather. Waves of hair from a blonde wig peek out from underneath the cap. As soon as I see her I realize that everything about this house is her – sharply modern, oozing with understated design, and ultimately rather sterile.

'You always were too stupid for Art,' she says.

I stare at her pinched face and hard, dark eyes. And in that moment it hits me.

'*You?*' I say, my brain struggling to accept what must be the truth. '*You're* the woman who took my baby?'

'Well done, Geniver,' Morgan says sarcastically. She's wearing pale blue leather gloves that match her cap. In a single, terrifying moment I realize that she is the woman Bernard O'Donnell saw going into the lock-up with Art. Which means Morgan must be the woman who killed him.

I stare at her, completely bewildered.

Lorcan stamps his feet, rocking in his chair. I fumble with the knot tying his gag. It's too tight to unpick. I move my hands down to the rope that holds him to the chair and start tugging at that again. I don't take my eyes off Morgan. She is still watching me, a look of contempt in her eyes.

'Leave him alone,' she orders. 'Or I'll call Jared to make you.'

I glance towards the door into the kitchen. It has swung slightly open and I can just make out the bulky profile of the large man. He's standing like a soldier, his hands clasped behind his back, legs slightly apart. He looks brutal. I let go of Lorcan's bindings, aware I haven't loosened them at all.

'What the hell is this, Morgan?' I say. An image of Ed flashes into my mind. 'What did I ever do to you?'

Morgan rolls her eyes. 'It wasn't about *you*,' she says. 'It was about me and Art.'

'What does that mean?' I frown, remembering Art's words . . . that giving away our baby was . . . what had he said? . . . an *atonement*. 'How is our child anything to do with you?'

Morgan tilts her head to one side. 'How dare you break into my house and make demands?'

'*Me* make demands?' I can't take in what she's saying. 'You . . . you stole my baby from me!'

'He came to me before you even knew who he was,' she says. 'I think that's a far cry from what, if I'm very much mistaken, you and Lorcan were just attempting: the kidnapping of a small child away from the only mother he knows.'

I stare at her. I can't believe what I'm hearing. I can't believe any of this.

'Art has you so wrong,' Morgan sneers. 'He said you would back off if he warned you, that you always did what he wanted. But I knew you wouldn't be able to. And I was right. You went straight to the police after he saw you, didn't you?' She snorts. 'Art didn't believe you'd be prepared to flush his entire career down the toilet either ... not until Jared brought back Rodriguez's CCTV footage.'

I glance at Jared. He's still standing guard by the door, blocking most of the light coming through from the kitchen. 'You sent him to mug me?'

Morgan nods. 'Jared was my father's driver. After Daddy died, my mother kept him on. He's known me since I was a little girl. He'd do anything for me.'

I glance over at the giant again. His eyes are dark and hard and fixed on Morgan's face. I have no doubt she's telling the truth about his loyalty.

'Why did you want the CCTV film on that memory stick?' I ask.

'Because it's incriminating to Art,' Morgan says softly. 'After Rodriguez told me you'd stolen it, I had to get it back to protect him.'

'Protect Art?' I shake my head. 'I don't get any of this, Morgan. Art's your *brother*. What have *you* got to do with our ... our baby?'

Morgan taps her elegant feet on the floor. She seems to be considering something.

'I would have spared you this, Geniver,' she says. 'But, frankly, right now I'm so angry with you I don't care any more.'

'Spared me what?'

Morgan points to the door. 'This way,' she says. 'I'll show you.'

I glance round at Lorcan. He's rocking more wildly in his chair now, clearly not wanting me to leave. But I don't see that I have a choice. Even if Morgan isn't armed, Jared has that gun.

Anyway, I'm desperate for answers.

I walk into the kitchen and past Jared. Morgan removes her cap and blonde wig and lays them on the counter. She directs me through the kitchen, out into the hallway and into a living room. It's a large, square space, full of the same pear-wood furniture as much of the rest of the house. A large-screen TV stands in the corner opposite a leather couch. Two sleek armchairs sit on either side of the sofa. It's a more lived-in space than the rest of the house. Books and magazines are spread across the coffee table and a stack of children's DVDs teeters on the floor in front of the TV.

Morgan crosses the room, pushes the DVDs aside and opens the cupboard underneath the TV. She draws a disk from her coat pocket and places it into the machine, then she steps back.

'This is a copy,' she says. 'The original was made on video.'

'Original of *what*?'

'You'll see.' She faces the screen. 'This is who your husband really is, Geniver.'

As the screen fizzles into life, I get the impression Morgan's in her element. That, despite what she says, she's been dying to show me whatever is on this disk. A picture appears. It's grainy . . . colour, but poor-quality – a shot of a bedroom, a girl's bedroom, with white lacy drapes around the bed and a row of dolls propped on the pink-painted shelf above it. A warm pink light glows from the bedside lamp.

'What is this?'

'My bedroom at home in Edinburgh. I was home from college – the Easter holidays. I was nearly twenty.'

I stare at the screen, my heart beating wildly. What the hell am I about to see?

A very young Morgan fills the screen, backing towards the bed. Slim and tanned, she looks amazing, dressed in a mini-skirt and a pink top with thin straps. There's a softness about her I've never seen in all the years I've known her. She's smiling at someone beyond the camera, flicking her dark hair – longer than it is now – off her shoulder.

She sits on the bed and holds out her hands. Art walks into the frame. He's wearing jeans and a T-shirt and looks unbelievably young. I frown, trying to work it out. If Morgan was almost twenty here, then Art must have been eighteen. He sits on the bed so both of them are side-on to the camera. Neither of them looks at it. I'm certain Art has no idea it is there. He would hate the idea of being filmed. He reaches out and pulls Morgan towards him. They kiss.

My stomach retches. I look away.

'What is this?' I say. 'Why are you—?'

'Watch!'

I turn reluctantly back towards the screen. Art is peeling Morgan's top up, his mouth is on her breast, one hand fumbling under her skirt. Morgan's face is tipped back, her hair sprawled over the white bedspread. She looks ecstatic.

A furious mix of hurt and jealousy and repulsion surges through me.

I turn back to the Morgan in the room beside me. She's watching my face, a mean, thin smile curling about her lips.

'*This* is what you wanted to show me,' I snap. 'It's disgusting.'

'It wasn't disgusting.' The smile falls from Morgan's lips. 'Certainly a lot less disgusting than you and Lorcan sneaking around in shabby hotels. Art and I loved each other.'

'What?' The ecstatic look on the younger Morgan's face flashes before my mind's eye. 'Maybe you had some revolting crush on him, but he must have been drunk to have . . .' I'm trying to keep my eyes off the screen. I don't want to see what I know the film shows. But I can't resist a quick glance. It's enough to confirm what I've already imagined. I look away again, quickly, but the image of Morgan and Art together has seared itself on my brain.

'Art wasn't drunk.' Morgan snaps. 'That wasn't the first time we made love, either. We did it every time my parents were out. We couldn't keep our hands off each other.'

347

'But he's your *brother*.'

'We'd only just met,' Morgan says impatiently. 'Art had turned up at the house the week before. Daddy refused to speak to him but Art insisted, and there was a big row at the front door. I was watching from upstairs. Heard everything. I was almost twenty by then and knew the rumours about Daddy having other women, so it wasn't hard to work out what was going on. Then Art left. I ran after him.' She pauses. 'Remember, I told you all about that, didn't I?'

I refuse to nod, but of course it's true. Morgan did tell me – so vividly that I could almost see her flying out of the house in tears, offering support and friendship. The sister Art had never known. And I'll never forget the hurt on Art's face – when I finally got him to talk about it – at how cold his father had been . . . how desperately rejected Art had felt.

It hadn't occurred to me for a second that there was more to the story than two children united against a bullying father.

'We talked for a bit, then we met later,' Morgan says. 'One thing led to another. It was chemical. Inevitable.'

'And *wrong*.' I feel sick to my stomach.

Morgan raises her eyebrows. 'Who are you to judge us?' she says. 'Who is anyone to judge us?'

'Why did you do the tape?' I ask. 'Art didn't know you were making it, did he?'

Morgan shrugs. 'We'd met every day for nearly a week. Then Art had to go home and I realized that I wanted a proper memento to remember him by.' A blush creeps across her cheeks.

I stare at her, realising what she means. 'You really fell in *love* with him,' I shudder, horrified. 'Oh, my God, you—'

'I got pregnant.' Morgan's words cut the air like a whip. 'I was pregnant with Art's baby. But he said we couldn't keep it. That he loved me but no one would accept the baby.'

My chest tightens. For a second it hurts so badly I can't feel anything else.

'What happened?'

Morgan keeps her cold gaze fixed on my face. 'I did what he wanted. I had the termination. Something went wrong – some rare, one-in-a-million, chance thing – and the doctor told me I'd never be able to have any more children.'

The film on the TV in the corner is over. I can hear the white noise fizzling away. It's too much to take in. 'An abortion.' The words whisper out of me. 'Morgan.'

She grimaces. 'It was the worst time. I told no one. No one apart from Art *ever* knew. But I knew. I knew as soon as I'd done it that I'd made the mistake of my life.'

'Oh, God.' My hands are over my mouth. Surely this is a nightmare. Surely in a second I will wake up.

'I was lost for a while,' Morgan says, her voice low and sad. 'I didn't see Art again for four years – the next time was when he and Lorcan went to the States. I said they could stay in the house at Martha's Vineyard – then I made sure I was over there for their visit. I couldn't believe it when they turned up. Art was a mess. Doing drugs. No direction. A total mess. And Lorcan was such a loser . . .' She pauses. 'I pleaded with Art to clean himself up. I offered him as much money as he wanted, but Art was too proud. The next time I saw him was two or three years after that. He'd turned things around. He'd set up Loxley Benson. He kept talking about you . . . this girl he'd met . . . but I knew, even though Art couldn't put it into words, that the feeling between us was the same as it always had been. And, as soon as I heard you were pregnant, I knew that Art owed us that baby.'

I can't breathe. So this is what Art meant when he said our baby was 'atonement'. A new life for a lost life.

'But it was *our baby*,' I gasp. 'Mine and Art's.' My mind

scrabbles frantically to get a purchase on what I'm being asked to believe. How could Art have given Ed up like he did? For love? No, he loved *us*. He wanted *us* to have a baby . . . *still* wants us to have a baby.

'Art *agreed* I should take Ed,' Morgan's expression is proud, defiant. 'He *helped* make it happen. He even gave you the zolpidem that sedated the baby the day of the c-section. He slipped a tablet in with your vitamins.'

I stare at her, my mind rushing back in time. So *that* was why I'd felt groggy and lightheaded all day. Art had drugged me, tricked me. It's unbearable.

'And Art did all that for me,' Morgan goes on. 'He knew I'd be a wonderful mother.'

'But what about *me*?' I insist. 'Didn't you stop to think for a second that letting me think my baby had died was cruel? Inhumane? Unfair?'

Morgan smiles again. 'Daddy's favourite saying when we were growing up was: "Who told you life was fair?" It isn't. You get what you can, when you can. It's all about survival. And the only thing that gets you what you want is money.'

'That's rubbish.'

'Is it?' Morgan arches an eyebrow. 'Money paid for Doctor Rodriguez to fake a stillbirth certificate. Money paid to keep staff at the hospital and the funeral home quiet. Money paid for all the papers I needed to prove Ed was mine. And money kept the trail secret until you and that idiot O'Donnell tracked us down to Shepton Longchamp.'

The image of Bernard's lifeless body flashes in front of my eyes.

'I know you killed him,' I say. 'And his wife, Lucy.'

'Don't be ridiculous,' Morgan sneers. 'O'Donnell was an accident. I . . . I panicked and pulled the trigger. I had nothing to do with his wife.'

'Not directly,' I said slowly. 'But you sent Jared, didn't you? You sent your driver, to run her down.'

Morgan stares at me. Her eyes give nothing away.

'How could you, Morgan?' I say. 'The O'Donnells were good people. They were just trying to help me find my child.'

'Good people?' Morgan folds her arms with a disdainful sniff. 'They were after Art's money.'

'No. No way.'

'You sure about that? Think, Geniver. Are you seriously saying that, when you spoke with the O'Donnells, the subject of a reward never came up? Do you think that they would have bothered to report Mary Duncan's deathbed confession to you if they hadn't known Art was a successful businessman worth a small fortune?'

I think about Lucy's anxious face, blushing as she confessed her money worries, and Bernard's embarrassed relief as I paid him twenty grand.

'Hoping for money doesn't justify murder,' I say, holding my voice steady. 'And what about Gary Bloode, the anaesthetist? You had him killed too, didn't you? What did he do, threaten to expose you?'

'Bloode got greedy,' Morgan snaps. 'He demanded more money than I was prepared to pay.' She pauses. 'You see, Geniver? None of them was innocent. And only the truly innocent should be protected.'

'Like children, you mean?' Anger rises in me again. 'How exactly have you protected my son by keeping him away from his own mother?'

'I am his mother.' Morgan fixes me with steel in her eyes. 'Ed doesn't lack *anything*.'

'Who else knows?'

'No one apart from us and Art.'

351

'So money buys you everything,' I say sarcastically.

'Almost everything,' Morgan says without irony. 'Art comes to see Ed and me whenever he can. That's love.'

Fury boils inside me again. 'Ed was *my* baby, Morgan. Mine and Art's. How can you live with that?'

'I've lived with far worse.'

A long silence falls over the room. It's raining outside – dark through the bare windows. I shiver, even though it's not cold in the living room. I don't believe Art loves Morgan. Not like she claims. So *why* did he let her take our baby? Morgan walks to the DVD slot and ejects her disk. An image from the film burns its way into my head.

'You threatened him, didn't you?' I stammer, working it out. 'You said you'd show people that film if he didn't give up our baby.'

'It wasn't that simple.'

'Yes it was. You used that film to blackmail him.'

Morgan's expression is ice-cold. 'You don't know what you're talking about.'

'Yes, I do.' I push on, sensing I'm right. 'You know that film really just shows two confused, screwed-up teenagers who let their hormones get the better of them. But you used it to punish Art for . . . for not loving you as much as you loved him.'

Morgan says nothing but I can feel I've hit home.

She places the DVD in her coat pocket, then indicates the door.

I think back to what Art told me in the woods. Was any of that true? He certainly didn't mention the film of him and Morgan. 'So . . . back then, when I was pregnant, did you threaten to hurt me if Art didn't give up our baby?'

'Is that what he told you?' Morgan sniffs. 'Poor Art. No. Art gave me Ed because he loved me.'

'Not because you threatened to hurt me if he didn't? Not

because he threatened to show people this film of the two of you?'

'You didn't come into it. And the video wasn't the main issue. It was . . . just my safety net, like the CCTV film of Art at the Fair Angel was Rodriguez's. But yes, Art definitely didn't want people knowing about . . . what we did.'

Even me.

'But I would have understood if Art had just told me.' The words blurt out of me but I'm not sure they are true.

Morgan laughs scornfully. 'Listen to yourself, Geniver. Do you really think it was your reaction Art was worried about? You were a long way down the pecking order, believe me. Art is the head of a company built on ethical practice. If the film of us together had got out, it would have ruined him.'

I stare at Morgan. Whatever she says about Art loving her, and whatever he says about trying to protect me, *this* is surely at the heart of his actions. I can just see the way the press would have presented the scandal eight years ago when Ed was born. They would have emphasised the hypocrisy of Art's ultra-ethical public stance and highlighted all the sordid details, using the video as proof. It would have ended his career, just as it was taking off.

My legs threaten to give way underneath me. All the lies. All the pain. To enable Art to retain his status as an ethical business-man . . . so that Art's ruthless drive to the top remained unimpeded. I want to yell at Morgan that what she's saying isn't true. But I know Art too well for that.

Some terrible dark place, deep inside me, cracks and bleeds.

'All for power and money.' The words slip out under my breath.

'Obviously I took care of the money,' Morgan says,

misunderstanding what I've said. 'Art helped. We paid everyone in cash. Over a million altogether.'

My head reels. The £50,000 Art paid MDO for Hen suddenly seems inconsequential. And innocent. *Oh, Hen,* I think to myself. *I'm sorry.*

'You just don't understand Art. Not like I do,' Morgan says, tight-lipped. 'He's like our father was – a huge, huge man who can't be tied to convention. He loves me with a power you can't even imagine. We love each other.'

I shake my head. Morgan indicates the door back to the hall-way. 'Now you know how everything started,' she says. 'It's time for this to end.'

'What do you mean?' Fear clutches at my throat.

'Jared?' At Morgan's shout, the big man appears in the door-way. His face is still half-hidden by his hood, but I can see the set of his mouth. Grim and determined. 'Get Lorcan into the car. We're leaving.'

She motions me to the door. 'Come on, Geniver.'

I look round, desperate for something . . . anything . . . I can use as a weapon to fight off Morgan and Jared. There is nothing.

In the hallway Morgan steps ahead of me. She's almost at the kitchen door. Through it I can hear Jared grunting and Lorcan's muffled yells.

My instincts take over. I rush at Morgan, shoving her over, then I tear back through the hall and out through the front door. It's properly dark now. I run as fast as I can, across the drive. I haul myself up onto the gate. If I can just climb over I can flag down a car . . .

'Geniver!' Morgan's voice rings out from the front porch. 'Don't be stupid.'

I stop. Look round. Morgan is leaning against one of the

columns, watching me, her glossy dark hair shining in the light flooding out from the hallway.

'Jared has a gun pointing at Lorcan right now,' she says quietly. 'If you don't come inside now I will direct him to fire it. Lorcan will be dead before you reach the street. On the count of three,' Morgan goes on. 'One . . .'

I hesitate. My instincts are telling me to run away. Morgan herself isn't armed. There's only one gun. And yet I entirely believe she will give the order for Lorcan to be killed.

'Two . . .'

If I go back there's still a chance for us both.

'Geniver?' Morgan's voice is cold and steady. 'What's it to be?'

So then I woke up and looked out of the window and there was the Bad Lady again – right in our drive! And I felt cross with her because letting her take my picture had put me in trouble and Mummy had made me go to bed really early. I remembered about being a brave knight and I got my sword which was silly really because even then when I was a little kid I knew it was only a toy sword which wouldn't hurt anyone.

So I was scared but I was ready to do the Special Fighting Plan because that is what I had promised Mummy. And I looked out of the window again and now the Bad Lady was walking across the drive towards our house. Mummy was down there too and that was the first time I realized Mummy was going to need my help.

I went over her Special Fighting Plan. There were only two things I had to do.

Under my breath I promised again to do them.

CHAPTER TWENTY-FOUR

Morgan is still standing there. She opens her mouth. 'Three.'

'Okay,' I say quickly. 'Okay, I'm coming back.'

As I walk back towards the house, a single thought lodges in my mind. I have to get that gun off Jared – even if it means shooting him with it. I have no idea how to work a gun – other than the obvious fact of pulling the trigger – I've never even held one. But it is quite clear to me that Morgan is going to push this situation to the very end – that, as far as she's concerned, it's my life and Lorcan's life versus her freedom.

Right now, she holds all the cards. Lorcan is tied up. Jared is huge and has that gun. Even if I could get away and call the police, everything is still stacked against me. I will be charged with Bernard O'Donnell's murder and before I can convince anyone I'm innocent, Morgan will disappear. And my son will vanish along with her.

Morgan grips my arm and leads me around the house to the car parked in the drive. The headlamps of the 4x4 flash on. Jared is inside, sitting in the driving seat. Lorcan has already been bundled into the back, still gagged and bound. Our eyes meet and the strength in his gaze eases my own fear, giving me hope.

And an idea.

I take a deep breath, forcing a note of calm into my voice.

'What about Ed?' I ask. "Are you leaving him alone in the house."

'Kelly's with him,' Morgan snaps.

'What's he like?' I persist. 'He reminded me of Art when I saw him at his school.'

I can feel Morgan stiffen beside me. She wasn't expecting anything other than terror from me.

I press on. 'I just want to know about him. I mean, he's nearly eight . . . what does he like doing? Who are his friends? He looks like my father, though his colouring is the same as Art's, don't you think?'

'The same as Art's and mine.' Morgan takes a length of rope. I let her bind my wrists behind my back. It's true, Art and Morgan both share their father's dark hair, olive complexion and intense brown eyes.

'How much time do you spend with him?' I say. 'I mean, I didn't even know you had a home in Somerset. I thought you were based in Edinburgh . . . and you travel all over the world on business too.'

'I do travel a lot,' Morgan acknowledges. 'But I don't spend as much time away as you'd think. Maybe ten nights in every month. I'm always here when Art comes.'

I swallow, hating this reminder of their family life together.

'Ed's nanny – Kelly, is it? – looked very young. Has she been with him long? Is he close to her?'

Morgan shoots me a withering glance. 'Kelly's got two degrees. She does an excellent job. We're not talking about this any more.'

She opens the nearside back door of the car and shoves me in, next to Lorcan. Our eyes meet again and I know he is telling me to hang in there. I give him a swift nod, indicating I have understood.

Morgan gets in the passenger seat in front of me.

'You should take off Lorcan's gag,' Jared grunts. 'If we pass anyone on the road, they might notice.'

Morgan hesitates a second, then clearly decides he's right. She nods and Jared reaches round and slices through the cloth around Lorcan's mouth with a large, steel knife.

I'm icy calm. Okay, so there's a gun and a knife to deal with. I make a mental note, then store the information away and shuffle closer to Lorcan, ready to put my idea into action.

As soon as the engine starts he looks at me. His eyes are fierce and strong.

I glance over my shoulder, towards my hands, then gesture with my fingers, trying to simulate the sawing action of his Swiss Army knife.

Lorcan frowns for a moment or two, then his eyes light up. He glances down at his trouser pocket. Keeping one eye on Morgan directly in front of me, I twist round slightly so that my hands can reach.

Jared drives through the gates and out onto the road as I slide my fingers inside Lorcan's pocket. Several cars pass us. I stare through the window, hoping to catch someone's attention, but nobody notices me.

My fingers light on cold metal. Smooth and circular. Coins. We take a right turn and my hand is pulled away. As the car straightens up, I reach in again, this time deeper. There. My fingers curl round the panelled side of the Swiss Army knife. I grip the metal between my finger and thumb and withdraw my hand.

It takes a moment to free the lethally sharp edge that I know is there, and another to position it against my rope.

I glance over at Morgan. She's peering through the windscreen, muttering something to Jared.

'If it comes to that,' she says softly. 'You can get the money from Bitsy.'

I have no idea what she's talking about. It doesn't matter. All that matters is getting myself and Lorcan free. I saw at the rope. It's hard to hold the knife in position while my hands are tied, but this is our only chance.

Beside me, Lorcan's breathing is shallow and tense. He's trying not to draw attention to what I'm doing, but every few seconds he can't help but look over to see how far I've carved through my binding.

We drive for a few minutes. I've nearly cut the rope. Then we turn off the proper road we've been driving along and bump onto a dirt track. Morgan looks around. I stop sawing at the rope.

Has she noticed?

She shoots me a withering glance, but doesn't look down at my wrists.

Good. Maybe Morgan's certainty that she is smarter – that she has had, and always will have, the upper hand . . . maybe that arrogance of hers is my biggest weapon.

I start carving away through the rope again. It's harder now, the dirt track is ridged and bumpy as hell. Morgan is holding onto the handle above her window to steady herself. Lorcan and I are being thrown around the back seat. A particularly large jolt jerks me forwards and I almost drop the knife. I've broken about half the threads now, but the binding is still tight round my wrists. I don't know where we're going, but I'm guessing it can't be too far away. There isn't much time.

'Down there.' Morgan points to a right turn.

Jared slows the 4x4, then swings it onto an even bumpier narrower dirt path. Our headlamps cast spooky shadows over the hedges on either side of the road.

'This used to be the local "lovers lane",' Morgan says with a sneer. 'Very appropriate.'

Jared drives slowly on. At last I slice through the final thread on the rope. My hands are free. Without shifting position, I reach the knife behind Lorcan's back and fumble with his wrist bindings. I catch the edge of the blade on my finger and wince with the pain. Then I find the rough edge of the rope round his hands and carve. It's not the easiest angle, but my movements are freer now my own wrists aren't tied. I cut through the first rope in seconds. The second hangs looser. I cut again.

'This will do.' Morgan is peering through the windscreen.

I give the rope around Lorcan's wrists a final slice. The bind-ings give way. As Jared stops the car, Morgan turns. I whip my hands together, so she won't see my own rope is cut through. The knife is jolted out of my fingers. It falls silently to the floor of the car. *Shit.*

Jared turns the ignition off, but leaves the headlamps on full beam.

'Get them out,' Morgan orders.

As Jared and she open their doors, I glance at Lorcan. He stares back, his eyes intent.

'I'll deal with the man,' he whispers. 'You go after Morgan. On my mark, okay?'

I nod, my heart thudding. I'm only going to get one chance to catch Morgan off-guard and I know it. I duck down as Jared pulls Lorcan out of the car.

'Come on, Geniver,' Morgan snaps, getting out of the car too.

I scrabble on the dark floor, my fingers desperately searching for the knife.

There. I clutch the handle, hiding it again in my palm.

'Out!' Morgan's voice is raised.

I scramble out of the car, careful to keep my wrists together, praying Morgan won't look too closely at the rope hanging limply from my fingers. The knife is sharp and cold against my sweating palm. I clutch it tightly. The tip pricks my skin.

Morgan peers along the deserted road.

'Now!' Lorcan yells.

I hear him thump Jared. Morgan turns to look, her mouth open.

In a second I'm there. I grab her arm . . . wrench it behind her back . . . I bring the knife up against her throat.

All I need to do is press the sharp edge against her skin.

Lorcan yells out. I hesitate. Distracted. Uncertain.

In a flash, Morgan twists away from me. The knife falls to the ground. In the second it takes me to lunge down, clawing for the blade in the dirt, the tables are turned. Jared's gun is in Morgan's hand, the barrel pressed against my neck.

'Bitch,' she hisses in my ear.

'Stop!' Lorcan shouts. 'Leave her alone!'

I look over. He is backing away from Jared, hands in the air.

No. He's giving up his fight. He's giving up in order to save me. But I won't be safe. Morgan will carry out her plan. She will kill us both. That's why she's brought us here. My eyes plead with him, but his gaze is fixed on the gun at my throat, his mouth open in horror.

'Don't shoot her,' Lorcan begs.

Jared grabs his hands and starts tying them behind his back again. Morgan picks up the Swiss Army knife and pockets it. Her gun points at me the whole time. I can feel the panic rising again, through my guts, tightening my chest and pinching my throat. I struggle to focus.

'Whatever you're planning, it isn't going to work,' I say quickly. 'Think about it, Morgan. No one will believe that Lorcan and I would get mixed up in some random countryside shoot-out.'

'That's not what they're going to think,' Morgan says smoothly. 'They're not going to think you're dead at all.'

'Then what . . .?'

'You and Lorcan are lovers. You decide to leave Art and run away together. Exvept of course you're really buried here.' She points at the damp earth at her feet.

I shiver.

'I was going to get Jared to use his knife, a gun is so noisy – but this thing . . .' Morgan pats her pocket containing the Swiss Army knife . . . 'this is much better. It's your own weapon, untraceable to me, if anyone ever digs you up, which they won't.'

I stare at her aghast. This can't really be happening.

'So how exactly are we running away?' Lorcan demands.

'You use your car, Lorcan,' Morgan replies smoothly. 'Currently parked outside my house.' She smirks at the look of surprise on Lorcan's face. 'What, did you think I wouldn't spot it?' Jared is going to leave it at the station later while I use your credit card to buy a couple of tickets.'

I gulp. Morgan sounds like she's thought of everything. Except . . .

'Why on earth would Lorcan and I run away together?' I say. 'Nobody will believe we would do that.'

'Is that so?' Morgan sniffs disdainfully. 'You're having sex with each other. That makes it entirely believable, even to Art.'

I gasp, seeing at last the cleverness of her plan. It fits in with what Art expects me to do. He won't like me going away with Lorcan, but he will believe it.

'It will seem odd though, just running away without saying goodbye to anyone.'

'Not really,' Morgan sneers. 'Everyone who knows you, or anything about you, thinks you're unstable.'

363

'No, they don't.' I stare at her. The wind rustles the leaves of the nearby hedge, its dark edges silhouetted in the car lights.

'Yes, they do,' Morgan insists. 'Everyone, from your best friend who thinks you're obsessed with the baby who died, to people who've only heard about you or met you once, like Bitsy and Bobs.'

I shake my head. 'What about O'Donnell?' Even if people think I'm unstable, no one will believe I'm capable of murder.'

'For goodness' sake,' Morgan snaps. 'Your prints are on his phone and his clothing. The police hardly needed my tip-off. The taxi driver you used to get to the lock-up will remember dropping you . . . not to mention witnesses to the argument you and Lorcan had with O'Donnell in London.'

My stomach falls away from me as I remember the small crowd watching when Lorcan slammed Bernard against the wall near his house. How does Morgan know about that?

Morgan sees my confusion and smiles. 'Bernard explained what happened just before he died.' She pauses, pressing the gun harder against my skin. 'So you see, they might not understand your motive, but you – and Lorcan – look guilty as hell.' She turns to Jared. 'We need to get them through there,' she orders, pointing to a particularly thick set of bushes.

Jared has finished binding Lorcan's wrists again. He shoves him along the road. Morgan drags me after them.

My mind whirls. I can't focus. What can I do?

'Why on the other side of the bushes?' I gasp.

'It's where you and Lorcan die.'

Jared and Lorcan reach the row of bushes. Lorcan is straining to turn round . . . to see me.

Tiny dots of light appear on the lane ahead. They're heading towards us. My heart leaps. It must be another car. We'll be seen.

We'll be saved.

'Shit.' Still gripping my arm, Morgan turns to Jared. 'Quick, get him out of sight.'

The headlamps are bigger now, like the eyes of a prowling animal. The car they belong to must be travelling very slowly. Jared drags Lorcan behind the biggest bush. As they vanish from view, I can see Jared has managed to bind Lorcan's mouth again. Morgan holds her gun against my ribs. I let her push me out of sight, behind a bush a few metres along the row from the others. She places her hand over my mouth.

I imagine shoving her away, grabbing the gun, running out in front of the car.

My heart races. I don't know if I have the nerve to do any of those things with Morgan's gun pressed into my side.

The car is getting nearer. A slow car is good. It means more likelihood that the driver will notice me if I jump out.

The car's headlamps grow bigger. The 4x4 is parked to one side of the track, and the car coming towards us will have to drive carefully to get around it. I can't see the driver but he or she has obviously clocked the big car in front and has slowed further.

'Get down.' Morgan pulls me down beside her.

I'm hunched over, my knees pressed into the mud. Through the leaves of the bush in front of me I can just make out the car travelling towards us. I don't have much time left if I'm going to make a move. My heart is pounding in my ears. How can I possibly get away from Morgan without her shooting me? Her gun is right against me.

I have to stop the driver. This is our last chance. The headlights are two moons now. The car is crawling along. So slowly.

And then it stops, just in front of the 4x4.

Yes. Maybe the driver senses something suspicious. Or maybe he just can't get past the big car. It doesn't matter. If he gets out of the car we have a chance.

Beside me I feel Morgan stiffen. I strain my eyes, peering into the darkness. The headlights of the car are so bright I can't make out the shape of the car, let alone how many people might be inside.

The car door opens. The engine is still running. The 'door open' indicator sounds, punctuating the still night air. The driver emerges into the glare of his own headlamps. I'm about to leap up . . . to yell a warning . . . to push Morgan out of the way . . . and then I see who it is.

Art.

Immediately Morgan stands, dragging me up beside her. Her gun is in plain sight, pressed against my side. Art and I stare at each other. He walks towards us.

'Art?' Morgan's voice is brittle. 'What are you doing?'

Art's eyes are on the gun. 'I guessed you'd be here. I came to help,' he says. 'You were right.'

I stare at him, horrified.

Morgan frowns. I can tell she's not sure whether to trust him either.

'It's time,' Morgan says. 'We can't wait any longer.'

I want to yell out to Art to save us but my throat is twisted into knots.

'Give me the gun, then,' Art says. 'I'll shoot her myself.'

CHAPTER TWENTY-FIVE

Art must be bluffing? *Surely* he's bluffing?

Morgan gives him a sceptical look. 'All of a sudden you're prepared to shoot her? I don't think so.'

Art keeps his eyes on the gun that Morgan is still pressing against my ribs. 'There's no choice and there's no time.' His voice is steady. 'Though we should deal with Lorcan first; he'll be harder for us to control physically.'

Morgan stares at him. I can see she doesn't believe him.

'Jared will do it,' she says. 'You wait there.'

A cold sweat rushes over me in a wave. Jared and Lorcan are both, still, on the other side of the bushes. Lorcan's muffled yells are the only sound in the night air.

'Fine.' Art holds out his hand. 'I'll watch Gen while you help Jared.'

I stare at him in horror. 'You can't do this,' I breathe.

'Shut up,' Morgan hisses.

She gives me a shove. I stumble forwards. Art steps up and grabs my wrist as Morgan half turns back to the bushes.

'No.' The word sounds strangled, as though all the breath is being squeezed out of me. And then I find my voice. 'No!' I scream.

'Keep her quiet, Art,' Morgan says, as Jared hauls Lorcan out from behind the bushes.

Art clamps his hand over my mouth.

'No!' My cry is a low moan. Unheard. A terrible fear swamps me. Not Lorcan. I can't lose him. It's my fault he's even here. 'No!'

Art pulls me against him, holding me fast. I watch as Morgan reaches Lorcan and Jared. She points her gun at Lorcan's chest. His eyes above the gag are wild with fury, but he stops struggling.

I try to pull away from Art but he holds me still. 'Stop it,' he hisses in my ear.

I kick out, making contact with his shin

'Ow.' Art swears under his breath, then he leans in closer to my face and whispers, 'For Christ's sake, Gen. Trust me.'

What? As Morgan fishes in her pocket, Art, still holding me tightly, takes a step backwards, away from her.

I have no idea what he's doing. I'm transfixed by the sight of Morgan slowly drawing the lethal Swiss Army knife out of her pocket. She holds it out to Jared.

'Here,' she says.

Art, his hand still over my mouth, pulls me back another step. We have reached his car, but I barely notice. My whole focus is on Lorcan. Morgan can't make Jared kill him. She can't—

Art opens the car door.

'Get in,' he hisses.

Morgan turns. Her roar fills the air.

'Art!' she yells. 'What are you doing?' She points the gun at me.

'Get *in*,' Art orders.

I scramble inside. An empty click sounds as Morgan fires. She runs towards us. I slam the door shut as Art dives across the car, into the driver's seat. Morgan is still charging towards us. Almost here. The split second that passes lasts an eternity, then Art turns the ignition and the car pulls away.

I look round. Morgan is standing in the middle of the track behind us, her face consumed with rage. I grip the sides of my seat, frozen with shock.

What about Lorcan?

'I took the bullets out of her gun after O'Donnell,' Art explains in a low voice, his hands gripping the steering wheel. He glances sideways at me. 'Gen, I'm so sorry. I didn't know things would . . . would go this far.'

The car is already travelling at nearly sixty miles an hour, far too fast for the bumpy lane we're driving along. My breath is coming out in short, jerky gasps.

'We have to go back.'

Art ignores me and swerves the car onto the main road.

'Please, Art, she'll kill Lorcan.' I turn and look through the back window of the car. The 4x4's headlights are visible in the distance.

'Morgan won't hurt Lorcan. Not until she's got you back," Art says. 'Making sure you don't get away will be her priority.'

I look round again. The lights in the distance are getting closer, though from the jerky way they're moving, I'm guessing Morgan hasn't yet manoeuvred the 4x4 onto the main road.

'Where are we going?' I ask.

'To Morgan's house,' Art says. 'To get Ed.'

What is he saying? My mind careers about, a million thoughts and feelings colliding with each other.

'*Get* Ed?' I say.

'You're going to have to take him away,' Art says. He glances round at me and I'm shocked by the agony in his eyes. 'I've screwed everything up, Gen. This is the only option now. I see that. I should have stopped Morgan before but . . . but it was impossible.'

My guts twist into a knot. I glance out of the window. The

Somerset countryside is zooming past. Is Art *really* taking me to Ed? My head is a chaos of fears. And yet, bizarrely, there's something so familiar about the two of us driving along. This could be any night from the thousands we have spent together.

'God, Art, how could you do . . . what you did with Morgan? How could you have let her take our baby?'

'I told you.' Art shoots me a grim glance. 'Morgan threatened you. She made me choose between losing Ed to her and losing you altogether.'

I don't believe him. Not now.

'But I've seen the film of you and Morgan,' I look down at my chewed fingernails. For some reason I can't explain to myself, I feel utterly humiliated. This is Art's wrong, I tell myself. Art's and Morgan's. And yet I feel shame at the thought of what they did – as if it's my wrong too. My darkness. 'Morgan showed me and . . . I saw what you did and it's obvious she was *blackmailing* you. I mean, taking Ed wasn't about protecting me, it was about protecting yourself . . . wasn't it?'

Art ignores me, his eyes on the wing mirror. We are still some way in front of Morgan's car, but its twin headlamps are visible as bright disks on the main road.

'Jesus, Art.' The words escape me in an angry burst. 'She was your *sister*, for God's sake.'

'I know,' Art says, his voice a mix of shame and defiance. 'But you have to understand she was also beautiful and available and she didn't *feel* like a sister. I didn't even know her, remember?' He pauses. 'I've thought about it a lot, though, and mostly I think it was revenge.'

'Revenge?'

'On Brandon,' he says. 'My dad. *Our* dad. It took everything I had to get up the courage to knock on his door. I knew he'd think I was after money, and I said I wasn't, straight off . . . but

370

he just didn't want to know.' He hesitates. 'The truth is I'd built him up in my head. I'd thought he was this great man ... captain of industry ... like he was some amazing guy who'd be delighted to meet his long-lost son. You know, like in a fairy-tale. I was so stupidly naive. And then, after he'd rejected me, I was so angry. You have no idea, Gen – I've never hated anyone like that in my life. I'd gone off the rails and hurt Mum by push-ing things to the edge and it was only Kyle and his family look-ing after me that stopped me ending up in jail when I was sixteen ... seventeen ... I was still out of control – though I thought I was such a big man ... I mean, I was already really screwed up, and Brandon acting like I was a piece of crap he was trying to wipe off his shoe made me even more screwed up. I stayed screwed up for years ... until I started working in the City, really ... then setting up Loxley Benson finally straight-ened me out, and by then I'd almost forgotten about Morgan and the abortion ...'

'But she hadn't.'

'She told me she was going to take our baby when she came to see us in that place we rented in Oxford. At first I thought it was a joke, then she told me how she'd already bribed Rodriguez, offered to give him enough money to retire on. And how she and Rodriguez had found a nurse and an anaesthetist to go along with the plan.'

'So you knew she was serious.'

'Yes.' Art swings onto a much busier road than the one we were on before. The landscape is suddenly illuminated. I look around at the trees on either side of the road. Cars are visible both ahead and behind us. I check the wing mirror again. The 4x4 containing Morgan, Jared and Lorcan is just a few cars back. Is Art right that Morgan won't hurt Lorcan until she's got me back?

'I told you, Lorcan will be fine as long as you're alive.' Art's

371

voice cuts sharply across my thoughts. Again, it strikes me how well we have come to know each other. And how little this fact has meant . . . how easily I have been kept in the dark . . .

'He's such a chancer, Gen,' Art mutters.

'You've got no right to judge Lorcan.' I turn on him. 'You're a total hypocrite.'

Art rubs his temple. 'You're still my wife, Gen,' he says. 'He saw we were having problems and he leaped right in to—'

'Having *problems*?' I shake my head. 'You can't honestly—'

'I mean that's what Lorcan saw,' Art says, '. . . back at the party. He's a predator.'

'Like with the client's wife from years ago?' I snarl. 'No, Art. That was *you*.'

Art looks out of the window. The hedgerows speed past – blurs of shadow. It's like the world is going on somewhere else, and in this car, for this moment, Art and I have been locked into hell together.

'I didn't force Lorcan into that lie,' Art says softly. 'He went along with it. I paid him and—'

'God, you're just like Morgan. Money this. Money that.'

Art shakes his head. I fall silent. I know that money isn't the reason Art let Ed be taken away. He will never admit it, but Morgan was right. He gave up our son in order to save face, to retain status, to achieve his full potential as a business success.

Those were his priorities.

This is the man I married.

Here is our truth.

I sit back and stare out at the night sky – it's dark with cloud. No stars. We approach a sign for Shepton Longchamp. We aren't far from Morgan's house.

'So how are we going to do this exactly?' I say. 'Morgan's not just going to let me take Ed – and what about Lorcan?'

'I'll help you get Ed into the car. I'll help Lorcan get away, too . . . You'll have to go away for a bit, let me sort things here.'

I stare at him. How does he possibly hope to accomplish all that? 'Are you serious?'

'Deadly serious,' he says. 'I can see now that it's the only way to finish this.' He pauses. 'Are you in love with Lorcan?'

I say nothing. Art's knuckles tighten on the wheel but he doesn't speak and we drive on.

'If I take Ed, Morgan will send that guy to kill me.'

'Jared?' Art nods. 'That's why you have to leave the country until I can take care of it.'

I take a deep breath. 'Suppose you *can't* take care of it?'

'I will.' Art sets his mouth in that determined line I know so well. I'm reminded of Ed again.

My instincts tell me Art is for real, that he wants to save me . . . to let me have Ed.

Art takes a right, then a left turn. We're almost at the house.

'You know I never wanted to hurt you, Gen,' he says. 'I only saw Ed every few weeks. We never went anywhere in public except around Shepton Longchamp – the little shops, the play park. It wasn't like you think . . . like I had some alternative family going on . . .'

I bite down hard on my lip. We're passing a street of semi-detached houses. A streak of cosy-looking living rooms flash by . . . a family around a table . . . two little kids bouncing on a sofa . . . a TV blaring out to a couple in matching armchairs.

Ordinary life.

That's surely gone for me now, whatever happens.

If I take Ed – and if Art is wrong and he can't deal with Jared when Morgan sends him after me – I'll be in hiding for the rest of my life. Even if I can convince the police that Ed is mine and that I'm innocent of Bernard's murder, I will lose everything I've ever cherished . . . my home, my family, my friends.

And Lorcan . . . supposing he survives all this too, would he really be prepared to give up everything and come with me and a child he has absolutely no connection to? We hardly know each other. And what about his life? *His* son? No, it's impossible.

I'm so lost in these thoughts that it's a shock to realize we've arrived at the house. Art slows the car and presses a key fob that opens the gates. We stop inside. Art gets out and strides to the front door. I follow as he lets himself in. As I pass the vase on the hall table I realize why it looked so familiar before. It's the same as the one Morgan sent to our rented house in Oxford, when I was heavily pregnant. It arrived overflowing with beautiful white roses and I remember how deeply touched I was by her thoughtfulness, just as I was when she gave me the bracelet the other day. I shake my head, thinking back to those moments and the years in between and how many lies Art must have told me.

Art is pushing open doors, calling out for Ed and for the nanny, Kelly.

She appears from the kitchen, her hair pulled back off her face in a ponytail. She smiles when she sees Art.

'Hiya,' she says. 'That was well heavy earlier. Ed woke up and I haven't been able to get him back off. He's in the playr—' She catches sight of me standing behind Art and the smile vanishes. 'What's—?'

'You have to go.' He hands her a thick bundle of banknotes. 'Grab your bag and get out. Is anyone else here?'

Kelly stares at him, her mouth falling open.

'Kelly?'

'No, there's no one else here. Just me and Ed. I've been waiting for Mor—'

'Go on, Kelly.' Art gives her arm a gentle shake. 'Leave. Now.'

Kelly looks at me again. 'But I'm not—'

'Go!' Art roars.

Kelly blinks rapidly, then backs away a few steps. She picks up a bag and coat from the bottom of the stairs then, still staring open-mouthed from me to Art, she scuttles through the front door.

Art marches through the kitchen to the door opposite the garage. Morgan's blonde wig lies on the countertop where she left it earlier. I suddenly think of Charlotte West and my earlier suspicions. God, I couldn't have been more wrong. Charlotte was simply a sad woman who thought she saw something to aspire to in my life – from my books and my hair and my handbag up to and including my husband. Like me, she has no idea who he really is.

I follow Art into the playroom.

It's a big room – and quite different from the rest of the house, with bright blue paint on the walls and toy soldiers decorating the long curtains that hang either side of the French doors. Toys are strewn everywhere – there's a full train-set laid out in one corner, a large box filled with action figures and plastic robots and a whole wall of shelves crammed with games and jigsaws. A huge TV stands in one corner and there's a wooden playhouse opposite, complete with front door and tiny window.

Art heads straight to the playhouse. 'Ed?' he says.

'Rah!' Ed bursts out of the playhouse. He is tensed, his little hand clutching a toy sword. He doesn't notice me. 'Daddy!' The tension fades from Ed's face. He drops the sword and hurls himself into Art's open arms.

'Hey, buddy.' Art picks up the little boy and hugs him tight. 'You should be in bed.'

'I was, but Mummy made me go too early,' Ed says. 'I woke up.'

I stand in the doorway and watch Ed's chubby fingers clutch at Art's hair, his face nuzzling into Art's neck. Again, I'm filled with a love I didn't even know was possible. It doesn't matter what I have to give up. I can't give up Ed.

It's unthinkable.

And then he looks up and spies me at the door.

'Daddy, it's *her*,' he whispers loudly, his eyes widening with fear.

Art turns and faces me. 'This is . . .' He falters.

'I'm going to take you on a trip, Ed,' I say.

Ed shakes his head. From outside, I hear the crunch of wheels on gravel. Morgan is here.

Art motions to the French doors. 'You can get out to the front that way. Take Ed. Now.'

I move towards them, but Ed clings more tightly to Art.

'No.' His mouth forms that determined line I saw in the school playground. The resemblance between him and Art is even stronger than it was earlier. 'No!'

'Sssh.' Art sounds desperate.

I look round. Morgan will have heard that. She'll be here any second. There's no time. I reach out for Ed's arm. Ed kicks out with his bare foot, then clamps it back around Art's waist. Art tries to disentangle him but every time he frees one limb, Ed clutches at Art with another. I step back, distraught.

For a second I see us as if from across the room – a parody of a loving family.

'I want Mummy,' Ed wails.

'Mummy's here, baby.' The door slams open. Morgan stands in the doorway. She is smiling at Ed, but her eyes are icy cold.

Ed is struggling to get down from Art's arms now. Art reluctantly sets him on the floor, but holds on to his wrist. 'Gen, take him outside.'

'No.' Morgan pats the pocket of her cream overcoat where the outline of her gun is visible. 'I just loaded this, Art,' she says. 'Don't make me use it in front of the child.'

My chest tightens. 'Where is Lorcan?'

Morgan ignores me. A beat passes, then Art lets go of Ed's wrist. The little boy tears across the room to Morgan, ducking behind her legs, then peering out at me from one side.

'Go into the kitchen, Ed,' Morgan orders. 'Be my brave knight, like we talked about. And remember everything I told you. Everything you have to do.'

'But, Mummy.' Ed's lip wobbles.

'Go!' Morgan's voice rises. 'Let Daddy and me deal with the bad lady.'

I look at Morgan and feel absolute hatred.

'*Now*, please, Ed.' Her tone is cold and harsh. 'Don't let me down.'

The little boy picks up his toy sword and stomps off towards the kitchen, kicking at a teddy bear.

It flashes into my head that, for the first time in my life, I'm capable of killing someone. In fact, in that moment, the clean murder of a gunshot to the head seems like a death too good for Morgan.

Once Ed disappears, Morgan takes the gun out of her pocket.

'I took the bullets out,' Art says.

Morgan raises a contemptuous eyebrow. 'I just told you, I loaded it. You think I don't keep bullets in the house?'

'Where's Lorcan?' I ask.

'He's still in the car,' Morgan says. 'You need to get your ass in there too, Geniver.'

'What, so you can drive us back to the middle of nowhere and try murdering us again?' I take a step towards her. I'm itching to run over and knock the gun out of her hand. She could be bluffing about those bullets and, at this precise moment, I'm willing to take the risk.

'Morgan, *please*.' Art strides up next to me, then stops as she levels her gun at him.

'Stay where you are.' Morgan draws herself up. She glances at me. 'Art belongs with me, Geniver. He's trying to help you because he feels sorry for you. But his heart is here, with me and Ed.'

'You're delusional,' I snap.

'For God's sake, Morgan,' Art pleads. 'It's not too late. I was there, with O'Donnell. I can tell the police that was an accident. But you can't do this. Not to Gen.'

'I can't let her take Ed, either.' Morgan curls her lip into a snarl. 'Why did you bring her here, Art? This is our home. She doesn't belong here.'

'Stop talking like that, Morgan.' Art lowers his voice. 'You *know* the choice I've made. I'm with *Gen.*'

My head spins. How can Art be talking to his sister like this? How can Morgan have these feelings? How is it possible I've known them both for such a long time and had no bloody clue?

'Oh, Art . . .' Morgan stares at him, her mouth trembling slightly. I have the strong impression she's almost forgotten I'm in the room. 'We can't let Geniver walk out of here knowing . . . what she knows.'

'I thought it didn't matter whether I walk out or not,' I say. Morgan looks round. 'You've already said you'll send Jared after me.'

Morgan stiffens. There's only contempt in her eyes as she looks at me. 'I didn't say that,' she insists. 'You don't get it, Geniver. You don't understand anything about real love. Real loyalty. Real sacrifice.'

'Of course I get it.' Morgan's earlier conversation flashes into my head. 'I even heard you talking to Jared about it before, in the car. You said if it came to it, he could get the money from Bitsy. That's what you were talking about – killing me.'

Morgan shakes her head.

'The details don't matter,' Art says. 'Come on, Morgan, face the facts. There's no way you can make this work. The truth is out now.'

'The truth isn't "out",' Morgan snaps. 'Only Geniver and Lorcan know about the past. Anyway, even if Ed isn't my son biologically, he is in every other respect. It might take a fight to make the courts see it but I am Ed's mother. No one can take that away from us.'

I lean against the wall of the playroom. Here, surrounded by Ed's toys, it seems surreal to be talking of court cases and biology. For all that I hate Morgan, I have to acknowledge this is Ed's home.

'There must be a way through this,' I say.

'Shut up,' Morgan snaps.

'Please, listen.' My voice shakes. 'Maybe if everyone calms down, we can find a way that allows Ed to be with *all* of us.'

'I'm not sharing him,' Morgan says. 'Now, for the last time, I'm taking Geniver outside and—'

'No.' Art and I speak together.

Morgan cocks the gun. Behind her, Ed has reappeared. He is peering around the kitchen door. Art notices him too. A terrible look of fear and guilt crosses his face.

'Go to your room, Ed,' Art orders.

The little boy's eyes are wide and round with shock, but he slinks away out of sight.

Morgan raises her hand and points the gun at me. 'If I have to, I'll shoot you here.'

All I can see is the barrel of the gun. My legs are shaking, but I stand my ground. For a moment I truly believe I am about to die. And then Art steps in front of me.

'If you're going to kill Gen, you'll have to kill me first.'

'Get out of the way, Art.'

'No.'

He means it. He will not let me die. I reach up and put my hand on Art's shoulders. I squeeze his arm. Whatever else Art has done and whatever is going to happen next, I want him to know this counts.

My eyes are fixed on Morgan.

With a roar, a figure flashes across the room. It's Lorcan, a long-bladed kitchen knife in his hand. Before I can even register what's happening, he's reached Morgan. He grabs her arm with one hand and holds the knife across her body with the other.

My heart pounds as Art darts forward to take Morgan's gun. And then she twists away. For a second everything slows down. I'm trying to run towards them and Art is reaching out and Morgan is lunging and Lorcan is backing away from them both, the knife unused at his side.

For a second Morgan and Art stand and stare at each other.

And then the gun fires.

CHAPTER TWENTY-SIX

I freeze. Time slows to a crawl as Morgan reaches forward, holding her arms out to Art. He backs away, the gun dangling from his fingers. Morgan's hands fall to her sides. Her eyes close and her body folds in on itself. With a thud, she crumples to the floor.

Lorcan and I look at each other, dumbstruck, then down at Morgan. She is perfectly still. Blood is seeping out of her chest . . . bright red against the blue carpet.

I rush over. 'Morgan?'

Her eyelids flicker open and she fixes me with a triumphant look.

'He'll get you,' she whispers. 'I've made sure of it. He'll get you both.'

For a moment it's still her, staring up at me – angry and brittle – and then her eyes lose their focus and their expression and suddenly she's no longer inside her own body. Gone.

Art sinks to his knees, the gun still in his hand. I look up, to see Ed standing in the doorway. More slow seconds pass. They feel like for ever. Then Ed draws in a huge breath and lets out an agonized wail.

I've reached him before I knew I was going to move. I pull him towards me but he wriggles away, tearing across the kitchen. I can hear his footsteps crossing the hall. He's running upstairs.

I move to run after him, but Art grabs my arm.

'Wait a minute, please,' he urges.

I look behind me. Lorcan is kneeling by Morgan's body. He is holding her wrist, feeling for a pulse. His other hand is over her mouth, checking for breath. Blood is everywhere. He shakes his head. 'She's dead.'

A wave of nausea surges through me. I close my eyes.

'Gen?' Art gives my arm a shake.

I realize he's been speaking. I haven't taken in a word.

'What?' I stare at him blankly.

Art sets the gun on the floor at his feet. 'I'm leaving this here,' he says. 'It's got my fingerprints all over it. Don't touch it.'

I nod.

He turns to Lorcan. The two men stare at each other with untempered loathing.

'Where's Jared? How did you get away?' Art asks.

'I knocked him out,' Lorcan says. 'He's outside, on the drive.'

Art walks across the room to the French windows. As he unlocks the door, Lorcan looks up from Morgan's body, eyes blazing. 'Where are you going?' he demands.

'Jared might come round,' Art says. 'We need to make sure he doesn't run off. I'm going to tie him up.'

'Like hell you are,' Lorcan snaps. 'You're not leaving this room.'

Art steps back from the door. 'We have to deal with Jared,' he insists. There is a terrible pain in his eyes but I recognize the fixed set of his jaw . . . the determination in the press of his lips. 'It's the only way to keep Gen safe.'

'You're staying here,' Lorcan stands up. 'I'll do it.'

'No, listen.' Art looks from Lorcan to me with desperate eyes. 'I know where the rope is. I'll come straight back.'

'I don't believe you,' Lorcan says. He strides over to Art. The two men glare at each other, fists clenched.

'I don't care what you believe. I'm doing this for Gen,' Art says.

'I think you've lost the right to do *anything* for her.' Lorcan moves closer. He and Art eyeball each other, neither one backing down.

'Stop it. What about Ed?,' I say, horribly aware that the little boy is upstairs somewhere, frightened and alone. 'And we should call the police. Right now.'

Lorcan gives Art a final glare.'Fine. I'll stay with Gen.'

Art holds up his hands in a gesture somewhere between self-loathing and defeat, then he points to the gun that he left on the floor. 'Call 999, Gen. Show them that. Tell them everything that happened. Except, there's one thing you shouldn't say.'

'Oh, and what's that?' Lorcan demands.

Art points to the knife, which Lorcan brought in from the kitchen. It's lying a couple of metres away on the floor. 'I'd wipe your fingerprints off that and put it back in the knife block in the kitchen.'

Lorcan blinks. This was clearly the last thing he expected Art to say. 'Right.' He gets to his feet and strides into the kitchen, picking up the knife on the way. A second later I hear the tap running.

A moment passes. I glance down at Morgan. She is still bleeding into the carpet. I cover my mouth with my hand.

'Oh, Gen . . .' Art says quietly. 'If it has to be him, then make sure he looks after you. I know I have no right to ask you for anything, but please be careful.'

His face is as haunted and unhappy as I've ever seen it, and yet behind his eyes I catch a glimpse of all the warmth and force of Art's personality.

I want to say something, but my feelings are too huge and too complicated to put into words. A part of me still loves Art. Will always love him.

All I know for sure is how much wasted life is in this room right now.

'I'm so sorry, Gen. Please tell Ed I love him.' Art's voice cracks, but before I can reply, he turns on his heel, flings open the French windows and walks out, into the darkness.

I look down at Morgan again . . . at the dark pool of blood that now surrounds her body. I cross the room to the phone and dial 999. I explain as calmly as I can that we need police and an ambulance as soon as possible.

As I answer the operator's questions Lorcan comes back into the room and puts his arms around me. I finish the call and let him hold me for a second. I want to close my eyes and shut out the sight of Morgan's body . . . the desperation in Art's expression . . . the terror of the little boy hiding from us upstairs . . . but I know that none of it will go away.

And that it's my job to face it all.

And then I pull away and go in search of my son.

A day passes. Then another. Before I can believe it, a week has gone by. A month. Two. Six. And my whole life has been turned upside down.

Art was as good as his word. He tied Jared up, then came back to the house, just before the police arrived. We were all interviewed separately, of course, but I learned later that Art confessed everything immediately. He told the police the whole story – how he'd taken our baby and why – and how he'd witnessed Morgan kill Bernard O'Donnell. Dr Rodriguez managed to slip into the shadows and has so far escaped detection. I'm sure he's living in luxury in some distant backwater – but I hope he spends the rest of his life looking over his shoulder.

Jared admitted his involvement as soon as he discovered Morgan was dead. I didn't see him, except in court, but it was clear he was too devastated by her death to try and cover his tracks. He pleaded guilty to the murders of Lucy O'Donnell and, years before, of Gary Bloode, the anaesthetist. He confessed he had mugged me and kidnapped Lorcan. The only thing he refused to admit was that Morgan had ordered him to kill me and Lorcan in the event of her death.

For a long time Morgan's final words, "He'll get you both", haunted me, permeating my dreams and jolting me from sleep with a pounding heart. But, six months on, no hitman has emerged from the shadows, and Jared himself is safely locked up for at least the next ten years.

Art was arrested and charged with murder, later reduced to voluntary manslaughter. The statements Lorcan and I gave supported Art's own account of what happened, so his sentence is less than it might have been. But he's still in jail. He's become a different person since he went inside – it's not just the stoic resignation. He seems shrunken inside his prison clothes, a smaller man without his sharp suits and his iPhone, a permanent air of shame about him.

In spite of my anger, I can't help but feel sorry for him. After all, Art has lost virtually everything . . . not just his freedom, but his marriage, his home, his business and his reputation. Loxley Benson has been bought out by the board and Kyle is continuing to keep the company going, but I'm not sure it will survive. News of Ed's existence and Art and Morgan's incestuous liaison were never formally reported in the press. For Ed's sake, I didn't want Art prosecuted for taking him away from me, which meant many of the details were kept out of court. Nevertheless, the information has leaked and this, coupled with Art's manslaughter conviction, has lost Loxley Benson half its clients already.

Kyle visits Art every week – and Tris and Perry have both been to see him a couple of times, but most of the board have turned their backs completely. I guess it's hard to blame them. Art's taken it badly. I mean, I know he deserves his punishment – and a lot of the time I'm still furious with him. But it's hard to stay angry with a man whose destruction is so total and whose remorse so all-consuming. And Art is devastated. The only times I ever see him smile are when I take Ed to the prison for a visit.

Ed himself has been my biggest worry – and my greatest help – in getting through the past six months. As I write, he's playing with a stick in the back garden, pretend-shooting at the flowers. I worry that he spends too much time playing guns. Of course, he didn't see the shooting itself. But he heard it, and he saw Morgan afterwards and he knows that she – his mother for nearly eight years – is dead. The child psychologist says his obsession with guns is probably just a normal developmental phase. We haven't told Ed that it was his father who shot Morgan. There's no need for him to know that now, but I worry that, as he gets older, it will be impossible to protect him from the information. Many of the details, including plenty of inaccurate ones – are on the Internet. And all the official newspaper stories name Art as Morgan's killer, with headlines like: 'Trials Guru on Trial for Manslaughter'. Ed's had so much to deal with already. Not just losing Morgan and having to visit his father in jail, but being taken into care while the DNA test that backed up my story came through.

Social services allowed me to take him home after a few days. He didn't speak for a week and there are still times when he curls up under the duvet and refuses to come out. I worry that it's not just how Morgan died that will damage him, but that he's inherited my own dad's obsessive, depressive nature as well. The child psychologist is hopeful. Ed's been seeing her for a few months now. She recommends he should start school again as soon as possible. It will be a new school, though, just as this is a new home for him. I thought long and hard about it, but having weighed up the pros and cons of letting him stay in Shepton Longchamp or start a completely new life here, it had to be here.

One of the first things Ed did was ask what to call me. The psychologist explained to him – with me alongside – that I was his birth mummy, but Ed hasn't so far used those words. Which is fine. I don't want to push him.

I'm trying to mend bridges with Hen. I still wish that she and Art had told me sooner about him lending her all that money, but in the context of everything I've learned since, it doesn't seem all that important. Hen's busy with her new baby now, of course, but most of my other friends have been great, bringing their own kids round to play with Ed – not that he has really engaged with them yet, he's always so wrapped up in his own head – then staying on when the children are in bed, and listening to me talk over a bottle of red wine.

I've given up all my teaching commitments so I can be at home for Ed. Charlotte West called a few times, asking if we could meet for private sessions and hinting she'd like to visit Art in prison, but I ignored the calls and eventually she stopped ringing and texting.

At least money isn't a problem, thanks to Art. He has signed everything he can over to me and isn't fighting the divorce, which I've already set in motion.

I sit back from the kitchen table and close my laptop. I can see Ed through the window. He's poking his stick at the ground now, spearing something on the end. His little face is screwed up with concentration.

Having him with me is a million times more challenging than I could ever have imagined. And yet he makes sense of everything

– as if nothing was in its right place when I had lost him. And now that he is found, I have found myself again too.

The best proof of this, to me, is that I'm writing again. I'm writing about finding Ed – just to get the whole story out of me . . . I feel hopeful that, once I've done this, I'll be able to write fiction again.

Lorcan thinks I will. We've spent a lot of time together recently, though not here – and not with Ed. There'll be time enough for that in the future. Anyway, Lorcan's back in Ireland now. I could have taken Ed and gone too, but that wouldn't have been fair. Ed needs time to get used to being with me here, just as Lorcan and I need time to find out if we have a future. We both know that coming together in the white heat of my search for Ed skewed everything. It's funny . . . though no relationship that starts like ours did should work, I can't help but believe ours will.

Ed is still outside. I get up from the table and wander over to the sink to make him a drink. Now, where I once stored Arts and Crafts china, I have a stash of plastic cups and bowls. I'm still getting my head round it. This is what I wanted, after all.

My son, my child, my holy grail.

I stand by the sink, running the tap, letting it become real.

Today is three years exactly since Mummy died. They don't know I know this but I do, just like they don't know I saw it but I did.

I am nearly eleven. Soon I'll be at secondary school. I saw my dad last night at visiting time. He was happy because he'll be out of prison soon and I pretended to smile at him like always but inside I'm still following Mummy's Special Fighting Plan. I even know where I'll get the gun. Darren Matthews's older brother told me. He says he knows a gang in Archway where you can weapon-up for like a few hundred quid. I'll steal that off Geniver, no problem. Yeah, Geniver. She wants me to call her 'Mum'. So do all the social workers and psychologists, I can tell. But it's her fault Mummy died. So she's just Geniver. I don't care whether she likes it or not.

All I care about is what Mummy told me before she died. Because it all came true. She said the Bad Lady was coming and she did. She said the Bad Lady would say she was my real mum and that she would have papers and test results and lawyers that would look like they proved it but that, whatever happened, I should never forget Mummy was my real mum because she loved me the most.

I am just waiting for Dad to get out of prison. No one at school knows he's there, I don't even know if the teachers know. It doesn't matter. When he's free I will get him. And I will get her. And Mummy will see. I know she is watching me. Watching me right now. Waiting.

Mummy told me I had to be her brave knight. She said that if anything happened to either of us, then I had to find a way to pay back whoever did it.

That was the first thing. She said I must never forget it.

The second thing was that I must not let her down.

I won't. I will get the gun soon. I make my promise to Mummy every night before I go to sleep.

I will be your knight.

I will pay them back.

I won't let you down, Mummy. I won't let you down.

ACKNOWLEDGMENTS

If books were babies, then *Close My Eyes* would have had many midwives. I'm deeply grateful to early readers Dana Bate – a wonderful author in her own right – Roger Bate, Philippa Makepeace, Eoin McCarthy and Jodie Marsh, who all helped when the book was at an embryonic stage.

My thanks to Sarah Ballard at United, who kept faith with the story as it developed and to the team at Simon and Schuster UK for their fantastic support all the way.

Thank you also to Zoe Pagnamenta and to everyone at St Martin's Press in the US for taking on my book with such enthusiasm. I'm especially grateful to Jennifer Weis, who brought a fresh pair of eyes to the story, offering some excellent advice as it neared completion.

And, finally, a massive thank you to Maxine Hitchcock, for not only having the most brilliant insights but always communicating them in the most encouraging and helpful ways.

Close My Eyes

by Sophie McKenzie

Reading Group Questions

Close My Eyes Reading Group Guide

1 One of the things which makes this novel work
   so well is the way the author gives us several
   possibilities, all equally credible, as to what
   might have happened to Geniver's baby. Discuss
   how this is achieved.

2 Which option is the one you are most inclined
   to believe until you find out the truth at the end
   of the novel?

3 As Geniver is a first-person narrator, we experience everything from her perspective. How does
   this bias your perception of people and situa-
   tions from the beginning? Does it ever make
   you doubt her decisions?

4 There are multiple clues throughout the novel
   that point towards the several big reveals at the
   end. Do you think these are intentionally placed
   as hints or are they meant to further the paranoia and sense of unreliable perceptions?

5 When we first meet Lorcan he comes across as
   charming but untrustworthy. By the end of the
   novel his true character is revealed. Discuss his
   role in this novel.

6 A well-respected businessman who clearly
   adores his wife, how does your opinion of Art
   change during the course of the novel? How
   does the author achieve this?

7 The child's narrative that intersperses the story is a mystery until the very end. Who did you think it was? Discuss how the reveal of the child's identity and his specific loyalties change the way you think about the novel.

8 Throughout the novel there is an underlying tension and sense of paranoia. How does the author create this?

9 Both Morgan and Art are severely affected by their childhood relationships with their late father. How much does this early trauma contribute to their life decisions and personalities? Does the knowledge of their difficult childhoods make you more understanding of their adult actions?

10 What about Gen? Do her memories of her late father influence her actions in any way?

You can keep up to date with Sophie McKenzie online

News – reviews – author interviews

Website: www.sophiemckenziebooks.com

Facebook: www.facebook.com/Sophiemckenzieauthor

Twitter: @sophiemckenzie_

nd out about more great books from the same publisher

Website: www.simonandschuster.co.uk

Facebook: www.facebook.com/simonschusterUK

Twitter: @simonandschusterUK

LIKE YOUR FICTION A LITTLE ON THE DARK SIDE?

Like to curl up in a darkened room all alone, with the doors bolted and the windows locked and slip into something cold and terrifying...half hoping something goes bump in the night?

Me too.

That's why you'll find me at The Dark Pages - the home of crooks and villains, mobsters and terrorists, spies and private eyes; where the plots are twistier than a knotted noose and the pacing tighter than Marlon Brando's braces.

Beneath the city's glitz, down a litter-strewn alley, behind venetian blinds where neon slices the smoke-filled gloom, reading the dark pages.

Join me: WWW.THEDARKPAGES.CO.UK

AGENT X

@dark_pages

Kristina Ohlsson
Silenced

Fifteen years ago a young girl was brutally attacked in the meadow behind her parents' Swedish country home. The crime went unreported; the victim silenced.

Cut to the present. It is a bleak February morning in Stockholm, when an unknown man is killed in a hit and run. At the same time, a priest and his wife are discovered dead in their apartment. Meanwhile, out in Bangkok on a business trip, a young woman finds that her flight has mysteriously been cancelled and, whichever way she turns, all contact with home has been cut off.

Following a trail that leads all the way back to the '90s, Alex Recht's team at the Stockholm Police, along with Investigative Analyst Fredrika Bergman, uncover a terrible crime that was hushed-up, but whose consequences reach further and deeper than anyone could ever expect.

Intense, urgent and full of surprises, *Silenced* is a treat for anyone who loved *The Bridge* and *The Killing*.

'Compelling' *Sunday Times*

Paperback ISBN 978-1-84983-131-4
Ebook ISBN 978-1-84737-962-7

Penny Hancock
The Darkening Hour

Dora on Mona

'Mona is, I guess, a few years older than me. Crooked teeth.
Poorly nourished, pale brown skin. Health care is expensive
where she comes from. I'm helping her, I think. I'll improve her
life. A fair exchange – after all, she's here to improve mine.'

When Theodora Gentleman employs Moroccan immigrant
Mona, she has little choice but to invite this perfect stranger
into her home.

But when two women are forced to make their home under the
same roof, power struggles are quick to occur. And Theodora
soon begins to suspect that Mona is not all she seems.

Mona on Dora

'When I arrived, Theodora opened the door herself. She smiled,
though I know from experience that looks can lie. I could see
straightaway that Dora needed me. This is good. Need creates
opportunity. It gives me power.'

Mona knows that this job is the only hope left of supporting her
elderly mother and daughter living back in Rabat.
But with each passing day, Mona begins to realise that Dora
might not be the kindly employer she had hoped for…

Hardback ISBN 978-1-47111-124-2
Ebook ISBN 978-0-85720-626-8

Kimberly McCreight
Finding Amelia

Single mother and lawyer Kate Baron is in the meeting of her
career when she is interrupted by a telephone call. Her
teenaged daughter Amelia has just been suspended from her
exclusive prep school for cheating. When Kate eventually
arrives at the school an hour later, she is greeted by news that
no mother ever wants to hear.

A grieving Kate can't accept that her daughter would kill
herself. But she soon discovers she didn't know Amelia quite as
well as she thought. Who are the friends she kept, what are the
secrets she hid?

And so begins an investigation which takes her deep into
Amelia's private world, and into the mind of a troubled young
girl. Slowly, Kate reconstructs Amelia through her online world
of texts, social networks and chat rooms – the ordinary
obsessions of a living, breathing girl; now, the precious final
words of a dead one.

Then Kate receives an anonymous text: AMELIA DIDN'T
JUMP. Is someone toying with her or has she been right all
along? To find peace and the truth about her daughter, she
must face a darker reality than she ever imagined…

Paperback ISBN 978-1-47111-129-7
Ebook ISBN 978-1-47111-130-3

Camilla Grebe & Åsa Träff
More Bitter Than Death

Sometimes reliving the past revives old demons . . .

In a Stockholm apartment, five-year-old Tilde watches
from under the kitchen table as her mother is brutally
kicked to death.

Meanwhile, in another part of town, psychotherapist Siri
Bergman and her colleague Aina meet their new patients – a
group of women, all of whom are victims of domestic violence.

From Kattis, who was beaten by her boyfriend and lives under
the constant threat of his return, to Malin, the promising young
athlete who was attacked by a man she met online, and from
Sofi, the teenager abused by her stepfather, to Sirkka, an older
woman who had a troubled marriage – each woman takes her
turn to share her story in the safety of the sessions.

But as the group gets closer, it is not long before the dangers
lurking in the women's lives outside invade the peace with
shattering consequences. And somehow, the fate of five-year-
old Tilde is intertwined with that of Siri and the other women,
so that what started out as the search for peace will swiftly turn
into a tense hunt for a murderer.

Trade Paperback ISBN 978-0-85720-949-8
Ebook ISBN 978-0-85720-951-1